CUT FROM THE EARTH

THE TILE MAKER SERIES BOOK 1

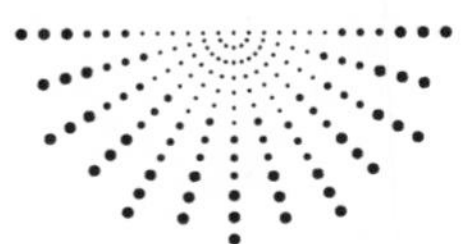

STEPHANIE RENEE DOS SANTOS

Published 2021 by Next Chapter

Edited by Lisa Gibson Dutcher, Donna Russo Morin

Cover art by CoverMint

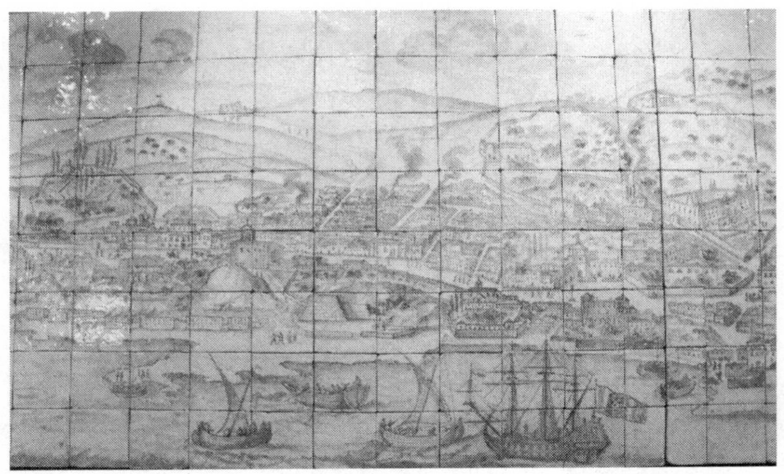

'A Grande Vista de Lisboa' Mocambo barrio (panel 7 of 16 panels) by Gabriel del Barco, National Tile Museum, Lisbon

"Figura de convite" *by Master PMP*

To my grandparents who introduced me to the beauty of tile,
to my parents for their unending support,
and to all those lost in the Great Lisbon Earthquake

A HISTORICAL NOTE

Wealth and extravagance ruled mid-eighteenth-century Portugal due to gold and precious gem extraction from its colony, Brazil, as well as the slave trade from Africa. While the Inquisition enforced its medieval Catholicism throughout the country, other parts of Europe embraced the Enlightenment.

The Inquisition sought to root out heresy against the Church, and to persecute those who did not adhere to Catholic orthodoxy. Conversely, the Enlightenment's objective was to reform society with reason and to advance knowledge through science and intellectual exchange, instead of relying on faith and revelation as promoted and controlled by the Church.

During this time, the art form of tile making flourished with Portugal's peerless affluence and produced one of the greatest world-wide advancements in tile creation: the *figura de convite,* a life-sized cut-out of a human figure. These elegantly dressed figures of a nobleman, lady, or footman were placed at the entrances to palaces, on stair-landings, and patios to welcome visitors. For the first time in the history of tile fabrication, the medium deviated from the square composition and embraced the outline of human form. This innovation is attributed to an eighteenth-century Portuguese tile maker, known only by the monogram PMP. Though PMP's works can still be viewed today in Lisbon, the artist's identity and life story remain a mystery.

Cut from the Earth imagines the lost story of the master tile artist PMP, beginning in the fateful months before the Great Lisbon Earthquake erupted on November 1st, All Saints Day, in 1755.

He who works with his hands is a laborer.

He who works with his hands and his head is a craftsman.

He who works with his hands and his head and his heart is an artist.

—Saint Francis of Assisi

PROLOGUE

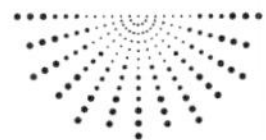

IN THE YEAR OF OUR LORD 1743

Cries of anguish cut Lisbon's noontide heat. Then stopped. Followed by a stream of air-slicing snaps and a man's angry commands. "Get up! Get up, you *burro*!" Tile making supplies under his arm, Pêro pushed through the gathered crowd. Paulinha trailing him, arriving at the edge of a scene of horror. A man lay collapsed in the dirt, dust plastering one side of his face, his nose, his lips. His black back lacerated raw and bloody.

"I'm going to miss the ship, the sale!" the master roared. He pointed to the handcart loaded with heavy sacks of wheat.

For a split second, Pêro and Paulinha looked into the fallen man's eyes, his soul, pleading for mercy, for relief, for escape. Pêro dropped his materials and lunged forward, arms outstretched. "Jibo! No! Stop!" He gasped, his tongue dry. It was visibly too late.

Paulinha gripped his arm, steadying herself. "Pêro! Wait!"

The lash-wielding master turned on the crowd. He cracked his whip and yelled: "What are you looking at! Get out of here! Be gone! All of you!"

Pêro broke forward, hands reaching to comfort the downed man.

The wax-coated and knotted whip lashed out, a viper's tongue, coiling with lightning speed around his right third and fourth fingers, lacerating them to the bone. Pêro fell to his knees alongside Jibo. "He's departed." He closed his eyes and squeezed his limp hand.

Pêro's vision blurred as he looked at Jibo, his bloodied fingers, the killer, and the dispersing crowd. Paulinha rushed to Pêro's side.

With blinding force, Pêro stared at Jibo. Pain seared him. "Never again. This has to end."

Tears in her eyes, Paulinha carefully placed her hand on Pêro's. "Yes, this has to end."

CHAPTER ONE

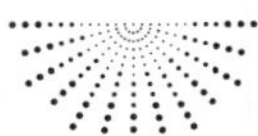

IN THE YEAR OF OUR LORD 1755

Sketchbook in hand, Pêro Manuel Pires squinted at the sky, an ironed blue sheet without a crease of cloud. From the corner studio windows, he followed a carrion crow wheeling over the Atlantic, casting an ominous shadow. He drew the bird's form as it cut inland to the outskirts of Lisbon, sailing aloft the Tagus River dotted with merchant ships. In the distance seven church-spired hills blessed the horizon. Pêro etched in the landscape as the bird circled above terracotta roofs, cork orchards, and tile factory smokestacks. It swooped before him, coming to rest on the kinked branch of an olive tree in the Fabrica Santa María's geranium-lined courtyard.

The earth trembled and a shudder rippled up through the ancient tree, causing his hand to stutter across the paper.

With a caw of warning, the crow took flight.

Pêro stopped drawing and turned toward the busy tile making shop.

Diogo, a boy black as squid's ink, burst through the entryway. "*Pai! Padre!* Help!"

Ebony faces looked up from their worktables pushed against whitewashed adobe. A worker slapped a ball of clay onto a gesso tabletop and halted. Another abandoned the pricking of holes into transfer paper.

Pêro stuffed his pencil behind his ear and swiped the charcoal from his olive-brown hands onto his smock. He sought Rafa, who stood, like an obsidian statue before a trimming pedestal.

Diogo, Rafa's son dashed to his side. "They've come for *Avo*." The boy's lower lip trembled. "They said for Grandfather Bagamba to ready himself to be sold to another cork farm."

Pêro hurried over, his cassock sweeping a path clean.

Rafa spun to Pêro. "It can't be. They promised."

Pêro coughed on an inhaled scent of loam.

"Padre, are you going to let them *take* him?" Tears coursed down little Diogo's cheeks.

"They've agreed to release him to me." Pêro struck his thigh. "I've near enough for the final payments to the de Sousa family for his freedom." He knelt to Diogo, offering welcoming arms. "Come here."

"Please don't let them take him, *please*..." Diogo pleaded.

The boy clung to Pêro's neck, staring up at him.

Pêro rocked Diogo and then set him down, turning to the boy's father, taking Rafa's hands into his. "Try not to worry. I'll do all I can. Soon he'll be as free as you and I. I must go now to see about your father. Finish this order, so that we receive our payment. It won't be long now; we must be diligent in our efforts. And pray for God's assistance."

Rafa placed a hand on Diogo's shoulder. "Go home and tell them Padre Pêro won't let this happen." He leaned in and whispered. "Tell your mother to send word to the Blacks of the Rosary."

Pêro watched the boy scuttle out into the looming twilight. Above the shop's doorframe their statue of Saint Anthony quivered on its shelf, as it had several times throughout the day.

Pêro hurried over to the ceramic saint, steadying it until the shaking subsided. He looked up to the rafters. "The earth is restless today. What more?" He made the sign of the cross.

Pêro brushed sweat from his forehead and strode into the Mocambo barrio. Lifting his coarse robe, he quickened his step. A white spotted guinea fowl scurried past, disappearing into the maze of earthen homes. Children with protruding bellies and spindly legs stood in open doorways and darted inside as he rushed by. Blue smoke streamed into the pathway, as women tended their evening pots over open fires. Hot pepper bit the inside of his nose. He dodged a woman with strong black arms, who steadied a basket of salted cod atop her head. *"Peixe! Peixe! fish!"*

Rounding a corner in front of Rafa's home, Pêro stopped, releasing his hold on his habit. Diogo sprinted to him, cheeks wet. Pêro embraced him and looked at Rafa's family huddled before their home: Grandmother Gogo, Rafa's wife Josepha, and his three oldest sons, ages seven to sixteen. Pêro's stomach sank as he saw Rafa's father, Bagamba, flanked by one of the de Sousa family's transport men.

"Stop!" Pêro said.

The hired man prodded Bagamba with a polished stick.

Bagamba lifted his eyes, meeting Pêro's in a silent plea. Light glinted off streaks of silver in Bagamba's wiry hair and from the iron ring around his neck attached to a heavy chain weighing him down.

"Move, Benedito," the man said, using Bagamba's Christian name, pushing him forward.

"Wait." Pêro blocked Bagamba. "He's to come with me."

The transport man's arm tensed, as he swung the shiny stick in front of Pêro, blocking his way. "No! You defaulted on your payments, monk, and I have my orders."

Pêro's face flushed. "This man's been promised to me. I'm a layman deacon, not a sworn friar." He placed a hand on Bagamba's shoulder. He shuddered at the long faces of the family before them. His blunder exposed, their disappointment radiating like scalding heat from a newly opened kiln.

"Go consult with Senhor de Sousa. I must carry out my duties." The transport man grasped the chain and jerked the old man who stumbled towards the waiting cart.

Pêro gripped Bagamba's shoulder, fingertips pressing, until he could hold on no longer. His hand slipped off. Bagamba tripped and peered back at him, eyes blazed with betrayal. Pêro glanced at his own right hand, to the stumped third and fourth finger, his mouth a tight white line. Yes, he'd go see Senhor de Sousa at once.

CHAPTER TWO

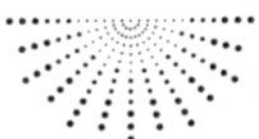

"Padre Pêro, you know I have every right to sell him to whomever I choose. You've broken our agreement." Senhor de Sousa stood tall and commanding, the fine lace of his shirt billowing forth at the neck and wrists. He looked Pêro squarely in the eye.

The waiting buyer sneered at Pêro, cocked his Northerner's wide-brimmed hat, flung his cape over his shoulder, and recounted his coins.

"Yes, but you promised him first to me and you already have a substantial sum," Pêro said. "Do you not?" Pêro looked over Senhor de Sousa's shoulder at Bagamba slumped against the wall of a converted horse stall among manure and soiled straw.

The buyer dropped his coins, one by one back into a velvet sack. "Let us proceed." He locked eyes with Senhor de Sousa.

"No. I'll have the payments to you shortly. Please, I just need a little more time," Pêro said. "I'll make good on the past due payments and pay you in full soon. I promise…in the name of Our Lord."

Senhor de Sousa drew his bejeweled hand to his chin and glanced pensively out the stable doors at the cork orchards and road lined with fragrant fuchsia oleander, both tended for years by Bagamba.

"We've already come to an agreement." The buyer snapped at Pêro. "Here's the payment." The man offered forth the bag of coins, regaining Sehnor de Sousa's attention. The full sack swung back and forth like a hypnotist's pendulum.

Senhor de Sousa reached for it.

Pêro placed his marred hand upon Senhor de Sousa's. "Please, I beg of you."

The buyer dragged the toe of his boot through the dirt. "Christ!" He glared at Pêro and pointed at Bagamba with his gold-capped cane. "Why do you want this cork orchard mule? He's not worth anything to anyone without trees."

"Senhor, careful. Do not defile the Lord's name, nor this decent man's." Pêro matched the rival and swept his robed arm toward Bagamba. "His son works in my tile factory. I've vowed to the Almighty to free the enslaved and keep families together, whatever the cost." Pêro displayed his stumped fingers to Senhor de Sousa. "I've already sacrificed these for another man's welfare. I warn you; I'll seek recourse."

Senhor de Sousa stiffened and lowered his hand.

The buyer huffed. "But here are the coins." He shoved them forward.

Senhor de Sousa held up his open palm. "Padre, you have until All Saints Day. Otherwise, I'll go ahead with this sale, withholding your down payment as we agreed." He turned to the guard at the gate of the stall. "Let him go."

Bagamba stopped walking at the base of the Mocambo hillside and bowed his head. "Thank you, Padre."

"It's what the Lord wanted. Thank him tonight in your prayers." Pêro smiled at the weathered man. He prayed Bagamba could not sense his pounding heart. "Now, let's get back quickly. The evening mist is already settling in."

Pêro tried to enjoy the cool autumn air blanketing them and the lowland Lapa region to appease his worry. Before them stretched the magnificent valley, home to farms and estates like Senhor de Sousa's and the streambeds that supplied the abutting Mocambo neighborhood and its tile factories with fine-toothed clay.

Bagamba hesitated.

Pêro paused. "What's wrong?"

"Do you really believe they won't come for me in the middle of the night?" He fingered the "S" brand on his neck. "I can't bear another branding, not at this age. My skin will never heal. I've seen younger men die from infection."

Pêro embraced Bagamba's shoulders and looked into his eyes. "Senhor de Sousa has given me his word." Tightness crept into Pêro's shoulders.

"But he gave you his word before…And..."

"Yes, but are we not now heading home?" Pêro encouraged him forward, his stomach knotting.

Back in the Mocambo, they joined the flood of workers returning home. Here Pêro noted, the faces were every color of the earth's soils, a visible contrast to the land-owning cream and olive-skinned residents of the Lapa. Pêro and Bagamba ducked to avoid fishermen with their catches dangling from sticks and side-stepped so as not to collide with two laundresses, full baskets balanced atop their heads. In front of them, a vendor carried net bags full of mussels. Servants and cooks of the upper classes bustled by. People, both bound and free, swarmed the street.

"See you tomorrow, if God wills it," Bagamba said.

Pêro's eyes were drawn to the unease etched on his wrinkled face. It pained him to see the man's discomfort and feel his own in his stomach.

"Please, try not to worry, believe and have faith in God's will," Pêro said, as much for himself as he watched Bagamba go.

Pêro looked up to the open countryside backing the hilltop neighborhood and its single, two and three-story homes, all in need of fresh whitewashing, reminding him that when the tile factory smokestacks churned out plumes of soot, it settled over the predominately African quarter and its gardens, coating everything in a light ash dusting. *What a vicious circle to be caught in! Like my situation with those who continue to default on their payments to me!* Sometimes the smoke caught an onshore breeze and traveled up to the palace of the Countess of Sarmento poised high above on the hillside. The Countess would send a man on horseback to the offending shop. *But who could control God's winds? Or the choices of wealthy men like Senhor de Sousa?*

CHAPTER THREE

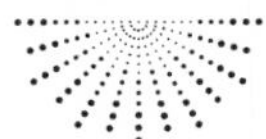

Church bells clanged, and on anchored ships sailors began to sing Vespers, their salty voices floating across the water on the early night breeze. Pêro waited alongside the potholed road, brow creased, overseeing the dark shadows of the comings and goings of Portuguese Naval ships on the Tagus River below. The anchored merchant vessels were heavy with freight from the colonies and Northern Europe. A few carriages and donkey carts clanked past him. He hailed a ride and stared out the open window as he traveled east into the city center towards home.

The cross of the Convent of Senhora of Jesus came into view and pierced the Barrio Alto neighborhood's horizon. Gold speckling the indigo sky was like a copy of a Giotto painting he had studied in his youth. *How is my mentor, Padre Danta, and my Franciscan Brotherhood*? It was nearly time for him to report on his deacon duties and responsibilities to the sick and poor. Obligations he had yet to properly attend to with the Fabrica's escalating workload and now the urgency of Bagamba's cause.

Dear Lord, I hope no one has fallen into irreversible neglect! He massaged his temples. *Should I inquire to the Order about support for Bagamba?*

One by one, lanterns of homes lit upon the slope below the

Senhora of Jesus priory. If only he'd been able to negotiate more time with Senhor de Sousa.

Along the route, turbaned musicians beat on drums and vigorously shook tambourines accompanied by the strumming of a viola and the sounds of an accordion.

Merriment pulsed in Lisbon, while blue devils hovered over his heart.

At Lisbon's central plaza, Rossio Square, Pêro descended from his coach and headed for a westerly side-street. Off in the distance to the east, All Saints Royal Hospital was alight, the tower of the infirmary's Dominican chapel soaring above its roofline. As he turned down the cobbled street leading to his home, he whispered a prayer for Bagamba.

Shrouded in shadow from the surrounding five-storied residences, Pêro worked the key into the iron lock. He entered the dark sala, where his wife, Paulinha kept a pewter plate and two sconces upon an ornate cabinet, the few precious pieces her deceased mother had left to her. But it was the items she kept within the escritoire that he considered of secret treasured value.

Laughter, punctuated by his youngest daughter Isabela's shrill giggling, led him to the kitchen. Lantern light haloed Paulinha's dark hair and slight figure dressed in her clay-chalked work skirt, as she and the girls cleared plates from the table. Their chatter subsided as he slumped onto a stool.

Paulinha dried her hands on a towel. "The tremors today nearly rattled the pots off their hooks."

Pêro rubbed his face with his hands. "Senhor de Sousa has given us until All Saints Day to pay for Bagamba. He must have the funds by November 1st, no later, or he'll go ahead with another sale. They came for Bagamba today, had him already caged and in chains for transport." Pêro met Paulinha's piercing blue eyes.

"But why would they take him? We're paying the installments for his release." Her arm fell to her side, the towel limp on her leg.

Pêro pinched the ridge of his nose. "I've gotten behind in our payments to Senhor de Sousa."

"What? How much? How could you let this happen, again?" She tossed the rag onto the table. "We've so many commissions."

"But you know how it is, *meu amor*." He reached for her hand; she leaned back against the counter. "We are only behind two payments."

"And that's only five weeks from now. We won't have enough time or resources to pay what is outstanding," Paulinha said. "And what about all we've already given Senhor de Sousa? Now, that's at risk? How could you, Pêro?"

"It will take every order we have and timely payment to make this happen. I promise I will not extend credit to anyone for anything else. Rafa's family — his father's well-being, Bagamba's life — depends on us. I know. Lord help us. I thought we'd have more time." He made the sign of the cross. "Bagamba's worried they'll come for him in the middle of the night. I should have brought him here, at least for tonight."

"Rafa will be relieved he's there with them and will see to his welfare. If something happens, he'll send word. Come to the table and eat." Paulinha retrieved the dishtowel, holding Pêro's stare.

His young daughters exchanged a worried look and finished drying the dishes in an uneasy silence.

CHAPTER FOUR

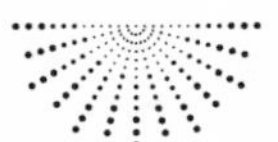

A raucous knock shook the wooden door. Bagamba bolted upright. Saucer-eyed, Rafa pointed to their sleeping room. He mouthed to Bagamba: "The window. Stay by the window. Ready."

Bagamba worked his way up from the mat and crept into the dark of the bedroom.

Josepha smoothed down her short-cropped hair, then folded her arms across her chest. She leaned against the earthen wall. Grandmother Gogo sat on a cushion beside her, opalescent eyes defiant. The four boys cross-legged encircled the glowing coals of the cook fire.

Another urgent knock.

Rafa headed to the door. "Coming." He held his breath then asked, "Who's there?"

"We've come to look in on things."

"Yes, and for what?"

"It's urgent. Please let me in." Rafa furrowed his brow, the voice somehow familiar.

Slowly, he cracked open the door.

"Sorry, one of us couldn't make it here sooner. We did receive word."

Rafa squinted at the lantern-lit face. "Oh, Brother Sambo. Come in." Rafa welcomed.

A midnight-colored man caped and capped in black entered. "Is your father here?"

"Father, it's all right to come out. Brother Sambo is here." Rafa escorted the man into their front room, grass-woven mats lining the side and back walls. An altar to the black Madonna sat in the far corner.

Bagamba stepped out of the dark. "*Boa noite.*"

"Water?" Josepha offered.

The man accepted the gourd cup, taking a sip. "A plan must be put in place. It's time."

Everyone looked at Bagamba.

Bagamba shrugged his shoulders and sighed.

"Trust in the Blacks of the Rosary." Brother Sambo gripped the cross at his neck. "I know how you feel about Padre Pêro. He's a decent Franciscan. But don't put your faith only in him. He's one man. There's greater strength in our unity." Brother Sambo's words filled the room. "With all of us who are now free here in Lisbon, there are still many enslaved like your father here." He motioned to Bagamba to come over, draping an arm over his shoulders. "Yes, living with a degree of freedom from his master who allows him to live here with you, while you bear the cost to care and feed him. Senhor de Sousa takes much and provides little. Yet Bagamba can be sold at any moment. Don't forget this."

Rafa ran his fingers over his eyes. "Yes. But Padre Pêro did intervene and is trying to secure his freedom like he did ours." He gripped his wife's hand.

"Padre Pêro was able to do so today. But what about next time?"

"What if they come for me again?" Bagamba interjected, his face contorting.

"Exactly, let us devise a plan of escape to keep you safe."

CHAPTER FIVE

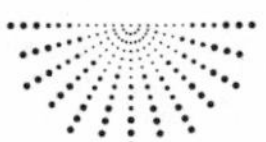

A week later, Pêro crouched in the Fabrica Santa María's courtyard organizing the tiles of a *figura de convite.* The life-sized figure would soon be inspected by the Archbishop's tile-setter. Pêro adjusted the tiles of the guard's welcoming hand, while the helmeted figure held a spear in the other.

Pêro paused from his work and cherished the last blooms of the red geraniums in the yard and the trellises of grape leaves turning from saffron to the color of claret wine growing along the walls of the court. The serpentine lines of the vines formed "S" shapes, reminding him of the de Sousa's brand mark, seared onto the necks of their slaves. Pêro let out a long sigh, whispering a prayer for Bagamba's ongoing safety.

A stout man in calf-high boots and a tricorn hat passed under the arched stone entrance to the Fabrica's inner courtyard. Dry heat rose in waves from the ground. The man squinted as he approached, blinded by the bright light reflecting off the glossy blue-and-white tiles, *azulejos,* laid out upon the earth next to the high wall of the main shop.

The ground quivered.

Pêro grabbed the stack of papers he'd set upon the tiles and stood.

The two men stared at the *figura de convite,* whose tiles clinked together before them.

"*Bom dia,* I'm Senhor Silva de Orvalho's new agent," the man offered. "The figure is magnificent, but is it trembling?"

"Welcome. *Santa María,*" Pêro said.

They glanced at each other, then quickly around the open court. Olives fell from the old tree to the hard ground, sounding like pounding rain.

Pêro tensed. The shaking of the earth felt somehow different, more urgent and forceful than before.

He looked down at the tiles. "Let us head inside."

Pêro hurried and gestured for the man to follow.

Upon entering, Pêro peered up at the wobbling ceramic statue of Saint Anthony. Wavering light shot through the front panes of the shop, as crates of tiles shook below. Pêro snatched the saint from its perch. He motioned for the agent to come with him around the sacks of silica in the doorway. Aghast, Pêro stared at the center of the open workroom as the vats of glazes, brimming with pastel pinks, greens, and creams, shook so hard that overspill ran down their sides.

Next to the far wall, Paulinha stopped moving her fingers along orderly rows of *azulejos* situated on the floor. She used both hands to steady the tiles in their place. They rattled against each other like stacked dishes. She turned to her oldest daughter, standing behind her, wide-eyed, Constanza, who abruptly halted making marks in a notebook, while Isabela, the youngest, stopped smiling and fiddling with her sister's rosewood tresses.

The earth stilled.

Then the room jolted with another shudder as if a stampede of carriages charged by. Pêro braced his legs. Out of the corner of his eye, he observed the visitor stealing a glance at Paulinha. She raised her head; their eyes caught, her cheeks flushed, and she turned away. She grabbed the tablet from Constanza and swiftly motioned the girls into the draft room. Paulinha gave one last look at her drafting table before she slipped out of Pêro's sight.

The shop workers glanced wide-eyed at each other.

Pêro looked down at the statue of Saint Anthony clenched in his marred hand.

What sign of God was this?

He stepped over to a shelf in front of the shop's wooden slat wall, setting down his stack of papers. His signet ring glinted as he let go of the commissions for *figuras de convite*. Then he steadied the shelf with his free hand. Buckets of brushes, molds, templates, and fluting tools jangled loudly on their shelves.

"Senhor? Padre Pêro? I've never been here, *into* the Mocambo. The ground continues to move," the agent said, his voice breaking. "Shouldn't we take to the outside?" Bits of plaster fell like hail from the rafters bouncing off the man's tricorn hat and Pêro's back.

"Quickly here! Give me a hand with this shelf!" Pêro yelled. "Save our master tiles!"

"Watch out!" someone blurted.

Hand on hat, the agent lurched forward as a section of the vaulted ceiling crashed to the floor. A cannon-like sound echoed throughout the space, followed by a cloud of motes, and flying chunks of hard earth and roof tile.

Pêro covered his face with his hands. He deflected flying pieces from his eyes. He espied his laborers' startled faces through the spaces of his missing fingers. They stared at him. And at the fellow who had "never been *into* the Mocambo", both narrowly escaping the falling ceiling.

Brothers Kujaguo and Jawoli gaped at the destruction. The lizard tattoos in the center of their mahogany foreheads contorted with concern.

"Here, come closer to me." Pêro motioned to the agent.

Pêro took stock of the shop and everyone in it, all of whom waited in silence for what would happen next. They craned their heads skyward, watching, listening to the shifting objects of the shop. A peep hole of blue sky shone through. *Would anything else come thundering down?*

Pêro brushed plaster bits from his shoulders.

Slowly, the shaking subsided.

Everyone looked around, mouths agape, eyes alert.

"Blessed God seems to have ceased his murmurings again… as He always does," Pêro said. He made the sign of the cross. "Lord, protect us. Now, let us not let His ways keep us from doing our service to Him. Let us see to this clean up and repair."

With cautious movements, everyone joined in to help clear the mess.

Pêro replaced Saint Anthony in his niche above the entrance doorway and retrieved his papers.

"Are you all right? Now, that we've had a moment to catch our breath. How may I be of assistance?" he asked the waiting man, who was hard at work cleaning his overcoat.

The fellow cleared his throat. "I'm agent Lico. That was close…I've been sent by Captain Rocha of the *Nossa Senhora da Luz*, to check on the progress of an order. The one for our client in the Amazon, Felipe Silva de Orvalho from Brazil, you know, the wood baron. I've been informed he's commissioned two tile murals as well as a large shipment of decorative tiles. Negotiated by his prior agent." Lico tilted his head forward, eyebrows raised.

"It's in process," Pêro said.

Lico reached inside the breast of his navy coat and extracted a letter. "There's been a design change."

Pêro raised an eyebrow, then broke the wax seal. He scanned it quickly. "This is quite a change — two completely different murals. We've already drawn the others." Pêro looked up and said in a low voice. "And we don't produce one of the subjects requested."

Lico nodded. "Senhor Silva de Orvalho worried as much."

"And what of the other designs? And compensation? Arranged with the other agent?"

Lico shrugged his shoulders. "I've orders to go to another

shop like Nicolau de Freitas or buy Delft tiles direct from Jesuit Padre João…"

From the doorway of the draft room, Paulinha shot Pêro a look.

Pêro eyed Lico and then said in a kind, controlled manner. "Full payment *is due* upon delivery as previously negotiated. Not a day later." He handed the letter back to the agent.

"Our departure has also been rescheduled for the eve of All Saints Day, after the day's celebrations. The captain believes firmly in sailing with the saints' blessings." Lico tugged on the front corners of his jacket.

"That's a month from now. We had until Christmastide before, I'm sure of this." Pêro blanched but recovered quickly. "But we'll deliver. Again, the shipment must be paid in full."

"Yes, I'll see to it," Lico said.

"It's an interesting place, the colony of Brazil?" Pêro asked, trying to calm his nerves.

Lico's jacket buttons glimmered in the shop's sun-infused haze. "This is my first voyage with Captain Rocha. I've been told the jungle goes as far as one can see, a wonder to behold. I know the captain is eager to ship your cargo and will be pleased to receive the delivery."

With a tip of his head, Lico stepped around stacked crates awaiting cargo in the entryway and headed back into the white light of the courtyard. Pêro placed his hand to his chest, resting it on the coral rosary, as he stood in the front entrance, looking on as the man set off into the noontide heat.

Bells chimed out of sync from the Mocambo's many convents. Pêro replayed the new agent's parting words, ones displaying his excitement at setting off for the colony of Brazil. He sighed. While many of his countrymen dreamed of the riches to be found in far-off lands, his concern was for those who'd yet to find the light of God, a much-discussed topic amongst his Franciscan Brotherhood.

Pêro turned to go back inside. At the far end of the courtyard, past the olive-littered ground, Rafa and Bagamba organized new wooden boxes for shipping. Suddenly, Bagamba dropped to his knees and bent over upon the ground. Pêro rushed over. "What's wrong? What's happened?"

"Here, *Pai*." Rafa said, helping him upright.

"Sit down, catch your breath." Pêro said. They propped him against a crate.

Bagamba closed his eyes and drew in long breaths steadying himself. "These boxes like the ones we were kept in before being transported to Lisbon."

Pêro shivered, coldness sweeping through him.

"When mother and I were kidnapped as are people fled north, following an elephant track because "elephants always know where water is". We tried to escape. But Rafa your grandmother, Gogo, my young mother, and I new to walking, we couldn't keep up. They caught us." Bagamba's face contorted, his shoulders slumped. He looked to Rafa, and then Pêro. "Every time I touch these crates, I still hear her cries when we were separated. Caged and sold."

Pêro's heart ached. It was an all-too common story. "Come with me inside for some water. Rafa can finish here."

Pêro entered the draft room, where he found Paulinha pacing back and forth.

"Girls," Paulinha said. "Continue counting without me. We left off on the third row. Constanza, here, take the ledger." Paulinha, hands on their backs, showed the girls out. They turned, looking at their father who gave them a supportive nod. Paulinha shut the door and turned to Pêro. "I heard everything. And the Lord's shaking is disconcerting."

"Everything?" Pêro rifled through piles of designs and commissions on his desk. "The Lord has His ways. With diligence we'll complete the Amazon commission on time. I know we've lost time and money on the other designs. What could I do?" Pêro threw up his hands. "Another concern of mine now is one of the design's questionable subject matter."

"What?" Paulinha placed a hand on her hip. "You should have at least suggested his employer pay some sort of fee for those other designs."

"You heard him; they were ready to abandon the whole project. Then where would we be? Fooling around trying to get payment on something they never received." Pêro scratched his temple. "Their full payment will secure Bagamba's freedom and get us out from underneath all of this."

Paulinha pursed her lips. "Yes, the Lord does have His ways. It upsets me that the new agent brought up the shop of your apprentice of all people, and Padre João and his Delft tile imports." She pointed a finger at the window. "What if we are unable to meet the ship's departure date? We are short by weeks to complete such a request with all these other smaller orders queued." She pointed to a Bible-thick stack of commissions. "And what is it about one of the designs that worries you?"

"We'll have to manage it. I don't see that we have any other choice." He rested his fingertips on a clean sheet of paper. "We'll start tomorrow. A man's life is at stake. No one will ever see Bagamba again if we don't follow through. The other buyer's farms are in the far north, in the Douro region. They will use him up like an old rag with no family to tend to him while they force the last of his strength out of him. It would devastate Rafa, thus the shop — all of us." Earnestly, Pêro looked at his wife, her face softened, sending a warm wave of reassurance through him. "Together, we will see this through."

Paulinha bit her fingernail. "What will we be designing?" She headed to her draft table and began clearing paperwork.

CHAPTER SIX

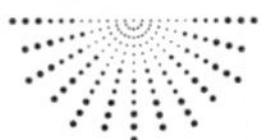

Stark morning light shone in rays through the square-paned windows of the drafting room, warming Pêro's back. He leaned over his desk sketching in the quiet of the closed space. "Do you know if Luis arrived on time today to help unload the kiln?"

Paulinha sat straight-backed upon a stool, studying her drawing. She glanced up at the corner where rolled designs rested against the wall. "He didn't."

Pêro shook his head, inspecting a courtship scene of an airy natural setting propped up on a miniature easel. It was a copy of an engraving by the celebrated French painter Watteau. He let out a long breath and drew an under sketch, rendering the life of a wealthy man in the company of sparsely clad native women. He pressed hard on the black lead, retracing the lines of the women's bodies, inwardly wanting to depict finely attired ladies in *rocaille* fashion dresses, the current vogue, featuring repetitive patterns of shells and feathers. Extravagant but acceptable. But the design began to reveal itself like secrets cajoled from its teller. Suddenly, he thought of Luis and how he wished he could get him to disclose his inner world. *Why was he continually late these days?*

Pêro closed his eyes in dismay at the vanity that was the current craze on the Continent and how Lisbon embraced it, living in excess and pageantry despite the Inquisition's preaching, prescripts, and punishments. He shuddered at the thought, the blatant and open disregard for humble well-founded Biblical precepts, and the harsh ways in which the Church sought enforcement of its maxim: burning, hanging, and dungeon imprisonment. *Didn't the Lord preach tolerance and understanding?*

He moaned and set down his graphite, shaking out his hands, stretching his fingers as if playing the pianoforte, still sensing the movement of his missing appendages. He placed his maimed hand on his heart and studied the design, then frowned.

Paulinha stopped drawing. "What's wrong?"

"Although I find drawing one of life's greatest pleasures, it troubles me to produce such a scandalous scene. What might the Church think of these less-than-dressed native women engaged in dubious interactions with a man of the Lord? What if they should find out about it?" Pêro said.

"Well, they might question how you've become so skilled in depicting the female figure," she said, lifting an eyebrow and smiling.

Pêro laughed with her. "The shop has an obligation to fill its orders and collect its payments, so we can fulfill our ultimate commitments: to liberate and employ the downtrodden and keep families together. And here we are, twelve years later after making this commitment to ourselves and God, creating a potentially controversial and frivolous scene to help liberate another."

Pêro wiped beads of sweat from his upper lip. He picked up his drawing tool and framed the scene with what would be its decorative tiles, images of plump cherubs and lush foliage.

Paulinha made bold strokes across her paper, arm dancing, drafting a repetitive shell-flower motif.

He stopped and studied her as she busily shaded with Toulouse blue pastel and added hints of yellow and white in other areas, to indicate where the colored glazes would eventually go.

She emerged from her trance, brushing hair strands from her forehead. "When this is affixed to Senhor de Orvalho's residence, the effect will be breathtaking. Oh, how I wish I could see this in the jungle."

"Could you take a look at this?" Pêro made room for her before his drawing.

She came over. "Pêro, we argued and agreed to this last night." From the table she retrieved gum elastic, removing some of the women's sparse clothing. With sure lines she enhanced the curvature of breasts and added in exposed private parts. Vigorously, she shaded and reinforced the sensual femininity of the women. "It's what was requested. Honestly, I'll confide I thought about it and I don't feel shame. Why should I? My body is similar."

"But last night you were adamantly against the whole idea."

"I don't want to belabor this."

Pêro resumed his spot on the stool and stared at what she'd done. "We can't do this."

"Just finish the rest of the scene. Be done with it, my love."

He fetched the gum elastic.

She stopped his hand. "No, I don't see any way around this. You agreed to it. Remember it will bring the proceeds we need for Bagamba."

"But what if the Church finds out?"

"It's not for them. We'll make it and crate it."

Pêro bit his lip. "I know the design will please the wood baron. Imagine all the insects there. How would the girls and I fare without you?"

"You'd all do well, I'm sure," she said. She returned her attention to her design, adding large border tiles and decorating them with blue and white ropes. "But imagine what it must be like," she said in a far-off dreamy voice, as she filled in more color.

"You have amazing imagination and courage." Pêro moved to her table and stood before her. He was proud of her design talent, her adventurous spirit, her commitment to their work. Yet, guilt swelled like an incoming tide. *Is it wrong to design such a scene? To love your wife so?*

"I deeply wish I could see the murals in the jungle."

He embraced her shoulders and kissed her dark hair, giving thanks for her present light-heartedness.

A familiar voice from the other side of the closed door interrupted them. "Padre Pêro? May I have a word with you?"

"Luis." Paulinha hissed, her eyes narrowed in irritation. She moved to the rolled designs in the corner and pretended to organize them. She waved for Pêro to sit down in her place.

Pêro turned over his design and sat before Paulinha's. "Yes Luis, come in."

Luis pushed open the door, pausing to gaze at his long white fingers.

"How are you? What can I help you with today, Luis?" Pêro asked, pushing himself up from the table.

Luis cast his eyes over Paulinha. "Hello, Paulinha, looking for a design, are you? Or…"

"Or what?" she said, refusing to look at Luis.

"How can I assist you?" Pêro asked.

Luis pressed his thin lips together, raising his aquiline nose. "How are the commissions coming along? We've been quite busy lately." Luis looked dead center at him. "I need an advance on my pay."

"You know I am not in a position to do so. We are saving to liberate Rafa's father."

Pêro examined Paulinha's drafting. "I must get back to work. Is there anything else?" He glanced up to see Luis's frown.

"Rafa's father is not my concern."

"He is ours." Pêro said. "And mind you, *please* arrive at the same time as the rest of us.

Your tardiness is beginning to wear on others. Is there anything else?"

Paulinha stopped her arranging and glared at Luis.

Luis turned and scowled at her. "No, that is all." He stomped out.

Paulinha rushed over and slammed the door. She held up clenched fists and brought them down in fury.

"I know, *meu amor,*" Pêro said. "Luis is becoming more difficult and demanding as the years pass. But you know why we need to keep him: to free Bagamba. Training another to Luis's tile making skill takes years." Pêro kept his hand firmly upon her design. "Remember it is because of you and your ongoing innovations of the *figura de convite* that we're able to continue freeing the enslaved."

Oh, how the rich loved the life-size *figura de convite,* Pêro mused, and as the new designs debuted a stream of commissions for them flowed in, but receiving final payments took months of follow up. But with the designs' popularity so grew the number of coins in his purse, coins of liberation, profits that facilitated the purchase of their workers' freedom and the subsequent hiring of them for pay.

Paulinha pressed her ear to the door, brow knit, and, looking about the room, came toward him. In a hushed voice she said, "And the secret of the *figura de convite's* current innovator, lest we forget. Speak softly, Pêro, we can't risk jeopardizing all this." She swept her hand across the room. She leaned in close. "Remember what I said about Luis? He's up to something. I sense it. And truly, we have God to thank for creativity, not me nor you." She moved behind Pêro's draft table and stared at the downturned parchment.

He switched over to his stool and she sat down upon hers.

Eyebrows pinched, she looked at the closed door and then at her design and again at the over-turned paper.

He watched her hand tremble as she reached for her drawing utensils. Finally, she picked up some ochre and set back to work.

In the late afternoon, Luis sauntered into the courtyard, smug-faced, bag in hand, smelling of cinnamon. The rest of the shop workers rolled up their pants cuffs, and Paulinha and the girls hoisted their long skirts, exposing knee-length bloomers, readying themselves to stamp air out of the clay. One by one, they stepped into the contained corral of moist earth in a compartment next to the other outdoor clay holding stalls. The high wall of the shop cast a cool shadow as the late afternoon sun of autumn baked the open yard. In unison, they worked their legs up and down. Luis hovered nearby observing, grooming his tawny hair.

"Welcome back, Luis," Pêro said, from the corral. "Long lunch…"

Luis shoved his nose up at Paulinha. "You're moving too slow."

"Shall you be joining us?" Paulinha asked tartly.

"Luis." Isabela flung a ball of clay at him.

Constanza laughed.

"I bring you a treat, and now this *mis*-treatment." Luis held up the bag, and opened it, helping himself to a cinnamon-sprinkled custard. He ate it and then the other.

Isabela and Constanza turned their backs on him. Constanza smartly readjusted her bodice, her budding breasts now visibly pushing forth from the fitted fabric. She looked to her younger sister and made an ugly face. Isabela mimicked her. Paulinha shot them a look that said: don't push him.

Pêro prayed to himself, and stewed over Luis's obvious malcontent, as he stomped down hard on the clay, working it through his toes. *Why is he late again? And so full of contempt?*

Pêro thought back to the day when Paulinha first had approached him about making *azulejos* herself. She'd spent hours observing him as she nursed Constanza, watching him shape and trim tiles. Her desire to work the clay had blossomed with their first child's growth and his increasing desire to serve the Franciscan Order.

"I want to make tiles. My hands ache to work the clay and my mind is ablaze with design ideas. I've already thought it through: I can work under your monogram. Our initials are the same, no one will ever know," she'd explained.

Pêro remembered how his stomach had panged with unease. "I'm afraid the men of the shop won't accept you nor take kindly to copying designs made by a woman."

"But I have ideas. I can help," she'd said. "Please, Pêro, please."

"I fear Luis will be difficult. He's already surly with the men."

"I've observed him. He lacks patience to execute delicate lines. There's little imagination to his renderings. Let me try my hand at it," she pleaded. "I'll stick to the shadows. Not let my effort be seen."

He'd studied his wife and was taken with her understanding of tile works. To make outstanding *azulejos,* it required more than merely copying a design. It necessitated the rendering of the soul, the giving over to God, patience, and inner stability — and practice. Plus, flair in the moment when the soft sable hairs of the paintbrush, loaded with pigment, swept across the prepared ground.

Finally, he agreed, "I'll support you, but the designs must be done in secrecy."

She excelled at the work.

Did Luis know she was designing?

He was bothered by Paulinha's recent suspicion that Luis was somehow conspiring with the chubby-faced Jesuit Padre João de Magella, who imported Delft tiles, and was one of their shop's longstanding competitors.

"Luis was particularly sour the other day when I overheard

the other shop workers' complaints about how Padre João is publicly speaking poorly of our shop's craftsmanship. He had the gall to guffaw," she confided.

"I pray Luis holds his tongue if he knows, or has somehow surmised, you're the designer of the latest *figura de convite* craze, of the masqueraded elegant couple. All our livelihoods depended upon silence on the matter as you well know."

"Yes, I do. We both fear if people found out I, a woman created it, they may not find it so wondrous, so brilliant, nor so in demand."

Pêro cut the exchange short to not reveal the true extent of his concerns. *And then how would we continue to serve those in need? What would the Inquisition really think and do if they knew a woman created such a playful work? And now this latest suspect design? What would a well-positioned priest like Padre João do with such information?*

Paulinha excused herself from the clay-stomping group and went to the front of the courtyard.

Pêro watched as she picked a red geranium from the potted plants at the entrance arch. She walked over and gazed at the *figura de convite* of the noblewoman adhered to the wall, who gestured to the door with a closed fan, welcoming clients. Paulinha reached up and placed her hand on the figure's chest, her heart, and mouthed a prayer. To the saints he was sure of it, and he imagined she said: *The family secret is safe within you and me and fired within us both.* She then enclosed the flower in the palm of her hand and squeezed tight, crushing its splendor.

CHAPTER SEVEN

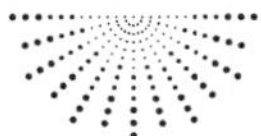

Paulinha let herself into the draft room, closing the door behind her, turning the lock. Sunday morning darkness lingered outside the windows, she grateful for its protective cover. Squinting in the dark, she made her way to Pêro's design table.

She'd gone to bed early last night, entering a deep sleep, one filled with artistic inspiration. Vivid designs visited her dreams. She'd risen before the roosters, the day's responsibilities, and church. Quickly, she'd dressed and tiptoed downstairs, leaving a note to Pêro of her whereabouts, not to worry, and to fetch her at first light at the Fabrica. She'd hurried and walked with the fisherman's wives and the early morning catch as they returned to the Mocambo from the riverfront.

Recovering the match box, she lit the lantern. Its light sputtered to life, casting a glow over the stacks of designs on the draft table. She riffled through a pile, locating the seductive scene for the wood baron.

With both hands she smoothed it out, setting stone weights at its corners. She stood over it, envisioning what she'd seen in her night vision, trying to recall each detail. She retrieved her sketchbook hidden in the folds of her skirt and reviewed her drawing.

This was always the challenge, to bring forth onto paper the magic and movement of the dream world, the gifts given in sleep. She reached for the graphite and sat on the stool. She let the lead glide over the parchment, her hand seemingly moving on its own as she brought forth slumber's insights.

Fluidly, she shaded the women's bodies as would be done at a later stage with blue glaze pigment. Each body held its own shape and size, every woman her own persuasion and power. From the silence of the space came feelings and emotions which she rendered in each woman's face. Her task now was to honor and bring to life the unique persona of each lady, easier imagined than done. Descending through her hands, fingers onto paper, she could feel the freedom of these women. Those with little to no clothing, the jungle heat upon their skin and the cool shade of the large, buttressed trees Pêro had told her about. Where some of the women reclined below the arbor's canopy, a parrot or two perched upon a hand, a shoulder. She took liberties in sketching. *Where else could she, if not here on parchment?*

She was tired of the restrictions put upon her. *How to bear it?* She needed to be free to do as she wanted somewhere! Paulinha sighed as her artistic flurry came to a close. She smiled, set down the pencil, and leaned back on the stool. She observed the drawing. Ah, the thrill of creative grace, the greatest of gifts and gratification. She removed the stones, and picked the paper up by the corners, holding it out, inspecting what she'd done, homing in on areas in need of improvement or adjustment. *Yes, that there must be removed, while the lines over there need to be extended, possibly more shading here.*

Outside a fiery pink-hue filled the sky, casting a glow and then a sudden shadow moved across the design. She froze. To her back she could feel eyes upon her. Swiftly, she brought the paper down, then spun on her heel toward the window, meeting only the pastel hues of the oncoming day. She rushed to the window, palms to pane, looking out. She could feel the presence of someone there. But no physical person stood before her. Yet an unfamiliar fermented dank scent seemed to seep in from the cracks of the windowsill. She sniffed and stepped back from the window, slowly retreating to the table.

She reviewed the design one last time. Later she'd make more changes. She stashed the parchment with the others.

"Paulinha?" Pêro called. "We're here. Ready?"

She smoothed down the skirt of her dress, snuffed the lantern. Upon exiting, she took one last look at the window, meeting only the light of the oncoming day, then closed the door.

Moments later, outside the draft room window, a long coil of smoke rose up, lingered, and played at the windowpane.

CHAPTER EIGHT

"Come, girls." Pêro beckoned to Constanza and Isabela who trailed behind. Constanza stopped and looked in on the gold and silver filigree works displayed in a window. Isabela lingered in front of a pastry shop, its pane filled with golden egg-yolk custards and doughy delicacies of *barriga de freiras,* "belly of nuns". As Pêro waited for them, he enjoyed the scent of burnt sugar and yeast.

Constanza touched lithe fingers to her ears. "I long for gold heart-shaped earrings."

"But your ears aren't pierced!" Isabela laughed. "*Pai,* may I have a treat?"

Constanza pouted. "One day they will be." She lifted her chin and feigned seeing something important ahead.

"Not now, Princess." Pêro smiled at Isabela before shifting his attention to Constanza. "No daughter of mine will wear gold while others remain in chains."

Constanza threw up an arm and walked on.

They worked their way through the crowded city-center street. Rua Ouro was packed with buyers and traders from every realm with daggers at their waists and the occasional fanciful sun parasol. While Lisboners in long black cloaks held tight the rosary in one hand and a sword in the other, engravers, jewelers, goldsmiths, and currency-exchange houses lined the busy commercial lane, a frog's leap from the port full of merchant ships.

Pêro and the girls passed the old import tax offices of royalty and entered Pelourinho Velho plaza, smelling of fresh ink. Clerks sat crowded at tables drafting letters, eulogies, petitions, and whatever else they were asked to write. The requesters milled around the writers' tables, chatting and exchanging gossip to the busy scratch of quills. A man shoved another fellow, accusing him of a misdeed. The accused ripped the writer's paper from the desk and tore it to shreds. Yelling ensued.

"Hurry along girls." Pêro quickly moved the girls forward, away from the dispute.

"Wouldn't it be wonderful to receive a love letter or poem?" Constanza said with a far-off look like her mother's.

Isabela rolled her eyes and shook her head, glancing back.

At the square's southern corner, they entered a side-street, where shops sold luxury items: damask silk fabrics the colors of the rainbow, Tunisian carpets, lemon-colored glass beads, elephant tusks and copper pots.

Pêro stopped before a window, cupped his hand to the glass and peered in. Paintbrushes of all sizes poked out of clay pots in the display, interspersed between lidded metal and clay pigment pots, potters needles and cutting wires. Mid-shop, rolled and stretched canvas sat in racks. A macaw with blue and yellow feathers the color of *azulejos* perched inside a cage attached to the wall of the display case. It stared back at them and squawked through the pane.

"Welcome, Padre Pêro!" The proprietor waved them in, the parrot repeating. "Welcome!"

Pêro watched as the girls fixed their eyes on the exotic bird whose beady eyes followed their every movement. Then they set their attention on the curious objects lining the back wall behind the counter: odd-shaped colored rocks, glass jars filled with brilliant blues, earthy yellows, browns, and vermilions. Out of sight, from the back of the shop, came the sound of stone grinding upon stone.

"What can I help you with today?" the owner asked, fanning his fleshy arm. "Rumor is you're extremely busy." The short semi-bald vendor winked.

"Is that so, Senhor Simões?" Pêro frowned.

"Yes. And that Jesuit Padre João isn't pleased. Heard you won the new commission for the Archbishop?"

"Word on the street travels faster than the Lord's." Heat suffused Pêro's body, his heartbeat picking up at the mention of Padre João and the Archbishop.

Senhor Simões grinned.

"We've come for brushes and pots of cobalt."

Senhor Simões set out an assortment of sumi and sable hair-brushes. Then he disappeared behind a sea-green curtain.

"See here, girls," Pêro said, pointing to a bushy brush with a bamboo handle. "These are for making full lines like those for outlining and shading large areas." Pêro picked up a slender paintbrush with a fine tip. "These are for the delicate lines and details. See the difference?"

"Yes," the girls said. Isabela beamed at him. Constanza's gaze remained fixed on the stones.

"May I hold it?" Isabela asked, staring at the slender-tipped brush.

"Yes, go ahead and pick it up. See how it feels. Hold it here with your thumb and index finger and place your third finger there. Good thing you still have yours," Pêro said, winking at her.

"Oh, *Pai*." Isabela bashfully took hold of the brush.

"Anything else?" Senhor Simões placed the pigment pots on the counter with the paintbrushes.

"*Pai*, what are those blue stones with the gold specks?" Constanza asked breathlessly.

"This?" Senhor Simões took an angular chunk, the size of

his hand, off the shelf. "This is one of God's most expensive creations, lapis lazuli. It comes from the Far East, where men with wild black eyes drive donkeys over desolate deserts with sacks of this hidden treasure inside." Senhor Simões ran his fingers over the stone as if caressing a beloved's cheek. "Ground down, it makes sea and sky in the finest of paintings."

Pêro placed his hand upon a pot of cobalt pigment. "Princess, sorry, we won't be buying any of that today. This pigment here allows us to create our blue gradations and is far more affordable."

Pêro pointed to the brush in Isabela's hand and to the other full-bodied one. "And we'll take three of these and three of those. Add it to our account."

The macaw squawked as they left, their wares bundled in old pages from the *Gazeta de Lisboa*.

They strolled back across the busy square.

"Wasn't the bird exquisite?" Isabela asked.

"I liked the gold bedazzled stones." Constanza looked to the sky.

Pêro gazed ahead and saw Padre João in front of the old tax duties office. He reached for Isabela's hand. "Let's take a different route back."

But it was too late. Padre João had already caught sight of their approach. He was cloaked in a cape and the Jesuit's black habit. His hands were full of leather-bound papers. Brothers circled him. How apropos, thought Pêro, since it is the Jesuits who truly now seem to control the coffers of this country, not kings.

Padre João glowered as they drew near, the fat of his cheeks making slits of his eyes. "Ah, the great Tile Master PMP, inventor of the highly sought after *figura de convite*." Padre João exclaimed through his knot of men. "The hoarder of commissions." The Brothers fell silent and stepped closer to Padre João's sides, creating a protective horseshoe.

Pêro cleared his throat, his face afire. "The Lord is the great Master, not I. And, like you, I'm merely his servant.'

"But this is where *you* go astray. For my now greatly reduced tile profits go direct into the hands of the Church and services for the poor and yours into your pocket." A burst of spittle fell from Padre João's lips.

Pêro's face and neck flushed. Padre João was still jealous, after all these years, and was now visibly furious that the Fabrica Santa María continued to win the Archbishop's esteem. This time the Fabrica was to provide *figuras de convite* for his countryside summer palace instead of the now out-of-favor Delft allegorical panel Padre João proposed. Soon, the Fabrica's work would be affixed to the palace's wall.

Pêro cleared his throat. "You know as well as I that the Fabrica Santa María's profits go to buy freedom for the enslaved and to help the poor and sick."

"I'm not so sure that I do," Padre João said, jutting his head forward. "Your girls seem to be as finely dressed as any wealthy merchant's daughters."

Absurd! His girls stared at the cobbles beneath their feet in silence. *How dare he bring my daughters into this!* Blood surged in Pêro's veins. His muscles tightened.

"Good day, Padre João, Brothers," Pêro said with a nod, clenching Isabela's hand. The girls curtsied, held tight their wares, and stepped away. Pêro walked in long strides.

Padre João's voice trailed them. "You'll be hearing from me. From the Jesuits…"

"Dear Lord," Pêro said under his breath. He picked up their pace.

CHAPTER NINE

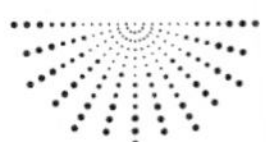

What to do? Rafa scratched his head, hovering over a design in the Fabrica's second story of the warehouse. "I'm not sure what Padre Pêro intends here." He pointed to a section of the drawing.

Kujaguo and Jawoli half-listened as they arranged tiles on a nearby table.

"Should I cut away the clay around the head of curls to the corseted waistline?" With his clay cutting knife, Rafa pointed to the square tiles before him and the charcoal perforated lines upon them. He studied the original mock cartoon again of the masqueraded noblewoman. "What do you think?" he asked Kujaguo and Jawoli.

Kujaguo and Jawoli stopped arranging tiles. "You need to ask Padre Pêro. I certainly don't know what he's thinking," Jawoli said. "Is this layout correct?"

Kujaguo shrugged and smiled, causing the tattooed etched dark lines fanning from the corners of his mouth like cat whiskers to perk up.

Rafa batted his lips with his index finger. "You're right. I'll go take a look at some of our other work upstairs. Maybe there's a clue in one of them of what to do here."

Jawoli puckered his lips in agreement and returned to his own dilemma.

Rafa ascended the stairway to a wide, open room. Completed pictorial murals and other *figuras de convite* were mounted on hardboard backing, some lying flat on the floor, others propped up like scene backdrops for plays.

He approached an upright mustachioed figure of a footman, a *figura de convite.* Words floated from his mouth: "Come in Your Lordship," the print read.

"See here, the tile has been cut away for the words." Rafa called down to Jawoli and Kujaguo.

Rafa returned to the floor below and started for the main floor staircase to seek out Padre Pêro. Pêro hadn't come to the outlying shop to check on them all morning. This is where they made all refinement cuttings for *figuras de convite,* statues of saints and fanciful figurines, along with the final inspections of finished orders before their crating and shipment.

Paulinha rushed up the stairs and ran into Rafa, dropping the rolled designs she carried. "Here, Rafa." She thrust the remaining scrolls at him and caught her breath. "These are to double check the commissions below."

Rafa reached down, gathering up the fallen pieces.

"We have a backlog of orders to be shipped for the Church." She reached down to help Rafa.

"Quite a few other orders too." Rafa motioned to a vase of flowers for the outside of a building and a courtship scene in process. "There are a couple of maritime murals that need to be boxed and a hunting scene."

Heads down Jawoli and Kujaguo continued to arrange and mark each tile numerically and alphabetically, prepping them to be placed into crates for delivery and forthcoming installation.

"Senhora Paulinha, is Padre Pêro around?" Rafa asked.

"He just stepped out with a client. But he should be back shortly," she said. "What are you working on? Maybe I can assist?"

"It's Padre Pêro's new masqueraded noblewoman." Rafa set down the scrolls. "I'm not sure if I should cut or leave this clay here around the waist and upwards?" Rafa gestured to the tiles upon the table.

"Ah," she said.

Paulinha honed-in on the cartoon, alongside the tiles. "See here, where the decorative border tiles complete this line and lead into her dress there." She pointed to the paper design. "Cut away the clay from here to the other side of her body, connecting it all with the decorative borders on both sides, so it's symmetric."

She ran her finger first along and above the charcoal pricked line superimposed on each clay tile. "Do you see what I mean?"

Luis's voice called from the stairwell. "I am sure *Jawoli* and Rafa and *Kujaguo* too, understand now that you've instructed them. Right *Jorge*, Rafa and *Carlos*?" He used the men's Christian names. He came over to where Paulinha and Rafa now stood stiff before the work.

"Aren't you quite friendly with these slaves?" Luis glowered at her. "And so knowledgeable about this new *figura de convite*?" he said. "How might that be?"

Paulinha's face flushed. "They're no longer slaves." She gestured to the clay cutting knife in Rafa's hand. "From what I've observed and heard Padre Pêro instruct —"

Rafa offered her the tool.

She stared at it and Luis at her.

"Go ahead." Luis cajoled motioning to the tool.

She locked eyes with Luis and accepted the knife.

With one swift motion she began. "See here, cut along this line as Pêro...follow the contour of her waist and shoulder and neck and onward and over." She handed the knife back to Rafa. "I'm sure Padre Pêro will be up soon. Excuse me." She gathered up her skirt in both hands and headed for the stairs. "Remember to consult the scrolls."

Rafa and Luis looked at the precision of her cut. Perfection.

Luis scowled. "Give that to me."

Rafa held back the knife, away from Luis's reach.

They glared at each other.

Slowly, with reluctance Rafa handed it over.

CHAPTER TEN

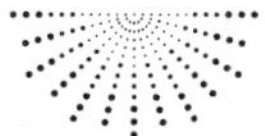

"*Jorge* and *Carlos*." Jawoli huffed, taking leave of the Fabrica's outbuilding. "I detest those names."

Kujagou and Rafa followed him into the bright light.

"Like trying to wear another's skin. White skin." Kujagou looked down on his cacao arm, shaking his head.

The three men sat on the ground, backs against the warm white wall of the building.

Jawoli looked at the sky as a cloud obscured the sun. "I long for home, across the water and sea of sand."

Kujagou smiled at his brother from their father's first wife. "Me too. I can still hear the night hyenas laughing and see the glow of moon on our hunts for honey."

Jawoli closed his eyes, bringing his knees up, gripping his upper arms with his hands. An ant crawled across his skin, the tickling feeling the same as in his village. "Home. Jawoli. My name is Jawoli." He opened his eyes, fury blazing. "Change my name. But can't take my memories." His nostrils flared. "I not give up the cool shade of the mango tree and conversations there. Or my hunting dog. The sweet nectar of the blooms in the trees after rain. The funny Baobabs. The pounding of millet and smiles of our mothers. Days tracking animals and tending goats among spiny trees. Our calabash drums, dance, and songs around the fire. The fields, planting, quiet of the land. Smoking whenever I want. Market days. *Our ways.*" Jawoli forced himself off the ground, grabbing his hair. "I am Jawoli! Never *Jorge*."

CHAPTER ELEVEN

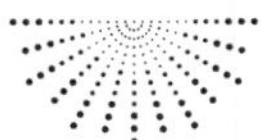

Pêro received the silver chalice from the parish priest. He set the sacred Eucharist in its place on the front altar, backed by the gilt three-tiered shelf and tabernacle box. He waited at the side of Padre Tomé as the priest closed Sunday Mass. Pêro gazed up at the plump plaster cherubs hovering in the cumulus cloud arcade. A sense of safety swept through him as he contemplated the small windowless chapel illuminated by candles, bathing the space in a fragrant glow.

Listening to the closing words, Pêro asked the Lord for his protection and guidance on how to handle Luis's inappropriate behavior towards Paulinha. Despite himself, he admired the blue and white tiles depicting the different life events of the Virgin lining the nave walls of Nossa Senhora da Oliveira, their neighborhood chapel in the city center. He bowed his head, asking for God's guardianship while scolding himself for being distracted in prayer by the beauty of art.

Paulinha and the girls waited in the second row of pews while Pêro finished his deacon duties. Fellow worshipers departed single file down the middle of the nave.

Isabela hummed the last hymn as Constanza prodded her to

slide out from the bench to meet their father. Paulinha leaned down and whispered into Constanza's ear. "Patience, Princess."

Outside the nondescript church facade, one large iron lantern hung over its entrance, indicating its location in the labyrinth of the center's warren.

Pêro greeted the milling congregation outside.

Padre Tomé stepped from the church and waved. "Brother Pêro." He rushed over, squinting in the sunlight, and patted each girl on the head. Constanza and Isabela winced.

"Padre, it was a lovely homily," Paulinha said. The girls stood by smiling at Padre Tomé clothed in a simple robe whose tonsured hair was now whiter than gray.

The priest pushed a drawstring pouch into Pêro's hand. "I nearly forgot. Please take communion to the Martins sisters."

Constanza scrunched her nose. This change of plans meant they couldn't go to the market. Shoulders slumped, Isabela and Constanza frowned at each other.

Paulinha nodded her head congenially.

"Tell them I send my blessings and wish for their swift return to our parish. That God is seeing to their well-being." Padre Tomé retreated into the chapel.

Pêro addressed the girls. "Often, situations and people possess the qualities we imbue them with. May I impress upon you both again, the importance of service. Thank goodness, Padre Tomé's eyesight is faltering. But mine hasn't, mind you."

"What's imbue?" Isabela asked.

"To instill or to inspire," he said.

Paulinha reached for his hand and held it tight.

The girls raised their eyebrows and rolled their eyes in unison.

"I saw that," Pêro said.

They all laughed.

. . .

They ascended the base of the Chiado hillside up a narrow flight of stone stairs. The hill's upper regions were home to affluent families and merchants. Pêro sought the Carmo Convent and the Church of the Carmelite Order above them. He looked over the city center and its jumble of tiled roofs. Saint George Castle on the top of the opposing hill, enclosed by fortified walls. Below the fortress, the Alfama barrio fanned around the hillside, with its maze of black cobbled switchbacks, hidden stairways, and tight alleyways. Residences of maritime families, New Christians, those who'd been forced to renounce their Jewish faith, and those of old Moorish descent, their homes sat one upon the other like stacked crates.

Constanza crouched down, plucking two stalks of rose hips growing from a crack in the stairwell. Isabela situated her pet turtle on her breast, holding it close and fiddling with the ribbon around its neck. She reached for Pêro's good hand, as she peered into the windows of the homes they passed.

"How are you, *meu amor*?" Pêro called down to Paulinha, who steadied herself with a hand on the wall.

They waited for Paulinha at the next stair landing. Houses jutted up on either side of the way like crooked teeth, overlooking the city center and leading out to the Tagus River in the distance. Constanza moved up the next stairway gathering the last of the fall flowers: miniature scented lilac-colored geraniums and a lonely lily, then she waited on the steps with her bouquet.

Before the Martins' black-painted door was a noisy group of magpies. Their deceptive chatter scattered as Pêro and family arrived.

"Boa tarde," Pêro called as he pushed open the door, flakes of peeling paint falling to the ground. The door creaked and dry leaves yellowed by time, blew in, swirling about the entry.

Pêro rapped on the bedroom door, opening it, the odor of illness escaping. The two sisters lay head to foot in a single bed, under threadbare covers. A rosary, draped in black lace and a silver cross, hung on the wall above the bed next to the shuttered window.

"Donna Udda," Pêro said.

The old woman opened a rheumy eye and sneezed. "Is that you, Padre Pêro?"

"It is. We've come to look in on you. May we enter?"

"Oh, for heaven sakes," Donna Udda rasped, waving them in with her bony spotted hand. "Where's my handkerchief? Good Lord, you don't need to ask, just come in, everyone else does." Her left eye remained shut, a yellowish liquid seeping from it. "Wake up, Rose."

Pêro could see Donna Udda prodding her older sister under the bedding. Rose rolled over and faced the wall.

"Let her sleep," Pêro said, resting his hand on Donna Udda's forearm, as he brought over one of the two chairs with worn leather seats.

Meekly, she looked at him with her one open eye. "All right," she grumbled.

Paulinha opened the window and shutters. Fresh air rushed in, while the stale lingered, refusing to dissipate.

"Fetch some clean water," Constanza said to Isabela. "And take care of this." She pointed at the bedchamber pot. Isabela scowled and placed her turtle on a chair, tying it there, and then set about her duties.

Pêro sat before Donna Udda and wiped the ooze from her eye with a clean handkerchief.

Paulinha took up the broom.

Constanza cleared the nightstand vase of its shriveled flowers and tossed the rank water out the window. "Has no one else brought you flowers since our last visit?"

"No one. Only you, dear heart, bring me flowers." Donna Udda flashed a toothless smile at Constanza, who blushed.

Isabela set water down for Constanza, who filled the vase and arranged the new flowers. Isabela replaced the chamber pot, retrieving her turtle, and stood by Donna Udda's hidden feet.

"What do you have there?" Donna Udda asked, trying to focus her good eye on Isabela's hands.

"A river turtle. Isn't he sweet?" Isabela inched closer to Donna Udda's inquisitive face.

"Good Lord!" Donna Udda said, as the turtle swam its legs through the air.

Rose hacked a few times and rolled over.

With a turtle in one hand and a glass of water in the other, Isabela hurried to Rose's side, while nearby Constanza inspected her skirt's embroidery.

On the nightstand, Pêro placed the thin wafers of Christ's body on a pewter plate preparing to deliver the Eucharist.

Paulinha slinked down into the chair in the corner.

Out of the corner of his eye, Pêro observed Paulinha withdrawing her small sketchbook and piece of graphite from the hidden pocket in the folds of her dress. With twinkling eyes and a grin of excitement, she opened the leather cover and flipped through each page, reviewing her drawings and notes. She began to sketch. A twinge of envy surged through him as he wished he could join her, but he knew this was one of the few places she could freely draw and was glad for it, even if he could not relish the moment sketching too.

Hands clasped, he returned to what he was doing and started the opening prayer: "O Sacred Banquet in which Christ is received, the memory of His Passion is renewed..." After Confession and Absolution, he took a wafer and placed it on Donna Udda's waiting tongue. "Thou hast given them Bread from Heaven."

"O God who in this wonderful Sacrament has left us a memorial of Thy Passion, grant redemption, who livest and reignest forever and ever. Amen."

Isabela handed him the cup and he brought it before Donna Udda's wrinkled lips.

"Amen," she said, as a dribble of liquid ran from the corner of her mouth. Isabela gave him the presider's towel and he gently wiped her chin.

After the prayer, the sole sound was the scratch of Paulinha's lead to paper. She stopped drawing, and they all paused and hung their heads.

Rose began to croak in a hoarse voice: "Oh! My little rose star of the sea…You will go to Lisbon; you will leave me?!" She fell into a fit of coughing, wracking her frail body.

"Rosinha!" Donna Udda said, reaching out to her sister.

Rose readily accepted a glass of water, coughed three more times, and then continued her song.

Arms linked, Pêro and family gaily sang Rose's song of the little rose star of the sea as they entered their street. He quickly halted their merry procession and released his arms from Paulinha's and Isabela's as a group of six black-cloaked men swept away from the front door of their home. Pêro squinted. *Was that Luis?* Swiftly, the knot of men drew up their hoods and rushed down the cobbled way, disappearing around the corner.

Pêro rushed forward. *What had they been doing? Why did they flee? Were they Padre João's men? Was that really Luis?* He stood before the door, his breath quickening.

Paulinha and the girls hurriedly approached, as he sought a sign of disturbance, a clue as to what had been going on before his door. He felt around the doorframe. *Nothing stashed.* He sniffed. *Nothing unusual.* He looked up at his bedroom window. *Nothing visibly askew.* He looked down at the cobbles. *Nothing.* He placed an ear to the door. *Nothing.* But he feared an evil spell had been cast. He made the sign of "the fig", closing his fist, sticking his thumb between the first and second finger, followed by the sign of the cross. He brought his hands together in front of his heart and mumbled a prayer, begging the Lord's protection for his family, himself, and the removal of any malevolent curse that may have been spun.

CHAPTER TWELVE

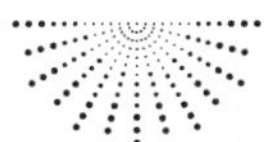

The next day, Pêro unlocked the alley door of the Fabrica Santa María and peeked into the kiln room and looked at the stairway leading to the clay drying room. He couldn't help but feel the presence of the group of suspicious men here too. Entering, he took stock of the shop, seeking for something out of place. A rat scurried across the dusty floor and disappeared under the shelves of tools. All seemed secure. *But was it really?*

Where a problem didn't exist, Pêro lamented, one could always be fabricated like in literature. From his experience, God's flock had an alarming tendency to do so. He bit his lip.

Rafa, Kujaguo, and Jawoli arrived at the shop as the sun crested Lisbon's seven famed hills.

"Clay is here!" Rafa called, stepping into the back alley, Pêro following.

Kujaguo and Jawoli came outside too.

"Where do you want it?" the delivery driver asked, as he drove his donkey cart in, leaving a splattered henna-colored trail behind.

"Place it here, today." Pêro motioned to an empty stall covered with a roof, next to three others.

Rafa, Kujaguo, and Jawoli's shovels scraped the bottom of

the cart, and with the last thud of falling clay, the holding stall was full. Excess water seeped out of the earth into a grooved trench at the base of the stall.

Pêro left the direction of the men to Rafa as he nearby double-checked his shipping list of the crates ready for delivery.

"Shovel clay into the smaller basin, the one lined with the chipped tiles," Rafa instructed.

"Where is Luis?" Pêro asked the men. He glanced at the Fabrica's entry arch.

"Late again as usual!" Rafa called back to him, leaning on his shovel.

Pêro shook his head and re-entered the shop. "I'll be inside. Checking on the drying tiles."

Each man hauled a large block of clay back inside to a workbench.

Pêro observed the men below from the drying room's wood-lattice floor.

Rafa took a *fouce* and effortlessly drew the crescent blade through the clumps of earth, creating smaller workable chunks. Jawoli sliced the pieces with a cutting wire. Kujaguo kneaded clay upon the gesso tabletop. Pêro smiled.

Outside a horse whinnied and snorted.

The alley door opened and slammed against the wall. Rafa picked up a large rolling pin, double the size of a baker's.

In stormed Senhor Guimarães, the owner of a nearby tile factory. His dark mustache quivered on his flushed face. "Where's Padre Pêro?"

Pêro peered down through the floor's grid. He remained quiet, waiting to hear what Guimarães had come for.

"Hand me the template," Rafa said to Jawoli calmly. Rafa placed the 14 x 14 metal template on top of a flattened slab of clay and began cutting tiles out with a knife.

"I asked a question you ignorant *peças*!" Senhor Guimarães bellowed. "Where is the Padre?" He shook his index finger at them.

Pêro cringed and shuffled to the stairs. He clenched his lucky malachite stone in his pant pocket, hoping for swift divine direction on how to deal with this man.

Rafa turned his back to the uninvited visitor. Systematically, he began to work from right to left. Kujaguo and Jawoli, foreheads creased, looked to Rafa and with hesitation began pulling away the excess clay.

Senhor Guimarães stomped past the kilns and thrust himself in front of the working men.

Rafa halted the removal of the tiles from the tabletop and stared down at the clay marks.

"Who's in charge?" Guimarães's mustache twitched with each word. "*Comer o pao que o diabo amassou!* Eat the bread the devil kneaded! I'm speaking to you!" Sweat ran down his temples and dripped onto his pressed linen shirt, pulled taut over his keg-belly.

Rafa put the scoring tool down and stared coldly at the intruder. "Padre Pêro."

Kujaguo and Jawoli clenched their embossing tools that etched Pêro's monogram PMP on each tile.

"Tell the Padre to come see me immediately." Senhor Guimarães looked at them with disgust. "Damn free slaves, *you* and Padre Pêro are ruining my business, giving my slaves crazy ideas. I just caught a group of them organizing trouble. Saying they want pay and liberation like you!" He shook his stubby index finger at Rafa. "I'll see to it that this ends!" He pounded his fist on the workbench, the tools jumping.

Pêro descended the stairs by twos.

"Senhor Guimarães!" Pêro placed himself in front of the men. "Let us discuss this in private." He gestured to the open door of the drafting room.

Senhor Guimarães glared at Pêro, sizing him up, and sneered at his simple brown tunic. "You're going to put a stop to this freeing of chattel, or I will see to it that the Church does."

"Mind you hold your tongue. As I too, will seek divine law

and support. For men were never meant to be bought nor sold." Pêro clenched the wooden cross hanging from his habit's hemp cord.

"You walk a wobbly line for a layman priest. You know as well as I how divided the Church is on the matter." Guimarães stared hard at Pêro. "And coins speak as loudly, if not louder than God's word in our princess of a city. Freedom is more expensive than subservience. You should know, your purse has been drained more than once from the looks of things here." He cast his stony eyes upon Rafa, Kujaguo, and Jawoli.

"A closed mouth captures no flies. I'm as committed to God as any ordained priest." Pêro squeezed the wooden cross, his knuckles turning white.

"You'll regret it, should you not change your ways. You'll see." Senhor Guimarães stamped out of the Fabrica Santa María, Pêro on his heels, watching him mount his steed.

Hoof beats struck the hardpan yard as Senhor Guimarães spurred his horse and galloped away.

"Pêro always says clay has a mind of its own, as do we," Rafa said to Kujaguo and Jawoli. Calmed by his words, they resumed working, dragging the metal combs over the backsides of the clay tiles, creating grooves.

Pêro hung in the alley doorway, watching the dust settle.

"Clay has memory like people. We've all seen it many times. *Azulejos,* if not handled with care, end up like meat fried in an overly hot pan." Rafa rounded his hands. "Raised in the center with the sides down curled. People end up that way too, disfigured, when not treated properly."

Yes, they did, thought Pêro. He turned and rejoined the freemen.

The brothers puckered their lips and nodded. Kujaguo's brown hands shook as he worked. Visible beads of perspiration broke out on Jawoli's dark face. Rafa continued talking incessantly, instructing, venting his anger through his words.

The three men carried the scored tiles on trays to the drying room.

Pêro watched their feet move across the latticework, freed feet, moving about as they deemed fit to move. *Why didn't Senhor Guimarães see that he could follow suit?* That his workers would perform better under the conditions of freedom and payment, that it was a God-given right for men to be free. *Was Luis somehow involved in all this?* He prayed that no one from the Church would get wind of this before he had a chance to explain his side of things. Any minor disturbance could be agitated into a tempest which the Inquisition would want to investigate and have final say.

CHAPTER THIRTEEN

"Paulinha, are you awake?" Pêro whispered as he slipped beneath the covers, bones tired from working late.

She lay on her side towards the open window, the full moon poised above the tiled roofs of their neighbors.

Bright light shone on the bedcover. Sleepy-eyed, Pêro gazed at the illuminated wooden cross on the wall at the foot of their bed. A briny ocean breeze floated through the window. He rolled over and draped his arm across her body. From the street below, a cat's mewing grew from a growl and exploded into a jumble of shrieks and hisses. Paulinha gently wrested herself free from his embrace and turned towards him, her brow furrowed.

"What is it, *meu amor*?" he asked.

"My mother's pewter plate is missing."

"What?" He bolted upright. "Are you sure?"

"I just noticed it."

"So, someone has been in our home."

"It would seem so." Paulinha looked at him and pulled the covers up further.

He rubbed his face and stared hard at the cross.

Paulinha propped herself against the wall. "Who would do such a thing?"

Pêro immediately thought of the group of men.

"Do you think it could have something to do with those men?" she asked, as if reading his mind. "You don't think they found out somehow about the redesign, do you?"

"I don't know, *meu amor*. Honestly, I don't know what to think." He bit his lower lip and drew his hand to his chin. He didn't want to tell her how uncomfortable he'd felt all day. He knew what she kept hidden inside that cabinet, that the pewter plate was not the whole cause of her concern. He felt uneasy. *Could the men of the Church have become privy to her risqué drawing? To the existence of her hidden sketchbooks?*

"And another thing..." She tossed her head back against the wall. "It is not easy for me to look as I do. I don't care for men's blatant stares like that agent weeks ago at the shop. I hid with the girls. Even men in the Church have devouring eyes." She clasped her pendent of Saint Anthony at her breast. "Beloved saint, the returner of lost things, hear my prayer…return my mother's plate and deflect attention pointed toward me."

Pêro turned to her. The sounds of the quarreling cats drifted in from off down the street.

"Hear our prayers Saint Anthony. May your protective bell ring loud here." Pêro closed the prayer. "Let's try to put this to rest for now. At least until the morning." He looked at the waning moon and its pallid orange glow.

"I can't get rid of the image of that knot of cloaked men before our door. Of course, I'm content for us to live here in the city center with the other craftsmen, and not amongst your class in the Chiado. I can no longer imagine staying at home all the time. I'm happiest now at the Fabrica, despite Luis," She gripped his forearm. "I think you better change the wood baron's design."

He reached over and pulled her close, not wanting her to worry and remembered all she'd suffered by marrying into his wealthy merchant family; the lacerating tongues that knew no limit, she without proper education, nor an important family name to shield her from the petty malice of his social class. He rested his head on her shoulder, inhaling the scent of her linen nightdress and loose dark hair. "Remember my family did not always live in wealth. It is only because my father forsook the tile trade. And I confess, I've already made the changes."

"Hum. Really is that so?" She mustered a smile and eased her body against his.

He wrapped her with his arms, holding her tight, wanting to comfort her.

"I'm worried too about this situation with Rafa's father, and Luis. He's up to something. You don't think from his accusations of my behavior that he could know something of my recent hand in that design?" Her hand gripped his and the moon shone on the whites of her eyes. "Luis seemed off the other day, when the other workers complained of Padre João." She paused seeming to search for the right word. "He seems subdued. Why is he always late now? The girls mentioned today that you crossed paths with Padre João."

A sudden tenseness seized him. He tried to keep his body from stiffening, from revealing his true feelings. He was thankful that Paulinha and the girls had not been present for Senhor Guimarães's visit. At least there was one thing to be grateful for.

"You said as much about Luis, and yes, we did see Padre João. It was a mere exchange of greetings. Try to sleep, *meu amor*. We've more work to do tomorrow than King José's court." He brought her further into his embrace, kissing her, and interlaced their fingers. She submitted, but he could feel her worry. His mind flooded with the contents of the ornate cabinet, the erased lines of the sensual drawing, the mysterious group of men before their door, Padre João's threat, Luis, and Senhor Guimarães. And now the missing plate. *What to make of it all?*

They turned to the window, to the night, to the flooding moonlight, but found no answers, just the moonbeam surrounded by darkness. He got up and shuttered the window, but there was no way to shutter his mind from the disquieting thoughts that would keep sleep at bay.

CHAPTER FOURTEEN

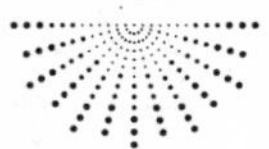

Finally! thought Pêro. It seemed far too long since he had had the chance to sit and draw painterly lines of their designs. The responsibilities of the growing shop and the manumitting of others, along with his deacon duties had all pulled him from what he loved most: the painting of tiles. Unforeseen problems he now must deal with as he confronted each new responsibility and the demands of the Fabrica. It was in the painting, when all the hard work of the clay preparation paid off and the tiles began to come alive with a soul of their own that he loved.

Pêro dipped the fine tipped brush into the glass jar of cobalt blue and glue extender, the grains of ground pigment visible as he swept the receptive hairs of the brush across the white prepared ground of the tile. His heartbeat with excitement as the soldier *figura de convite* took on life before him, as he made fish scale-like lines depicting the infantryman's leg armor. He briefly looked up and across the table at Luis and Rafa also at work. *Do they feel the same way?* Rafa at times displayed a similar glow of enthusiasm watching the tiles awaken under his fingers.

He couldn't say the same for Luis. *When had Luis lost his passion? His drive and desire for the work? Along with their friend-*

ship? Pêro dipped his brush into the jar and stalled, discreetly observing Luis.

Luis sat with his elbows on the painting table, his chin resting in the palms of his hands and intently stared out the second story window.

Pêro remembered back when Luis had been a good friend and confidant for so many years, their fathers' lifelong friends. But, after Luis' father passed away, and Pêro lost his fingers things began to shift and to drift like the glazes in the heat of the kiln. But Pêro had shown concern and given comfort to Luis, after he lost his mother and father.

While Pêro began to excel at the tile works despite his new deformity, Luis seemed to shift away from the artworks. It was as if Pêro had become possessed to overcome and prove to himself and to others that the loss of his two fingers could not prevent him from creating tile works.

Luis, as though sensing Pero's thoughts, chewed the end of a paintbrush and tapped his foot. Luis had always been right by Pêro's side, ready with a helping hand, taking over where and when Pêro needed assistance, as he learned new ways to maneuver the tools. Luis had been a great support throughout this time, despite his waning interest in the work itself.

But Luis did not develop the same spiritual sense that Pêro had, after he'd witnessed the death of Jibo. The Lord had not called out to Luis in the same way.

Yes, this event was the beginning of their friendship's divergence. And, in the weeks that followed Rafa's liberation the rift widened, like water in a channel working its way down, eroding the foundation of their friendship. But it wasn't Rafa's fault; he just did what he was asked and was eager to please, as he pursued the life and work he desired.

Luis smirked at the window.

As Rafa began to master the tile works, Luis wallowed, grew distant, aloof, like now, and seemed to float in another world, spending less and less time here with them. Luis no longer seemed interested in the work, instead disappearing into what haunts, Pêro did not know.

Luis stabbed his brush into the pigment jar, shoving back his stool. It made an awful scraping sound as he got up. "I'm finished." He tore off his apron and flung it onto his stool.

"But we have the rest of the panel yet to finish," Pêro pleaded.

Rafa didn't look up but kept his head down and focused, glancing at Luis from the corner of one eye.

"Rafa can finish it," he said.

"Luis." Pêro stood up and came toward him, arms wide open. "We need your help to finish this project. You know you're the best at painting the border tiles. No one paints them better than you."

"Not any longer. Rafa, does them just as well now." Luis looked Rafa up and down. "I need some fresh air." He grabbed his leather bag.

Pêro held his ground. "Stay and help us finish."

"The funds from this will free his father. He should do the work! Not me!" Luis brusquely shoved by and hurried down the stairs, yanking open the door, hinges screeching.

There was no use in arguing with a man who'd made-up his mind and obviously resented working on something that might help another. Pêro slumped onto his stool and rubbed his eyes. He smiled apologetically at Rafa who lifted his head now that the storm had swept out and away.

Rafa got up and went to the window. "He detests me. He wants nothing to do with helping my family, my father." His back to Pêro, Rafa's eyes widened as he peered down on Luis in the road with Senhor Guimarães who handed him coins.

Pêro looked upon Rafa's back. "What can I say? It's true." He had not intended this, such a grand divide within the workforce of the Fabrica. But some men take to responsibility and leadership better than others. Throughout the years of making tiles, he'd come to learn that sometimes others believe they are best suited to perceived positions of power and prestige, dreaming of wealth, and of importance of name, but they do not want to do the work, nor manage the many threads that must be tended to realize a position of importance.

It was not those attributes he'd pursued to become the well-known monogram: PMP. Instead, it was the unexpected result from pursuing his heart's desire to create outstanding works of art, and help others to freedom, which drove him to take on more and more. Passion often gets mistaken for the pursuit of power and prestige. And this he suspected was what Luis misunderstood. Luis could not see that he often longed to return to simpler days, to the times when not so much was demanded of him. That all this here at the Fabrica came at great cost to him — to his creative free time and imagination, for they no longer were his, but now belonged to them all. He lamented this loss, but knew it was God's will, there was no other way. Not now.

Pêro hung his head. *What to do about Luis? How are we ever going to finish these projects to receive the needed funds for Bagamba's release?*

CHAPTER FIFTEEN

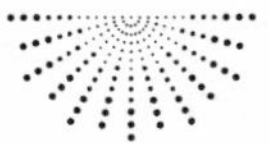

Pêro halted at the entry to the kilns, listening in on Jawoli and Kujaguo's conversation with hopes of overhearing something about Luis.

Jawoli stopped shoveling sawdust in front of the main oven. "Working these fires will put our feet back on African soil one day. We let Jibo's family know to sing for him with ancestors." He resumed scooping and moving shavings. "I long to laugh with our little brothers and sisters, to watch the children run through millet mounds and drink water from the Baobab trees."

Pêro's beating heart hit his chest like a sudden torrent of pelting rain. He prayed silently, recalling Kujaguo, Jawoli and Jibo's story of abduction from their village in a night raid, being forced across a sea of sand like tethered goats. Sold at market and stacked like logs at the bottom of a ship amongst the swill of vomit and shit. Jibo taken from the same bush hamlet as them.

At the conversation's end, Pêro approached the men. "We are ready to bring over the boards for the kiln's scaffold." Pêro pointed to the shop's earthen back wall and the lumber stacked there. Together, Jawoli and Rafa fetched the boards, as Pêro climbed the kiln's scaffold ladder. The other Fabrica workers filed into the shop and stood before the main kiln.

A circular brick chimney attached to the large rectangular kiln filled the back of the Fabrica, with the old beehive oven off to its right. The doorway of the main kiln was raised above ground level like an inaccessible cave on a sheer cliff, only reachable from the floor with a ladder to reach the scaffold. At its bottom, a portal fed the fire.

"Master, here." Jawoli lifted one end of the board while Kujaguo hurried over and held the other.

"Go on, get up there, *Carlos*. Start laying the mortar. You too *Jorge*." Luis ordered from the sidelines.

Pêro looked down at Paulinha with a frown. Seven days later he still felt the sting of Luis walking out on the painting project, on them all. Paulinha raised her eyebrows at him.

"Kujaguo needs mortar," Jawoli said, looking at Luis who stood by the pile of cement ready to be mixed. Luis stared at his fingernails, manicuring his cuticles.

Rafa shot Luis a seething glance and brought over a bucket of water, adding it to the cement, and began mixing everything with a shovel.

Pêro felt his agitation rising, watching Luis's apathetic manner when there was so much work to do, so much at stake.

Pêro handed bricks to Kujaguo. "Remember to leave one brick un-mortared in the lower right corner, three layers up from the bottom. And another in the upper left corner."

The ability to remove these two bricks provided windows into the fire, allowing them to read its temperature.

"Last brick." Kujaguo swept his hand over the sealed kiln door.

The next morning donkey carts arrived with the sun, their flatbeds heaped with fodder for the fire. They received sawdust and woodchips from the *carpintari*, the woodworkers' shop, down the way. Scents of fresh tropical wood shavings filled the air, followed by a cacophony of coughs and sneezes. The piles grew like termite mounds and brought with them a pollen-like haze that coated everyone by day's end. Everyone except Luis, who never appeared.

Kujaguo and Jawoli brushed off their clothes and hair as Pêro came over to them. "Tomorrow we'll start the fire before first light."

"You bring fried mackerel, snails, and bread, like the other time? I dream of oily hot pepper fish sauces from home. But I like fried fish and the funny little ground crawler with its house on its back." Kujaguo's eyes grew wide, displaying the eagerness of his stomach.

Rafa hurried over to Pêro and said in a low voice. "There's a page waiting for you at the arch entrance."

"Tell him I'll be there in a minute." Pêro and Rafa exchanged questioning glances.

"I'm going to be staying here tonight to work," Pêro said as he removed his smock.

Kujaguo and Jawoli looked at one another. "Is everything all right?" Jawoli asked.

"Yes. We just have so many orders lined up to design. I will see about getting us escargot for tomorrow." Pêro fetched the snail pail. "It's funny how a particular taste of a food stays with a person, no matter how many years pass without smelling or tasting it. Don't you think? I remember dishes my mother made that Paulinha doesn't." Pêro tried to make light of his mounting tension. "Wouldn't you agree it is also amazing how one learns to love new tastes? We are creatures of repetition and through repetition habits form, some good, some bad."

Kujaguo looked at Pêro curiously. "I like fried fish," he said.

"I know —" Pêro said with a grin, giving up. He walked away. He'd found over the years that Kujaguo and Jawoli had their own way of seeing the world; he tried to get them to see life through his eyes, but with little success; the cloth had been woven in childhood and the weave was strong.

He stepped outside, looking for Luis. *Where in the Lord's name is he?* The page shifted from foot to foot as carts creaked by and children chased after a three-legged dog. The young messenger presented a note. "A message from Padre Matos of the Santo-o-Velho."

Puzzled, Pêro accepted it. "Thank you. Is that all?"

"Yes. Good day, Sir." He bowed and was on his way.

Brother in Worship, Padre Pêro,
Your presence is requested in three days time at Santo-O-Velho. At the bell hour of mid-morn.
Regards under the Blessings of Our Lord,
Padre Eduardo Matos of the parish of Santo-O-Velho

Pêro folded the note and stuffed it in his habit's pocket. He hurried back inside, shaking his head. *What now?*

The next morning, Pêro and Jawoli awoke before Kujaguo. They stepped into the alley, each taking up his respective spot to kneel and urinate. Pêro rubbed his arm as the morning breeze blew off the Tagus River and the Atlantic. They both shivered and peered down the alleyway at two perched crows.

Their black feathers shimmered in the pink light of dawn.

Jawoli stared at his forward foot, the earth making it quiver. The birds suddenly took flight.

"*Buama,* God!" Jawoli said, quickly fumbling up his trousers. He barged inside.

Pêro followed.

"Wake up, get up!" Jawoli called to Kujaguo.

"What? What is it?" Kujaguo asked, startled awake.

"What's happened?" Pêro asked.

"The two black birds and the shaking." Jawoli paced the floor, refusing to look at anyone.

"So?" Pêro asked.

Kujaguo stared at his pacing brother, who finally stopped before him.

Jawoli hovered over Kujaguo. "You don't have memory because you are little. You did not finish your initiation, or you know birds like that and trembling — a bad omen. I see it all clearly now." Jawoli glanced hesitantly at Pêro.

"Really?" Kujaguo asked.

"It's taboo to start the fire today." Jawoli nodded his head at the men.

Kujaguo looked to Pêro for direction. Pêro stared at the wooden wall where a faint silver-blue was now visible between the slates. Kujaguo stood up.

"Two black birds and the trembling. The second time." Jawoli crinkled his brow and facial tattoo, puckering his lips and gesturing with his head toward the alley door. "An omen. I tell you it is. The shaking close together now."

Pêro raised an eyebrow. He tried not to judge or condemn Jawoli for his superstitions. He most certainly needed to keep quiet about this and not implicate Jawoli of wrong thought that could damn him in the eyes of the Inquisition. He still had much work to do with both Jawoli and Kujaguo and their understanding of the Lord and His ways — this was clear.

"Let's get started." Pêro smiled encouragement.

Instead of picking up his shovel Jawoli brought a footstool into the vicinity of the kiln and woodchip piles and sat.

Pêro took up Jawoli's shovel and together with Kujaguo began stuffing the fire chamber with whale-oil-soaked rags, lighting and tossing them in.

Jawoli observed, then got up and lumbered over. He offered to take over his shovel from Pêro. Jawoli then hurled a load of sawdust into the fire, setting off an explosion of light.

"I'm going to see about the snails," Pêro said.

Smoke plumed from the Fabrica's chimney as Pêro passed by

the red geraniums whose many blooms had now begun to wilt. Soon they would lose their petals. He strode, under the arch in search of the snail and sardine vendors who stationed themselves along the route heading to the river.

The Tagus River was a distant thread of silver against the ashen sky. Donkey carts kicked up dust along the route, as Pêro started down the hill. Humble homes along the way connected one to the other. He felt excited about completing the Amazon commission, and that he and Paulinha would both start tending to the new stack of design requests this evening, while the girls stayed the night with their neighbor in the city center.

Most of all, Pêro prayed that if everything went as scheduled, Bagamba would soon be free and his missed payments a part of the past. But Jawoli's concerns replayed in his mind like a popular folk song, adding to his already lengthy list of worries, including this impending summons with Padre Matos, the day after next, along with the need to focus more on the conveyance of the Lord's teachings to both Jawoli and Kujaguo. *What a weight the Lord asks one to bear!*

Hours later, Pêro let himself in the shop's front door, setting the pail down, and inhaled the burnt wood scent. He walked back to the kiln, taking inventory of the shop as he went.

Kujaguo stood in front of the heaps of woodchips and sawdust, the fire's heat exuding now from its chamber in a constant wave.

Jawoli pushed coals back into the corners of the fire's chamber with a long iron pole, a rectangular plate welded to its end. It scraped as it slid, distributing the coals so the fire would burn evenly, heating the upper chamber uniformly. The fire popped and Jawoli jumped. He dropped the pole and eyed the shadows around the kiln as he picked it back up.

"Jawoli, what's wrong? You're tense," Pêro said, coming up alongside him.

"Master, what?" Jawoli said, annoyed, turning to Pêro.

"You're restless."

"I never seen that."

"It's not something to see, it's what you're doing."

The fire hissed, then fell silent.

"The two black birds this morning." Jawoli locked eyes with Pêro.

"What is so unusual about seeing birds?" Pêro cocked his head.

"Where I come from, it's a sign of bad things. There was a shaking again, they flew away. I saw it with my own eyes." Jawoli puckered his lips, pushing them forward.

Pêro gazed at him and remained quiet for a moment, then said, "There are stories here in Lisbon about two crows. They accompanied the crypt of Saint Vincent from Spain and are considered heaven sent — *a good omen*. The flags of our caravel ships often have two crows on them. The birds are known to live under the Sé Cathedral's eaves where the saint now rests. So, as I see it, it's a good sign."

"No." Jawoli adamantly motioned with his puckered lips to the alley. "No stop to forces. Go in caution. *U tienu wani len laafia*, May God give health and protection."

Pêro touched his coral rosary hidden under his undershirt. He glanced at Kujaguo and back at Jawoli. "May God bless us so that we may finish this order headed to the colony of Brazil and receive the baron's payment."

As Pêro left the kiln area, he paused, and looked back at the brothers, before retreating to the draft room. *Patience, yes, patience…more patience.*

The daylight between the wooden wall panels waned. Pêro came back to the kiln. The brothers' faces now glistened. Using metal tongs, Kujaguo slipped out the lower brick and peered into the fire.

"Keep adding fodder," Kujaguo said to Jawoli, while he shielded himself from the fire's heat exhaling from the hole. "Soon it will glow hot orange."

"Excellent. I'm working on designs this evening. Remember if you need anything, knock first."

Jawoli and Kujaguo nodded and kept tending the fire.

Pêro cracked open the draft room door, slipped in and drew the latch. Paulinha peered up briefly from her work.

They worked by lantern light, one upon each draft table. A sooty smell filled the space. Into the night they sketched, rummaging through old compositions and copies of engravings by French painters Jean-Baptiste Pillement and Antoine Watteau and others from the reproduction collection of the Royal Palace.

"I'm exhausted. I'm going to rest," Paulinha said, snuffing out her lantern. She knelt before her palette and recited her daily prayer to Saint Anthony: "Dear Lord, Saint Anthony hear my prayer, please return my mother's pewter plate. I beg of you. For it is one of the few precious reminders I have of her. Amen, Blessed Lord art thou in Heaven."

Pêro waited until she'd finished and lay down. "I'll keep on, *meu amor.* Sleep in peace. I'll go out into the kiln room and work there. See on the progress of things," he said.

Pêro eased out of the draft room with his lantern, parchments, and drafting tools, slipping into the darkness of the main shop. The area around the kiln port was bathed in chiaroscuro light, where Kujaguo and Jawoli worked. He moved to a workbench near them.

"I rest first," Kujaguo said.

"No, I will." Jawoli stopped shoveling sawdust.

"You watch for black birds," Kujaguo joked. He grinned and bugged his eyes at his brother.

Pêro set down the lantern and looked on, as Jawoli picked up his shovel and thrust more woodchips into the fire chamber. They crackled and snapped.

Kujaguo made his bed at the back of the fodder piles, soon he was snoring.

Pêro breathed in the sedative scents of red cedar.

Pêro sat facing the kiln, gazing periodically at the fire's glow.

Humming a tune, Jawoli shoveled in a rhythmic pattern, shifting his weight onto his outer leg, resting, and repeating. Hours passed as Pêro reviewed the design orders, the figuring of sums, who he needed to make a personal call on for payment, calculating which orders would be needed yet to free Bagamba.

When it was Kujaguo's turn to work, Jawoli nudged him. Jawoli nestled down in the warm patch where Kujaguo had lain. Before dozing off, Jawoli called to Kujaguo. "Be careful, attention tonight, remember the birds."

Pêro rested his chin in his hand, elbow on the desk, dozing on and off. The lantern light sputtered.

Kujaguo worked and then took a break. He crouched on the floor and rolled a *cigaro*. He inhaled slow and deep; the tobacco singed as the *cigaro's* end burned red-orange. He held in the smoke and then released it. It rose in tendrils, disappearing into the night. In the effulgence of the fire, Kujaguo gazed at the slits in the shop's wooden wall.

Pêro sleepily looked at the wall too, watching for a shift in light, a sign of the oncoming morning. He'd sleep later in the day.

From Kujaguo's crouched stance, he flicked the butt of his smoke into the fire hole. It quickly incinerated.

Pêro and Kujaguo watched the fire.

A sudden canon-like explosion shot through the space.

Kujaguo crumpled to the floor.

Pêro jumped up, knocking over the burned-out lantern. He smelled the metallic odor of blood.

A stream of smoke rose from a nearby sawdust pile.

Jawoli scrambled onto all fours. "Kujaguo! Kujaguo!" In the shadows he sought his brother.

Pêro rushed over to the kiln. Kujaguo's body lay between two woodchip mounds. Blood seeped from his head.

Jawoli crouched next to his brother.

Kujaguo's chest heaved.

Jawoli looked around, his arms shaking.

Blood covered most of Kujaguo's face.

"Tear a strip of cloth from your pant leg, stop the bleeding," Pêro said, scanning the area to find where the smoke was rising from.

Jawoli tore a strip and began carefully to wipe away blood. The fire illuminated Kujaguo's face. A straight gash traversed Kujaguo's right eyebrow, running over his facial tattoo to the left eyebrow: splitting the lizard in two.

A gleaming brick sat in a sawdust pile.

Pêro lunged over to it. One end radiated blood-orange as smoke streamed up. He grabbed a shovel, and frantically scooped up the hot brick and placed it in front of the fire door. He lifted the hem of his habit and stomped wildly on the ignited shavings.

Feverishly, Pêro shoveled the burning chips into the fire chamber. The fire exploded. A brilliance of light. He continued his panicked clearing until nothing remained but the ground. Breathing heavily, he turned to Jawoli and Kujaguo.

Pêro rushed to Kujaguo's side. "How is he?" he panted.

Jawoli glanced at the wooden slat wall, where rays of light filtered through the cracks. "He's breathing."

Pêro bent down listening to Kujaguo's breath. "Keep vigil."

Jawoli gazed at his brother's face.

Pêro hurried to the draft room, kneeling before Paulinha. "There's been an accident. I'm surprised the commotion didn't wake you."

"What's happened?" she asked, sitting up.

"It's Kujaguo. He was hit by one of the window bricks. Somehow it dislodged. He's unconscious."

Paulinha lifted her hand to her mouth. She set to making a cool wet rag, following Pêro back to Kujaguo, and cleaned his forehead.

Rafa arrived for the morning shift and rushed over. "What's happened?"

"Rafa, we need you to call upon your grandmother." Pêro said. "Kujaguo needs his head looked at. He was hit by something while tending the kiln."

Rafa's grandmother, Gogo, was an old woman of the old ways, steeped in herbal healing and known in the Mocambo for her power to cure.

They waited in silence as Rafa left the shop, until blinding slits of light shone through the wooden wall and crossed Kujaguo's face.

Kujaguo's eyelids fluttered. The whites of his eyes beamed up, two quail eggs, and then he rolled his black pupils forward meeting Jawoli's. He lay wide-eyed for a moment, and then asked, "What happen?"

"The smell of smoke woke me. Two black birds at work, I tell you," Jawoli said.

"There was an accident at the kiln. Blessed, you've awoken," Pêro said.

Kujaguo slowly pushed himself up, legs outstretched, and removed the blood-stained cloth. Tenderly, he felt his forehead, tracing the cut with his fingertips.

"I not dead," Kujaguo said, forcing a faint smile at Jawoli. But Jawoli did not smile back. "Why you sad? Something hit me not you."

"Two black birds: one came, one more to come." Jawoli looked to Kujaguo and then Pêro and Paulinha. "You understand now?"

Kujaguo nodded.

But Paulinha looked at Pêro, her jaw slack.

"The Lord works in His own ways," Pêro said.

"No. Two black birds work this morning. They want to burn the shop down. Look, look at Kujaguo. Big brick on his head." Jawoli pointed to Kujaguo with his lips. "More to come. *Two* birds." Jawoli warned again, holding up two fingers.

Pêro studied Jawoli and Kujaguo, trying to understand their world. It was so different than his and Paulinha's and Luis', and even Rafa's. Bringing them into the Lord's ways was proving difficult. He looked around the shop, as if by searching he could see and find what these two black birds of Jawoli's would do next. But nothing revealed itself.

Rafa returned with word from Gogo as the girls arrived, in the company of the neighbor lady. "She asked that Kujaguo be brought to her. How is he?"

"Conscious now." Pêro groaned inwardly. Now they were short of another person since Luis was so unpredictable. The orders were piled up, commissions that would bring in the funds to release Bagamba, orders that must be filled, payments that must be secured. But at least Kujaguo was alive and would recover.

The shop took on the hurried feeling of market day. Pêro asked everyone to pitch in and help with Kujaguo and Luis's workload. Rafa arranged to transport Kujaguo to Gogo, while he lay resting.

The fires were left to burn out, the kiln left closed and cooling, while Pêro thought about what to do. He paced back and forth, rubbing his chin, the hem of his habit swinging side to side.

"Should I go now?" Rafa asked.

"Is Kujaguo going to be all right?" Isabela asked Pêro.

Pêro placed his hand on her head. "Yes, go now, Rafa. There's always a dog getting into the chicken coop. Why do I ever think it will be different? Let's all arrive early tomorrow."

The girls let out a "no."

But Paulinha reprimanded them and hurried them along. "Gather your things. Let us start home."

Rafa looked to where Luis should have been working and cleaning up. Rafa's green eyes were as cold as an emerald winter sea as he escorted Kujaguo out into the crisp autumn air.

Pêro came outside. "Senhora Gogo will help you, Kujaguo.

We'll unload the kiln and start crating tomorrow. Go with God." Pêro held up his cross, his habit hanging from his center like a candle snuffer, as Rafa and Kujaguo passed under the courtyard archway and into the night.

CHAPTER SIXTEEN

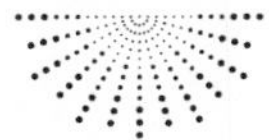

"Grandmother?" Rafa called into the windowless room where Gogo rested. Kujaguo slumped further on Rafa's shoulder. Rafa shifted his weight onto his outside leg to bear the burden as his youngest son, Diogo, came up alongside him.

"Oh good, you're now here." Gogo's voice drifted out of the black like thick smoke.

Rafa set Kujaguo to the ground, bracing him against the wall.

"Light this." Gogo offered a stub of candle.

Diogo hurried to retrieve it for his father.

Rafa dripped wax onto the earthen floor and set the candle. It emitted a sour tallow smell and faint glow. "Here Grandmother, feel here." Rafa guided Gogo's knobby fingers to Kujaguo's head bandage.

Gogo ran her fingertips along the blood-soiled cloth, squinting her cloudy eyes in the dim light.

Diogo stood by, ready to help.

"Comfrey. We'll need a bushel of fresh and dried leaves, a pinch of turmeric and powdered crab's eyes. A calabash of clay. Ash from the fire. A cutting from my aloe plant." She pointed to the rafters. "Hand me the medicine bowl."

Rafa fetched it.

She rummaged through its contents. "We'll make do with what we have now. But tomorrow at first light buy fresh comfrey and more dried and the other things from the market."

Rafa nodded.

"Did he have the fits? Shaking?" Gogo asked.

"No." Rafa looked at Kujagou.

"See if Ajay has any of his African '*abutua*' and '*fastio*' roots. Wake Kujaguo up in the night, make sure he wakes up. Cut me some aloe." Gogo began the poultice preparations.

In the morning, Rafa, accompanied by Diogo, arrived on the outskirts of the Mocambo's westerly edge, home to disorderly gardens and single-story dwellings. From this vantage point a vista looked down upon the Lapa lowlands and the Church of Our Senhora of Lapa on a far distant hill. The valley's fertility contrasted with the dryness of the Mocambo. Here the soil had to be coaxed to reap a yield.

They entered an alley that delivered them to an open-air market. With a rooster's call, buyers arrived. Families set up their stalls, placing wares on mats and old pieces of cloth. Young men worked overhead securing shade covers.

Rafa, holding Diogo's hand, perused the market as he sought Gogo's medicines. Women organized baskets of various sizes and wide-mouthed clay pots and called out morning greetings. Others made pyramids of fresh vegetables or doled out ladles of honey from basins. Heaps of salted sardines and pelt-like stacks of *bacalhau*, cod, and piles of small red *piri-piri* peppers lined the path. Black pigs on tethers snorted as they passed.

They stopped before a stall with bushels of dried and fresh herbs hanging from the rafters. Round plate-like baskets filled the ground before them, containing dried oddities: shriveled animals' feet and claws, mangy pelts, an assortment of beaks and seeds, barks and pods. A twiggy man with gray at the temples, his skin the color of indigo with four lines cut and scarred over on each cheek. He used a stick with a hook on its end to hang herbs overhead.

"*Bom dia,* Ajay. Today I need fresh and dried comfrey, turmeric, and crab's eye powder. My grandmother hopes you have *'abutua'* and *'fastio'* roots." Rafa crouched down, sitting on his haunches.

The vendor plucked a bushel from the roof and brought it down before Rafa. "Dried comfrey." Ajay then searched amongst bags at the back of the stall. "This is the last of the *'abutua'*. I don't have any more *'fastio'*." He handed two dried roots to Rafa. "Tell your grandmother sorry, it's the last I have until the next slave ship arrives." He pointed down the alleyway. "A couple of tables down, Senhora has fresh comfrey. Go into town for the other items. You will find them at the fancy Two Crow Concoctions apothecary."

Rafa looked at the sun; if he hurried, he could still make it back to the Fabrica to help unload the kiln. *What had made the brick dislodge?* He was as curious and concerned as Pêro, who referred to the mishap as "this random accident".

"Diogo, hurry home with this. Let your great grandmother know I've gone to town to try and find the other ingredients. Hurry now. Don't stop anywhere along the way."

Diogo took the proffered goods and sprinted off.

Rafa rushed down a flight of stone steps, entering the subterranean apothecary. Floor to ceiling, the walls of the pharmacy were lined with shelves housing china-white and azul ceramic jars. Shop workers eased out the large urn-shaped containers from the bottom shelves to retrieve ingredients. Copper pans and oversized iron spoons hung on the column supports. A deer rack chandelier with two stuffed crows perched upon it, hung from the center of the octagonal space. Rafa stopped cold under the stuffed birds, goosebumps crawling across his forearms, replaying Jawoli's warning. *Was this yet another ominous sign?*

Customers milled around investigating the medicine jars lining the walls. Others waited around three tables to be served, as druggists at each ground and mixed compounds. Rafa bypassed a boisterous group of men in powdered wigs who discussed the properties and prospects of the plant medicines coming from the New World colonies and East. "With this laudanum…" The man held a bottle of reddish-brown liquid up towards the cellar window. "My wife has become more agreeable. I can't recommend enough the benefits of this treatment."

Rafa made his way towards a table where a mulatto boy fed a fire beneath a distiller. Above it, condensation dripped into an awaiting vessel. The thump of pestles in floor-based wooden mortars accompanied the clientele's chatter.

Moving to a less busy table, Rafa settled in behind a line of men. He eavesdropped on a nearby conversation and watched the stocking-capped pharmacist busily grind. "You see my father is still terribly ill. The doctor says the hashish seems to work best for his condition."

"Again, who is his doctor? He seems to be prescribing larger dosages than usual," the pharmacist said. "You've been in more often these past months. Is your father terminal?"

"My father's in a terrible state I'm afraid. But Doctor Lopes thinks with the ongoing treatment that he is at least stabilized, and he could go on for quite some time."

Rafa strained to see the inquiring man but couldn't catch a glimpse of him. But he knew the voice well…

"Hum, I see. Yes, I think I know of this Doctor Lopes. He's a countryside doctor? Out along the viaduct," the pharmacist said, stopping his grinding and emptying the mortar's contents onto the table.

"Yes. My father feels more at peace resting in the countryside," the man said.

"Very well. Miguel, a block of the hashish for this man." The pharmacist waved the servant boy off to fetch the goods. "But this must be paid for now, not later. You've already accrued quite an outstanding bill with us."

The man grumbled and produced the coins, Rafa catching sight of the long white fingers and manicured nails — Luis! *I'd know his voice anywhere. But his father is deceased! Scoundrel!*

Rafa started to push back from the waiting crowd. The last thing he wanted was for Luis to know he was here, that he'd overheard the whole deception. But the boy returned, and Luis pushed through the men just as Rafa stumbled into a bench and a woman there sifting seeds into a basket. The container tipped onto the floor, kernels scattering everywhere.

Luis stopped and stared at him sprawled on the ground. He walked over and hovered above Rafa. "You're spying on me," he said, suspicion riding on every word. "You'll say nothing of this, or I'll have your head. What's another dead slave, after all?" Luis raised his foot.

Rafa grabbed the boot as it plunged toward him. Letting go, Rafa pushed himself up, yanking up his shirt collar to make sure his damned "S" slave brand was well-hidden. "Not if I have your head first."

Luis's eyes flared at the matched threat.

"Keep your distance," Rafa said, then turned to help the woman.

CHAPTER SEVENTEEN

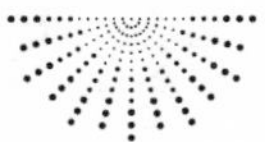

"How's Kujaguo?" Pêro asked.

Rafa briskly approached him and Jawoli before the kiln. "He's all right. Made it through the night. Grandmother is tending him now." Rafa climbed up to join Jawoli on the scaffold, relieving him of the sledgehammer, taking over breaking down the sealed kiln door.

Scalding air escaped from holes, and the men worked more carefully and slowly than usual as not to be burned by the hot air's forceful exit. They removed the broken bits gingerly as if afraid the bricks were cursed and might somehow leap out and strike them.

Pêro watched as they hopped, staying light on their feet, and looked around as they worked.

Soon, a thick wall of heat exuded from the body of the kiln.

Pêro paced below. Beads of sweat rolled down his temples. "Rafa." Pêro stopped dead in his tracks.

Rafa looked down and rested the sledgehammer's head on the scaffold board.

"Monday, I have a meeting in the morning. I'd like you to look at our new design requests and start in on one of them in my absence." Pêro said. "I don't want to fall any more behind, now that we are down a man. Two really."

Rafa shook his head, eyes earnest. "Yes, down two."

Pêro rubbed his face with both hands. "I'll leave the orders on the farthest draft table. Choose the one that appeals to you the most."

"I'll do my best, but I can't promise..."

"Just do what you can."

When the kiln was cool enough to enter, Pêro stepped inside the cavernous chamber. Tiles rested on multiple brick shelves filling the interior. He wiped his forehead with a handkerchief. *What had dislodged the brick?* He picked through the tiles — nothing, no clue.

They removed the ultramarine blue, white, and egg-yolk yellow *azulejos* and boxed them into transport crates, then placed them by the entrance door, ready to be taken to the *Nossa Senhora da Luz*.

Pêro stood again on the scaffold, alone, peering inside the kiln's empty chamber. Jawoli's warning seeped from the space.

Pêro shivered, despite the heat. *More to come. Two black crows…*

CHAPTER EIGHTEEN

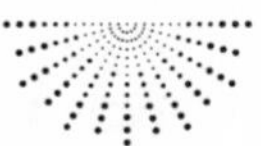

The late fall sun beamed down, basking the courtyard of Pêro and Paulinha's home in a warm amber. Seated upon a mat and cushions, Pêro rested against the stucco wall in the shade and exhaled long, trying to set aside the stresses of the Fabrica for a few hours. He picked up the *Gazeta de Lisboa* and read.

Nearby, Paulinha sketched in her little drawing book the fruits of the yard that the girls artfully arranged before her: pomegranates, figs, and tangerines.

"Place a couple of leaves here, beneath the pomegranate," Isabela said to Constanza.

"It says here that Prime Minister Melo *is* in support of abolishing slavery. I agree with him on this point. But I'm not sure if I concur with his attitude towards the Church. From what I gather, it seems he's in favor of secularizing affairs here, like he saw in England during his time as Ambassador. But we most certainly are not the British, despite our ongoing commercial exchanges with them." Pêro looked at Paulinha. "What do you think?"

Paulinha vigorously finished the shading of a fig and then

raised her graphite to her lips. "The Inquisition must be furious with this blasphemy."

Pêro continued. "Pamphlets are circulating information about the 'Enlightenment', as the philosophers of the North refer to the movement, like by this popular Parisian, Senhor Voltaire. Their thoughts are in feverish circulation now here too in Lisbon. I found this on the ground the other day." Pêro removed a pamphlet from his pocket and waved it. "I fear they are undermining the Christian world, despite some of my own disagreements with the Church. I've never supported the public *auto-de-fé*."

Paulinha looked at him eyes wide, mouth agape. "Pêro," she said, in exasperation. "Careful what you say aloud," she whispered. "Those men…the ever-diligent ears and tongues…"

There was a clapping from the street.

"Someone's at the door," Constanza said, looking from mother to father.

Paulinha stuffed her drawing book into the pocket in her skirt.

Pêro rose and headed inside. Paulinha followed, tidying her dress, forehead furrowed. Constanza and Isabela trailed behind.

Pêro opened the door.

"Blessed, Saint Anthony's answered my prayers," Paulinha said. Paulinha reached for the pewter plate and clasped it to her breast. "A true saint, He is!"

The young man at the door smiled exposing a black tooth.

"Where has this come from?" Pêro asked. "How did you come by it?"

"Found my thieving little brother with it. He must'a climbed in through one of your unlocked windows," the young man confessed. "Mother heard the talk on the street that you were missing it, knew it was yours. A good scolding little Luis got when I showed it to her."

Pêro placed his hand upon the young man's shoulder. "May

the Lord bestow blessings upon you and your family. Thank you for returning it."

"My brother said it came from a high shelf. I can put it back in its spot for you." The young man offered, peering in behind them with searching eyes.

"No, that's quite all right. I'll see to it," Pêro said.

The young man craned his head to see further in, and then spun on his heel and was off.

Pêro peered out their front door, glancing at the houses that flanked them on either side, owned by other master craftsmen: the hat maker, the leather boot fabricator, and master wood carvers proficient in gilding. Each of their houses connected, creating an endless chain. He shook his head and stepped back inside, the vision of the group of hooded men before his door well burning in his mind. He locked the door.

"Who would've guessed a little thief was behind this and by the name of Luis. I'm pleased to have it back." Paulinha hugged the plate to her chest. "Saint Anthony did hear my prayers."

"It wasn't the plate he was after. The little brother is the culprit behind this? I doubt it. I'm relieved the plate is back in our possession, but suspect there's more to this," Pêro said. He ran his hand over his head.

Paulinha looked square at him. "Yet, one doesn't really know. Now do we? The little boy theft could be a ploy. I've already relocated the hidden treasure. As Barbary pirates have been known to set such innocent traps, before they sack the Mother ship."

CHAPTER NINETEEN

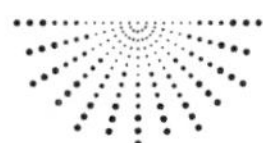

Three graveyard cypresses at the riverside edge of the Mocambo neighborhood marked the entrance to the Church of Santo-o-Velho. As Pêro's coach approached, bouncing along the stony road, he felt queasy as if he'd eaten something disagreeable that morning. *Why has Padre Matos called this meeting?* He shifted in his seat and stared at the chapel poised on a precipice of rock along the Tagus River.

The coach passed the Templar cross monument in front of the Flor da Murta Palace and then the Convent of the Bernardas. Pêro paid the coachman and the buggy lurched forward, the horse clopping away echoing his heartbeat.

Pêro entered the dim church, built on the site where the three saints for whom it was named were martyred: Veríssimo, Máxima, and Júlia. He thought of their sacrifice for their beliefs. His skin crawled. *Will I too be put to trial for mine?*

Mildew and dusty old tapestries made his nose itch, as his eyes adjusted to the changed light in the vaulted space. Padre Matos, the local Mocambo parish priest responsible for overseeing the welfare of the barrio, stood before the front altar. Pêro was beholden to Padre Matos and his decisions regarding concerns within the neighborhood's affairs. *Dear Lord. What is this?* Standing next to Padre Matos stood Luis, Senhor Guimarães, and Padre João. Pêro resisted gripping his wooden cross and tried to clear his throat.

"Come forward, Padre Pêro." Padre Matos held his right hand out, his white vestment cloaking his thick middle.

Pêro walked the nave's main aisle slowly, as if seeing his mother to her grave. Stark light shone in from the eastern windows, casting a beam of light before the waiting men.

Padre Matos stepped from the circle of men, placing his hand on Pêro's back, escorting him into the group.

"Thank you for coming," Padre Matos said kindly.

Pêro stood flanked by Padre Matos and Luis.

Tension hung in the air like the toll of the death bell.

"Now that we are assembled, it has been brought to my attention there is discord within my parish. And at the center of this unease is the Fabrica Santa María," Padre Matos said, turning to Pêro.

Pêro's heart beat like a thousand-winged birds trying to escape a cage. He gulped, looking at the faces of the band of men.

"What sort of discord?" Pêro tried to steady his voice.

Senhor Guimarães folded his arms above his keg-belly and cocked up his dark mustachioed lip. "As I said before, you and your freed slaves are disrupting the peace of my factory. My slaves clamor for freedom. I caught them planning to run away. You're hurting the stability of my workforce, my commerce."

Pêro held Senhor Guimarães' angry stare. *Why could this man not see the rightness in his workers' desire for liberation? Why Lord?* He would benefit from their freedom, both here on earth and in heaven.

"And you, Luis, why are you here? We've missed and needed you for days now," Pêro said. He looked with narrowed eyes at Luis.

Luis shifted from foot to foot and stared coldly at Pêro.

"May I intercede?" Padre João said smugly, the fat of his cheeks obscuring his eyes.

Pêro shifted his attention to Padre João. "Yes, of course, by all means."

"I have learned —"

"There are —" Padre João hesitated. "Questionable goings-on in the Fabrica Santa María."

"And what might be these things in question?" Pêro asked, brow furrowed.

"It has been brought to the Church's attention that Christian names have been discarded for the profane. And there were two lantern lights ablaze in your shop's draft room late the other evening, with a woman performing inappropriate work at an inappropriate hour on more than one occasion," Padre João said.

Pêro looked from face to face, all eyes harshly gazing upon him.

"And pray tell what is the problem with this, should any of it be true? And who should be looking upon my draft room windows at such an hour?" Pêro asked. He could feel Luis' eyes scorching him.

"God-given Christian names please the Lord, not the use of the pagan. The Church has clear and appropriate conduct for all persons of the Catholic faith, does it not?" Padre João intoned.

"Yes, of course." Pêro met Padre João's suspicious stare.

"I suggest you and those working within the Fabrica Santa María take heed of my words. Otherwise, the Inquisition may need to look into this matter," Padre João continued.

The group fell silent, each man looking at the other. Pêro's mind raced thinking of how the Fabrica Santa María now received the vast majority of the commissions that had previously gone to foreign tile makers, mostly the Dutch. Padre João had served these tile makers as the importation middleman long ago, brokering lucrative deals for the Church and wealthy clientele of Lisbon. *Was he now trying to maneuver the Fabrica Santa María out of its lucrative position? Creating some problem to try and reinstate his position of past profit? Did he really think it possible after so many years of the decline of general Portuguese interest in Delft tile?*

"Is what Padre João is saying true?" Padre Matos asked.

Bile worked up from Pêro's throat. Beads of sweat burst upon his upper lip, as all eyes skewered him.

"It is true Padre Pêro?" Padre João repeated.

Pêro felt as if lightning were about to strike him.

"Answer the question, Padre Pêro," Padre Matos said.

Closed mouthed, Pêro looked at his accusers before answering. "Yes, it's true. I and my wife were working late into the night the other evening." Pêro looked at his accusers again. Padre João's mischievous eyes danced, while Pêro's hands shook.

"And what was your wife working on?" Padre João asked.

Padre Matos folded his arms upon his white-clad belly.

"Our accounts," Pêro said quickly.

"What type of accounts?" Padre João frowned.

"Our tile projects."

"Was your wife designing?" Padre João asked. "Something —"

Pêro looked to Luis. "No." he lied, *Dear Lord how could he sin like this!* He drove his fingernails into the palm of his hand.

"I've heard differently," Padre João said.

Luis's nostrils flared.

"Hearing and seeing are two different things," Pêro said, turning to Padre Matos.

Padre Matos regarded each of the men, his gaze coming to rest on Pêro.

"Yes, but we all know hearing of misbehavior can lead to investigation by the Inquisition." Padre Matos nodded his head paternally at Pêro. "And what of this insinuation over the use of non-Christian names in your shop?"

Pêro looked over the shoulder of Padre Matos, his eyes on Luis. "I will see to it that the Lord's given names are adhered to.

I will be more attentive to these exchanges in the shop. Please forgive any oversight on my part. I am sure Luis will be helpful with this." Pêro forced a smile at Luis.

"All right then, so you agree to heed these good men's concerns. And for this not to be brought to my attention again for it could result in dire outcomes and closure. We wouldn't want anyone higher up to get wind of this conversation nor the female in question and her keeper." Padre Matos said. "Now join me in prayer."

Pêro could not bring himself to look at Luis again. He put his head down, wishing for the Lord's intervention. It was time for him to seek counsel with his mentor Padre Dantas. The recitation complete, Pêro briskly excused himself, escaping into the street. He hailed the first cart that passed by.

"To the Barrio Alto, to the Convent of Senhora of Jesus," he said to the sedan driver.

He drew the red curtains on both of the chair's windows. *Padre João is as slippery as clay slip.*

"Where should I let you off?" the driver asked.

Pêro drew back the curtain and peeked out at the enclosure walls of the Convent of Senhora of Jesus. The persimmon orchard in front of the three-story priory hospital was heavy with fiery sun-colored ripe fruit, rolling countryside a backdrop to the sacred grounds.

"The front of the chapel."

Climbing a flight of stairs, Pêro pulled at the door to the church, but found it locked. He looked up at the imposing façade, then walked to the stairs' edge. Far below at the riverfront, people worked at the docks of Santos. Down the waterway to the east, the Palace of the Almada family, purveyors to the House of India, and the wealthy Barrio Alto stretched before him. He made the sign of the cross and descended.

At the convent's iron gate, he waited until a clergyman with a newly shaved tonsure noticed him. "I've come for my monthly counsel with Padre Dantas."

"You will find him in the cloister courtyard."

Pêro slipped in, the gate clicking behind.

He passed through the arched passageway leading to the cloister. It led to a manicured quadrangle court, bordered by the dormitories that housed the monks. In the open space, pathways converged on a stone cistern, surrounded by contemplation benches.

Padre Dantas sat on a bank; his back hunched, knobby fingers clasped on his lap. Brothers encircled him, a lively discussion at hand.

"Welcome, Deacon Pêro," Padre Dantas said with a quizzical face.

The other Brothers stepped aside making space for Pêro to enter the enclave.

"It's been sometime. I've been expecting you." Padre Dantas lifted his arms.

Pêro bowed his head, and Padre Dantas blessed him with tremulous hands.

"Brothers, could you please excuse us. We'll return to this discussion later," Padre Dantas said.

Hands in prayer before their hearts, the obedient flock took leave.

"Come, sit beside me."

Pêro took his place next to his revered mentor, whose skin was now like that of an oyster shell, thin and discolored by time, weathered by the endless tides of life. Pêro let out a long breath, being in the presence of this man calmed his swirling mind. Peace swept through his limbs; tension slowly ebbed away. He sought his adviser's eyes, his reassurance that the wisdom of the Lord could ease his present concerns. *Where to begin explaining everything?*

"Something is bothering you, Deacon Pêro." Padre Dantas placed a hand on top of Pêro's.

"There's discord in my life. I feel a great weight upon me. My promises to the Lord are wrought with resistance and conflict." Pêro looked up at Padre Dantas' kind eyes.

"Confide in me. And let us ask the Great Father to guide us to a resolution on these matters." Padre Dantas tipped his head toward the cumulus clouds that churned out like the plumes of smoke from the Mocambo's tile factory chimneys, hovering above.

"I've been accused of blasphemy." Pêro dropped his head.

"Blasphemy? This is serious indeed, Deacon Pêro." The elderly priest's forehead furrowed, resembling the many pages of a manuscript.

"With the liberation of slaves who've come to work for the Fabrica, we've begun to call them by their given names in their native tongue. I didn't think anything of this as we came to do this slowly, over time," Pêro explained. He stole a glance at his mentor, and then gazed at his hands once more. He would not reveal the other matter of Paulinha designing at night nor questionable subject matter. *Lord forbid and forgive!*

"Is this so?" Padre Dantas stared at the cistern for a long silent moment. "This is a serious deviation from the Church's teachings, an undermining of our efforts."

Pêro felt his heart pang and his heartbeat thumped in his ears. *Am I hearing correctly? Even Padre Dantas believes I've done wrong!* He looked up sheepishly. "But…"

"Deacon Pêro, you've been a good and devoted man in service to the Lord. A man of good heart and intentions, yes, this I know. You should know better than to have slid into the ways of these men in need of guidance."

Dear Father! Something in him rebelled violently against his trusted mentor's words, his heart.

"You must bring an end to this and immediately. Who knows of this?" Padre Dantas looked sternly at him. "I will speak with whomever I need to. I will let them know of our support and of our disciplinary action in regard to you over this deviation, as a way to deflect further chastisements on this matter. The Lord *is* forgiving. You will repent. I will assign you further service to the community. You'll tend upon the sick and ill here weekly at dusk, Thursdays, at the convent's hospice for your penance."

The color washed from Pêro's cheeks and he stared ahead. *Is this happening?* His body became as heavy as a block of clay. He decided not to mention the knot of men before his home's door, the Inquisitions' inquiring men no doubt. No, instead he would keep silent on this matter, with prayers that Padre Dantas' intervention and his punishment to minister weekly upon the ill in the priory's hospital would appease the inquiring men. And they, no doubt, were at the root of this. Jealous, spiteful men.

Now, how will I ever complete all the commissions on time?

Padre Dantas signaled the waiting clergy. Brothers gathered again around them. He motioned to a novice to reinstate the conversation. "Again, the article states that the role of the Church in life matters..."

Pêro sat still, mouth clamped shut. As these men here too discussed the same article he and Paulinha had seen the other day at home in their own courtyard. Maybe he didn't quite agree with the defined role of the Church and its place as much as he'd thought...

CHAPTER TWENTY

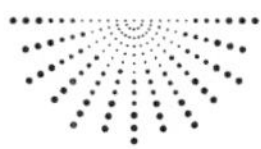

Rafa stood at the draft table and picked up the commissions Pêro had set aside for him. Carefully, he looked through each one, praying one would strongly capture his imagination. *Where in the Lord's name did Pêro and his clients come up with such requests? Like the Chinese themed murals with pointy hats and parasols?*

Rafa pinched his eyebrows and reread again, his eyes straining to make out the preliminary sketches. Designing was so different than copying, he sighed. Transferring and rendering he could do. *But working out the composition and creating something new?* He struggled with this as he also now wrestled with whether or not to mention to Pêro the exchange he'd witnessed from the window and apothecary? He forced his thoughts back to this task. And yes, the difficulty of getting all the objects and detail proportions correct, Lord… Pêro kept calling on him to help with designs, and he tried. Really, he did. But it was so hard to come up with designs whereas Pêro seemed to have an endless stream of inspiration and creation.

The only drawings he truly felt comfortable creating were those of his people: the fishermen in their boats with nets and the daily catch, women selling baskets of salted cod, the laundresses, children, and women preparing fish like his wife. These people he *knew*. He knew the shape of their heads and their hair, their bodies, their noses, their eyes, and lips. He also knew their worries, loves and concerns. They were a reflection of him and there was comfort there, mapping out what you know.

He sat down on the stool and placed the three orders in a row before him. He pulled up the collar of his shirt, hiding the "S" brand. *Cursed mark.* He looked around the room, at the other table, and back down at the papers. Pêro wanted new *figura de convite* designs: a pair of Roman centurions, a musical duo, or a warrior. Rafa set his elbows on the table, resting his chin in his hands. *Choose what? Where to begin?* He recalled the blue and white Chinese porcelain vase in the window of the de Sousas' estate home he had loved as a boy. He'd admired its simplicity which he wished he could apply here.

As he stared at the requests, daylight grew brighter and stronger through the windowpanes. Voices began to filter into the main shop, followed by the sounds of the final closing of crates to be delivered today.

"Rafa," Paulinha said, poking her head into the draft room.

He gazed up, crinkling his forehead, and shaking his head. "I've been here all morning and I've accomplished nothing."

"May I take a look?"

"Yes, certainly." Rafa stared down again at three sheets of paper. His hands joined in his lap; shoulders slumped.

Paulinha picked up each request, scanning the rudimentary sketches and then set them down.

"This one." With her index finger she indicated the middle parchment.

Rafa read the commission description aloud. "A musician duo." He glanced at Paulinha, who flanked his side smiling down at him. "Why this and not the others?"

Paulinha pointed to his heart. "Because you have the musicians' music here, here in your heart. I've observed how you light up at the sound of the street players. Draw from real life.

Pêro always says the most arresting designs are drawn from the heart. I know this to be true."

Rafa stared at her a moment and then back down at the simple example outlines of the musical pair.

"You know Rafa, Pêro deviated from his family's established line of work when he was a tile making apprentice at del Barco's shop. He wanted to be an oil painter, not a tile maker. He studied with a visiting French master of oils at night, and recently with Pillement learning more about landscapes. As a young man, every evening after painting, in the privacy of his own room, he copied prints of the Royal Ribeira Palace's collection: Titians and Correggios with their dramatic scenes, the Flemish Baroque Rubens, of open countryside and allegorical subjects. But as you can see," She gestured to the draft room. "His father's legacy and connections within the tile craft won out. Pêro's carrying on the family's original trade, since his father abandoned tile works to expand into the lucrative importation of gems from the colony of Brazil, which in turn, elevated the family's social standing, making it possible for us to free you. But it is Pêro's training and his continued studying in painting that allows us to out-design the Dutch here in Lisbon."

Rafa stared at the paper before him. "I guess, I didn't quite understand how much copying and practicing he has done and continues to do. You're right. I need to work on my sketching before live musicians. Maybe this evening or later next week, or after the All Saint celebrations." Eyes twinkling, he smiled at Paulinha.

"Excellent idea. Now you're thinking like an artist. Practice, practice. Draw from real life when you can, and work from Pêro's many copies of engravings too." She grinned at him and looked fondly upon the three waiting design requests.

"Pêro mentioned that Padre Monsignor Sampaio of the Sé Cathedral recently told him that the Church likes our shop's tiles significantly more than the Dutch. They find the free-flowing spirit in our works reflect the local tastes here," Rafa said.

"Yes, he shared this with me too." Paulinha gazed off, looking out the windows.

"It's settled then, the musical pair it is. In the meantime, I'll ready the wood baron's delivery." Rafa stood up. "Yes, a musician duo!"

And now, he needed to find Mother Conga Carlota the Astrologer, to map the duos' charts, to help better understand the true characters of this musical ensemble!

CHAPTER TWENTY-ONE

A crowd was gathered before the newly opened Phoenix Opera House. Its wooden domed cupola arched up to the heavens. Elegant painted scrolls with gold details made the exterior white walls shine bright like the exquisite musical librettos performed within. Blind men sat before the grandeur selling the text of opera songs and plays attached to sticks with string.

Pêro and Paulinha pushed through the throng of people. "If we can get past this you can make it to the next scheduled appointment. Remember Pêro, you promised to meet with them before noon."

They both stopped. Pêro's muscles tightened, seeing a husband and wife arguing in the crowd. The man struck the woman across the face. The people around the couple turned their heads away from the scene. The man pushed people out of the way, leading the woman by the hand, she lowered her head in shame.

Pêro's face became earnest with concern.

Paulinha nervously ran her hands over her pulled back hair, and then intertwined her sweaty fingers into his and said in a soft voice. "Let it go, it is in our past. Leave them be. Come now."

Pêro looked at Paulinha with sad eyes. "I will always regret —"

Paulinha mustered a faint smile and tugged him forward. They reached a gridlock of people and stood behind a drove of devotees who knelt on the ground in black robes, pointed hoods drawn. Before them was a group of barebacked men. White cloths tied at their waists, the men all donned white cone pointed hats, their faces masked in white hoods. They were not elegant egrets, but spooky. Men clad in black stockings and belled coal-colored coats, cone hats upon their heads flanked the moving procession and blew brass trumpets. A priest led the group, an open Bible in hand, his lace finery contrasting the crude nakedness of the repenting men behind him. At different moments, the men raised their whips and lashed at their backs, groaning in penitence, blood flying like cast seeds.

Pêro's knees started to buckle, his body growing weak; the rawness of the men's backs, and the bright crimson blood recalled too intimately Jibo beaten to death before his eyes. Paulinha clamped her hand upon his forearm, as if bracing herself against the spectacle. Pêro knew the men before them were not slaves but worshipers of the Lord, choosing self-punishment, whereas the slave had been subjected to it, an unwilling "Christ", imposed and subjected to suffrage. Pêro's gut forcibly turned over at the sight of the floggers. His throat constricted.

The Pentecostal banners of the march limply bounced along while wooden crosses were held erect and high, guiding the large, gathered crowd. The men's ankle chains clanked along the cobbles as they inched forward. The knotted waxed hairs of their self-mortification whips swished through the air and then landed with whacks upon their open wounds.

An effigy of María with her golden crown rode on a platform carried above the masses, serenely smiling at the blood splatter before her.

"No, María would not condone such violence," Pêro whispered to himself. This was not a display of public piety, but repentance for deeds that more than likely should never have been committed, if the men had practiced self-restraint and goodwill. Regretfully, he was familiar with the lack of self-control and the likes of the man today who'd struck his wife. He cringed, remembering his own dark secret. He placed his maimed hand on his heart, grasping his habit.

One of the flagellants turned in Pêro and Paulinha's direction. Two onyx eyes stared out at them from under the hood. The masked man hefted his whip into the air and viciously brought it down upon his back, pain shooting from the penitent's eyes like knives. A light shower of blood rained on them, the whip once again cutting through the sky. The procession trumpets blared, the cloaked women kneeling before them wailing out prayers and psalms. No matter how many times he'd witnessed this scene, Pêro could not stomach it. It always returned him to the thought of Jibo who'd begged for mercy but received none.

Paulinha's elbow bumped into Pêro's side.

He looked down as she clenched her sketchbook through the folds of her skirt. He grabbed her wrist. "It's too dangerous to draw here," he whispered sternly. "What are you thinking?" He squeezed more tightly. "Record the scene in your mind, etch the lines there and put them on paper in the privacy of our home."

Paulinha wrested free of his grip. She wiped a tear from her cheek before letting go of the drawing book.

"You *know* a woman artist is scorned and seen as lowly as an actress and a woman of the pleasure profession —"

"But I don't have your same gift of memory," she said in a hushed voice. "It's an ongoing strain, this secrecy."

"Yes, but you have other talents which I don't, the fluidity of delicate expressive lines for one. God has given each of us a gift to nurture and bring forth. He's been generous in our cases. But we must continue to be careful and not reveal our secrets." He smiled at his wife. "Let us get away from this madness."

They turned away from the procession, meeting the stone-cold stares of three men in black cloaks, making their own markings in little black books.

CHAPTER TWENTY-TWO

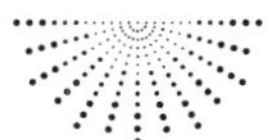

"No, I won't go with him." Luis stood defiant before Pêro.

Rafa was a black marble statue, his calm eyes fixed on the crate of tiles in front of them.

Pêro sighed. "Luis, there's a backlog of work to be done. Go with Rafa and oversee the beginnings of this installation. He's your assistant. You're in charge." Pêro gestured to the waiting box. "I cannot go right now. I have a meeting soon."

"No, I don't want to be seen in the company of an ex-slave." Luis thrust his nose up into the air.

Pêro's face turned red. "Look, there's no time for this. You've been seen in his company for years. Whether or not you like it, if you want to be paid this week, I suggest you go."

Luis snorted in disgust and turned to leave, disappearing into the street.

Pêro threw up his arms, knowing Luis would stand before his draft room door come the end of the week, whimpering for his pay despite blatantly abandoning his work.

"What's going on with him?" Pêro asked. "What's wrong?"

Rafa eyed Pêro and opened his mouth to speak.

"Yes, what is it?" Pêro asked.

"Well…" Rafa said, turning toward the crates. "I'll get these loaded. Kujaguo and Jawoli can you give me a hand with these?"

"Rafa…" Pêro said.

"Yes?"

"Remember they must now be called by their Christian names. It's imperative."

Kujaguo and Jawoli came over.

"Everyone you must now remember to only use your Christian names. People are watching. I can't stress enough how important this is. Now Carlos and Jorge …" Pêro looked squarely at Kujaguo and Jawoli, who lifted a box of tiles and placed it onto the flatbed of the cart, eyebrows raised, mouths shut.

"What about Rafa?" Kujaguo blurted.

"Rafa is a shortened version of my Christian name, Raphael, so it shouldn't be a problem, correct?" Rafa asked, looking to Pêro.

"Yes, I do believe it should be fine."

"Once these are loaded, Carlos, please tell the crate maker we'll stay with our regular quarterly order. I'll come see him as soon as I have a moment."

Pêro massaged the creases of his forehead as the cart entered the congested flow of carts, carriages, animals, and foot traffic, passing the House of India and entering Terreiro do Paço. The Tagus River was in full view. The plaza smelled of chocolate drinks brewed with exotic spices, mixed with wafts of rosemary marinated meats roasting on charcoal braziers. Under the arches of the new riverside quay, the Cais da Pedra, merchants discussed business while waiting for outlying skiffs to come ashore with newly arrived goods from far-off places. Their slave bodyguards waited patiently alongside them, some aloof, others alert. In the middle of the wide-open space men worked at erecting a wooden platform, a solid post rising from its center, the stage of an *auto-da-fé*. Pêro cringed at the sight, as carts passed loaded with logs for the fire.

One of the workmen yelled. "Look! Look! The Royal barge!"

Work halted, everyone turned to the ribbon of river the color of sardines. Bands of homeless children and men ferrying water barrels made for the river's edge. Rafa's and Pêro's cart was caught in the stream of curious onlookers eager to see the incoming procession. The mass of people halted behind waiting military escorts.

A choir of awed voices rippled along the bank.

Muleteers doffed their hats as the nobility neared.

Pêro took hold of his waist belt cross, gripping it ever more tightly as the Royal vessels advanced, excitement building at catching a glimpse of the incoming display.

Pêro could not help but smile at such a regal water entrance at close range. The street children danced at the water's edge. These were not desperate times Lisbon found herself in, yet there were many children in need of homes and care. Pêro frowned, wishing for a solution.

All of Lisbon lived under the city's thick, protective cloak of piety and lavish wealth where pedigree meant everything. The Church, the alms to saints, and the proceeds from gold, diamonds and slaves funded constant ostentatious displays such as at the Jesuit Church of São Roque and the Chapel of St. John the Baptist, despite the poverty lingering on the Church's footsteps.

Pêro lamented to Rafa. "Watching this wealth row in with the poor upon the banks tears at my heart —" Pêro caught himself, cutting his words short.

He and Rafa looked at each other knowingly.

The Royal family was leagues apart from their populace, not quite of them. The family arrived in sovereign fashion, carried by an elegant one-of-a-kind vessel, long and sleek upon the waterway. Sculled by forty oarsmen in perfect unison, it spliced the craggy waters like a sword's blade. It did not seem of earthly origins. Painted in an opulent navy blue, its embossed planks were detailed in gold leaf, each oar painted with a fierce dragon eel. Pêro imagined depicting the whole scene in tile.

Princess María sat on a bullion footstool at the feet of her mother, Queen Mariana Victoria of Spain, who was poised in a copper gown on a low throne of gold, under an awning protecting them from the glare of the sun. King José I leaned over to speak to his wife, he cloaked in a crimson velvet cape lined in white fur with black spots. The other three princesses were not present. An entourage of attendants flanked the royal group. A massive fleet of barges backed the incoming vessel.

Pêro and Rafa looked on with everyone else in the square. The scene reminded Pêro of the Fabrica's mural creations: once installed, the spectacular panels caused spectators to stop, eyes stunned by the beauty. Nothing compared to handcrafted works of art, finely executed, with the simplest of tools and materials. It was amazing what clay, wood, and minerals could produce, worked by a skilled hand — even awe-inspiring at times. Like this boat carrying the House of Braganza.

Cheers rang out as the craft glided in followed by chattering and speculation.

The Royal Appointed Priest dressed in a white lace habit greeted Princess María as he helped her out of the boat first. She was draped in a butter-cream floor length cape that plumed around her like a delicate tulip. Her features were framed by her hood, the white skin of her noble line contrasting starkly against the cream. Each cheek was rosy from the sea air and her lips brushed in faint merlot. She was not striking like Paulinha, it was her bloodline that enchanted and enthralled. Wealth and royalty had a way of making those who lacked outer beauty seem exceedingly beautiful, mused Pêro, but then, beauty is solely in the eye that perceives, and tastes vary depending on each soul's unique lens.

Princess María did not look up or out, but kept her head bowed, as the Queen and King were helped to disembark. All of them swept into waiting coaches, while attendants saw to their things. The coaches passed the platform in the center of the plaza, and then headed for the Palacio dos Corte Reais.

"The Royal family —" Rafa said, gesturing to the moving vehicle that carried them. "I'm relieved that our Mocambo healer Doroteiada Rosa is no longer in danger of being put to the stake here in the plaza. This platform isn't for her, is it? She was convicted but nothing ever came of it. Her master is too powerful." Rafa shook his head. "It seems the enslaved are often more protected than those of us who are now free. I fear what life would be like without your presence Padre Pêro." Rafa stared at the solitary wooden pillar.

"I think it's for another unfortunate soul," Pêro said in consternation.

The riverside crowd began to break up. Rafa maneuvered the cart out of the fray and into open space. They crossed the square at a trot and headed to the Alfama, the Sé Cathedral peeking above the tile rooftops of the hillside neighborhood. White marble homes gleamed in the afternoon sunlight.

Women sat crossed-legged on cork and rush mats on their balconies gazing down coquettishly on Pêro and Rafa. They peered out from their sheer mantillas and made hand signals to each other. Rafa and Pêro paid no mind to the women's gesturing as they wound their way up into the Alfama labyrinth.

Multi-storied homes crowded the narrow ways, and tight alleys spilled off the main cart path. Homes leaned into each other, and from some upper story windows one neighbor could pass salt to another across the street. Drying laundry snapped in the breeze like colorful flags. Rafa jostled the reins, moving them along.

"Rafa, you were about to say something back at the shop," Pêro said, as they arrived before Senhor Reis's residence.

Rafa reined the cart to a halt. He stared at Pêro a long moment.

Senhor Reis's footman approached and greeted them, smelling of cheroots. His card playing friends looked at the cart as they smoked, waiting for their friend to return to the game.

Rafa sat closed-mouthed, clenching the reins and looked at Pêro.

Pêro addressed the footman. "Go ahead and unload. Remember these are tiles, handle them with care." The footman motioned to the other men to come and assist.

They began unloading the crates and carrying them into the residence's double doors and marble checkered foyer with a white marble staircase.

"Luis," Rafa said.

"Padre Pêro, Senhor Reis is waiting for you. He's pleased you've come instead of your help," the footman said, hands clasped behind his back as he bowed forward.

Pêro looked once more at Rafa. "Tell me later."

Pêro and Rafa entered the home. "*Bom dia*." They followed Senhor Reis in his high-heeled boots up two flights of stairs.

Pêro inspected the walls where the Roman centurion *figuras de convite* would be affixed, connecting into tile panels of faux balustrades decorated with flower garlands, lining the whole stairway. Pêro ran his hand along the cool white plaster.

Rafa did the same.

"I suggest the tile installers lay out the upper panels on the second floor first." Pêro pointed to the wide-open hallway with an enormous hanging crystal chandelier at the top of the stairs. "And, that you use your other entrances until the tile setting is complete. Rafa here, will oversee the installation," Pêro said, introducing Rafa.

Senhor Reis smiled curtly in agreement, rice powder from his wig raining down. "How did the final design turn out?"

"I'm very pleased with the Roman centurions. They are vital and robust, and will be the talk of the town, surely. The first of their kind always are," Pêro said to Senhor Reis, whose smile grew to a grin as he twisted the end of his thin black mustache and cocked a painted eyebrow, obviously pleased.

"Indeed," he said, looking fondly upon his now empty walls.

Senhor Reis saw them to the door.

"Rafa will return here at the beginning of next week to oversee the installation." Pêro nodded his head congenially at their patron. "Final payment is due at this time."

"I'd prefer to pay at a later date," Senhor Reis said, pouting.

Clouds the color of drab wool obscured the sun.

"That won't be possible," Pêro said.

"But it always has been in the past. I can't possibly be expected —" Senhor Reis bit his lower lip. "You can't go making changes just like that." He raised a bejeweled hand and snapped loudly.

Pêro paused and scratched the back of his neck. "If you are unable to pay in full at the time of completion and need more time to do so, I can extend that time, but with an added cost."

Senhor Reis gasped. "Well, I most certainly will be letting others know about the changes at the Fabrica Santa María."

Pêro's stomach churned. The last thing he needed was more negative gossip pointed toward the shop. *But what else can I do?* He ran a hand over his hair.

Senhor Reis spun on his heel and looked over his shoulder. "Fine. Good day." His servant closed the door.

Pêro threw up his hands then sat in the cart. "Now Rafa, what were you going to tell me about Luis?"

CHAPTER TWENTY-THREE

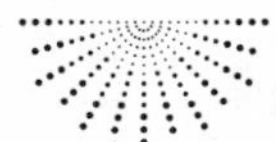

The Convent of Senhora of Jesus hospital ward smelled of cider vinegar. Light shone through the large windows onto the rows of beds and patients under pressed sheets. Pêro headed to the first bed. Paulinha situated the wicker basket in the crook of her arm and came up alongside the other side.

Pêro kneeled, placing his hand upon the ill youth. The boy's hand was cold like the sea. Paulinha pulled from the basket a white and blue tile with a lively duck painted on it.

The boy's eyes lit up at the playful image.

"Take it, son. It's yours to keep," Pêro said.

The boy smiled, accepting the gift. He held it up. "It's wonderful and reminds me of home." He propped the tile upon his chest and beamed at it, a little color returning to his pale cheeks.

"May the Lord continue to aid you in your recovery." Pêro made the sign of the cross over the boy and touched his forehead. "Receive the Lord's blessings."

The boy beamed. "Thank you, Padre and Senhora."

Pêro and Paulinha walked through the ward, gifting extra and slightly flawed tiles to those who were awake to accept them. Pêro also made sketches on scraps of paper as they made their rounds, leaving a drawing at each bedside for those sleeping.

Pêro noticed the special care Paulinha gave each patient. She smiled kindly at each child, softly touching his or her cheek, then carefully adjusting and straightening the bedding. Each person's demeanor brightened with the motherly care and affection. Pêro was inspired by her loving touch, courage, and her ability to ease pain and loneliness of others.

As they climbed the stairs to the next floor, Paulinha paused mid-flight and turned to Pêro. "Padre Dantas has been generous in his punishment. I don't find this a hardship in the least, but a blessing. I'm so pleased to be able to assist you and show my thanks to Saint Anthony for the return of my mother's pewter plate."

"I'm happy you see it this way, *meu amor*. It lessens my worrisome load. If I must pay retribution for my error, I too now see this as a kind penance." Pêro reached for her hand, helping her up to the next step with him.

Is this the right time to tell Paulinha what Rafa had revealed yesterday about Luis? That Luis is unabashedly lying, using his deceased father's name to buy hashish, which explains his lack of interest and detachment from the work. While this is disturbing in of itself, it is the deception and the absence of respect for family and the departed that is most alarming. If he now so blatantly disregards the dead to what end will he go? Should I say something? He paused at the last stair and turned to her.

"Yes, dear?" Paulinha said.

No, no he'd not further burden Paulinha with the sad news, for he did not yet know how he was going to handle the situation.

"Do you think it would be all right if I drew a little here? Especially, since the nurses are on the second floor?" Paulinha asked.

"Oh, *meu amor,* there is nothing more I'd wish for you to be able to do but —" *Oh, how I wish she could partake in this aspect of the service in the same way I can. Why Lord was it so questionable for a woman to do so?*

"Just a few sketches."

"We both know the risk, *meu amor.* No."

Paulinha retrieved her sketchbook from the folds of her dress.

"Put it away now," Pêro insisted.

"Deacon Pêro!" A voice echoed from the stairway corridor below, accompanied by the pounding of up-bounding footsteps. A young monk rounded the stairwell, eyes alert and opening wide as they homed in on Paulinha's hands holding a drawing pencil and notebook.

CHAPTER TWENTY-FOUR

Rafa, Gogo, Diogo, and his sons joined the stream of people heading for the day's procession in honor of their venerated Virgin María held on the seventh of October every year. Young men rap-tap-tapped on drums hanging from straps around their necks, welcoming and summoning the gathering crowd to celebrate this year's Our Lady of the Rosary celebration, the special day of reverence for Mother María's crowning day in heaven. Procession leaders dressed in white silk robes holding spindly upright palm fronds directed the crowd, the white of their garments gleaming against their dark skin.

A statue of María was raised up on a platform carried by eight men the color of coal. Today, the Mocambo's laundresses, household cooks, and nannies all thumbed their rosaries made of simple knots on a cord and repeated recitations of *Ava María*. They called upon the Virgin for her intercession in their community's unified goal of freedom for all, liberation for the enslaved. Mother María was their grantor of salvation, of hope.

Rafa helped Gogo along through the jostling masses. Gogo leaned into him and said, "A new slave ship arrived last night while our Brothers were out collecting alms for today. Word is that our people are almost all gone now." She made a clicking sound with the sad pronouncement. Rafa patted Gogo's forearm. Gogo clenched tight the crook of his arm and looked ahead, chin raised. "Oh, Grandmother, I am sorry to hear and know of this."

Up ahead Rafa saw a brilliant flash of gold amongst the black and white. Mother Conga Carlota the Astrologer slowly turned, covered from head to foot in white-gold threaded cloth that gleamed in the morning light, she as brilliant as the sun. She was surrounded by a sea of admirers, her fleshy body dark and wide like the ocean itself.

Rafa itched to approach her and see about a meeting time, to consult with her for guidance on how to proceed with his musician duo design, the threat of Luis, and most importantly, to know how a reading of the stars would decide the fate of his father, Bagamba. He needed counsel. Mother Conga Carlota was his direct link to the wisdom of the night sky and most importantly the knowledge of the ancestors. But here and now was not the right time nor place. Later he'd send Diogo to arrange a time.

CHAPTER TWENTY-FIVE

Three weeks later, scents of anise and roasted chestnuts filtered from under doorways and out windows, women busily baking *pão-por-Deus,* small cake-like breads for the morrow's festivities. Tomorrow, children would go door-to-door to receive their special fare of bread, chestnuts, and pomegranates, in celebration of All Saints Day.

But despite the festivities, Pêro hurried by coach to the Fabrica and distanced himself from The Church of Santo-o-Velho and that morning's disturbing encounter with Padre Matos. The Padre had received word of Paulinha and her sketchbook in the empty stairway of the hospital ward. Despite her claims that she was merely taking notes for him, keeping track of the floors they'd served, the young monk had eyed them suspiciously and reported back on what he saw exposed upon the page: a nude female figure. One the fellow claimed had been in a suggestive position.

Pêro shook his head, lips pursed, and held tight the formal letter summoning Paulinha before the Church inquirers in three weeks' time. Carefully, he folded the note and placed it into his undershirt pocket, next to his heart. In his mind's eye, he saw the approaching black cloaked men; heard their pounding fists on the door of their home. Anguished, he gripped the wooden cross at his waist, a flash of heat, of horror spreading through his body as he imagined them escorting her into the accusing daylight.

Pêro forced himself to walk on, glancing back occasionally, making sure no one followed him. He fumed at Luis's betrayal that Pêro believed started all this observation and suspicion now plaguing them, along with his ill guided decision to take on the wood baron's design request. He replayed the words of Padre Matos in his head. "Your wife must answer for her questionable actions."

Today, the tile order destined for the Amazon would be delivered and payment secured, Bagamba freed, and he would no longer need to keep such long hours, freeing him up to devise a plan, seek his own Church assistance in this escalating matter, somehow deflect all this.

Pêro strode into the Fabrica's courtyard, coming upon Paulinha who pulled her cloak tight over her shoulders, her cheeks rosy in the fall morning air. She and the girls were tending to the removal of shriveled flowers and stems from the yard's red geraniums. Pêro clasped Paulinha's hand tight and kissed her forehead.

"Everything all right?" she asked.

Pêro just squeezed her hand more tightly and smiled.

Nearby, Rafa and Jorge, their Jawoli, loaded the boxes of the tiles destined for the Amazon jungle onto the donkey cart, maneuvering the crates into rows.

"Crates of colorful rocks, this should do it," Rafa called to Pêro. The cart creaked and the planks bowed as they placed the last box in.

Rafa harnessed the donkey, which brayed as Pêro spoke with Paulinha. "I can manage things now *meu amor,* so you can go home to take care of the holiday baking." He turned to the girls and hugged them. He leaned down and kissed their rosewood-colored hair.

"What did Padre Matos want to see you about?" Paulinha asked, trying to catch his eye.

"Let's discuss it later."

"Are you sure?" Brow furrowed, worry spread throughout Paulinha's face.

"Yes, for now let's keep focused on this delivery and payment." He looked at her. "Today, this is what we can see through."

The girls released their hold on him and went to their mother's side.

Pêro reached again, for his wife's hand, holding it tenderly, trying to reassure her.

Then he let go and hurried to Rafa. "I shall ride with you, to secure this payment. Make sure all is in order," Pêro said.

Rafa nodded eagerly.

Paulinha returned to her pruning, occasionally glancing at Pêro.

"How is your design coming along, Rafa?" Pêro placed a hand on the donkey.

"The musicians are coming along slowly. I am not happy with my preliminary sketches," Rafa said, fastening the last of the animal's straps.

"I think we have a copy of an engraving that might be helpful to work from. I'll try to find it for you."

Pêro and Rafa clambered into the cart. Rafa cracked the whip and the animal jerked forward. Paulinha and the girls stood with Jawoli waving them off. The donkey's slate mane flip-flopped, pulling the heavy load, the beast's rear trumpeted gas as the cart left. The girls giggled and placed their hands over their mouths, looking at their mother.

As they passed other carts piled high with sacks of cereals headed for the tide windmills along the Tagus River, Pêro let out a long sigh and rubbed his forehead, relieved that the Amazon commission was complete and that they were delivering it. Bagamba's release and payment weighed upon him like an unshakable illness that he was desperate to cure, given his new set of problems. He looked forward to spending tomorrow's holiday with Paulinha and the girls.

They rode without speaking, accompanied only by the sound of the donkey's clop and the jingling harness. Pêro glanced over and grinned at Rafa, shifting his thoughts from his problems and thinking back over the years that they'd worked together. How their friendship had developed during Rafa's apprenticeship with him. A friendship he thought he'd also had with Luis. He considered Rafa one step shy of a master *azulejo* maker, although the Guild would not recognize him as such. Rafa possessed the patient temperament of a professional; he'd developed precision line control and understood how each clay type behaved during the tile making process. He had yet to uncover his own full innovative spirit, but like Luis he copied well.

Creativity, Pêro mused, was not something that could be taught. He'd found that one had to toil and surrender to the process until new ideas bubbled forth. One often worked hard but an advancement could be long in coming; or in the extreme, never arrive. For a decade, he'd hoped to assist Rafa in opening up the wells of creativity within himself, for he sensed his design aptitude, but the right set of circumstances had yet to bring forth his full potential.

Whereas for Paulinha, new designs sprang forth like miraculous visitations from saints: the dimensional shading of cloth, the new masqueraded couple design, and the innovative shadowing on the back of the decorative panel of the female *figura de convite.* The ideas just appeared to her after analyzing prints or after moments of silent reflection.

Looking at Rafa, he knew one day he would need another man to take over the shop, as Paulinha had yet to deliver a son, but there was still time. And there was the problem that the Guild would never accept Rafa, despite his status as a freeman. They'd have to wait and see, for things were also always subject to change.

Vendors lined the way along the dirt road toward the river, selling bunches of flowers for the oncoming holiday: lavender, lilies, sunflowers mixed with thyme and marjoram.

Pêro enjoyed the fresh flower scents, reflecting on how greatly he valued Rafa and his work ethic, so like his own, and how pleased he and Paulinha had been when they were able to liberate him and Gogo from the de Sousa's estate. The cart passed a group of slaves chained one to the other at the ankle, with a disconcerting hollow sound of iron dragging along the earth. A man on horseback driving them down to the river. A wave of sadness swept over Pêro, recalling how Rafa's own mother and other brothers and sisters had been sold off to faraway places throughout Portugal, before there was a chance to free them. But Bagamba was needed at the farm, and so he remained — his back permanently bent, his strength spent. But he would be free soon. *Lord, make sure of it.*

Rafa glanced at the procession, whipped the donkey, and they hurried past.

Pêro internally said a prayer for those retained and then admired Rafa, the youngest of seven children, he'd benefited like the rest of Lisbon, from the wealth coming from the colonies. For Rafa it manifested in his size, health, and education. He spoke Lisbon's Portuguese dialect immaculately and had an inclination for learned things. Rafa had grown fascinated with *azulejo* works as a boy, willingly helping Bagamba with clay deliveries from the de Sousa's portion of the Lapa clay stream beds, where the Mocambo's tile-making factories obtained their ongoing needed supply.

It was his friendships with Paulinha and Rafa, and not the Fabrica's prospering, and especially their desire to help the downtrodden that truly sustained him. Because he was noticing with success came complications. As the proverb said: "*Grande Nau, Grande Tormenta,* Big Ship, Big Storm —" and how true the wisdom of the words rang.

Rafa's self-control and ability to make light of things in difficult situations helped him to deal with the shop's increasing commitment to freedom and workload, both of which brought prying eyes and the busy tongues of Lisbon to their doorstep.

Rafa snapped the reins, turning the corner at the base of the Mocambo hillside onto the main road along the Tagus.

The clangor of iron-shod hooves arose from behind them, overtaking their cart, along with a cloud of dust. Pêro covered his mouth. Out of the particles came a procession of Lisbon's finest vehicles: a Meninos of Palhava coach, followed by a Spanish-made Philip II coach.

Rafa and Pêro looked on at the exquisite spectacle.

The first coach quickly passed them, like a traveling jewelry-box, bouncing along with gold trimmed glass windows and drawn emerald curtains. The Philip II traveled behind.

"The Philip II transports the royal family's princesses," Pêro said. "I've seen it depart on a couple of occasions, while looking in upon one of our installations for them."

"I've never seen anything like it." Rafa leaned forward eyes wide.

"I know." *And how many mouths could be fed from the cost of such a vehicle?* Pêro held his tongue.

The *boleeiro*, the princesses' security guard, sat poised next to the coach's page who lashed his whip. The horses swished their braided tails and leapt into a canter, the open-air two-person coach bumping along the road as it galloped forward. Behind the men, two princesses sat like rare vases. The red leather seat cushion gave their pale skin a rosy tint. The outside of the Philip II was painted to simulate a wicker basket. Its golden background and plumes of peacock feathers intermingled with strings of pearls.

"Look at the paintings," Pêro said in wonder. "The craftsmanship is spectacular." He inspected the coach's back panel of an angel holding a banner and the arms of Portugal. "Extraordinary. They are probably on their way to the country palace in Belém."

The coach pulled away.

From a side street came the pounding of more hooves, loud breathing, and then a command: "Out of the way!"

Pêro watched as a wild horse and rider stampeded towards them.

Its driver yanked and held the horse's bridle strap up by his ears, the silver bit cutting deep into the horse's jaw. The steed reared up onto its thick hind legs.

"Watch out!" Pêro cried.

Rafa lashed the donkey and the beast cried out.

Pêro yelled "No!" staring at the hairs of the underbelly of the horse. Pêro reached out and pushed hard on Rafa's back, forcing him down, and then crumpled his chest onto his thighs.

With the last crack of the whip, the donkey lunged forward, right as the bay Lusitano squealed and crashed down onto the back of the cart. Wood snapped and cracked. The sudden impact threw Rafa and Pêro forward and out. But the donkey's movement was instantly halted, as the steed barreled through the loaded bed, the crunch of hooves breaking wood and clay. The donkey cried in fear as he buckled forward onto his front knees.

Planks of wood splintered; crates burst open. The weight of the horse broke the cart's axle and two wooden wheels popped off, rolling away. The steed found its footing and bolted into a group of olive and lavender vendors along the way.

It was no ordinary mount. The rider rode in pure silver stirrups, and the horse's silver bit and bridle glinted in the morning sun.

The horse faltered, launching its driver into the olive brine mixed with lavender cuttings. Sprawled on his back, the rider swore and swatted at the crushed baskets and the vendors.

Pêro and Rafa struggled to their feet and Rafa limped over to their cart and animal, kneeling to inspect the frightened beast, which shrieked and hawed. He laid a hand upon him, trying to soothe him while searching for injuries. Pêro brushed himself off, then stood in silence above their load. Crates were still intact, but one box had taken the full weight of the horse.

Pêro turned to glare at the rider of the runaway steed. *What in the name of María is going on here?*

Swearing and coughing, the rider dislodged himself from the oily mess. His sword dangled from his waist, the scabbard's decorative ribbons caked in dirt and oil.

It was a wonder he did not impale himself on that thing!

The horseman's long waistcoat buttons had popped off; his coattails oil stained. Each wide jacket cuff was folded down, hiding his hands. The ruffles of his fine linen shirt had torn from their seams and drooped like two dead doves.

A group crowded around the spectacle while the reckless man tried to stand and continued to thrash about.

"What in God's name are you doing in my road?!" the rider yelled.

"My olives! My flowers!" A vendor cried, as he scrambled around scooping up handfuls of green and black olives, shoving them into his apron.

Pêro's cheeks grew hot, watching the young man teeter and weave in an effort to stay upright.

"What are we doing on *your* road?" Pêro cried, aghast and indignant.

"Yes!" the horse rider demanded, gesticulating — his hidden hands popping out of the down turned cuffs like jacks-in-the-box while he stomped on the ground.

"I think a better question is what are you doing riding *drunk*?" Pêro asked stiffly.

"I am Tiago of the Rivera; how dare you talk to me that way —" The horse rider slurred, spewing fumes of brandied wine that Pêro could smell even at a distance.

Pêro pointed to his ruined cargo, where Rafa bent over, salvaging from the broken crate. "You're aware, Tiago, you have just purchased a costly crate of *azulejos* and caused our shipment to be undeliverable." Pêro's body shook as he looked at the broken tiles. "Do you understand how long it took to make that shipment? Weeks, no, months and...and a man's life depends on this shipment." Pêro could barely speak the words out loud. He didn't care at this moment whose rich son Tiago was, nor what the consequence would be in standing up to him. "You're going to have to pay for your recklessness."

"Pay?" Tiago returned, slitting his eyes.

Pêro knew it was impossible to deal with a drunken man and a self-righteous rich one doubly so. Tiago stumbled in the street, continuing to rant. Pêro eased away to assist Rafa. Together they kept an eye on Tiago and sorted their load.

"Tiago will not be going anywhere soon." Pêro held his forehead in his marred hand.

"Lucky for him it's not All Saints Day. The Inquisition would hang him by his ruffles," Rafa said.

The men smirked at each other.

"Truth be told," Pêro said.

Tiago was young, obviously foolish, and out of control. Pêro felt sure Tiago's father would be mortified at the commotion his son had caused, in public, upset with him for tainting their family name, and doubly angry as he now would be responsible for paying for the Fabrica's damaged cargo. *But how soon would payment be secured? Within a day?* Highly unlikely, he bemoaned. Rivulets of sweat ran down his back.

The young man limped and circled in the dust-covered olives, one foot in a silk stocking, the other clad in an expensive wide-heeled shoe. He gimped on the one elevated foot, looking in vain for the shoe's lost mate.

"Blasted shoe, blasted Padre João!" Tiago blurted.

Pêro stopped cold from their sorting.

"He did just say Padre João? Didn't he?" Pêro asked Rafa, his face turning to stone.

Rafa stared at him. "Yes, I heard him say Padre João too. What of it?"

Pêro paced back and forth, then stopped. "I have reason to believe this is no accident. Dear Lord, have mercy."

Word was sent to the *Nossa Senhor da Luz* explaining the circumstances and delay.

"Rafa, we need to work tonight and tomorrow. It is the only way," Pêro said.

"But it's All Saints Day. The Inquisition?"

"I know. How many tiles are ruined?" Pêro asked.

"Twenty-one."

A finger to his temple Pêro massaged. Paulinha could not help them this evening, for the risk was too great. Eyes were watching him, them. It was strictly forbidden to work on a religious holiday. He knew better, as a secular deacon. He knew the punishments, potential imprisonment. But a man's life, a family's well-being already weighed on the scales. And this was work for God, a vow he'd promised. If he failed Bagamba, he failed God.

Pêro bit his upper lip and said in a whisper: "We'll paint the already bisque-fired tiles this evening and pull them in the morning for delivery. We need to let Kujaguo and Jawoli know of the change." He winced and internally chided himself for forgetting to use their Christian names in this moment of urgency. "They can meet us tomorrow when the sun is up after tonight's effort. We'll work with drapery over the windows. Working tonight is not forbidden." Pêro let out a long sigh and crossed himself three times.

"Tomorrow, you'll fetch me at the Terriero Palace square just as the sun crests the hills," Pêro instructed stoically. "This must be done. There is no other way. The de Sousa's and the ship are waiting. We must liberate your father. We won't be working but delivering."

CHAPTER TWENTY-SIX

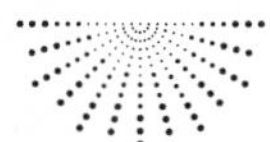

"Where is he?" Jawoli complained to their puppy who was amusing himself with a dried fruit pit. Jawoli poked the cooking fire with a stick, careful not to send ashes into the black pot awaiting water to boil.

Jawoli lay down on his bed mat, hands behind his head, staring up at the low soot-blackened rafters of their single room dwelling. The walls of the place were made of an assortment of odds and ends, wooden planks and adobe bricks. Smoke from the fire lingered at the ceiling and filtered out the open door, while he gazed into the black of night for Kujaguo. He rubbed sleep from his eyes, thankful the late night of work at the Fabrica was now finished until morning. He rose and went to the single nail securing their clothes, located another long-sleeved shirt and put it on.

He leaned in the doorway, rolled a *cigaro* and waited.

Panting, Kujaguo entered their courtyard, the moon already making its way across the starry night. The dog wagged its tail in greeting.

"Where have you been? What's taken you so long to fetch water at this hour?" Jawoli asked.

"There was a long line for water. The public fountain is only putting out a trickle and the water is muddy. Look." Kujaguo lowered the water bucket from on top of his head and set the pail down. He massaged gently the scar where the brick had struck him.

"Strange." Jawoli lifted the bucket and poured water into the pot.

"And all the fishermen are talking about the unseasonable afternoon fog and the late tide."

A pack of dogs yelped, barked, and swirled by in a cloud of dust in the road.

"Put out the fire," Jawoli said. "Gather your things, we're leaving."

"What? I just got back. I'm tired," Kujaguo said.

"I know, but I see the crows' signs of warning all around us. The water has tasted strange for days. It's time to go, take shelter away from here. Come on, get your things." Jawoli lifted his clothes off the nail and set them in the middle of his sleeping mat. "Put the water into the leather goat bag. I'll carry the pot with the food." Jawoli poured the water into their gutted goat bag, Kujaguo came over to help.

"I'm so hungry. Can't we wait and go in the morning?" Kujaguo asked.

"No, we have to go now." Jawoli finished tying shut the mouth of the water bag. "Hurry."

Jawoli closed the cloth that served as their home's door. Then he went to the back of their room and ran his hand along the far wall in the dark corner. He worked the bottom brick, sliding it out. He flipped it on end to reveal a bored-out hole and removed their few saved coins. Then he carefully replaced the brick.

Jawoli waited by the drawn curtain, a rolled mat under his arm, the cooking pot filled with food in his other hand: a half sack of grain, a salt pouch, a chunk of squash.

"Let's just wait till morning," Kujaguo pleaded again.

"Come." Jawoli drew the cloth, holding it open.

Kujaguo snuffed out the remaining coals, placed his bundle

on his head and ducked under the curtain and into the night. From somewhere nearby came the sound of a spoon scraping the sides of a cooking pot.

Jawoli put his roll on top of his head, the puppy nipping at his heel. "To the hillside behind the Mocambo."

Into the night like refugees they traveled. Jawoli looked up at the dark sky, sniffing the air tainted with a scent he did not recognize, an odor of something old escaping its confines. But of what he did not know. But what he did know was that these were signs and warnings that was clear, at least to him. *Should I go tell Rafa about the warnings? Let Senhor Pêro know? No, they think me crazy. In the morning, I'll send word of our whereabouts.*

An eerie silence mocked them as they fled the neighborhood, until a night owl hooted and swooped before them. *Yes, I've made the right decision, another sign.* Jawoli looked up the black hillside, picking up their pace.

CHAPTER TWENTY-SEVEN

Pêro awoke to tolling church bells and cooing pigeons. Abruptly, the tilting stopped, and the birds took flight, drawing him to the window. He sniffed and knitted his brow. Something in the air was different, charged with power somehow.

Outside, a wooden head of Christ bobbed, the painted-on blood oozing from the rose thorn crown. Below, the priesthood ferried a Brazilwood crucifix. Its sepia timber stained the white cloaks of the clergy as they passed through the city streets on their way to Mass at São Domingos. Behind the cross floated carved doves mounted on long poles with streaming ribbons. A procession of effigies, carried on elevated platforms, of Lisbon's Patron Saint Vincent, Saint Anthony, and three Portuguese Princesses, followed.

"*Pai*! You're late —" Isabela called from the stairs.

Chants and the scent of fried batter drifted up. Pêro scratched his face, the peeling skin on his hands catching on the dark bristles. He looked one more time down on the procession, and then quickly set to shaving.

He reached for his undergarment shirt and trousers, habit, and coral rosary. He slipped the prayer beads over his curls, clasping the cruciform, and gazed at the blue and white tile he had made for his mother prior to her death. The tile called to him. He took it and swiftly admired its design, turning it over, and held it up to his nose inhaling its earth scent, a familiar smell unlike what now lingered in the early morning air. Images of the multilayered clay deposit appeared before his eyes. He retrieved the summons letter, folded it once more, and hid it beneath the tile he replaced back on the nightstand.

He felt his pants pocket, making sure his malachite stone rested there. With a black ribbon, he tied back his hair. He packed into a pouch his church outfit: his official stole, a new russet-colored habit, linen trousers and shirt, recent gifts from a client who'd commissioned their new noblewoman *figura de convite* with Paulinha's innovation of the dimensional cloth skirt.

Inside the kitchen, Constanza and Isabela arranged their white dresses and braided ribbons of white into their hair as they bantered at the table. It was cloaked today with the family's finest lace cloth, a bowl of figs, and a plate piled high with *pão-por-Dues* at its center. A fire burned in the hearth, the soot creating a perfect half- moon at the back of the nook. Coffee brewed on the iron plate, sending out wafts of tropical aromas.

"We've missed the first procession," Isabela said, making a face at her father.

"My love, words are silver, and silence is gold," Paulinha said, as she tossed crumbs to the birds milling outside the window. Paulinha moved about the kitchen with purpose as if she were at the Fabrica. Pêro admired her and smiled.

"Father, your face looks like a crazed tile," Isabela said.

"How so my love?" he asked, in tired amusement.

"You know when it rains hard, the little rivers that cut into the clay banks? That's what your face looks like."

"We have a poet here, not a tile maker."

"Clever. I'll still take gold over silver," Paulinha said, minding the hearth, stealing a glance at Pêro.

It was true: after the previous day's events and the late

evening of work, his face displayed acutely the fissures of stress and fatigue. He'd seen it in the little round mirror as he shaved.

"I smelled frying batter?"

"Dreamcakes, but you'll have to wait like the girls."

Paulinha swiveled and mustered a coy smile at her husband, as Isabela asked, "When shall we leave for Mass at Saint Anthony's? Right after we get back from collecting our treats?"

As Pêro listened, he reached behind Paulinha, snatched, and then bit into a cake.

"Pêro," she said, with loving hopelessness.

Each of the girls' hands darted out and grabbed a warm dreamcake, but Pêro intercepted Isabela's hand and popped her cake into his mouth. He beamed at her.

"*Pai!*" Isabela pleaded, turning sour.

Paulinha and Constanza laughed, and Pêro gave Isabela a nudge. She smiled.

Paulinha began preparing another batch of dreamcakes, continuing to fill the kitchen with the smell of hot oil blending with Porto wine, cinnamon, grated lemon, and orange peel. The girls begged for dreamcakes regularly, but Paulinha made a point of only baking them on holidays; her attempt to tame overindulgence in a city where overindulgence was the norm, despite fervent religious orders touting otherwise.

Pêro kissed each girl on the head, and Isabela asked, "How long until we go?"

Pêro bent down and looked into Isabela's face. "Princess, I must go meet Rafa. I'm going to help at the shop this morning with something. Consult with your mother about your rounds with the neighborhood children. I'll meet you at Saint Anthony's. Where shall I find you?"

Paulinha glanced up from her stirring and drove her crystalline blue eyes into him, as she leaned over her bowl. "Yes princess, *Pai* has some things that need tending to. He'll meet us at the chapel."

Pêro took a deep breath, cleared his throat. "But I'll be with you all before the singing begins."

Paulinha whisked vigorously, the batter sloshing up the sides of the bowl. She swallowed hard, looking at both the girls and then Pêro. "We'll be at the back, on the left side, waiting under the statue of Saint Anthony. Remember where we lit candles last spring?"

"Yes, I'll look for you there. Buy us tapers."

Paulinha paused in her whisking; Pêro placed the coins in her outstretched palm, brushing his fingertips along her skin. She closed her fingers, the corners of her mouth turning up into a slight crooked smile. She tucked the coins into her apron and continued whisking.

The girls vied for their father's attention.

"One day, may I go with you to visit a rich client?" Constanza asked.

Pêro looked into her eyes, just like her mother's. "Princess, I will try to arrange it, after the holidays."

Constanza grinned at her father and smoothed her braids. "Me too! I want to see the palaces and work with clay." Isabela hopped up and down, extending her arms into the air.

Paulinha shot him a worried glance as to not encourage her too much into the tile trade.

Pêro reached for Isabela and engulfed her in his arms, drawing her near. "Yes, you too will go to the palaces and continue to learn clay works. But let us be quiet about these things." Isabela wrestled herself free from Pêro's embrace and together they moved into the front room, Constanza following.

"Princesses, open the shutters."

The rectangular wooden lattices opened onto the city street. Pêro and Isabela peeked out and up.

"Perfect morning," Pêro said. Despite his tight, aching neck muscles, he tried to remain calm and cheery.

"Look at the pigeons!" Isabela said, pointing to the sky as hundreds of birds dashed across it, heading inland.

Pêro and the girls turned from the window.

A blinding light shone into the room as the sun reflected off the whitewashed and tiled homes across the street. Church bells continued to peal throughout the city center, calling the devout to Mass. Pêro grinned faintly, thinking of how *figuras de convite* would be greeting the affluent worshippers to and from chapel services. Immediately, he cringed at the thought of what he must accomplish this day. *Will we be found out? Can I secure this final payment?*

"Girls, fetch my bag."

They raced upstairs to the bedroom, Isabela snatching the pouch first. Dispirited, Constanza trailed behind and walked to the front door, pulled the iron latch, and pushed. The doorway connected with the cobbled street, its intermittent potholes brimming with fetid waste-water.

Paulinha hurried over to Pêro wiping her hands upon her apron and whispered into his ear. "Be careful no one sees you going in. We'll be waiting for you at the back of the church. Don't be late. I really wish you didn't have to do this today. I am worried Pêro, very worried. I hope Luis doesn't know about any of this." She stared at him, her mouth downturned, eyebrows pinched.

She held tight to his forearm.

He leaned down and said in a low voice, so the girls could not hear. "Don't worry *meu amor,* since we completed the Sé Cathedral's Baptismal Chapel panels I find it hard to believe anyone would say anything. The Bishop and the Archbishop love our work. And remember, Luis hasn't been around for days."

With the last of his words, Tiago's comment rushed into his mind, the ones he'd blurted out yesterday: *'Blasted Padre João!'* He'd left this information out when he told Paulinha what had happened at the accident yesterday, not telling her about the true details of his most recent meeting with Padre Matos: the summons letter. He didn't want her worrying about this laundry list of problems: there'd be time enough later to explain it all and find solutions.

"But this is not work for the Bishop or the Archbishop. And Luis not being around worries me. Where is he?" she said, her eyes wide and focused.

Carefully, he put his hands on her shoulders and kissed her. "See you at Mass. We both know what must be done. I love you."

They looked into each others eyes and stayed a moment there, two pieces of a tile mural completing an image.

CHAPTER TWENTY-EIGHT

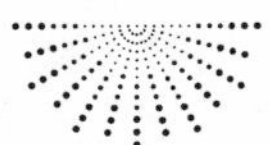

Pêro stepped out into the first of November sea air, and waved goodbye to Paulinha and the girls who smiled from the doorway. He brooded as he went. *Before honoring the saints today — it's true — I'm sure the Inquisition would not condone the unloading of a small batch of tiles nor their delivery. Nor would Padre João and Padre Matos. Senhor Guimarães would have a heyday with the information. And Luis, where has he gone off to? I'm placing myself on a precipice, but Bagamba, Rafa and family are already at its edge.*

He walked alone. *I know what Padre João would think: 'A fine opportunity to halt the progress of the Fabrica Santa María." Does he not know that others' lives are the true cost of his selfish desires?*

Cold seeped from the earthen buildings where the sun had yet to reach. He rubbed his hands together, thoughts of Padre João's fat face and how when he spoke the fullness of his cheeks squished up into his eyes, making them difficult to see. *How can he eat to such excess when so many go hungry? How could anyone trust or deal with a man when they could not clearly see his eyes? Yes, Padre João would take any opportunity to undercut the Fabrica Santa María.*

He reached up out of the building's shadow and let air into

his habit as he continued to reflect. *God must be working with us in the Fabrica. I come from a long line of azulejos makers traced back to a place my grandfather called Persia. My grandfather said our bloodline has a holy connection, that our works follow wealth and where riches flourish so do our works. I know this to be true. And now we must serve the poor with this abundance. The Lord understands and wants this.*

There are days when I feel God working at the tip of my paintbrush, carrying out its strokes, blending subtle hues or orchestrating soft lines — acts that can only be divined by the divine. But there are also times when I sense another presence, an older and a wiser one like the one connected with the malachite stone my grandfather gave me. Do I dare think this presence wiser than the saints?

Clanging disturbed his thoughts; as a pair of lyre-horned oxen, joined by a yoke with bells and little white tassels plodded past, the old cart creaking as its wooden axles emitted a shrill whine.

Southwest, he wended through the city center warren. His artist eyes took note of every detail of this bright clear morning. He passed low roofed shops, closed taverns with sprigs of protective laurel hanging over their doors. Lisbon's center was a mix of construction efforts. Eighth century Moorish structures endured beside storefronts decorated with new tiled facades, and North African influenced spires jutted into the sky. The mixture of building materials and styles exemplified the community's creativity, as well as its pockets of poverty.

Today, out of respect for the saints, all shops were closed. No one wanted to court potential problems with the Inquisition.

At a corner hat shop, owned by a business acquaintance, the middle-aged proprietor sat outside on a bench, his stockings loose around his ankles. He tipped his hat to Pêro. "Best to live in fear of God, wouldn't you say Padre?"

Pêro averted his eyes, offered a simper of agreement, and quickened his pace. He pushed to blend in with the church going masses, hand over his pocket, clenching the malachite stone with its orbiting deep-sea green lines. He recalled his grandfather's story of its attributes, how the stone could help him attune to spiritual guidance. "Place it between your brows, Pêro." It could activate visualizations and psychic vision, scry into other worlds, stimulate intuition and insight. "You can journey through the stone's encircling patterns. To release your mind and stimulate pictures for tile making and life counsel."

In this moment, Pêro wished for reassurance and protection from the stone and God.

At the slave market, men, women, and children slouched upon the ground, feet chained one to the other under the watchful eye of a guard and his whip. Pêro said a prayer for their emancipation and strode forward.

Rossio Plaza was abuzz with those eager for the day's celebrations. So many people were on their way to Mass, that there was not enough space for the pigeons that lived there. Displaced flocks flew up and relocated just to start the process all over again. Pêro stepped aside, making way for old ladies who hurried by with colorful baskets filled with squawking chickens and bunches of fresh cut rosemary, broadcasting the herb's scent.

Everyone from all corners of the world was outside this morning. Many headed to São Domingos place of worship in the city center. Its canyon-like nave alone could hold a great portion of the populace currently in the square. Others streamed up the plaza's side streets, heading uphill to the lavish Jesuit Church of San Roque and Saint John the Baptist Chapel in the Chiado neighborhood. Others climbed the Alfama district's alleys and staircases that flowed from the hillside like mountain streams, to attend Mass at the ancient Sé Cathedral or, just below it, at Saint Anthony's Chapel, birthplace of Lisbon's own Saint, where Pêro and his family would meet.

Pêro brushed shoulders with blue-eyed and thin-faced transplants from the Azores Islands and Arab-African Moors from haunts along the North African coast. A man with black-ringlet curls lining his bearded face, a New Christian, strode head down as if consumed in thought. The races blended with one another, creating a moving mosaic of skin colors and garments, weaving rich colored patterns.

Despite the outward appearance of piety amongst the mixed population, dressed in their best church attire, Pêro knew from working with Rafa, Kujaguo and Jawoli that each ethnicity secretly harbored its own talisman from their ancestral land. They obscured old faiths with an outward appearance and display of honor for Lisbon's feverish Catholicism, while holding strong to beliefs passed down through generations. The thought made Pêro grip his own family amulet in his pocket once again.

He passed a group of industrious Protestant merchants from Britain, and French traders steeped in the new ideas of the "Enlightenment". They milled around observing and conversing, clearly not on their way to a church or a roadside shrine to partake in the All Saints Day worship. One of the fellows with gold rings on each finger boasted. "Lisbon is Europe's most church spired capital and Europe's most decorated *'Princess'* of a city. Just look at it today. I've never seen the likes of this anywhere, not London, Paris, nor even Rome."

It was true, thought Pêro, Lisbon and its outlying areas were home to multitudes of convents and churches all the way from Belém to his home in the city center and strung out east along the Tagus River.

Pêro hurried across the central square, greeting robed clergy who scuttled about, all wearing their best silk cords and tassels that swayed, to and fro, knowing the slightest connection with each one could possibly aid him and Paulinha in their forthcoming situation. A group of fresh-faced nuns descended from the Convent of Carmo from the Chiado hillside above the Martins sisters' home. He admired the eyes of a nun that peered out from her wimple-framed face, her features delicate like his daughter Constanza.

A group of ordained Franciscan monks — his Brotherhood — approached, with halos of hair, their brown tunics tied with simple hemp cords. One of them called to him. "Padre Pêro!"

"Beautiful morning." Pêro stopped to embrace each man.

"And where are you headed this fine blue-sky morning?" an older monk asked him.

Too quickly he said, "A house call, won't take but a moment." Instantly guilt overtook him. "I must be off, to get back to meet my family at Saint Anthony's Chapel. God be with you and the poor." Pêro smiled wide, before bowing his head and taking leave.

Once again, Pêro mulled over his decision to unload and have his men deliver the replacement tiles on such an important holiday. The billows of smoke churning from the Fabrica's kiln chimney would surely call attention to the shop, but fires were often left to burn out and produced smoke. He'd planned an explanation for this. And the *Nossa Senhora da Luz* was awaiting the cargo, and he, his money, and the de Sousas' their payment, and most of all he was anxious for Bagamba's release.

He had no choice. He carried on. He needed the payment in hand.

Pêro inhaled the fresh air of celebration mixed with soulful reverence for saints who had passed onto the next world. As he summoned his strength for this day's work.

At the Terriero Palace square, fronting the river waterfront, Pêro looked on as a sturdy boat rowed in, built to transport millstones to the wheat millhouses stationed along the river. But today the vessel hauled passengers from the other side of the Tagus. Boats tied up, bringing people in from Lisbon's outlying areas.

A flash of gold diverted Pêro's attention away from the busy waterway, as a swarm of ornate carriages glided by, towed by dark men or horses harnessed in twos and fours. The earth shook as they passed. Pêro watched the road and river movement, tapping his foot as he waited for Rafa's arrival.

Over the Tagus, a flock of purple herons flew inland in a shifting V formation. *North? Not south at this time of year? Why are all the birds flying inland this morning? Something is odd.*

CHAPTER TWENTY-NINE

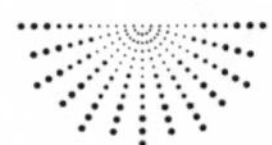

The sun already shone above the Alfama hillside as Rafa brought the borrowed cart to a halt. "Sorry I'm late. A herd of goats blocked the way, headed to the hills they were. No way around them."

Pêro hurried into the cart. "I'm afraid we're going to be late to Mass. Let's go quickly and get me back as soon as possible."

Rafa cracked the whip and the cart jumped forward. The dirt road paralleled the Tagus. Rafa cut a corner and traversed the square in front of the Royal Ribeira Palace. As they sped past, Pêro thought of the exquisite painting collection of Titians, Rubens, and Correggios housed inside, wishing he could see and inspect them firsthand.

They trotted along the royal fortification wall and turned where it met with a slaughterhouse. Rafa wound the cart through the narrow-cobbled streets, passing under the clock tower that showed seven minutes past eight.

"The Phoenix Opera House is magnificent this morning." Pêro said, as it came into view, trying to distract himself from his growing fear. "The cupola is a masterpiece."

At the Royal Shipyard, a naval *Nau* and a *Fragata* were under construction; two masts punctuated the skyline high above the tile roofs of the nearby businesses and homes.

On the Tagus, boats of every configuration cut and scudded, flying flags of the Continent of their nationalities: Britain, Germany, Holland, Norway, France, Italy, Spain, Denmark.

"Look there, we are not alone." Pêro pointed to a vessel coming in from the open sea, its hull full of sharks.

"It's the nets that do the fishing," Rafa said, flashing Pêro a grin.

"True and our kilns that do the firing," Pêro said.

They exchanged doubtful glances.

"You're as worried as I," Rafa said, looking to Pêro.

"Yes, of course. But we've no choice. Let's just hurry." Pêro stared ahead.

"At least there's a northeast breeze to carry the kiln smoke away from town and inquiring noses," Rafa said.

Pêro nodded and focused his attention on the boats from the Algarve anchored offshore, their bows carved and painted as snake heads to ward off evils lurking in opaque waters. He squeezed his malachite stone.

"Yes, we are not alone," Rafa said.

"We are not."

On the hill overlooking Pêro and Rafa, a crowd gathered at the stone Cruz de Pau, the same kind of rock cross that explorers posted on newfound lands. They passed the Convent of Hope, the Convent of the Bernardas, and the Our Lady of the Porciúncula Convent. Crowds moiled around the cart as they pushed toward the Mocambo.

The road became congested with cart and foot traffic, interspersed with whole families riding donkeys, fathers leading the beasts. At the Church of Santo-o-Velho on the front steps three black-capped men stood in counsel with Padre Matos, their backs to the road.

"Dear Lord, Rafa, veer right as fast as you can, get off this road and out of sight." Pêro kept watch on the men as they started their ascent to the Fabrica Santa María.

"*Tio!* Uncle! Coming through!" Rafa called to the stream of moving people.

Pêro placed his hand on Rafa's forearm and said in a low voice. "Discretion. Best to keep your voice down now."

Rafa winced at his error.

Time slowed, as Pêro looked at Senhor Guimarães' smoke-stack, where smoke snaked into the sky. *Amen.* He crossed himself. He then quickly glanced toward the west as the Fabrica's road came into view. He looked at the Tower of Belém and the spires of the Monastery of Jerónimos. The Tagus River connected Portugal to the world, and this hilly panoramic view welcomed all those arriving.

The borrowed cart clunked as they turned onto the Fabrica's roadway, leaving the commotion behind. To the east spread Lisbon's city center, a brisk twenty-minute walk, or less by horse and donkey cart, when the roads were not steeped in mire.

A black pig with her piglets squealed and dashed in front of them.

Pêro noted there was a strange silence today as her squeal tapered off. Gone were the wives of fishermen with their baskets of salted cod, bellowing the call of the Mocambo: "*Peixie! Peixie! Peixie!*"

It was here, that the poor lived and worked, where Lisbon's and the world's decor was conceived and fabricated. Like himself, other master craftsmen supplied the rich of Lisbon, statesmen of the colonies, and wealthy merchants with hand-crafted finery for their mansions, palaces, and the Church. Today, as they rolled by the workshops of master wood carvers and the gold gilders, doors were closed and locked. But as Pêro had suspected, smoke did seep from the other tile factory smoke-stacks piercing the skyline. His heart pounded as they entered the Fabrica Santa María's courtyard.

CHAPTER THIRTY

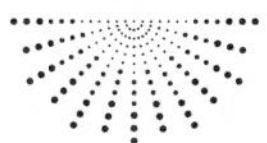

Before the little oval mirror in their bedroom, Paulinha parted her dark-brown hair down the middle and then put it up into a bun, wrapping it in white lace. She sniffed, looking around the room. *What's causing this odd scent?* She shrugged her shoulders and pinned a gold brooch set with a topaz gem, the color of her eyes into the lace, a recent gift from one of their customers who'd commissioned a gallant pastoral panel. It had become the custom in Lisbon, adorning those who performed work for you with riches from the family. Some families had become so wealthy from the gold and diamond extraction in Brazil that they could afford to give such gifts, even to their servants. She relished clasping the golden piece in her hair, despite its opulence which did not align with her faith, and she chided herself for the extravagance and silently asked the Lord for forgiveness.

She reached under her bed pillow, retrieving her latest sketchbook. She clasped it tight, feeling the embossed floral print in her palm, a dear gift from her husband. She ran her fingers over the cover, a leather strap and knot holding it closed. Looking down inside its spine, she checked for the piece of graphite wedged there. She then slipped the drawing book into the hidden pocket of her dress, a pocket she lovingly sewed into all her skirts. Quickly, she ran her hands down the robin's-egg-colored dress, patting and brushing down the crisp linen, making sure her book was well-hidden in the folds.

She began to make the bed, swiftly she moved to Pêro's side, knocking her knee into the nightstand, causing Pêro's mother's tile to move. She reached down to rub her knee, noticing the corner of paper peeping from beneath the ceramic piece. She removed it and sat upon the bed, unfolding it. She read. With a quick breath in she braced herself on the bed with her hand.

"Mãe! We're back!" The girls called from downstairs.

Paulinha sat for a moment staring at the wooden cross at the foot of their bed. Dear Lord. She tucked the folded summons letter into the sketchbook inside her hidden pocket, and hurried downstairs.

The girls' cheeks were rosy, from their neighborhood rounds, their colorful patterned Chita cloth bags full of *pão-por-Deus*, chestnuts, and pomegranates. Isabela pirouetted in the front room in her best dress with floral embroidery at the hem and cuffs. Constanza adjusted her bodice and panier skirt, to exaggerate her hips.

"Come here," Constanza said gaily. She took Isabela's wrists and tied a white ribbon around each one, copying the current court style of little bows at the wrist to elongate one's hands and give one's arms a more elegant air. Constanza held her pinky fingers and ring fingers slightly out like the British women drinking tea from porcelain cups, as she had seen in print copies. Isabela chirped with excitement and made a silly face. They picked up white lace mantillas, and draped them over their heads, folding them back, leaving their faces open to the air.

"Let us go. We don't want to be late," Paulinha said. *Yes, I most certainly don't, not with this damning note and situation before me.*

. . .

Saint Anthony's Chapel rested on the uphill side of a square surrounded by apartment buildings. They passed under the chapel archway, entering the ascending crowd. They let down their mantillas. Candle vendors peddled along the stone stairs.

"Four please," Paulinha said.

"But you are three." The vendor raised an eyebrow.

"The other is for my husband, thank you." She placed the coins in the seller's palm.

Eagerly, he wrapped his fingers around the *cruzudos*.

Candles in hand, they approached the marble font. It was set below the Tau Cross symbol and the image of Saint Anthony accompanied by a pig while holding an open book. They dipped their hands into the holy waters, crossing themselves, and entered.

Saint Anthony's Chapel was Paulinha's favorite place of worship. She liked its small size, finding the Sé Cathedral and São Domingos too expansive. She felt an intimacy at Saint Anthony's, the church being built upon the Saint's very birthplace. And now, more than ever she needed the Saint's support.

Golden light infused the space. Paulinha dropped into a low genuflection, head bowed.

Saint Anthony's feast day was June thirteenth, but today Paulinha wanted to give special thanks to the Saint for the return of her mother's pewter plate, for answering her prayers and to beg for mercy from this summons.

"Look at the front altar," Constanza said, as they made their way towards the left side of the nave. Pure gold chalices and small glass bottle cruets set with rubies, emeralds, amethyst, and blue lapis graced the altar.

"Girls, see the front altar antependia is decorated in *azulejos,*" Paulinha said in a low voice, she fought to keep steady.

"Oh Mother, it's wonderful! Did you design it?" Isabela asked. Paulinha lowered her head and said softly: "Yes, dear, but keep your voice down. See how the tiles imitate fanciful oriental fabrics of calico and chintz."

The credence table was plated with gold, and the priest's finger towels the finest on the Iberian Peninsula. Presiders' chairs set with cushions of scarlet velvet lined the backdrop of the altar, while the gold Processional Cross reflected the morning sunlight, sending out bullion beams in all directions like a lighthouse.

Flames danced atop pillar candles while black iron-terraced candle stands led to the front altar, supportive and patient soldiers to God, to the Saints: bearing their eternal servitude and light.

As Paulinha focused on admiring the scene before her, she noticed the flames suddenly flickered side to side and then resumed their upright stance. She glanced around discreetly, craning her head up to see above the sea of heads to the statue of Saint Anthony.

Paulinha leading, they went towards the ceramic saint. Sunlight permeated the church space, a celestial presence, as if every saint was there in the temple with them, sharing their protective glow. Light warmed the straight-backed pews of black *jacarandá* wood. The front benches were still empty, waiting for Lisbon's elite: nobles, dignitaries, and the families of well-off merchants.

People continued to stream in the double doors of the church.

"*Bom dia,* Senhora Pires and girls!" The elderly Martins sisters waved from a back pew.

"Lovely to see you here and well this morning." Paulinha greeted, clasping their hands.

"And where's our beloved Padre?" Donna Udda asked, eyes twinkling. "Oh, and is your little turtle here?"

The girls shook their heads "no", while Rosinha sat petite and demure.

"He's behind us. Will be here soon." Paulinha reassured, motioning the girls forward.

Together they slipped under the temple's inner arches,

praying hands, sending entreaties to God. Everyone hurried, trying to find their respective place.

The organist settled himself on the bench before the organ. He began to play. Its pipes trumpeted, calling to God, and then eased into a solemn tone. The priesthood hum was heard between the lulls of the instrument and the bustling crowd.

Poufs of talc powder wigs covered with lace veils rose above the heads of seated commoners, while like Paulinha, other women had chosen a high-set bun wrapped in lace.

"Over there." Constanza gestured to Isabela. Their eyes fixed upon a woman who displayed on her wig a diamond surrounded by rubies that caught the candlelight sending an aura of color that haloed her head.

"Come now, don't make a scene. Keep your eyes down, lest someone else recognize us here and wonder where your father might be." Paulinha whispered sternly to the girls. "Keep going, find us a place under the statue of Saint Anthony. Focus on why we are here, not this idle eyeing of others."

The two girls looked at one another, rolled their eyes, adjusted their head pieces, and moved forward behind Paulinha.

Lanterns of guttering light hung along the aisles of the nave. Paulinha, Constanza, and Isabela passed below, finding a spot for the ceremonies under the larger-than-life statue of Saint Anthony and Mother María. Rows of candles were lit under the two statues, giving off a warm glow. Paulinha welcomed the fact they stood at a distance from the elite's overly perfumed attire mixed with body odor.

With their place secured at the smoke blackened feet of Saint Anthony's icon, they waited for Pêro. They each lit their candle at the Saint's feet and said a prayer. Their tapers melted in with the others, while Paulinha held the candlestick for Pêro tight in her hand.

"*Mãe*, when will *Pai* be here?" Isabela asked.

"Speak softly child, soon, very soon," Paulinha said, trying to keep her voice kind and reassuring.

She looked fondly upon her girls, shoving away worry about Pêro's absence and the letter in her pocket. Oh, how swiftly the years had passed. Constanza was already a woman, her hips round, her breasts formed. Despite this, she still had the heart of a young girl. Not long ago Constanza used to construct small thrones, *tostaozinhos* to Saint Anthony. Altars made out of scraps of paper, old lace, adding miniature clay figurines, little pieces of metal, and small dried flowers. She would position herself with the neighborhood children along the sides of streets, displaying their decorative creations, in hopes of collecting coins for candles to offer to the Saint, but often they spent the proceeds on fireworks instead.

Isabela looked up at her. "Just think, when I go with *Pai* to a palace, it will be wonderful!"

Paulinha smiled and nodded. At ten years, Isabela, like Constanza was enamored with the wealth of Lisbon's noble and merchant families, but she still liked to play with the neighbor boys in a game of charging heads. Isabela and her friends made makeshift *estafermos,* dummy statues, using old pieces of cloth and mismatched buttons, mounting them on revolving pedestals. Each player tried to knock down the dummy with a pretend lance made from an old broomstick or a piece of wood as though it were a pistol. The children played at this game for hours in the alleyways close to home. Isabela usually came back with scratched knees or an elbow, and a tear in her dress where a lance broomstick missed its mark.

Paulinha looked at the light streaming in from the temple's high stained-glass window, blending colors of a painter's palette with the candlelight.

"I can't imagine anything more beautiful than this place," Constanza said.

"Me too." Isabela looked starry-eyed upward.

To the left of the front altar, Padre João genuflected and then pardoned himself, and headed towards the back of the nave. Paulinha cowered as Padre João moved towards them. *Why is he here in our place of worship?* As Padre João progressed in their direction, she felt moisture under her armpits soaking into the material bunched there, her heart palpitating.

Does the Padre recognize me and the girls? Know of this indictment?

Close to their vicinity, he shuffled in front of them. His full face illuminated by the candlelight displayed circles under his eyes, making them seem more prominent, more severe.

"Pardon me," he said in a low voice. Paulinha did not respond but made space for him to pass. As she stepped back, Padre João looked at her. "Senhora Pires, good to see you and the girls. Alone are you?"

Before she could reply, the other priests and attendants filed out onto the high altar, single file, their starched white chasuble stoles resting on their breasts. A priest swung the incense-burning thurible, sending the scent of frankincense, myrrh, and copal drifting up and throughout the nave. Off the swinging ball, light sparkled. Paulinha smiled at Padre João. "My husband will be here soon."

He smiled, looking unconvinced, the fat of his cheeks squishing into his eyes.

"Very well *dear*...you both know God does not look kindly upon tardiness nor deviance." Padre João looked sternly at her and the girls then took leave, continuing towards the back.

Paulinha shivered as her face reddened. She clenched Pêro's candle tighter. Both the girls looked up to their mother as she fixed her gaze on the front altar. *He must know!*

The bishop rose in his pulpit, shafted crosier in hand, a shepherd with his crook. He was cloaked in white, a stole with gold piping draped over his shoulders. A silk miter sat on his head, a messenger of God himself. He stood in silence as the choir began to chant the Morning Prayer in low tones: *"Gaudeamus omnes in Domino, diem festum."*

The main nave and side aisles packed, the crowd spilled out and down the chapel stairs, the singing filtering out the doors and into the square. Paulinha wiped her brow as the sonorous singing of the choir droned on. The parish joined in, while everyone continued inspecting each other's finery, and who was with whom.

Pêro is on his way, he'll be here soon, she repeated to herself instead of singing.

CHAPTER THIRTY-ONE

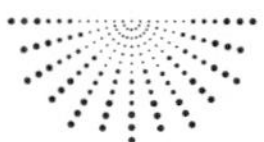

Rafa drove the cart up to the alley door. Pêro descended and said quietly: "I'd hoped Jawoli and Kujaguo would be here waiting. Drive the cart to your house, leave it there until we need it, so no one sees that we are here. Hurry back but be careful to enter through the side door unseen."

Rafa backed the cart out onto the main road and headed home.

Pêro glanced to the roadway and then stared dead center at the door. He held his breath and unlatched it. He slipped in, making sure his habit did not catch. He closed the door. Once inside, he released his breath, a plume of steam billowing forth, the heat of his exhale combusting in the cool fall air. He set down his satchel. *How many times have I performed this act of invisibility since the Fabrica Santa María's opening?* Before the shop even had a name.

He went to the beehive kiln and opened the cone's door, recounting the money in his mind he would earn with this order's completion, finally securing Bagamba's freedom. Hot air escaped the chamber.

He bent down and opened the kiln's fire port hatch, looking in at the red-hot smoldering coals, then closed the door.

With iron tongs he began to remove the tiles, setting them on a drying rack. He smiled at the monogram, PMP, remembering how before he and Paulinha were married, they'd both laughed that their initials were going to be the same, not knowing, as the years passed it would prove fortuitous, for it allowed Paulinha to work clandestinely under the monogram. He presented her work as his own, but they knew the initials represented both their contributions.

He unloaded the three shelves of the beehive chamber but needed the leather-canvas gloves to retrieve the tiles enclosed in the saggar box on the bottom. Now, he had only six more tiles of the twenty-one to set out to cool and the order would be complete.

A fine dust floated in the Fabrica Santa María, the particles highlighted by the morning sun shining through the long rectangle studio windows of the shop. The front windowpanes were still covered in the makeshift drapery from last night. He felt again, an uncanny stillness, as a coal hissed from within the fire chamber. The local convents' church bells tolled the new hour. He still had time to make it to Mass. *Where are Kujaguo and Jawoli?*

He walked to a worktable, looking for the leather-canvas gloves. Finding them, he returned to the beehive oven. The air smelled of old riverbed sediment, of iron. He picked up a cooling tile from the open box with the tongs.

A frightful noise, hollow and distant like the rumble of thunder ripped through the earth.

A shock reverberated through Pêro's bull-hide sandals, rippling up and throughout his body. He held the tongs clenching the tile in his marred hand; the tile shaking violently, wanting to spring free from his grip. He lurched forward, reaching out with his other hand, struggling to place it on the main kiln. The floor buckled under his feet, breaking into pieces like dropped tiles. He fought to stay upright.

His muscles clenched, his stomach churned, his eyes darted about the space.

Dear Lord, what's happening? Have mercy! I beg of you!

CHAPTER THIRTY-TWO

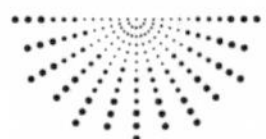

The floor of Saint Anthony's burst upward as if a rolling wave surged beneath. Paulinha gripped her daughters' shoulders as the church was tossed like a piece of seaweed yanked into a turbulent sea, torn from its stable rock foundation.

Heads swiveled, saucer eyes seeking a reference point to explain why their Godly ship was shaking. Terror ignited faces, accompanied by a split-second breath of silence. Before howls of fright ripped through the holy space.

The nave's central aisle cracked like a cleaved pomegranate. Front pews slid into the chasm. Wild screeches emanated from the abyss. Pleas to heaven, pleas to God.

The masses stared in horror. Gasps emanated forth, followed by tearing screams.

The righteous rich and privileged were swallowed up.

Those who flanked the sides of the nave pushed backwards, forcing those at the temple doors outside and down the steps.

"*Santa María!*" the multitudes cried.

The crazed populace surged, crowding and shoving, clawing to escape into the open square.

A second shockwave struck.

The twin bells of the nearby Sé Cathedral rang out in violent chimes.

Inside Saint Anthony's Chapel, stone and rock dislodged, tumbling down. Candles toppled, igniting the high altar linens. Others were snuffed out in an instant, spewing black smoke. The stained-glass windows exploded. A rainbow of deadly shards poured down. Timbers snapped and splintered. Marble capitals plunged off their pillar mounts and archways collapsed, crushing the unfortunate below.

The statues of Saint Anthony and Mother María pitched forward, then rocked side to side, a wind blowing out their candles. Isabela looked up into Saint Anthony's eyes. Constanza grabbed Isabela's arm and her mother's dress sleeve and pulled.

"*Mãe*! Isabela!" Constanza screamed, as she pushed her mother and sister.

The statues wobbled violently, splattering hot wax. Shawls and dresses absorbed the burning oil; welts swelled on faces, chests, and arms.

In unison, the two effigies fell forward.

Saint Anthony's clay hand and brown cloak blasted down on Isabela's shoulder.

"Jesus!" Isabela's eyes bulged as the ball of her shoulder bone popped out of its socket.

"Falling Saints!" Constanza screamed, moments too late.

Isabela's arm jolted back into its proper position. She started to cry.

The statues broke into pieces, revealing hollow interiors. The dead and wounded bled out dark pools, while others, pinned, moaned in agony. Paulinha, Isabela, and Constanza stood stone-still, rocks in a charging stream of people, the crimson blood running out the temple doors.

Isabela cradled her injured arm. Paulinha dropped Pêro's candle and stepped in front of the girls.

"Turn around. Go to the back. Now!" She pushed them forward.

Together, they were swept into the rush of people, their lace veils stripped from their heads. Out of the corner of Paulinha's eye she saw the elderly Martins sisters frozen in panic upon their pew, she'd return for them if she could. As she and the girls carried out the high arched doors and down the steps, into the square. Like a litter of helpless puppies, the girls and Paulinha huddled together, vying for the safest spot.

CHAPTER THIRTY-THREE

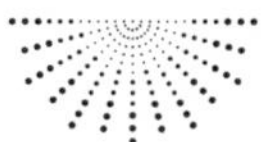

A jolt shot through Pêro's body, ejecting the tile from the tongs' grip. It shattered on the floor. He dropped the iron-tongs, which clattered upon the shards. Barrels of chalky glazes shook, their thick soups boiling over their rims, mixing paddles churning. The viscous substances ebbed and flowed: manganese-browns, copper-greens, cobalt-blues, iron-oxide oranges, creating a chaos of colors on the ground.

Rolling pins fell off counters, and ricocheted end-over-end before congregating in a pile next to the vats. Dried goat balls the size of peaches filled with liquid glaze vaulted to the floor, paints squirting out their nozzle ends. Buckets of paintbrushes careened, brushes scattering like plucked feathers. Work pedestals spun. Small glass jars of pigments vibrated across tabletops; others wobbled off, exploding.

Pêro gasped, paralyzed amongst the broken tiles at his feet. Water spilled from barrel containers, housing gooey slip used to join clay pieces, and formed puddles on the floor's low spots. The holding tank of white iron-oxide cracked down its front, contents oozing out. Stacks of clay blocks toppled, hitting the floor with loud *thuds*. Pails of wires, paddles, anvils, and ribs shimmied off back shelves, while the shelves themselves threatened to pitch forward.

Pêro dashed from spot to spot, arms outstretched, catching items, and picking up others. He filled his arms.

What is going on?

The earth heaved again, a second more severe shock, like a violent undulating ocean wave.

Overhead, the drying racks collapsed, sending bone dry tiles to the lattice floor. Splinters of dried clay rained down, covering him in a fine dust.

The trembling unlatched the kiln's fire door. Hot embers jumped from their earthen cave. Wisps of smoke spiraled. He sprinted to the coals, kicking them back in, dropping everything in his arms. Quickly, he latched the door again.

Coughing, he rushed to the front windows of the shop, tripping on the crumpled drapery fallen to the floor. His hands visibly shaking, he stabilized himself in the window frame. *Paulinha…girls!*

He heard a loud groan outside. An explosion.

The planked walls of the Fabrica Santa María gave and flexed.

An awful grinding sound of houses and buildings grating one against the other coursed through the neighborhood. Before him, a two-story edifice broke into four large blocks and fell in on itself. The ground convulsed beneath his feet. Star-shaped cracks burst across the floor like shots from a pistol — stars mimicking the shop's pentagram tile designs.

"Saint Anthony save and protect!" he cried.

Pêro looked above the front door, where they kept their statute of Saint Anthony on a shelf. In slow motion, the ceramic saint teetered then launched off its mount, headfirst, breaking into two even halves, right down the middle, right where a man's heart would be; one half holding the book of purity, the other the infant Jesus.

"Santa María, no!"

The elongated windows exploded, a deathly rain of shards.

He dove for the front door. Unlatched it and hurled it open. As boxes of knives and fluting tools plunged down, a knife grazed his forearm while others punctured bags of salt and silica.

He stumbled out the door.

Clamping his bad hand over the abrasion.

Screams. Pleading. A suffocating cloud of dust.

Trapped citizens begged for help. Their cries floated on the cascading motes invading his hair and ears. A chill. A surge of energy. His heart throbbed. Then silence. It enveloped him.

He turned toward home.

Before his eyes, images of his wife, his two girls waiting for him in the side aisle of the nave at Saint Anthony's. *What of Rafa and his family? The other men of the shop?*

I need to get to Saint Anthony's.

Now.

He let go of his cut and scrambled over piles of debris that blocked the street.

Some people ambled about dazed, others clawed and scurried. Shrieked.

Where is the sun? The morning's clear blue sky?

In the haze, he slowed and then stopped. *I forgot my bag of church clothes. Paulinha will be upset with me for arriving in my work clothing, but I don't want to be late. She'll understand.*

From behind, a blast of debris hurled into Pêro's back, sending him flying to the ground.

CHAPTER THIRTY-FOUR

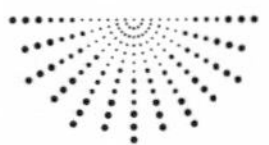

The donkey brayed wildly. Rafa rushed from his home, feeling the earth convulse.

"Out of the house!" Rafa cried.

Cracks broke across the walls of their home as sheets of earthen plaster cleaved off.

"What's happening?" Josepha, Rafa's wife, called from the sleeping room.

Rafa bolted back inside, as earthen chunks fell from the ceiling, pieces of dirt falling into Josepha's short-cropped frizzy hair and onto her sturdy shoulders. Rafa grabbed her hand, helping her scramble up onto her feet. "Gather up the food. Take as much as you can. I'll get the water!"

"Boys, the bedding! Help your mother, hurry! *Ava,* here let me assist you." Rafa bent down and picked up Gogo off a woven mat in the main room. "Grab Gogo's mat!"

Rafa carried Gogo to the flatbed of the cart. The donkey violently pulled back and forth at its post, the cart creaking with each jerk. He plopped Gogo down and rushed to the beast and placed his hand on its mane, whispering calmly into its ear. "It's all right. Try to stay calm. Soon we'll be on our way." He stroked the donkey's flank a couple of times, as the quaking of the earth tapered off.

Bagamba shuffled in and out of the house, carrying Gogo's things, along with his own and the family's.

Rafa rushed back inside and worked the clay water vessel from its groove in the hard-packed earthen floor, hefting it from its place. "Where's Diogo?" He set the clay water container onto the cart next to Gogo.

Josepha stared at him from the doorstep of the house.

"He's still not back from this morning's rounds?" Rafa asked.

"No, no he's not," Josepha said in a high-pitched tone. "He left with his friends for their *pão-de-Deus* —" She brought her hand up to her mouth and hurried back into the house, returning with a squawking chicken hanging by its feet. Her other arm was loaded with a half-bag of wheat flour, one bulbous squash, and a sack of dried salted cod.

Their three other sons followed with the cookware, a machete, and a pot of hot coals.

Gogo scooted off the cart.

Rafa returned from the house, hurling their bedding onto the cart. "He could be anywhere. Dear Lord."

"Gogo!" Rafa bellowed. "Everyone into the cart! Where's she gone off to?"

He rushed back inside, the earth shifting anew. "What are you doing?"

Gogo was hunched over the ground in the far corner. She ferociously dug at the earth with a stick, beneath the family altar table. Above, their black statutes of Mother María and Saint Anthony were draped with their Brotherhood of Our Lady of the Rosary beaded strands. The saints shook on their simple wooden table.

"Grandmother!" Rafa snatched up both saints and their rosaries.

"It must not be left. She must come with me," Gogo cried.

"What? What must come with you?"

"Her!" She held up a dirt encrusted blackened wooden statue. Its head was grossly enlarged, breasts drooping, body lank and straight.

"What in the Lord's name? Hurry up!"

A wall swayed and caved. Rafa jumped and covered Gogo with his body, as the earthen wall broke upon his back.

"My medicines!" Gogo whimpered from within the cocoon of Rafa's sheltering body.

"Where are they? We need to get out of here before the room completely collapses."

"Above there in the rafter," she said, pointing skyward to the halved calabash.

Rafa forced himself up, rubble falling from his back, while he kept cover over Gogo. He reached up. "I've got it. Now let's get out of here." He helped Gogo up and out of the house.

As they exited the earth heaved again, Gogo stumbled and fell to her knees, clutching her precious object to her chest. Chickens cried and darted as if being chased for the pot. The donkey brayed wildly.

"Hurry!" Rafa's family cried from the cart.

"Diogo!" Josepha bellowed. "Come home. You should be leaving with us now." She clutched the front of her blouse.

The earth rippled like an ocean wave hitting shore as Rafa hefted Gogo off the ground and onto the cart, abandoning Mother María and Saint Anthony to the earth. He scrambled to untie the wailing animal.

Walls of the single-story earthen homes around them shook, swayed, and crumbled in on themselves. People fled from their homes like scattering fowl.

The rumbling ceased.

Rafa drove the donkey into the street. "Diogo, Diogo! *Vai!*" They bounced forward. The donkey eagerly broke into a trot. They headed toward the Mocambo's outskirts, dodging mounds of debris and families rushing into the street. The cart careened dangerously, jumping side-to-side as they sped over uneven ground, nearly colliding with another cart, and fleeing populace.

"Secure the water!" Rafa cried. He whipped the donkey with a great lash.

He maneuvered the cart up the hillside behind the Mocambo. Again, the earth rattled violently, like a crazed shaman summoning spirits. Rafa maneuvered the cart as far up the wind-swept grass incline as he could. He brought the cart to a halt, tying the donkey off to a tangerine tree devoid of fruit this late in the season.

"Take everything up to the old olive tree. Hurry. Go." Rafa helped Gogo and Bagamba from the flatbed.

"What about Diogo? And Padre Pêro?" Josepha stood hands full, wide eyes, blinking.

Diogo and the neighborhood boys…And yes, Padre Pêro?

"As soon as you're all secure here, I'll go seek Diogo first," Rafa said, his voice strained.

What else can I say? There'd been no time to search for Diogo or fetch the Padre.

He prayed Diogo and Padre Pêro had found safe havens, somewhere out of reach of God's wrath. For this was far more than a murmur, this seemed to be a Godly blow like none other he'd ever felt nor witnessed before.

Where is my dear son, Lord? Keep watch.

CHAPTER THIRTY-FIVE

Jawoli and Kujaguo jumped to their feet as the hillside dried grasses rose up like the spine of a disturbed cat ready to attack. They looked at their feet, one other, and upon Lisbon. Mouths agape. Eyes wide. Each drawing a hand over his mouth. Great clouds erupted from the city center and its outlying areas as buildings collapsed.

"Watch out!" Jawoli cried. He yanked Kujaguo to the ground and forced him to rollover as a large boulder careened by nicking Jawoli's knee.

Jawoli thrust his hands over his kneecap, and then drew up his pant leg. The spot where the rock had hit was swelling. He winced, watching the stone bump and jump its way downhill.

Kujaguo sat up. "Two black crows."

Jawoli lolled back, massaging his knee, and mumbled. "Yes".

They looked up the hillside to the patch of rocks where they had made their home, providing shelter from the elements last night.

The earth heaved again, rippling through the countryside. Swiftly, they moved out of the way of the stones and turned their attention back to the city and river way.

Jawoli squinted and looked east and then west towards Belem and the open sea. He put his hand up over his brow. In slow motion, he brought it down. He crumpled onto his knees upon the earth with a cold thud. "*Buama*...dear Lord —"

CHAPTER THIRTY-SIX

M*other María! Pêro!* Paulinha reached for her girls and tugged them into her bosom, holding tight to their backs, pushing their hearts close into hers. *Should I go back after the Martins sister?*

"*Mãe,* my shoulder hurts." Isabela whimpered and clutched it.

Paulinha drew Isabela further into her embrace. *Oh… Pêro where are you? I need your reassurance, your strength. Who will help the Martins?*

"It hurts," Isabela said.

Paulinha breathed deep, closed her eyes, and gently held Isabela. "I know Princess. It will be all right." She stroked Isabela's hair.

Isabela did not say more, nor did she fight against her mother's arms. Instead, she nestled in and Constanza leaned against them both. They held each other. Isabela started to weep. Constanza draped her arms around her shoulders with care and rested her head down onto Paulinha's chest.

People pushed up against them. They swayed with the crowd's movements. Paulinha looked down at her children's heads, their white ribbons lovingly woven into their rosewood hair. She said nothing, holding her daughters steady and firm.

Sounds from the injured filled the air.

Paulinha's heart raced and she worked to keep her body from shaking. More and more people flooded into the square, boxing them in. They came from the surrounding two-story buildings and apartments, and from Saint Anthony's Church. People packed the already filled square.

A third shock rumbled through the earth.

Paulinha looked up, her eyes meeting with a slender man's dark stare and a little girl who peered down at them from their apartment. Fear swept across their faces as they raised their hands to their mouths.

Paulinha looked over her shoulder, following the man and girl's gaze.

"Push forward," she said to the girls. "To the street, get to the street. Now!" With both hands Paulinha forced the girls forward. Isabela cried out, but she kept pushing toward the cobblestone street.

Paulinha fixated on an auxiliary room of the Church and watched in horror as the third tremor struck. The Church shook, along with its side buildings and arch. They began to crumble. Buildings outlining the plaza gave way. She screamed as the structures fell inward on the square. The snap of timber and the grinding of mortar, brick and stone mixed with human cries. Flames and black smoke billowed, creating a sooty cloud over them all.

CHAPTER THIRTY-SEVEN

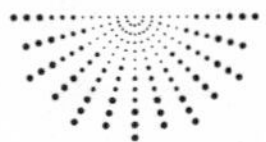

Pêro worked his way up onto all fours and brushed the debris from his hair. He looked back on the Fabrica as flames engulfed the wood paneled wall, the front and studio windows blown out.

"No!" He kneeled on the ground, watching in horror.

He scanned the landscape for recognizable landmarks, locating the cross tower of Santa Brigida's Convent. He fled east, downhill toward the convent.

Arriving, Pêro paused at a spot where he could see the Palace of the Countess of Sarmento above on the distant hillside. Its fortress wall snaked through the dry countryside grasses, smoke billowing up from the mansion and meadow.

Pêro rushed toward the river.

He crawled over downed buildings.

Around the next corner he came to a stop and gasped.

Some cried, some flagellated themselves senselessly; others knelt on the ground begging to God or screamed and tore at their hair, hovering over their dead: a child, a mother, a father, a brother, a sister, a family.

A sour-salty breeze blew off the riverfront.

Then a third shock rippled through the earth.

It knocked Pêro off balance, even though he was on his hands and knees. He craned his head up after the tremor had passed. Jaw slack, he blinked his eyes to register Luis before a lone wailing child who was buried up to his knees in rubble. Luis looked towards the Tagus and fled.

Seagulls skirled in swirls in the sky.

The sky darkened.

Lisbon's bright natural light morphed to a gloomy ominous hue.

Pêro clasped his chest as a piercing pain clamped down on his heart. He clutched his habit and gasped for air. Then the constriction of breath halted. The grasp on his heart released. He felt light and spacious. Out over the Tagus River a sunburst broke through the cinder haze; an island of light alight on the river. He choked and inhaled, releasing his breath. As if it was his first of life.

He hurried to the little cacao-colored boy, stuck and weeping.

Pêro clasped the boy by the shoulders; his own body becoming heavy and cumbersome as he touched another's fear. The child's swollen eyes met his. *How could Luis have looked into this boy's eyes and abandoned him?* Pêro frantically dug. His hands touched hair. Uncovering another little person trapped below. He clawed at the earth, until he freed the two boys.

The boy who had been completely buried sat mute upon the rubble, while the other cried.

Pêro searched the area, spotting a dark leg sticking out from a collapsed structure. He scrambled over, removing bricks and timber until a dirty face and stunned chocolate eyes stared at him. With care, he propped up the young woman. Muffled cries of people trapped in downed homes and buildings echoed around them. *What should I do?* Brow furrowed; he scanned the area.

The crying boy bolted to his mother, blood running down his shins as he embraced her.

"Daughter of the Lord. Are you all right?" Pêro asked.

Dazed eyes stared back at him.

"We must hurry. We are late for Mass," she said. She sat with legs outstretched, unblinking. Goosebumps rippled over Pêro's body. The mute boy remained unmoving.

"I'm late too," Pêro confessed, cringing at how ridiculous his words sound. "Can you move?"

The young mother with disheveled hair, no older than Constanza, tried to push herself up. But she could not move below her waist.

He looked down into the woman's eyes, tears swelling in his own.

"I can't," she said, staring wide-eyed at her immobilized legs.

How can I leave this woman and her children? And the others encased around them?

"Do you know where your husband is?"

She pointed.

A motionless body lay in the distance in front of them, missing limbs.

"I see." Pêro winced.

"We live here together. My husband sells olive oil," she said dumbly, pointing.

"Oh my, Blessed Lord," Pêro said under his breath, crossing himself, recalling immediately Saint Francis of Assisi's teaching: "It would be considered a theft on our part if we didn't give to someone in greater need than we". Pêro went to the corpse, took off his habit, and blanketed the body, sweeping his right hand over it, reciting a prayer for the dead. "Blessed be God for our brother, the death of the body, ever more. Amen." Even though he knew he was not yet authorized as a deacon to perform such rites. He prayed anyway for this man, this father, this deceased child of the Lord.

"Watch out!" the woman said.

Pêro lurched forward but there wasn't time.

Pêro fell to his left side and rolled. Adobe bricks rained down from above, burying him with the deceased man. Pêro tried to move but earthen clods weighed him down. He managed to kick a leg free. Gasping for air, he inhaled dirt particles and coughed violently.

Little hands pawed through to his face, removing earth from his mouth and eyes.

"Start removing bricks. Whatever you can, Fernando. Start with the smallest ones." The paralyzed mother instructed.

Pêro worked himself up onto an elbow. "Now, you've saved me."

The little boy stared at him blankly.

"Thank you, son." *I must get to Saint Anthony's before I'm killed. Lord knows what has befallen Paulinha and the girls.*

Pêro looked to the woman and the twins huddled before her.

They were surrounded by the dead and maimed, while the living pleaded to God or offered crazed confessional repentance: "*Livra-nos do seu leito de morte*! Deliver us from your deathbed!" A man limped along, crawling in front of them and lashed at a rubble pile with one arm. The place where his other arm should have been was a bloody mess. Nearby, two old women huddled over each other, their clothes torn and bloodied, uncontrollably shaking their heads and ranting prayers.

What can I do to help this woman and her children? He did not know them, they were not his family, yet they had saved him as if he were their own father. Looking around, he tried to physically locate the solution, but the answer welled from his heart. *Take them with you. The next answer will present itself.*

Pêro hobbled onto his feet and checked himself for injuries. He stared for a long moment at the section of brick wall upon the fallen man, before consoling the now silent woman and children.

"Let us say a blessing for your husband. Will you say a prayer with me?" Pêro asked softly. "Thank you for saving my life, for instructing Fernando to free me."

The young woman's tear-filled eyes met his. She lowered her head and whispered. "God give me strength."

Pêro stood before the pile of impossibly heavy rubble that

had buried the man and began: "Eternal rest grant unto thee, O Lord, and let perpetual light shine upon thee. May thee rest in Peace. Amen," they said in unison.

"I'll carry you. Hold onto my shoulders," Pêro said to the woman.

"Where are we going?"

"To my wife and children at Saint Anthony's Chapel. How we'll get there I don't know. But I can't leave you all here."

She called to her son who sat alone. "Pedro, come here. Say your prayers." She held Fernando's hand and looked into his hurt-filled eyes. "Go on, say a prayer for your father. You did a very good thing. I know, your father is pleased."

"Bye, *Pai*," Fernando said, barely audible. He began to sob.

The stunned boy did not move nor respond. He stared ahead like an animal that's been tethered too long — beaten and defeated.

Pêro kneeled and picked up the woman. "Does this hurt?"

"I don't feel a thing." She hung her head and held Fernando's hand.

Pêro carried her over to Pedro. "Come, take hold of my shirt." The dazed boy stared up at Pêro. He burst into tears, releasing a wail of anguish. Pêro cringed. But he got to his feet and grabbed Pêro's long undershirt, holding it with a quaking hand, staring at his father's makeshift grave.

They climbed endless hills of rubble, traversing a relentless rocky coastline. Pêro negotiated one pile and another. He said little prayers as he passed a lifeless limb or distraught wounded survivors unable to move from where they'd been struck down. His stomach clenched and bile worked up his throat. He, they all were lucky to be alive.

"Let us rest a moment," he said.

They watched as others limped along the mounds, injured animals lost in a desolate land with strange outcrops: a roof beam on fire, a leg, the half torso of a donkey.

A crowd of people came from behind, streaming towards the waterfront.

Encouraged by their energy, Pêro resumed their descent. He shifted the weight of the woman and struggled to keep up like a piece of driftwood caught in a strong ocean current. His body ached and he weakly let the masses carry them downhill.

"To the waterfront! To the docks!" The hordes bellowed, a conglomeration of young, old, and injured. Some held cloth bundles, others small children half-dressed, or a lone animal.

Pêro spied a young girl carrying her own intestines. He choked at the horror. He stared straight ahead, surrendering to the downward heading mob, focusing only on staying upright.

The throng picked up more fleeing people, all intent on escaping the unstable land and the fires it had triggered. The herd took on a panicked energy.

Another tremor hit.

The crowd surged forward.

Off in the distance, the expansive Tagus River came into view. Pêro peered down as people crammed onto the docks along the river's edge. Some ships were loading passengers, packing their decks. Others were moored to the docks with people scrambling up their sides, while the vessel's crew lashed at them with whips, fighting back the hordes.

The whole of the waterfront: a frenzied moiling swarm.

Alongside Pêro, a lady screamed as she shook her crucifix in the air: "We must get to the other side!" Others clutched icons of saints, pleading to be carried away from the earth's tremors—from God's wrath. People bellowed out their hopes for escape, for exodus to the other side of the river, anything that would grant them safe ground, to ferry them across to a secure place.

Pêro halted, a snag in a stream. Before his eyes, the river receded, pulling away from its banks. He looked to the west, to the Atlantic.

Silver liquid rushed into the mouth of the Tagus. A giant frothing and rising wave.

Like an additional hill to be added to Lisbon's famed seven.

The crowd stopped.

And watched.

Below, unaware of what was coming, people filed onto the newly built marble quays, half-clothed, caked in blood and dirt. Pedigree no longer held meaning. The rich now filthy and disheveled crammed alongside beggars and servants and slaves.

Pêro looked beyond the building masses to ships from every port in the world, and the Portuguese fleets anchored in the waterway, newly arrived from the colonies of India and Brazil. Each ship was laden with gold, diamonds, sugar, spices, and more human freight. But their mighty hulls and lucrative cargo could not stop what was coming. He clasped Pedro's head to his leg.

Pêro searched the waterfront as the water in the bay continued to withdraw, revealing a littered muddy floor: crates, pieces of old ships, rotten pilings, sunken skiffs, netting and a plethora of other items. Stench swept up the hillside. Pungent and rotten, the smell of paper-thin seaweed along the river's banks, a visceral warning, the reeking of decay.

Others stopped alongside them, frozen in horror, as the river continued to suck out.

"*Santa María! Santa María!* Save us!" the people cried on the docks "What's happening?". As ships keeled over, their passengers tossed, screaming into the river's muck. Everyone darted, colliding into one another.

"Run!" The crowd surrounding Pêro screamed.

A wild torrent of water rushed in, engulfing the docks and the multitudes of pulsating people trapped there. Shrieks and groans echoed around them. The hillside crowd looped back onto itself, a school of fish desperate to evade a predator.

Sixty-foot ship masts crashed into one another and disappeared along with everyone and everything in them. Vessels anchored on all sides fought to stay upright. Their anchors jerked off the river's floor.

The water pushed up over the land, submerging all in its path. From their hillside vantage point, Pêro and the crowd craned to witness the oncoming consuming flood.

Boundless, the water surged, doing as it pleased.

It rolled and tossed barrels of wheat, baskets of salted cod, bolts of cloth, caskets of Porto, crates of vegetables, cotton, and salt sacks end-over-end. The water was a cold wet blanket covering everything yet offering no comfort.

Pêro strained as he fought to go back uphill, hearing the whinnies and snorts of horses as they and their carriages were swept away, doomed. Indian peppers, fruits, hardwoods, sugar, tobacco, and gold were carried away by the water's greedy force. Far off wails rode the winds as people on the quays were swallowed up in whirlpools of ravenous water. Boxes of coffee and tea, merchant stalls, bundled goods, overturned boats, earthquake rubble, and families were swept to a watery grave. Nothing escaped the seething waters.

Violent gurgling cries reverberated over and within the churned liquid, the water now rushing downhill, retreating in crashing waterfalls. The wall of water ripped shrubs, rock, houses, anything left standing after the earthquake's shocks. Colossal *Caravel, Nau,* and *Fragata* ships were whipped about wildly, their grandeur no match for the water's chaotic force. Their wooden hulls, decks, and masts — now sticks.

"Run! Move!" people shouted.

A shoving stampede.

Pêro shifted his legs and secured his load. He struggled as people thrust into him. He fell onto one knee. Hands and arms clawed above them, knees knocked at his sides and back. *Dear Lord, we're going to be trampled!* He fought to stand upright; the woman in his arms, but the crowd forced them down. The boys pulled and clutched at his shirt. He craned to see through the flailing bodies. He caught a glimpse of the Santo Alberto Convent, sitting on the bluff with the Conde of Obidos Rock to its front. Pêro leaned into the chaos, head down, and tried to force his way up. From behind someone forcibly knocked into him. He fell onto both knees.

The masses overwhelmed them like a sea anemone closing up. Pêro's head popped up, as two hands forced him from the ground. Pêro braced himself and the woman and turned. He and Luis's eyes meet, both growing large. Pêro registered compassion in Luis's panic-stricken face as he was forced away from them, and down toward the water in a stream of crowd confusion.

"Luis! Luis!" Pêro called.

Luis thrust a hand into the air, displaying his elegant fingers. "I am sorry! I've been so jealous of her! Of them!" And he was gone.

Jealousy of Paulinha and Rafa. So that is why. Plain and simple. The plague of many. Pêro, mother and children stumbled forward, forced uphill by a separate throng of people moving in the direction of the nunnery.

"Don't let go!" Pêro commanded the boys, as the mob pushed and shoved them all.

Get to the side street before the Santo Alberto Convent. Get inland. Now.

The next wave.

Larger than the first.

Massive.

Water barreled in, carrying with it timber and debris from the first wave.

Foamy and filthy it struck the land with the force of thunder.

The ground convulsed up through Pêro's feet, legs, and gut. The woman cried out like a wounded animal. The crowd exploded. Pêro clasped hold of the woman with all his force as the water monster rushed uphill. "Don't let go of me, Fernando! Pedro! Don't let go!"

Up, up they fled.

Pêro turned and looked down as the next wave crashed inland.

The black veil of water charged towards them. His thighs burned. The boys' fists were full of his blouse, as they scrambled and stumbled to keep up.

Pêro peered through a break in the houses. On the street below, a man on horseback raced up the road over and around rubble, water at the horse's hooves. The steed's coat was lathered in foam, froth dripped from its mouth, its large almond eyes glazed with fear. Pêro fixed his vision ahead like the horse. He veered away from the fleeing masses and heaved up a side alley. He collapsed into a doorway. The horse whinnied and screamed. Pêro breathed in gasps. He looked down over the fleeing masses, down to a sea of horror, then to the dead-end way from which they'd arrived.

Another wave pounded in.

Pêro's heart beat like a funeral drum. Tears streamed down his face. They could run no more. Sweat drenched his shirt. His legs shook. The two little boys cowered in the door-well next to him. Pêro eased the mother down, resting her back against the door frame. As he moved away, the woman's hand caught on his rosary and coral beads scattered before them. He lurched to pick them up as water rushed up the street and alleyway. Frantically, he grabbed for his beads. The water engulfed his hands. His fingers searched for the round coral, fixing onto a lowly piece.

The water gushed up over him and the woman's waist, swallowing the children. Pêro let go of his bead, plunging his arms into the murk.

The mother cried. "Pedro! Fernando!"

The water rose to their chests.

"Grab the door latch!" Pêro called out.

Pêro held tight to what he hoped were two arms. He jammed his feet into the doorframe and fought to hold his position.

The water relented and then furiously retreated. A rushing river, it streamed downhill, clutching its newly acquired treasures, life.

Pêro knew all rivers return to the ocean, some way, at some point.

Sitting in a puddle, he tried to block out the cries of the water's victims as they were swept away. His hands still clasped two arms firmly. Pedro and Fernando coughed and spit up water, they began crying.

Pêro dropped his head and slumped over, tears flooding his eyes. His tears did not come in waves, but a torrent. He wept until he was left like a leather-hard tile relieved of all its moisture. Only then did he glance up. They were all still alive.

The woman and children sat transfixed. Mute. Silently, they shared the void, the gap of despair and pain.

Was there more water coming? Would the earth shake again?

The street was now vacant below them. Pêro looked to the river. Bodies, human and animal floated on the water's surface. Survivors clung to broken parts: planks from the docks, anything buoyant. Merchant and naval ships turned bottom up, bobbing like giant whales, others oddly beached. The hard goods and the men and women who brought them to Lisbon were sunk and drowned.

Pêro's eyes traveled to the city center, to the Alfama hillside, to where Saint Anthony's Chapel should be, where he prayed his wife and children had found a safe refuge.

Or…dreadfully…a vision of bloodshed flashed before his eyes, the wails of mothers and daughters…Pêro trembled and inhaled in short quick breaths. Lisbon, once a clutter of creativity, was now crumbled chaos, utterly destroyed. A black cloud hovered over the valley of "The Queen of the Seas" severing her from eternal light.

Pêro reached for his rosary. But it was no longer there.

CHAPTER THIRTY-EIGHT

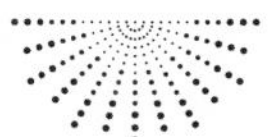

"Diogo!" Rafa darted from place-to-place, calling out with the other ghostly black figures covered in chalk-colored dust. People crawled among the fallen homes and rubble littered streets throughout the Mocambo. They stared fixed-eyed, attending no particular thing, their breathing ragged, hair filled with broken bits. An acrid cloud spewed from the city, hanging low in the sky like scum on water. Rafa held his hand to his mouth, as he made his way through the barrio.

Rafa struggled toward home. His cries joined the choruses of others' in search of lost loved ones.

"Diogo! Diogo! It's *Pai*. Call out to me. Let me know where you are. I've come for you." Rafa rasped over and over, his voice hoarse. "Come home, Diogo. Meet me there."

Rafa peered into each open doorway, their roofs caved in, walls half standing. He searched skyward to open-faced multi-storied buildings whose jagged broken bricks exposed halved interiors. Carpets dangled from destroyed floors with toppled chairs and tables, crushed and teetering on exposed edges. A lone woman stood and looked out vacantly from the threshold, her exposed shoulders bloody, her dress ripped, revealing her bodice.

"Diogo!" He and the woman's eyes meet. She stepped forward.

"No!" Rafa cried and held up his hand.

But she walked out into the floating dust and disappeared into an impossible to reach jumble of broken buildings.

Rafa clapped his hands at his temples. "Dear Lord…Rest in peace, Sister."

Moans and groans from unseen places filled the air. Rafa called out and then rushed to where sounds emanated, crouching on his hands and knees, or leaning against an intact wall. "Diogo is that you?"

Behind a wall he discovered a broken soul beyond repair, beyond retrieval, beyond hope. He wiped the old man's brows and held his shoulders, for he no longer had hands to be held.

Rafa whispered a blessing as the man departed to the other world. "Black Madonna, Mother of the endless night, receive this old soul."

Rafa sat on a lone chair and wept, looking at the dead man. "Where's Diogo?" he asked over and over.

He worked his way out of the building and back into the street.

A shower of broken tiles and debris rained down. Hands on his head, Rafa careened his eyes skyward, lunged and stumbled forward. "Diogo!"

CHAPTER THIRTY-NINE

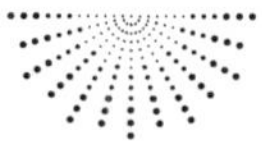

Pêro's face hardened. He ground his teeth.

Was it only yesterday that he and Rafa had the unbroken parts of the tile shipment delivered, destined for a place the ship's messenger claimed: "...was the end of the world, Fort São José of the Rio Negro, Brazil..." *Was this not the end right here in Lisbon?*

He stared at the Tagus River and outlying countryside spotted with plumes of smoke and fire. *Where are you Paulinha? Girls? Rafa and your family? The men of the shop? What of our home?*

Smoke drifted through the door well. Pêro peered in the window of the home where they'd taken refuge, discovering a dismantled kitchen hearth and toppled candlesticks. Lisbon was on fire.

Pêro sought the ocean, watching everything turn calm. *Is it safe to move from here?* He looked at the woman and boys — *where's my family?*

"Let us go," Pêro said in a hushed voice, and carefully picked up the woman. "Come boys."

They entered the vacated street, accompanied by an eerie silence and smoke. Pêro headed toward the Santo Albert Convent.

The waters had spilled over the nunnery's walls, pushing open its doors and undermining its cloistered confines. Brick sections fell every which way like old tombstones. The structure's second story had collapsed like a fallen soufflé, but its rear portion appeared intact. Pêro made his way to the back where he found a group of matronly nuns doling out orders to the younger sisters.

A middle-aged woman approached him. Her wet black and white habit stuck to her body, like her skin taut on her face. She looked severe, but when she spoke it was with kind eyes and voice.

"What is it, my Brother?" she asked, not recognizing Padre Pêro in his simple undergarments.

"Sister, this young woman has lost her husband and home. She's unable to move on her own. These are her sons." Pêro embraced the boys. "I have my own family to locate. May I please leave them in your care?"

Fernando stared coldly at the nun, while Pedro looked helplessly up at Pêro.

"As you can see, we are in a difficult position. But yes, leave them here. We'll do our best to see to their welfare. May God guide and grant you reunion with your family." She held out her welcoming arms for the boys.

"And may God's grace also be upon the convent. Thank you, Sister," Pêro said.

Pêro knelt down to the young woman and met her fearful eyes. "You and your sons will be taken care of here. I am sorry to leave you, but I must go find my wife and children." He kissed her forehead as he would his own daughter. Then he turned to the boys and embraced them. "Take care of your mother."

At first, the two lay helpless in his arms. Then the boy, Pedro, who had been completely buried and mute, lunged and clung to Pêro's neck, whimpering: "Don't leave me." *Clinging to me like Isabela, my own.* Weakness overcame his body.

He held the boy, cradling him gently. Reluctantly, he

unclasped Pedro's arms and set him into the nun's care before turning to walk away. A few steps forward, he looked back.

The nun stood behind the family, hands on Pedro's shoulders. Fernando sat on his young mother's numb lap. They stared at him with the most painful longing he'd ever seen. He turned away from their anguish and walked, a tear falling upon his hand. It was not fair that a woman with two young sons should be left in such a way, and honestly, how could two little boys care for their mother: so young, so in need of care themselves? He regretted saying it. Head hung, chest caved in, Pêro made his way toward the river now that the sea's swells had subsided.

At the riverfront, people worked rescuing survivors, while constantly glancing toward the mouth of the river where the monster waves had risen. In groups, the populace set right overturned skiffs from tidal strewn debris. Vessels headed to shore; others backed out amongst the flotsam.

Pêro sensed disillusionment among the living. No one knew what to expect next. *How to get to Saint Anthony's Church?* On foot it seemed impossible. Refuse blocked the way and was strewn in every direction. He broke out in a sweat at the foolishness of being at the water's edge after witnessing its savage force. But the desire to find his family overrode his fears.

A subtle ripple wracked the earth, halting all work momentarily, sending others scrambling uphill.

Pêro held his ground and then approached an old man bent over a skiff. The fellow fiddled with a rope. The *Batel* boat had lost its two sails but its wooden rudder was still in place, along with the steering pole.

"She held on, can't believe it. Seen many a storm but this takes the whole net of fish," the man muttered, peering up at Pêro. The ancient face was creased with deep furrows like the bark of a cork tree. "What do you need?"

"I must get to Saint Anthony's Chapel in the Alfama."

"Sorry, won't head out on the waters." The old man continued to thread a cord.

"Could I beg of you to let me take the boat myself? I can pay you." Pêro pleaded.

The old man closed one eye. "No. She's all I have now." He turned back to what he was doing.

Resigned to walking, Pêro headed east along the river, getting as far as where the docks of Santos should have been. The great hull of the ship he and Rafa had passed earlier that morning was missing. Nothing was left but barren land.

At the Palace of the Alamada family, the famous purveyors of the trading House of India, Pêro made his way through the rubble, nobles, and their attendants nowhere to be seen. Pêro stopped and crouched behind a fallen granite pillar as wild hoots rang out. He spied a group of suspicious-looking men rummaging through the broken palace. They shouted with glee at their booty. Pêro looked on as a rotund fellow held a silver plate and goblet above his head while a sinewy lad leapt up trying to confiscate it. A third man with a scar-riddled face uncovered a monstrance inset with topaz. Pêro averted his eyes and hid beneath the pillar, waiting until the thieves moved on.

The shoreline was a ragged cloth edge; large chunks of the riverbank had literally cleaved off and disappeared. Ahead, an enormous *caravel* sat on its side on the embankment, beached. Out on the water, Pêro spotted a man in dark pants and coat, hair slicked back, poling a boat slowly upriver.

"Sir! Sir! May I hitch a ride with you? I'm trying to reach my family in the Alfama," Pêro called over the cluttered waters.

The man continued poling.

Pêro kept up with the boat and man, repeating and shouting: "In the name of the Lord — let me go with you! I can help row!"

The man kept on. Pêro scrambled over the broken bank and into the river, waving his arms wildly. "Please!"

The man stopped, letting the boat glide towards Pêro. "Wade over, get in," the man said annoyed.

Pêro steadied himself in the boat. "I'm Pêro and your name?

Where are you headed?" His questions met with silence, the man stared ahead, keeping the skiff moving forward.

They waded through the dead: corpses, birds, dogs, goats, donkeys, cats, horses, mules, people. Fruits of every shape and color bobbed colorfully alongside the deceased. The man maneuvered, keeping the skiff as close to the riverbank as possible.

Pêro could see in his mind's eye, Isabela and Constanza excitedly waiting along the bank for a glimpse of the new bolts of colorful cloths arriving from far off lands. He shivered and looked up to Lisbon's hillsides. The *Cruz de Pau* still standing, but the Church of Santa Catarina of Liveiros had fallen.

"Look there," Pêro said, in a cracked voice.

Out in front of the craft two arms splashed frantically.

Pêro strained to see, his skin becoming clammy. "It's a girl struggling for her life! Pole over. I'll help her in!"

The man continued to go forward.

"Sir, just over there! Go over so we can help her," Pêro said indignant, his breath rapid and shallow.

"No."

"What do you mean *no*?" Pêro braced himself on the skiff's rail.

"I can't swim."

"Nor can I, but if we don't help her, she'll drown, like the rest here." Pêro swept his arm out, gesturing to the bodies surrounding them.

The man stopped and took the pole into both his hand and thrust it into Pêro's chest. "This is my boat. I command here!"

The girl continued to thrash at the water. The vessel passed within feet of her. The girl looked to be Constanza's age. *Could it be my own daughter? Please, no!* Pêro tried to submerge the hateful thoughts entering his mind and control his escalating breath. He repeated the Lord's name and reached down, splashing water onto his face. Given the choice between saving his own life and that of another, this man has chosen to think of only himself. It was true they both risked drowning should the boat overturn while trying to save the girl. But the grandest measure of a man is not what he chooses to do that is easy or safe, but what he chooses to do in times of immense challenge and conflict that may cost him his life. With this clarity, Pêro leapt across the midsection of the boat and punched the man, who crumpled to the floorboards. Pêro took the pole and pushed back to the girl.

Slowly, he approached. *Constanza? Hold on, just a little bit more, I'm coming!*

The girl grabbed for the boat's rails, one hand grasping on then slipped off. Pêro reached for her as she spewed water and spit. Her waterlogged attire weighed her down like a full fishing net. The boat pitched dangerously to the side; the downed man rolled adding deadweight. Pêro struggled at the stern as the girl flailed her arms at the water as she began to slip down beneath the hull.

The boat rocked…tipped…

CHAPTER FORTY

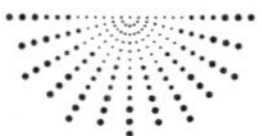

At Pêro's feet the man awoke. The girl thrust her hand up one more time as her body drifted under the boat. The rail of the skiff dipped down into the murky waters. Pêro snatched the shoulder of the girl's cloak. She forced her hand up again and gripped the rail of the skiff; it careened down. The man grabbed Pêro from behind, causing him to fall back. As he fell, Pêro kept his clutch on the girl's coat, dragging her up as he dropped.

She came up, he went down. A gush of water flooded in. She landed on top of Pêro, and he on top of the man. The skiff rocked violently.

Pinned, the man beat the water in the bottom of the boat.

In a quick burst, the girl scrambled off Pêro, as punches exploded into his back.

"Damn you! Get off me! I'll kill you!" The man below him thrashed and cursed.

"Control yourself! We're all alive!" Pêro said.

The pole to propel the boat floated in the water at the boat's bottom. Pêro placed his hand on it, and then rolled on top of it, off the man.

"I command here!" The man burst onto his feet ready to attack.

Pêro and the girl cowered back from him, waiting.

"Give me that!" the man said, lunging towards Pêro. Time seemed to stall as the two men eyed the pole lying beneath Pêro. The man growled, revealing rotten broken teeth.

Pêro rolled off the pole.

The man snatched it up.

"Do that again, I'll kill you!" The man squinted rabid dog-like eyes as he dipped the stick into the water. The boat vibrated with his anger.

Pêro turned toward the river. The young woman cowered in the bow. She was not Constanza, but her features deeply resembled those of his dear daughter.

With each thrust of the pole the man drove the skiff into bodies that thumped as they deflected off its sides, driving into the Royal Shipyard's now adrift lumber. Some logs were stuck upright out of the mud, as if replanted to grow again.

Pêro focused on the heartbeat in his throat as they passed and pressed through the dead, and alongside destroyed landmarks: The Royal Ribeira Palace and House of India.

The magnificent marble architecture of the stately buildings was now a wreckage of stones and filthy river sediment. Pêro cringed and his throat constricted as the Royal Ribeira Palace burned: flames ravaging the collections of the Masters' paintings and the Royal Library. He crossed himself. A tear rolled down his cheek.

The House of India's contents bobbed in the water around them, hundreds of closed baskets and sacks filled with imported goods. Precious magenta and indigo silk cloths were soiled with bright orange turmeric and floated by in heaps, rats lying dead upon their colorful funeral mounds.

Pêro turned from the scene and inspected the girl's attire: brown and white cloth peeked out of the top of her cloak.

"Sister?" he asked.

The girl looked up. "Yes?"

My God, this foolish man was going to let a nun drown, a costly sin!

"From which Convent?"

"The Convent of Carmo."

"Blessed Lord, it is a miracle of God you're still with us," Pêro said, shaking his head. She was young, her skin fair, untouched by the sun, so much like Constanza.

Tears swelled in her eyes and his.

Pêro shivered and clutched his arms around himself.

She lifted her hands up to keep her tears from falling. "It is a miracle. You saved me."

"Sister, how did you come to be outside the Convent?" Pêro wiped his eyes.

"The Convent did not withstand the tremors. We all fled. I saw the hillside's ancient dragon tree weeping red resin and I was afraid. It was so blood like…I was separated from my Sisters and carried to the river by the throngs of people and then the rush of water."

She stared at him. "It's because of you and God that I am alive." She reached under her cloak around her waist, revealing a pouch and pulled out a delicate gold cross with one red ruby set at its apex.

She held it out to Pêro, the cross lying upon her delicate palm.

"Please take this. May God always protect you, as he has protected me," she said. She handed the cross to Pêro.

"No Sister, please, I can't." He tried to explain.

She insisted. "You saved my life. I will paint a *retablo* to the Saints, in thanks for this miracle. But I want you to have this. Please, take it."

Pêro sighed, accepting the gift. There was no need to pay for his help, for he had vowed to serve God and his people. All he asked in return was for the heavens to protect his family. He hoped others were able, in this dire time; to find it within themselves to help those in need, to act selflessly and remember what seemed like a small gesture could have great consequences.

The man glared at Pêro and fixed his eyes on the gold.

"I saved *you*." The man blurted out.

Tension rippled throughout the boat like a frayed cord about to break.

Pêro sat still, and then said, "You're right. You did save her, please have this." Pêro turned to the man and gave him the golden cross, the red of the ruby glimmering in the gray haze. Greedily, the man seized the treasure, dropping the pole into the water. Swiftly, he stuck the pendant into his jacket pocket.

The man reached for the stick. A hand shot up out of the water and snatched the man's arm. Headfirst the man plunged in, his body disappearing into the darkness. His feet kicked a moment at the water's surface. Splashes of water leapt into the boat. Then they stopped.

Pêro and the nun rushed to the rail of the skiff.

Only dark submerged logs and bodies drifted below: a horse still tethered to its carriage, trapped in its harness, eyes bulging, tongue afloat.

Pêro and the nun looked at each other, their foreheads deeply creased as they waited for the man to return.

The pole began to wander away.

Each of them watched as the boat drifted further from the stick. Pêro scanned the craft, searching for anything that could propel them forward, something that could help him reach the pole. Running his eyes along the water and gunwales he saw nothing of use, only shriveled sardines and an odd sun-bleached crab claw. The pole lingered beyond reach, threatening to leave them stranded.

"Sister, please come here. Secure my ankles."

Hands shaking, she obeyed. She moved behind Pêro and

crouched down into a low position holding onto his ankles, her wet habit and cloak mushrooming around her.

Pêro held his breath and counted to three. In a single movement, he extended himself out and over the river. With his right arm and damaged hand, he reached for the pole. His shirt billowed down towards the dark deathly unknown.

CHAPTER FORTY-ONE

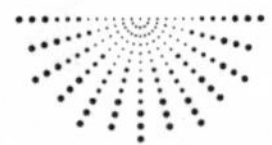

Rafa braced himself against the bottom of a wall and wheezed for air. The northeast wind continued to fan the raging fires, producing more soot, and mixing with the clouds of dust. On all fours, Rafa worked his way forward. Others crept out of the wreckage too. Some bled with broken limbs, others stumbled about in search of family, responding to cries for help and the wails of screaming children. Wounded animals whimpered and snorted. Rafa stopped and placed his hands over his ears, trying to block out the incessant agony of others, the moans and groans of not only people but their actual homes on the verge of collapse. He tried to imagine the street musician's merry melodies.

Fires leapt up from every direction of the Mocambo.

Rafa crawled until he reached his home.

The aloe vera plant pots were now all broken, littering the yard. Two chickens scratched at the newly exposed soil. One fowl let loose a startled "*swak*" as he entered, wings flapping but never taking flight as it scrambled up and over debris and out of sight.

Quickly, Rafa scanned the compound grounds for Diogo.

"Diogo!" he called, making his way toward their broken home.

He knelt and retrieved their abandoned statutes of Saint Anthony and Mother María.

Beads of sweat ran down his temples, down his neck. He sat, laying the saints in his lap, resting his back along an intact part of the concession wall. He looked at his exposed arms, now like the ghostly figures he'd first seen as he reentered the Mocambo from the hillside. Eyes closed, he set his head against the earthen wall.

"*Pai*?"

Rafa bolted up onto his feet, the statues falling to the ground. "Diogo! Where are you?"

"Over here. Over here, *Pai*."

Rafa searched. "Call out again."

"Here, *Pai*. I'm over here…above."

Skyward Rafa scanned.

In a mass of broken thorny orange tree limbs, Diogo hunched, arms wrapped around his knees: a little bird in a thicket nest. Dried blood covered him.

Rafa rushed over. "What's befallen you? All this blood —"

Diogo looked down at his father, brow pinched and stared blankly; trails of blood running down the tree's trunk, his clothes soaked a dark red.

"What's wrong? Where is all this blood coming from?"

Diogo shook his head side to side.

"It's all right, here —" Rafa began to work away the broken branches, creating an exit. "I am here for you."

"No." Diogo whined. "No, *Pai*."

Rafa stepped up, reaching for Diogo, prying his little hands from his knees. Blood streamed from a gaping wound in Diogo's right thigh.

"What happened? Did a dog bite you?" Rafa's nostrils flared.

Diogo continued to shake his head and swiftly clamped his hands back over his knees.

"What did this to you?"

Tears broke from Diogo's eyes.

"You can tell me what's happened. I need to get you to Gogo immediately."

"I wanted the powdered *pão-de-Deus* like Rodrigo's." Diogo's lower lip quivered uncontrollably. "The other boys rushed off when the rumbling started and I wanted to too, but Senhora Corriea was hurrying to get me my treat. She was dressed for church and as soon as she gave it to me. I was the last one, my *pão-de-Deus* —"

Diogo fell silent.

"Go on, finish the story." Rafa broke and removed more thorny branches, until he could inch in to extract Diogo.

Diogo whimpered, pouting his lips. "— it's terrible what happened."

"It's all right now, go ahead, as I get you out of here."

With hurt eyes, Diogo studied his father.

"I need to get you to help quickly." Rafa picked Diogo up, holding him like a newborn in his arms.

Diogo squirmed and stiffened, then cried out in pain, resting his head against his father's heart. "Sehnora Corriea's house fell on her. She fell onto me. She was crushed. She bit my leg and died." Diogo began to cry. "I had to unclench her mouth from my leg. She bit me. She took this chunk out of my leg, but she didn't mean to. I know. I had to find a way to escape —"

"Dear Lord." With a shaking hand, Rafa stroked his son's head.

Diogo's eyes rolled back into their sockets, his body falling limp.

"Diogo! Stay here in life with me! Have mercy, Lord!" Rafa wailed. He rushed into the chaos of the street. Diogo's lifeless body in his arms, Rafa jogged and maneuvered towards the hillside, towards the rest of the family, desperate to reach Gogo.

CHAPTER FORTY-TWO

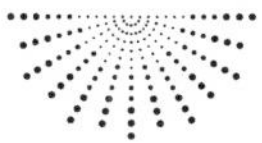

Pêro clasped his hand on the pole. He braced his feet firmly in the bottom of the skiff and with one swift movement brought his body and the stick back into the vessel. The pushing pole hung over the rail. He felt a disturbing presence lingering below.

"We must get out of here," Pêro said with urgency.

"God's waters giveth and taketh away," the nun said softly, as she resumed her perch in the bow.

Pêro thrust the stick into the water. He pushed with both hands with all his strength, driving it down into the watery depths, trying to propel them forward. It met something seemingly solid, and then suddenly plunged down a foot, nearly causing him to fall out into the murky depths. He pulled up, the pole disengaged, and the boat lurched forward. He had a sinking feeling that what he had just pushed off from was human.

He quickly crossed himself.

Up ahead, the Phoenix Opera House's masterfully-built wooden vaulted roof was a forest of flames. Naval cannons were tipped upside down with their iron noses buried in the riverside mud like old pilings. A series of gunfire shots cracked in the distance. The fountain with the statue of Apollo was missing, completely ripped from its mounting. From the water, central Lisbon resembled an amphitheater, with a tarnished copper cloud hanging low over its center as demonic licks of smoke snapped up, a den of disturbed cobras. It looked like the end of days described in sermons, thought Pêro, his eyes wide. Lisbon's grandeur was gone, destruction left in its place.

The nun kept vigil from her place in the bow and pointed when Pêro needed to steer clear of something impeding the way.

Open waters ahead, she turned to him. "God has His ways. Sometimes justice comes as it is due — divine law. But not always and this is what confuses me."

Pêro studied her young innocent Constanza-like face a minute. "I'm bewildered and distraught by God's will at this moment." He swept his hand before the destruction.

"As am I." Her voice wavered, as she turned back to the waters, to her purpose.

They watched the horror, the wreckage of Lisbon in mutual silence.

Pêro scanned the riverbank looking for a spot to beach the boat. Nothing more was said about the disappearance of the man, nor the golden cross. They left it with God.

Boats vied for places along the bank and knocked into one another, thudding, and bullying their way to land. Pêro drove the craft into the muck, taking in the scene before them.

People on land cut in every direction, the busy early morning Terriero Palace Square now a mass of desperate displaced persons. Merchants hauled and dragged and collected their salvaged goods from the Rua Nova dos Mercadores and Rua da Confeitaria wreckage: bolts of fabric, piles of pots, crates of consumables, pastry pans and rolled carpets. Stacks of household and merchant goods formed piles upon piles in the vast rubble filled plaza. *What of our home's precious things?* Broken and disabled members of family or friends kept watch on salvaged items as the able worked to retrieve and stockpile.

Canons in aubergine-colored robes, nuns and priests in their full vestments, and half-clothed women and children kneeled amongst the chaos. Mothers hit their breasts and cried out prayers: "*Misericódria meu Deus!* Mercy, my Lord, Mercy! María!" While clergy scolded: "God has been grievously provoked! Call upon the Blessed Virgin and Lord to intercede upon this sinful city!"

Madness in every direction. Pêro returned his attention to the skiff.

"Can I assist you somewhere?" Pêro asked as the nun helped herself out of the bow.

"Sister Inês!" A group of three nuns pushed through the panicked crowd to the skiff.

"Dearest Lord!" She embraced each woman and wept, then turned to him. "Sisters, this man has saved my life." She curtsied low, her head bowed in grace; the other Sisters nodded their gratitude. "I'm indebted to you. With my Sisters, I should be able to make our way back to the convent and alert the others of our safe keeping. God bless you. I can't thank you enough. And your name?"

"It was the least I could do. Go in peace and with God's protection. My name is Pêro." He quickly bowed back.

Inês and her sisters prepared to take leave, gathering up their cloaks and habits.

"God bless you, Sisters." Pêro rushed up the bank after them and into the melee.

Pêro headed toward the Alfama.

"Repent!" a distraught youth screamed at Pêro and lunged towards him. The young man brandished a useless piece of wood, waving it crazily at him. Pêro ducked and dashed out of the way of the moving stick, nearly falling on a deceased man. The incensed boy relentlessly paced back and forth before the body, wooden weapon in hand.

Out of reach of the distraught youth, Pêro slowed and caught his breath, searching for a glimpse of Saint George Castle. Valiantly it still stood poised atop the crown of the hill of the

Alfama neighborhood. The castle had provided protection for Lisbon from invasions; and throughout the tremors its fortress walls had remained upright; but the fortification couldn't shield Lisbon from the violence of the earth and sea — God's will, Pêro lamented.

Below the castle, the bell towers of the Sé Cathedral jutted up and out of the hillside wreckage. Pêro's heart beat rapidly at the sight of the towers and clusters of upright homes. *Saint Anthony's is below the Sé, follow the bell towers.*

Pêro sought the eccentrically designed House of Beaks and its studded stone facade of pyramid-shaped rocks to lead him eventually to the Arch of the Conception, an entranceway into the Alfama.

Pêro took the steps two at a time, meeting rubble at its exit. He trudged on until a ghastly stench hit him, cloaking him in a gross, unwanted second skin. Pêro choked and gagged. He thrust his hand over his mouth to stop the forthcoming bile. With his other hand, he covered his nose.

Through the sickening smoke of burnt flesh, Pêro saw a man and girl fleeing his way.

"They're all dead! They're all dead!" The man ranted and flailed his arms. His cries amplified, reverberating, like an echo trapped in a tunnel. With one eye cocked, the slight man locked eyes with Pêro and charged through the putrid haze, coming before him, and staring him down with a crazed glare and crying. "They're all dead!"

Pêro reached out and placed a hand on the man's shoulder, holding him back.

"Get a hold of yourself," Pêro said.

"They're all dead! D-E-A-D!" The man wailed. "Every last one of them!" Breaking Pêro's hold, the man stooped down shaking his head at the little girl next to him. "Dead they are. D-E-A-D!"

The girl cried, head jerking, her body convulsing.

Pêro watched them, wanting to calm the man, the girl. He

drew a long breath and then asked with kind urgency: "Every last who?"

"They're all dead!" The man wailed again.

"Multitudes have perished. But we are here alive, and you are not alone," Pêro said, trying to soothe him.

Hearing his own words, weakness filled him.

The man lifted his head and said, with weary bloodshot eyes. "Saint Anthony's Chapel. They're all dead. All of them. Their families too."

Pêro's legs buckled as the man embraced him, bursting into an uncontrollable sob. On his knees, Pêro was stone, the man hanging off him like a cloak. The girl clung to the man. Breathing into the pit of his stomach, Pêro shoved the man and girl away and dry heaved.

With a hand on his stomach, Pêro looked up at the bereaved duo.

"All of them died at Saint Anthony's?" he said in bewilderment.

In between gasps of air, the man cried out again. "All of them. Dead!"

"Heavenly Father, but my wife and two girls are there, at the back of the temple," Pêro said flatly. *This man is crazy. He knows not what he is saying.*

"Dead! Dead!" The man began again, deranged.

"Curse you! Stop repeating those words! Hold your tongue!" Pêro screamed. To no avail. The man kept on. Pêro got to his feet and lunged at the man, shaking him violently.

"Stop! Stop speaking!" Pêro pushed the man aside and dashed uphill. He clawed his way up the rubble and away from the delirious ranting.

But the words rang in his head: *They're all dead!*

Pêro tore at his hair, pulling the thick peppered strands at his temple as he went. He sensed the truth in the man's words despite the fact that the source was mad. A terrible feeling swept through him and images played in his mind: the dead, the dying trapped below the debris of his frantic ascent. He heard wails and screams from those encased in the rubble louder than ever.

Staked out on top of ruined homes, the neighborhood's fishermen wielded broken oars at him and other would-be looters. "Stay back! Go away!"

Family members worked frantically to recover a baby who cried, trapped somewhere below.

Pêro worked his way over a jumble of up-rooted olive and spiny orange trees, mixed with twisted grape vines and broken adobe bricks. A loud groan emanated from the three and four-story buildings still standing. Suddenly, two buildings imploded, burying the fishermen, their oars, and families.

Billows of thick dust obliterated the way. Again, the ground quivered and a loud crack emanated through the blinding dust, followed by more falling buildings. More plumes of dust barreled down, the earth shaking violently as the structures hit, accompanied by screams.

Pêro scrambled faster until he saw the bell towers of the Sé Cathedral above him. His hair tie was lost unleashing his wild curls, now matted in sweat and dust, giving him the hollow-eyed look of a madman.

CHAPTER FORTY-THREE

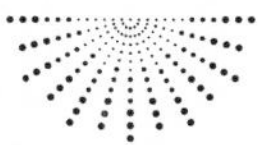

Rafa collapsed to his knees, Diogo in his arms, in front of Gogo at the base of the tree. The rest of the family rushed over, gathering around.

"Here, give him to me." Gogo held out her arms.

Rafa bent and kissed Diogo's forehead, delivering his favorite son, into his great grandmother's care.

Gogo supported the boy's head and draped his limp body across her lap, inspecting his thigh wound. She ran her bent fingers along Diogo's forehead, stroking it softly.

"Josepha bring water, my medicine gourd and some rags." Gogo closed her eyes, raised up her chin, gently rocking her body back and forth. She whispered a prayer that shifted into song in her native tongue. Bagamba joined in. Everyone else remained somber and silent, listening.

"The water," Gogo said.

Josepha's hands shook violently as she lifted the hollowed-out gourd to Gogo's open mouth.

Gogo drank until a little stream dribbled from the corner of her mouth.

Spat! Gogo sprayed water from her mouth onto Diogo's

sleeping face. She ran her fingers along his neck, feeling for a pulse. "More water. His spirit is far off."

Again, she rained water down onto Diogo. "Join hands, and each of you step your right foot forward, together stomping the earth in unison. Rafa you lead. Each of you call out Diogo's name. Summon his soul back here to us."

With drum-like steps they rhythmically followed Gogo's instructions. Each person repeated Diogo's name as they stepped in time with each other upon the ground.

"Josepha! Mother! Come rub the soles of our little Diogo's feet!" Gogo commanded.

Josepha broke from the group, falling before Diogo's small pads.

Gogo ran her hands over Diogo's body. "Here, Son of Rafa and Josepha! Your mother and father call to you! Your brothers long to play!"

"Thump, thump, thump!" Wildly the group beat the earth.

Gogo grasped the tree roots at her sides, clamping them as if clinging to the rails of a skiff in a violent storm. "Now the crown of his head, Josepha!"

Josepha scrambled on all fours to Diogo's head, massaging his cranium as she wept and said, "Diogo! Diogo! Your Mother Calls You! Come Home! Get Home Right Now! I Need You Here with Me!"

The family carried on, until their voices grew hoarse and weak…their stamping subsiding and Gogo released her hold on the tree roots.

Solemnly Gogo looked upon Josepha, whose desperate eyes could not leave hold of Gogo's milked over pupils.

Rafa crouched down and touched all parts of Diogo's body. "Son, we are here!" he cried.

Josepha released Diogo, buried her head in her hands and sobbed, dug her fingers into her face and then threw back her head and let out a heartbroken cry. "DIOGO!"

CHAPTER FORTY-FOUR

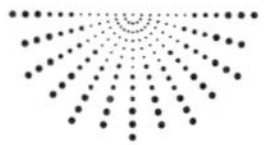

Pêro pushed through the hordes toward the front entrance of the Sé Cathedral. One by one, a group placed dead bodies on the cathedral's threshold. A crowd surrounded the deceased, praying for peaceful and swift entrances to heaven. Amazingly, the walls of the church remained upright, while everything around it lay in ruin. The side chapels had crumbled, along with the main nave ceiling. Its congregation was outside, a swarm of panicked bees whose hive had been suddenly struck, knocked to the ground. Hundreds of shocked worshipers shouted for family members. Before Pêro, a happy father and son embraced one another, desperate and overjoyed. In the chaos, Pêro found himself turning the malachite stone in his pocket over and over.

He scanned the living.

Is that Isabela over there?

There's the back of Paulinha's head, no?

Constanza?

But no, the only person he spotted whom he knew was the well-known Padre Gabriel Malagrida, who, in holy inspiration and fire bellowed: "Repent you sinners! Repent! *Miserecordia meu Deos!*" With dark, penetrating eyes, the fanatic Jesuit searched the rubble for sinners, his arms flailing about in wild gestures to the heavens, as he cajoled others and begged the Lord's forgiveness for his wounded earthly flock. Endlessly, he exhorted others to join him.

"Drop to your knees! Bow your heads to God and plead for forgiveness for your sins!" Padre Gabriel Malagrida shouted in a trumpeting baritone. "All you sinners are responsible! Repent! Repent! Repent for this curse you've brought upon us!"

Crazily now, the Padre pointed to the blackened sky and then down to the ground as if he'd been struck by lightning and commanded: "Go to the ground and repent!"

Responding to the priest's call, the wounded and maimed fell to their knees, crying to God, while others whimpered the few words they could pull forth from their anguished bodies and hearts.

With each command, heat consumed Pêro's body and the desire to flee overwhelmed him. *How can he charge the populace of Lisbon with the responsibility for this horror?* His feelings escalated and swamped him like waves rushing in, submerging everything.

Pêro fled towards the square of Lisbon's beloved Saint Anthony. Fires blazed. Smoke blurred his vision. His skin burned from the shifting waves of heat.

Landslides disfigured the landscape on the hills to the west.

Chasms had swallowed up alleys, lanes, and buildings.

He stopped and stared at the wreckage of Saint Anthony Church. Surrounded by rubble, flames churned out thick black smoke from the entrance of the broken main nave like from the mouth of a dragon.

The only standing building of the square was a three-story apartment. A thumping sounded from its direction. He hurried over to the buried front entrance. "Hello? Paulinha, girls, is that you? Can you hear me?" He crouched, putting his ear to the portion of the door peeking above the debris.

A singular muffled voice responded, of an old woman. "My cane is broken. I can't get up the stairwell."

Pêro looked up and down along the wall searching for a way in. "This way is buried. How many of you are there?" Secretly, he prayed his family was also trapped inside. "Are you alone? Or are you with others?"

"I…oh, no!" she said, followed by the clamor of falling blocks.

"Are you all right? What's happened?" Pêro asked and waited. "Senhora? Are you there? Have you been injured?"

Silence the only response.

Pêro dragged his hands down his face and mustered a prayer.

Where are you, Paulinha? Girls?

Slowly, he walked away, head down. A sparkle caught his eye: a golden candelabrum.

Pêro made his way to the candlestick. It had three white ribbons tied to its stand. Instantly he thought back on the morning and the girls inside the house adjusting ribbons of white in their hair. Carefully, he untied each silk strip and placed them in his pocket with his stone. He kissed the gold taper. His eyes glazed.

"Paulinha! Constanza! Isabela!" With quick movements he scanned the area. The few others in the rubble-filled square looked at him a moment, then returned to their own search. The plaza was strangely abandoned.

Ghostly calls emanated from beneath Pêro. On hands and knees, he tore at the stone and mortar until his knuckles bled, and his arms and back could no longer lift another stone. The chilly cries of someone trapped below abated.

Pêro slumped down upon the buried square. A clamping pain returned to his chest. He cried and stared at a fragment of a white lace mantilla, like Paulinha's, embedded in the debris, the crazed man's words replaying over and over in his head.

They died here…didn't they?

Nothing felt real.

From his perch, he gazed at the desecrated remains of Saint

Anthony Chapel. Splintered pews burned, broken blocks of marble were strewn about, along with pieces of shattered colored glass and blazing fires. Whirlpools of ash twisted and twirled upward into the sky like confetti, but this was no celebration. A great wave of sadness overwhelmed him, as if his heart was now broken in two like their statue of Saint Anthony at the Fabrica. A deep fissure split his soul. Acute unbearable pain. Mangled hand on his heart, he grimaced, the muscle cavity seemingly pulling apart as aching blood coursed through his body, spreading paralyzing pain. Confused thoughts scattered about his head. He saw double and he had the sensation he was no longer connected to his body.

A northeast wind swirled the ash over the buried square. And Pêro. It rained down on him, covering him, aging him beyond his years. He stared at the golden candlestick, but he did not dare take it for himself.

Why tempt God now?

Confused and disoriented people milled about the square. Seekers like himself, searching for family, those lost in the maze and destruction of the Alfama.

Pêro did not engage with anyone nor did anyone stop to talk with him. He sat on a mound and kept his eyes upon the giant heap of rubble that had been his wife's favorite place of worship. He should leave this terrible site, but he could not move — his heart tethered to the place, while hoping that he would find his family withered like a plant without water. *Wait for them here? Or go back to our home? Or to the Fabrica Santa María? Maybe they are searching for me too?*

The words of the disturbed man continued to reverberate in his head. "They're all dead!" Acute sadness froze him.

Eventually, Pêro clambered to his feet, but instead of following the earth's natural decline, leading to the city center, he trudged uphill. He bypassed the Sé and made his way to Saint George Castle.

He leaned against the fortified wall and cast his eyes down

on the city center and outlying hills. Plumes of smoke arose from every distant point. Their neighborhood, street, home, his church of service, all were now completely obliterated. In their places, a gorge and deep fissures, some twenty-feet deep. A grand earthen crack headed north from the river, slicing the city in two. Slowly, he slumped down onto his haunches on the ancient wall. His eyes fixed on the low hanging cloud of smoke, a heavy blanket tucking the valley into its nightmare. Above, a perfect blue sky. A lone white dove soared above the darkness.

Pêro sat, an immovable block of clay, contemplating this strange juxtaposition of heaven and hell. He talked aloud to himself, to God. "Why have you done this? Where's my family? Are they alive? Are they down there in that hell? Or up here in this one?"

Slowly, he swiveled his head towards the waterfront and the remaining docks where hundreds of citizens jammed into the upright ships and skiffs that had survived the tidal waves' onslaught.

A mass exodus was underway.

Legs shaking, Pêro rose to his feet and followed the road that wrapped around the castle's base, connecting to a partially intact stairway that deposited him amidst the rubble of multiple flights of stairs. Each stairway now buried in the talus of fallen buildings and haunted by the cries and groans of those injured and trapped inside fallen apartments along the way.

At the base of the Alfama, he merged into a large group of people huddled together, escapees from the Royal Hospital of All Saints.

Fire spewed out of the hospital's windows and from the arched buttress gallery, in dark sooty spirals, streaking its exterior walls. People trapped and ill, hung out of windows, pleading for help. Pêro gasped and thrust up his arm to cover his face, as a one-armed woman flung herself out the second-story window onto the cluttered street. But he could not escape the sound of her body striking the cobbles.

Flames leapt into the sky, igniting nearby buildings and homes, and shot down streets and alleys — demons' breath making the air thick with smoke as it burned the Dominicans' public library. Pêro's heart skipped a beat watching the horrific loss as he sought an escape route. The flames shifted direction and exhaled a scorching gust down on Pêro and those clustered outside. The deranged screamed in pain, some falling to the ground, while others rolled and cowered. Pêro lowered himself onto his chest, covering his head with his hands, then scrambled up onto all fours.

Others, crazed, bumped and tripped over him. Each way he turned he saw melee and misery. Enclaves of terrified groups splintered off in every direction. He reached for his rosary, finding only bare skin. He fumbled for his stone and held it on his forehead. Images of his girls and wife reeled before his eyes; the girls' early morning laughter and Paulinha's hand upon his arm. Her crystalline blue eyes stared at him in the stone's vision, accompanied by her crooked but beautiful smile, followed by a flash of how they'd maintained the love of their early years together, it, flourishing along with the tile making. The clay works had allowed them to grow close, where other couples grew distant and foreign to the other as the years passed. Instead, he and Paulinha intertwined like the roots of two great trees, their love a protective canopy. It all seemed like a dream of long ago…now ensnared in this horror, alone, without her.

What will become of me? What will I do without my family if I don't find them?

Other wives of craftsmen complained about the long hours of their husbands' absence from home, but not Paulinha, because she was there beside him, working and serving the poor too. She was a rare flower in a field of common grass. *There will be no end to this grief, no end to self-pity should I not find them.*

Next, words came to him from his mother, ones spoken on her deathbed, when the thought of living without her seemed unbearable: 'Son, sometimes we need to stay in the lonely and frightful interior grove, to rest, to come to know the dark, so we can recognize and appreciate the light again one day — All things pass, even the pain of the heart.' He was in the dark forest, lost, very lost and — alone, in pain.

People rushed over him like water, their madness mixing with his. Pêro released the green stone from his forehead, holding it tight in his hand as he crawled. Distancing himself from the scorching heat he noticed a break in the mass of people. He managed to stumble onto his feet, lunging toward the opening, but tripped and fell to the ground. Others tromped atop him. He protected his head as best he could. Home…he wanted to be home, home with his dear family. *Is my home truly swallowed by the earth? Did I actually see this? Maybe my family is waiting for me there?* He squeezed the malachite stone fiercely in his fist. *Get up, get up onto your feet!* The rock cried.

CHAPTER FORTY-FIVE

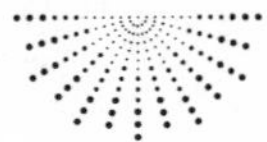

"Hand me the medicine gourd, fetch the black pot," Gogo said. "Place Diogo here alongside me."

Josepha removed the piece of fabric draping her shoulders and laid it on the ground. Rafa lifted Diogo and rested him upon it.

Gogo set Diogo's hands, palms down on top of the serpentine raised roots of the old olive tree, making sure his fingers connected with the furrowed bark.

"Children, go find firewood." Gogo gestured toward the hillside.

They jogged up the slope and fanned out, propelled by a sense of urgency, a mission.

"Undo the indigo-black cloth," Gogo said to Josepha. "Hand me the umbilical cord." Josepha handed her the dried shriveled part.

"Find the bird wings. I think they're inside the bag." Gogo placed the dried cord and wings into a small wooden mortar and began grinding with a rock pestle. "Josepha, collect five olive leaves from the ground there for me."

Gogo mixed the leaves with the other items and then transferred them into the black pot. "Add some water."

Josepha poured in water.

Rafa started the fire, feeding it slowly between the three stones and placed the pot over it.

Firewood in hand the youth returned.

"Children, now dig three holes." Gogo pointed to the area in front of Diogo's feet. "Remember, begin on the right with the smallest hole, working towards the left. The center hole is the largest, align the holes in a crescent moon shape."

Wielding a sturdy stick, they set to their task, taking turns at digging.

"Rafa, make the drumming sticks." Gogo pointed overhead. "Use strips of cloth from Diogo's pant legs to secure the five sticks together."

Gogo held her fingertips to the side of Diogo's throat and then down at his wrist.

Josepha looked eagerly as Gogo worked in silence, her face stern and stoic.

Rafa inched his way up the rough bark of the tree trunk, gripping it with his bare feet, knife tucked into the waist of his trousers. In the branches of the ancient arbor, he gazed out at the Tagus and city center. Fires burned in all directions with billows of smoke filling the sky in great plumes.

Back down on the ground Rafa set to making the drumbeat sticks. He fashioned three, each made up of five finger-like pieces of wood.

"Remove the pot from the fire and place it here next to me." Gogo stirred the medicine, releasing the scent of olive oil and ladled the concoction onto a clean rag, making a poultice.

Halved gourds of three different sizes were placed on top of the three holes on the ground. Rafa took his place before the largest central one, Josepha to his left and Bagamba to his right. The rest of the family took up their places behind the trio.

Gogo nodded and the drumming commenced, beginning with Josepha. With eerie scratching clicks they beat the calabashes with their hand-like fashioned drumsticks.

With a wail, Gogo cried out to the heavens, summoning Diogo back to them. As a shock wave reverberated through the earth, leaves fell from the tree canopy. The earth rattled, joining the ceremony.

"*Click, click, click*" Gogo slapped the palms of her hands violently down on the ground around Diogo's lifeless body. Milky eyes wide, she thrust her tongue out at Diogo and belted out "*Ahhhhhhh!*" She placed the medicine cloth over Diogo's wounded leg bandage.

Diogo's body began to shake. Or was it the earth? Gogo thrust her arms out to her sides, turning her head side to side, tongue still protruding. "Release him! From the netherworld of flight!"

Rafa leapt from his place of drumming and began tracing the intricate tile motifs his son loved with his index finger in the dirt around Diogo's body, creating a beautiful visual border. "Follow these lines back to us Diogo. See the beautiful patterns? Come home. There's much creating left for you yet to do, my son. We need you."

Diogo's chest slightly rose and fell in a rhythmic pattern, eyes closed, face angelic but silent.

Rafa and family kept vigil on Diogo's faint beating heart.

CHAPTER FORTY-SIX

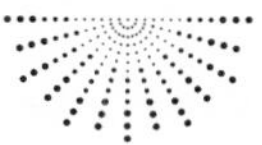

Pêro lunged towards the clear opening, a possible passageway which would allow him to go home. He stopped abruptly on the edge of a precipice. The earth split open like a flesh wound, stone cobbles broke away under his feet. He stumbled back from the edge. Below him, others, not so lucky, had been swallowed by the deep chasm.

Across the gap thousands of people were packed into Rossio Square, beating and tearing at their faces, wailing for lost loved ones. Crosses punctuated the crowd like grave headstones.

"Kiss the Cross! Kiss it!" A deranged old woman shouted. Her head shrouded with a black shawl, blood dripping down her cheeks as she shoved her cross in the faces of those around her.

Waves of heat swept across the square from the north, coming from the burning of the box-like Estaus Palace: home of the Inquisition and its prison. Pêro felt an enigmatic rush of happiness at this sight, immediately followed by guilt. *How can I think such things after committing myself to God?* But, at times the "*Santa Casa*" the Saint House, had caused more harm to the populace than good, publicly promoting and displaying cruel means with which to handle those who had fallen from the

Lord's prescribed path. And now Paulinha's summons. Pêro had questioned the *auto-da-fé* and forbidden his girls to attend the horrific public affairs. *Was it not the word of the Lord to show mercy and compassion to those who go astray?* If this disaster was God sent, it was a revelation indeed that the Inquisition's headquarters should be destroyed. The Lord's commands of tolerance had not been honored by the Church through pitiless acts on many occasions. And it was a well-known fact, that gold often liberated those who might have slipped from God's course, while those without the finances to free themselves were subjected to the misery of the Church's dungeons. It was a harsh double standard, an abuse of position and power — acts committed by those sworn to honor and protect and assist the lost and confused in the name of the Almighty.

The earth shook and the crowds cried with fear. Clefs of stone sheared off the façade of the Church of São Domingos, its iconic pillars jutting up with great slabs of rock now missing, cleaved from its circular supports. *How many had died here before from public executions? Now how many lay buried beneath the massive blocks of stone and mortar? God's message was strong, was it not? Had not the Church gone astray?*

Pêro retreated as the earth calmed. He repeated *"Santa María"* — starting the recitation of the 150 rounds as he searched for another way home. He wanted God to clearly know his intent of dedicated service, despite his growing mixed feelings about the Church's ways.

Off in the distance, brilliant light exploded from the Inquisition Palace. Pêro was caught in a sea of people pushing and shoving to escape the raging and growing fire. The flames rose higher than any other blaze Pêro had yet seen. He crouched as he moved and clasped tight his arms, keeping a constant eye on the panicked crowd and the fire's flames that curled out of the inferno. It was no use; he could find no way to get past the destruction, the crazed masses, the dead and dying that blocked his way to home. He'd have to find another way on another day.

Pêro gave in to the force of the moving mass, distancing himself from the hellish sites. Like an apparition, Pêro drifted with the crowd's movement; each footstep rueful, witnessing endless groups of terrified people huddled and hunkered down together. Others moved about aimlessly, some dodged and bolted into the remaining buildings, while other lonely souls like him navigated the endless hell.

Pêro let himself be carried along with the crowd only to find the way blocked with downed edifices. The group was forced to backtrack, to find another route.

Pêro splintered from the group, making it to the once pristine tiled central market, now a filthy depository of debris. Timbers were jammed against the few standing walls. In the middle of the mess stood a shining polychrome *azulejo* panel that lined the back walls of the market; the blue, white, and saffron-yellow tiles of flowers and shells the only thing of beauty left standing. At the sight of the tile works, Pêro smiled and thought of Paulinha, until he noticed the market's wayside cross ahead of him. Its right arm was broken off, leaving a stub, and atop the amputated symbol of Christ was a child's sandal, stranded, singular. *Cruelty abounded.* His body flushed with heat, sweat breaking throughout. He needed to get back to the Mocambo. Maybe Paulinha and the girls were waiting for him there.

CHAPTER FORTY-SEVEN

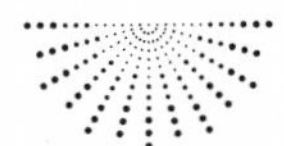

"Go quickly and find out if Conga Carlota the Astrologer has survived and can be consulted." Gogo said to Rafa. "I've exhausted all my ways, but she, The Oracle, will have more."

Rafa stroked Diogo's head and gazed upon his sleeping face. He squeezed Diogo's hand and hurried off.

Rafa stopped each person he encountered in the streets and alleys. "Do you know anything of Conga Carlota the Astrologer? Is she alive?" He sought everywhere for any crumb of information about the stargazer. He worked his way through the rooms of her destroyed residence, picking through the rubble hoping for a clue.

After hours of combing the Mocambo, following multiple false leads, definitive information appeared in the guise of one of her black-hooded cloaked attendants, Mercury. The little man nodded his head and said, "She's well, but working and can't be disturbed right now."

"Please, take me to her. I am desperate. My son's dying." Rafa's stomach clenched at the weight of his words.

The man drew his hood down obscuring his eyes. "I'm sorry. I must go." He stepped away.

Rafa reached for Mercury's arm, halting him. "I beg you. At least tell me where I can look for her. I'll go alone."

The attendant pulled back. "I'm sorry I can't reveal her location. It's too important for all our well-being that she's not disturbed right now. All our lives depend on her readings."

"But my son may die. He's in a deep sleep." Rafa brought his hands together in prayer. "We've tried everything. Don't you remember me? I am the grandson of Healer Gogo. Gogo's exhausted all that she knows. Our only hope now is with the stars, the planets, her diviner's sight."

The fellow drew back the cloth from his eyes. Brow furrowed, he inspected Rafa. "Is that you, Rafa? I'm sorry I didn't recognize you covered in all that dust. She's in an underground chamber, the earth's shaking has revealed an underground world of ancient galleries. We think, the Roman's . Let's go."

Rafa lowered himself down inside the circular corridor into the earth. Goosebumps covered his skin as he dropped and hit groundwater. He shivered and squinted, seeking his guide's torchlight in the arched stone tunnel. A hand on the rough-cut block he followed the light.

White chalk circles of the moon's lunar cycle covered Conga Carlota's face. Star constellations adorned the flesh of one arm, the planets on the other, giving her immense body an otherworldly presence. Seated upon a pillow on an upraised mosaic floor of earth tones, she sat in a trance. Soot billowed from sconces alight on each side of her on the stone wall to her back.

Her attendant knelt before her; the point of his hood aligned with the new moon at her third eye.

Rafa lowered his head, hands clasped and kneeled.

A funnel of wind entered the space, causing the sconce flames to gutter. Carlota opened her eyes wide. "Why have you come here to the womb of the earth? Your situation must be dire."

Shivering, Rafa raised his head and met her intense stare. "Yes."

The earth pulsed and then contracted like the beating of a great heart; filaments of ancient sediment rained down. Conga Carlota thrust out her arms, bracing the masonry, as a sulfuric stench filled the space.

Rafa swiveled his head and looked up, mouth agape at the subterranean chamber.

The falling motes subsided, and stillness returned.

Conga Carlota lowered her arms. "Is this about Diogo?"

Rafa gulped and wiped his brow. "Yes, my youngest son, Diogo. You could already see?"

She smiled at him and waited.

"He's wandering in the realm of the dead. We've tried everything to revive him, but he just keeps sleeping. Gogo's exhausted all she knows. The matters now rest with you." Rafa dropped his head and stared at his clasped hands.

As the stargazer continued to stare at him, he felt her visionary power. She craned her head toward the roof of the vaulted ceiling, then opened her eyes wide, like full moons, seeing through the stone and mortar, dirt and destruction, above and out beyond the night sky — to the stars, galaxies, and beyond. In slow motion, she brought her gaze back to Rafa. "Leave Diogo's birth time, place, and full name here. Come back in a few days and I'll share what I've discovered. Now, take care getting back to your family. The earth shall not lie quiet. This I can guarantee. Take heed. Go with caution."

CHAPTER FORTY-EIGHT

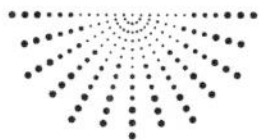

Pêro halted before the embers burning on the old sections of the Fabrica Santa María *azulejo* floor. Ash swirled throughout the footprint of the burned down shop and out the now nonexistent roof. The beehive kiln was a black cave with a hole in its cone where a ceiling timber protruded. Pêro stared at the still half-full swaggar box nestled inside its cavity, a coffin put to rest in a mortuary. Broken finished and unfinished tiles, with wispy burn marks, lay in scattered piles on the floor. Glazes and slip bubbled in pools. Blocks of clay had hardened into adobe bricks. Sacks of silica had melted, forming twisted colors of dark greens and blacks, creating rocks of obsidian.

Pêro approached the noblewoman *figura de convite* still adhered to an upright section of wall on the outside of the shop. In her elegant full-length dress, she stared out with a welcoming face and gesture, each fold of the full skirt life-like. With a closed fan, she pointed to the open air where the Fabrica's main entrance used to be. Pêro stepped on the rubble at her feet and gingerly placed his palm on the cool glassy cobalt, white, and cadmium glazed tiles. Paulinha had made the same gesture not long ago as they stamped out the air bubbles from the clay. This design was Paulinha's creation, her brushstrokes, her clever idea to add the filigree work simulating golden embroidery, celebrating the stream of gold coming from the colony of Brazil. Tears streamed down his face. He dropped his head onto the tiles and cried. *Where are you, meu amor, my life, my wife?* The cold of the tiles seeped and mingled with his despair.

He shoved himself away from the *figura de convite* and stumbled inside the remains of the Fabrica Santa María.

Twenty years of work lay in ruin.

The wooden shelf that housed the Fabrica's test and master tiles had collapsed and burned to the floor. In its place, pieces of a lifetime of innovation lay shattered. A broken clay shard with Paulinha's brush strokes and their monogram PMP caught Pêro's attention. He'd taken to writing his initials in monogram on the Fabrica Santa María's works, early on, before Paulinha began working under it too, as a way to preserve his autonomy amongst other tile makers, but in a way that he considered discrete, non-boastful.

Pêro stared at the monogram, traveling back to the early years of his tile apprenticeship. His grandfather, not his father, had impressed upon him the importance of humility, though it was hard at times to abide by. He traced the PMP with his index finger, recalling how his grandfather had been one of the finest *azulejo* makers in Lisbon after studying in Seville, Spain.

Dropping his hand from the tile, Pêro clasped the stone inside his pocket. His grandfather had been considered a gifted tile maker, and when he'd passed the malachite piece onto him, instead of his father, it had confused him at first. But his grandfather explained that his father knew nothing of the amulet; it was and needed to remain a secret in order to be its keeper. He'd chosen Pêro to be the next stone carrier, because his own father displayed traits marking him as unworthy. And this proved to be true, his father left the tile making trade to sell gems, at times pawning off fakes in place of real stones. To his grandfather's dismay, his own son was prone to greed, jealousy, vengefulness, and vanity. "The stone cannot work when someone possesses these traits," his grandfather had explained. Pêro realized early on in his career that he too was prone to the sin of pride, pausing daily in front of the windows of shops to stare at his own reflection. In this moment, standing in the destruction of a lifetime of work, he prayed for the stone's guiding powers.

No one knew about the malachite talisman, not even Paulinha, at least not to his knowledge. But he recognized wives often know much more than they reveal. If she did know, however, she never let on.

Pêro removed the stone from its hiding place and rubbed its smooth surface, recalling how it had arrived on the Iberian Peninsula, while he tried to locate his secret compartment in the floor of the Fabrica. His ancestors had traversed landmasses, crossed deserts, and open bodies of seawater; the malachite stone had originally come from the East, his grandfather said. It had traveled long distances and thus gained its power of sight.

In the waning daylight, Pêro held the ringed stone tight in his fist, searching through burnt wood scraps and clay shards. Sea winds blew on the shop's embers, changing their colors from ghost grays to radiant oranges. He stopped and held the rock between his eyebrows, closing his eyelids; he lowered his head as if in prayer.

A gust of wind blew in, a cloud of ash pranced around him, and with it came a vision. A dark endless body of water and soot coated his hair, salt crystals encrusting his peppered curls. He licked his lips — salt — as he crossed the silence of eternity.

Suddenly, a pop-like sound of a fired musket ripped through the space.

The saggar box lid flew out of the skylight hole of the beehive kiln and crashed down on the burning embers.

"Padre Pêro!"

Pêro dropped the stone from his forehead, hiding it in a closed fist, and spun around. Inside him a warm feeling welled. *Rafa.*

"Padre Pêro, it's you! I was on my way back to the shop

when the first shock struck. The donkey was spooked, so I gathered my family and fled. We headed for shelter under the old olive tree up on the hill. There was so little time. I prayed for your safety —" Rafa explained in one long breath.

"Blessed to see your face." Pêro came forward and embraced him. "Rafa, the Fabrica's Saint Anthony statue broke in two. I fled also in search of my family. Then there were these boys and the young woman, the girl with her insides in her hands, the water, all that water, the nun and the golden cross. *They're all dead, they're all dead* —" Pêro released Rafa as he rambled, easing his hand into his pocket to restore the stone to its hiding place.

"Paulinha and the girls?" Rafa asked, his pupils dilated.

Pêro let out a strained breath. "I'm searching for them. I've been to the Alfama. To Saint Anthony's Chapel. It all came down Rafa, the whole place," Pêro said, his stomach cramping. "They haven't showed up here yet?"

"Not to my knowledge." Rafa looked around at the destroyed shop. "Come stay with us."

"Where are Kujaguo and Jawoli?" Pêro asked, unable to look Rafa in the eye, nor caring that he'd used their native names.

"No one's come, just you," Rafa said.

"I'm going to stay here. So, I'll be here when Paulinha and the girls arrive." Pêro gazed about the surroundings. Deep in his heart he wanted to be alone to harbor this hope that Paulinha and the girls *would* find him here — that they were still alive. He didn't want to risk missing them, nor for them to have to search any further for him.

"I must stay and wait," Pêro said. "How's your father? And the rest of the family?"

"My father is fine and with us. The de Sousa's farm and residence are in shambles. We've yet to hear about their whereabouts. But —" Rafa stalled.

"What is it? What don't you want to tell me?"

Rafa drew his hands down his face. "Diogo's not well. He's suffered an accident." Rafa wiped his eyes. "I wish you'd come see him. But if not now, I'll bring you something to eat when I return," Rafa said pained. "You don't have anything to sleep with."

"I'm going to start going through things here. It's important I'm here when my family arrives. Diogo will be in my constant prayers. I don't have the stomach for anything else right now."

Pêro stood vigil while Rafa made his way over the broken pieces of the Fabrica's entrance arch in the last of the tragic day's light. A splotch of red caught Pêro's eye near the fallen entryway. He kneeled before the wreckage of clay pots and plucked a red geranium bloom, Paulinha and the girls faces reeling before his eyes.

Pêro held the red flower to his heart and watched the twilight skyline. Fires burned throughout the undulating hills. They burned brighter as night hovered in, emphasizing the Cimmerian nightfall hanging over Lisbon and its survivors and dead. Howls of dogs cursed the last of this wicked day. Over and over again he reviewed the day's events.

Pêro then resumed his search for the hidden spot in the floor.

He rummaged around the site. Using a tile, he pushed embers into a pile. The ashes left black streaks, forming a big black star that glowed in the middle. Lifting a piece of canvas, he found the place he was searching for and pried out the tile, accessing the box below. He opened the lacquered lid set with mother of pearl and pressed his hand onto the blue velvet purse of *cruzudos*. He'd stashed these coins away when his mother had passed. It was the last bit of his inheritance. He and Paulinha had used a great portion of the gift to manumit those who now worked in the shop, along with tile commissions. Not enough of the coins remained to liberate Bagamba minus the monies from the Amazon tiles and other unpaid works. A sense of unsettled peace awakened in him, knowing he had at least these few coins. *But now how to use them?*

Pêro arranged the piece of dusty canvas on the floor and counted what he had and then replaced the box, empty, into its hiding spot. He stuffed the blue velvet pouch into his pocket. With the canvas, he wrapped himself and stared into the embers, occasionally adding a piece of wood, stoking the fire.

To the west, the lowlands of the Lapa and out towards Belém, fires burned, also along the river's edge and its surface was alight. The light of the fires gave off an almost festive air with the darkening sky, but with every breeze, the stench of burnt bodies betrayed the twinkling lights, exposing the true loss and destruction underway. To the east, bright sparks burst from the Chiado hillside, backed by a cloud of pitch soot, rising from the city center's valley floor. The ancient city and its beautiful churches, woodwork, ornate furniture, grand ship building, homes — turned to ash, to dust.

The particles flying into the night sky and out across the river and sea like the covering of a once pristine canvas, now coated in a somber gray *grisaille*-like glaze. Pêro clutched his shoulders, knees bent, and watched the fire before him; feeling its warmth and contemplating how fire could give such comfort yet bring such devastation.

Paulinha and the girls danced in the flames.

Hours passed.

He fought to keep his eyes open, but his body begged him to lie down. He surrendered and gazed up at the night sky and pulled the canvas on top of him. The smoke clouds separated, revealing three bright stars. He imagined Paulinha and the girls as these luminous points, shining down on him, before smoky clouds obscured them. A hollow feeling hung inside him like an open waiting casket to be filled. *What to do next? How long to wait for them here? What to do about the Fabrica? What of the de Sousa family and payment for Bagamba?* He placed his hand on the coins in his pocket, securing them. There's no way to complete the Amazon commission at this time. *Does it matter now? Has the Nossa Senhora da Luz survived?* His body ached for rest, but the questions pursued him, and the malachite stone's vision of the dark endless silent sea haunted him.

. . .

The next morning, Pêro picked through the Fabrica's master *azulejos,* finding a well-executed majolica tile, glazed in sunflower-yellow, marine-blue, and china-white. The tile's geometric shapes pointing inwards to a yellow Fleur-de-lis. It was chipped in the lower right corner, but other than that it had survived the fall. Paulinha had painted it. Pêro took the blade of a clay cutting knife and used it to sever a piece of canvas, and tore the cuff of his pant leg, gaining a long sinuous strand. He wrapped the tile like a present and wound the remaining string around his midriff, letting the tile hang from his waist and covered it with his shirt.

"*Bom dia,* bread from Josepha," Rafa called, as he made his way into the shop over and around the debris. He handed Pêro the bread.

Roosters crowed off in the distance, some normalcy to the abnormal reality they found themselves in. They sat sharing and savoring each bite surveying the situation around them.

"How is Diogo?" Pêro asked.

"The same. In a deep sleep."

"I see. I'll write him a prayer for you to share with him from me. Any word on the de Sousas?"

"Thank you, Padre. Still nothing, but I'll continue to see what I can discover."

"Rafa, I spent the whole night worrying about my family. What I didn't tell you yesterday is that I met a deranged man on my way to Saint Anthony's Church; he incessantly repeated that everyone died there. I went to see for myself. What I found was not hopeful. I'm going to need to go back if they don't show up here soon. They have to be somewhere."

Rafa wrapped his arm around Pêro's shoulders and shook his head.

CHAPTER FORTY-NINE

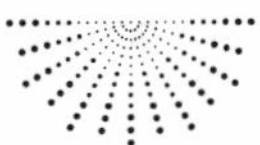

Rafa helped Gogo change Diogo's leg bandage. They cleaned the wound and reapplied the poultice. Josepha swept the area with a broom made of garlic straw and sprinkled salt on the ground as prescribed by the Oracle.

Stick in hand, Rafa drew on the cleared space again, a tile floral design at Diogo's feet and head. Afterwards, he sat alongside Diogo.

Josepha placed a cup of water upon the design at Diogo's feet and a lit candle at the crown of his head.

Rafa began to repeat the given prayer. "You, Diogo covered in the protective mantle of Conga Carlota's chosen deity, will be saved from the evil eye upon you, from all malefic energies. You walk everywhere without fear, away from the realm of the living dead. You will come back into your life here with your mother, father, grandfather, great grandmother, and brothers. You are under the protection of Archangel Gabriel. May the arm of Zambi restrain whoever wishes to do you harm. Lamb of God, Diogo!"

The dinner pot was removed and set aside the cook fire. Rafa started to feed the flames, again, at this twilight hour: 'The auspicious time of day when the veil between this world and the other,' Conga Carlota had said, 'was the easiest time to penetrate.' Rafa began to pray in silence the prayer from the Oracle. With each recitation he placed specific items into the flames: coffee grounds, the outer shells of garlic and rue. The fire crackled with each offering, sending out rich astringent smoke, traveling over Diogo's sleeping body.

Rafa closed the prayer sprinkling salt water onto each of Diogo's limbs, his torso and face. He sat back down in silence and watched his son and spoke to him. "Today I'll go back to see Conga Carlota again for more instruction. Remember how you love to go along with me to see her."

A ripple reverberated through the earth. Rafa took hold of Diogo's limp hand. "These earth murmurs are to be expected, Son. The stargazer says so."

Rafa placed Diogo's hand back on his rising and falling chest. As he let go, Diogo stretched out his fingers.

"Diogo?" Rafa asked. "Diogo!"

Rafa ran his hand along Diogo's forehead.

Slowly, Diogo opened one eye and then the other. "Pai?"

Rafa leaned over his face. "You're back! You've returned to us —"

Diogo blinked a couple of times and turned his head, stretching out his neck and whimpered. "What's happened?"

"Are you in pain?" Rafa asked.

Everyone in the family rushed over and gathered around Diogo.

Diogo tried to extend his arms and grimaced. "I hurt everywhere." He blinked a few times and smiled.

They all grinned and chuckled.

"Hurt. And you still make us laugh!" His older brother affectionately squeezed his arm.

Josepha fell upon her son, tears streaming down her face. "Blessed! Oh, how I've missed and worried about you." She draped her body over Diogo, hugging him.

Gogo smiled and rocked, hands clasped in prayer, one leg

crossed over the other. "Diogo's come home!" She then broke into song. "Cense with Jurema's herbs! Cense with rue and Guinea pepper! Let's all cense now, children of the Faith! Blessed Our Oracle of the Faith Conga Carlota the Astrologer!"

They all joined in, rejoicing in Diogo's return. A soul who was now with them to celebrate again All Souls day of reverence for the departed.

CHAPTER FIFTY

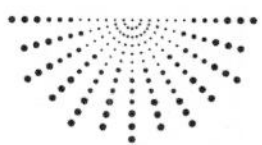

The following day, black flakes fell from the sky, an eerie early winter snowfall. Rafa rushed into the Fabrica. Pêro swiftly arose from where he sat leaning against the broken foundation wall of the large kiln.

"What's happened?" Pêro asked, his face ashen, his eyes weary.

"Diogo's recovered, returned to us!"

Pêro looked up from his entwined fingers. "Oh! Wonderful news." He let out a long sigh. "The girls and Paulinha are still not here." His shoulders slumped, eyes bloodshot and swollen. "Any word on the de Sousas?"

"Nothing I'm afraid. Paulinha and the girls probably found a place of refuge. They will come soon," Rafa said reassuringly.

"Maybe. I pray so."

"My father says the de Sousas went to Mass at São Domingos. He overheard Sebastião José de Carvalho e Mello has mandated all mills, stock houses, and ships with rations to share with those in need."

"Good," Pêro said, dropping his head down. "The money for your father, Bagamba's, emancipation is due. If the de Sousas are alive and want to complete the exchange, we still lack funds. We haven't been paid for the Amazon commission. We need to know if the ship survived, along with the cargo." Pêro sighed deeply. "We're just going to have to wait and see. São Domingos is in ruins. That I know."

"Yes." Rafa came over to Pêro.

"I'm going back to the Alfama today." Pêro took Rafa's hands into his and transferred a coin into Rafa's palm. "If they arrive here, take care of their every need and send for me immediately. All right? Start repairs here."

Rafa bowed his head. "May the Lord bring Paulinha and the girls back to us swiftly. I and my family will do all that we can here to receive them."

As Pêro left the Fabrica he whispered, "Paulinha? Isabela? Constanza?" Only the wind responded with a twirl of ash. He looked to the salvaged tiles for the Amazon cargo next to the crumbled main kiln, where bricks lay around its foundation like stones at an ancient ruin. He massaged his temples looking upon the destruction again. Tears streamed down his cheeks. He spotted a fragment of his official stole — now reduced to a charred square. A sense of nakedness overwhelmed him, he without his habit and alone. Vulnerable. Exposed. *How could God do all this? Where's my family? I beg of you Lord. I beg…*

His heart beat like a thousand bird wings as he left the Fabrica. But trilling birds did not accompany him as he passed the broken potted geraniums and the few red blooms that held their color, their dear life. He stepped over the disjointed pieces of the entrance arch and lugged his aching heart towards the river, once again, meandering through the trails now formed amid the rubble.

At the river's edge a group of monks in black robes worked in the mire, organizing the donated rations rowed in by skiffs from outlying ships. Pêro hurried towards them with hopes of obtaining information about the ship with his shipment of tiles destined for Brazil. As he neared the group of working men his eyes grew wide. He slowed his approach and sensed. *These are the very men who'd stood before my door.* To the right of them, Padre João held a white feather quill, a Brother at each of his sides. One secured an ink well, the other paper. The rest of the Brothers lifting and stacking sacks and crates. Padre João paused from his note taking, white feather raised.

Pêro came before him.

"Padre Pêro Manuel Pires is that you? What a surprise," Padre João said, looking upon his unrobed person with curiosity.

"Padre João."

"We missed you at Saint Anthony's," Padre João said, accusingly and looked at his men.

"You were there?" Pêro said in surprise.

"Yes, I saw your wife and girls. But not you."

"You saw them?" Pêro said with unrestrained eagerness. "Do you know of their whereabouts? Where can I find them?"

Padre João placed the tip of the feather into the inkwell. "I'm sorry, there was so much confusion. Saint Anthony is one of our greatest tragedies I am afraid —" Padre João stared at Pêro. "Have you not heard?"

"Heard, what?" Pêro said, his brow furrowing deeply.

"It is one of the places where we lost the whole square."

He knew firsthand what Padre João was talking about — the rubble strewn square, the main nave spewing black smoke and flames, the golden candlestick, and the three white ribbons now in his pocket.

Padre João tapped his quill upon the paper, the ink spreading in all directions. "A travesty it is. I do hope your beautiful and *talented* wife and daughters escaped as I did."

Eyes glazed, Pêro stared in disturbed silence upon Padre João's full face and double chin. Dots connecting in his mind… The Church, Padre João and Brothers, knew of Paulinha's designing, her sketchbooks…this is what they were after at their home. Luis.

"God has been gracious in my case, may he prove so in theirs and yours," Padre João said.

Pêro's face reddened. "Thank you, Padre. May it be so." Pêro lowered his head. "Good day and good works."

Heavy in heart, but now with a glimmer of hope as Padre João had escaped and seen his family, Pêro trod away from the Jesuits. Padre João's voice and instructions trailing off as he took leave. "It's a pity so many are missing. But let us keep our focus on the living. It is God's request now. We can let past transgression rest for the moment."

Pêro slowed for he knew precisely what Padre João was referencing, his intuition confirmed, the summons letter he'd placed under his mother's tile in his home.

"These items need to be accounted for, place the chickens there and then distribute —"

Then as if keeping pace with the fury of mad drummers, Pêro headed back to the Alfama.

CHAPTER FIFTY-ONE

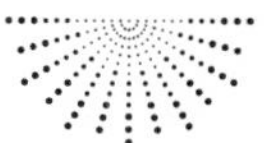

Saint Anthony's nave was an abandoned black cave surrounded by rubble. Seekers moved as haunted shadows on the buried square; pained souls drifting over those lost below. Throughout the nights they worked: grandmothers and grandfathers, aunts and uncles, a lone child, a lone wife, a lone husband.

Hope exists — Padre João saw them here — and he is alive. Pêro repeated over and over to himself.

Small groups tugged and shoved and hauled debris away from the square. Donkeys pulling wooden carts forced their way over leveled debris, transporting the material to place it in fissures on the hillside and in the earth's scars in the city center.

As Pêro cleared, it was as if a person had taken one of his clay knives and driven it into his soft clay-like heart, slowly cutting away pieces as the hours passed, the knife slicing a little further, diving a little deeper.

He was not alone in his search, but as time passed, his hands chafed raw. His lower back throbbed. It became difficult to see and think clearly. Heaviness sat upon him and pushed him down. *Can I go on?* He slumped upon the base of a large pile, in silence. Stooped over, he placed his hand upon the hidden tile beneath his clothes, his mind sifting through thoughts. *Why do people love azulejos?* He thought of Paulinha and her love of the craft. Each individual tile was hand constructed by various persons, thus in the end, each tile possessed its own personality. Each tile ended up unique in color, line work, and physical shape. It was the subtle and slight differences coupled with the overall sameness of the tiles that Pêro and Paulinha loved, the perfectly imperfect. This was the key to beautiful tile works. And like Paulinha; her fine feline features, clear iris-blue eyes, and crooked smile. Without that smile she would not be Paulinha. It was her blue sparkling eyes with creativity and kindness and the slight mischievous grin that set her apart from other women. He loved those eyes — her smile and the love they shared of *azulejos*.

A cluster of people passed and began extracting chunks around him, tossing pieces by his immobile body. As the debris hurled past, he tried to unleash himself from his stupor, but instead fell deeper into it.

Where is Paulinha? The lone daughter of paintbrush makers. Her mother had died during her birth and her father lost his senses at a young age, blamed on the meticulousness of the work, leaving Paulinha to be raised by an elderly neighbor. He'd noticed her one day at the shop where she assisted in the selling of brushes. Immediately, he'd perceived her curiosity about tile making. He'd watched her closely that first meeting as she placed his purchase on the counter, listening intently to him as he explained the properties of the glazes and how the different brushes worked with each pigment.

Pêro stared at the destroyed nave of Saint Anthony envisioning his wife and daughters there. Paulinha's looks drew stares from nobility and the church, for extreme beauty draws attention. Even when not desired by the recipient, and from those that have vowed to not be seduced by it. But it was not her physical beauty that captured his heart but her person: the caring and creative rebel. Not knowing once married, she would not only support his work, but join him. She not minding how the clay sucked the moisture from her hands, leaving them dried and cracked. Oh, how many nights he'd held her close; those hardworking and creative hands at his heart or resting on his shoulder, pressing into his back. Other women of her social standing and beyond were always trying to demonstrate their wealth, marry above their station, continually striving to associate themselves with those higher up the social hierarchy, but not Paulinha. She was happy with what she had; she loved him, their children, their simple life dedicated to tile making and service to the Lord. It was her need to innovate that caused her sleepless nights and frustration, as ideas sprang forth in the predawn, not the fussing over what women were saying about her or what she would wear each day.

Eventually, Pêro pushed himself up, back onto his feet, as more people arrived to help clear the square. As word spread, the local populace came from near and far to aid at the home of their revered and beloved Saint Anthony's birthplace. What had happened here was beyond fathoming; Pêro clenched his fists and shook his head.

They worked the plaza from all angles. Bodies slowly pulled from the wreckage; those that went unclaimed were placed in a cleared area and carted away to mass graves. Pêro wandered off, isolating himself, looking on from a safe distance as individuals and families found their loved ones. Yet their pained wailing still reached him, sending chills across his body. Not a person yet found alive, but at least the bodies had been recovered and could be buried and their souls prayed for, released to God.

Thick smoke coiled from the city center, encasing the Alfama in perpetual gloom. Four days passed, one blending into the other. Pêro rested on the flatbed end of an empty waiting funeral cart. His face now covered in a layer of grime, smeared with black soot marks like his fellow seekers.

A group cheer broke out as a sister and brother were recovered alive, but embraced by strangers, their own family still lost to them. As the siblings held each other, Pêro's heart ached for

Constanza and Isabela. Miracles were possible; he'd seen it now with his own eyes. He got to his feet, this spurring him and others on, stoking their inner fires of hope.

Keep clearing, keep digging, keep clearing.

Bodies dressed in the world's finest silks from the East were placed along those more humbly clothed in simple cloth attire. Jewels from nobility passed into the hands of the surviving Padres. A putrid smell exhumed from the recovery site, intermingling with smoke and mortar and dust.

The King's army arrived and pounded nails relentlessly as soldiers made gallows at the square's edge, a deterrent for would-be-looters, while Pêro and others continued to clear.

"I heard the plague is coming, from the city center. Puss oozing welts are all over people down there. The other cart driver told me with the last load," a bald man said to Pêro, as they painstakingly filled the back of a cart with newly discovered corpses. "And Barbary pirates attacked the port last night."

"They say the homeless are taking refuge in the Inquisition's dungeons, alongside the imprisoned that haven't been able to escape," another man added, helping load the cart.

Without comment, Pêro left the men. He needed to be alone, all this dismal banter tore at his heart.

As Church relics were uncovered, a silver goblet, a gold candle snuffer, the men of the church seized them. At certain points, Pêro wondered if the Padres were not just posting themselves at the recovery site to lay claim to the gold, silver, and precious gems, using the departed as an excuse to make sure the riches of Lisbon entered the vaults of the Church. As agonizing as these thoughts were, he couldn't quell the suspicions and dark thoughts. It was a sullen way of looking at the Padres, especially because he was one of them. Although his secular vows as a deacon were not the same as the ordained, they were all to be working in service to God; not merely for themselves and the Church's coffers.

"Soldiers are massacring looters throughout the city. They are hunting thieves and galley slaves," a stout old man dressed in black said. Pêro frowned at the circulating rumors as the city continued to burn uncontrollably.

Other disturbing gossip filtered through the Alfama that the encroaching flames were headed to Saint George Castle, riding the rooftops of the houses that surrounded it, and were going to ignite and blow up the stocks of gunpowder stored there.

Tremors continued as they searched. With each tremble, everyone froze in their spots. Anguish permeated each face, until the quivering subsided and went no further. With cautious slow movements they resumed their tasks.

Rafa knows I'm here and surely if they'd arrived, he'd have sent word by now? Maybe they are injured somewhere? Or have been taken in at a convent? Perhaps they have found refuge in one of the new encampments forming throughout the city? Or they've fled to the countryside? Across the Tagus?

Pêro continued to clear debris, praying for each possibility.

CHAPTER FIFTY-TWO

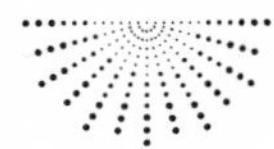

Five days into the clearing effort, the perimeter of the square was passable, a path for carts well established. A notification arrived at the clearing site with orders from Sebastião José de Carvalho e Mello, the King's Secretary of State that all rubble was now to be dumped along the river's edge.

Pêro was part of a core group of men, in search of wives and children. At first, they did not engage, but as the days passed, descriptions of whom they were seeking and what they looked like and what they were wearing on All Saints Day became nightly discussion topics.

"My girls had ribbons of white woven into their braids and Paulinha wore her light blue linen dress," Pêro explained to the group around the nighttime fire.

"María has a mole on her upper lip and my boys are ten and fifteen, thin like myself," another man said.

In this way, they passed the days and frigid nights, talking to strangers and sharing about loved ones. It felt good in a strange way to speak about Paulinha, Isabela and Constanza, and to hear about others' beloveds. Listening attentively to stories and discovering what was being said, in between tears and trembling voices, made Pêro feel part of something: a family of survivors, less alone. The days became progressively cooler and as winter's chill set in, so came the brutal cold facts of Lisbon's losses.

Massive blocks of downed buildings continued to clutter the plaza. Groups worked together to lift pieces of marble columns, stone windowsills, and beams of solid oak and cedar.

Pêro hunched over and sorted wood they'd later use for the evening fire.

"Pêro," a fellow worker said, coming over to where he stooped.

"Yes?" Pêro's heart sank then started to pound in his ears, sweat beaded on his brow. He looked at the wan man, standing before him. *Was this the moment he'd been working for? Was it really now upon him?* If so, he suddenly didn't want it. He stood still while others peered up from their posts with sad eyes and dirty faces.

They all had recovered so many dead from the square. The site of Saint Anthony's was being hailed as one of the largest congregations of the dead. Only in a few other places had entire churches come down with their surrounding buildings.

"Yes," Pêro said again softly.

"Please come."

Pêro walked with the man. He did not feel the ground beneath his feet.

The waiting group stepped aside, forming a corridor for them to pass through.

Azure eyes stared at him.

Paulinha's eyes.

He fell to his knees, hands in prayer.

Her eyes — transfixed — open. The golden brooch fastened to the lace wrapped around her bun shone, and the blue topaz gem radiated the same color as her blank stare. His daughters' heads were tucked into her bosom, with the ribbons of white woven into their braids. Paulinha had a faint crooked smile, the smile he'd cherished for so many years.

With a helping hand, he got up and went to his family. He

lowered himself, huddling in with them, embracing their bodies. Six days since All Saints Day and here they were, covered in dust, much like the dusting after a day's work at the Fabrica. Paulinha was as still as her life-sized noblewoman *figura de convite* and exuded the same fixed life presence. She and the girls preserved by the cold encasing of the rubble.

The group stood around them fighting back their emotions. He could feel their joint heartache.

This is not what I wanted — they are gone! Damn you, Lord! Damn you! It's not fair! Why have you done this?

His head leaning onto Paulinha's, he recalled a brisk morning on their way to the Fabrica, they each dressed in their previous day's clothes covered in a fine film of silt as they passed a group of women poised outside a church. They'd both felt the cluster of eyes upon her worn attire. The group moved in together like a sea anemone closing when touched. Their heads turned inward, each woman lifting a hand up to pursed lips, as if by putting one's hand over one's mouth, Paulinha would not understand what they were saying about her.

She'd turned to him. "I don't care about any of that silliness. I love working with clay and prefer it to idle posturing. Those women bore me." She walked on. He'd reached for her hand and squeezed it tight. *Now this incredible woman is gone, lover, wife, creative companion, mother of my children.*

Pêro stayed there against the girls' backs, his arms outstretched, holding all three of them, desperately wanting to bring them back. Never wanting to let them go. Never.

The group stepped back and left Pêro to his family. He thought back to his shortness of breath and the pain that had clamped and pierced his heart the day of the third large tremor, there in front of the little crying boy. Instantly, he knew this was the moment they'd been entombed. And he recalled his first night alone at the destroyed Fabrica, spent under the clouds and the momentary break in them, when the stars had winked at him. *They were saying goodbye, letting me know where they'd gone.*

"Master," Kujaguo said, touching Pêro's back. He turned, pain shining from his eyes.

"Kujaguo, Jawoli, you're here?" Pêro said, defeated.

"Rafa sent us." Jawoli looked over his shoulder at the Padres nearby then whispered, "Careful, remember to use our Christian names."

Pêro hung his head down. "Here are Paulinha and the girls. I've found them —" His voice trailing off.

An Inquisition appointed Padre arrived. Kujaguo and Jawoli stepped back, making space for him to reach Pêro.

Into Pêro's ear the Padre whispered: "Padre Pêro could you not mourn so openly, it doesn't set a good example for others. For this divine justice of the Lord."

Pêro's eyes flared open. He turned to the Padre and said aloud. "If it is a sin to show love for those one has lost and loved on this earthly plane, then pardon me Padre, damn me, and let God forgive me." Pêro cast his eyes to the ground, fighting back tears. *Divine justice! Blasphemy.* But he stood firm, his lips moving in prayer. He waited for the Padre to bless his family, as his blood boiled.

Lord commend these three souls back into the care of the Savior that created them, through the death and suffering and worthiness of his Son our Lord, please that he have mercy on their souls and pardon their sins, back into your care they dwell, Amen.

The Padre's words flowed into him, seeping into his heart like water filtering through sand meeting a bedrock chamber. His body light, he no longer sensed a separation between himself and the world; instead, it was as if he was melting into the space around him. *Now I must take care of business. They've been blessed properly by the Church. Next the ceremony to bury them which I will see to, as I deem fit for them. They will come with me to the Mocambo.*

They will be buried on the hillside where Paulinha loved to sketch, looking down on the Fabrica. Damn the Inquisition and this accusation of "divine justice". They will be buried in unconsecrated ground in God's overriding domain where she was and will be free of this unfounded blasphemy. Paulinha's eyes still sparkle like the blue glaze she loved, now, fired and fixed forever. Dear Lord! Help me!

"We need to prepare to take them to the Fabrica," Pêro said, without knowing he was speaking. Jawoli and Kujaguo lowered their heads to his instruction.

"Master, can I tell you something?" Kujaguo asked, lifting his head.

"Yes," Pêro said vacantly.

"Jawoli, Jorge." Kujaguo looked over his shoulder at the Padres then back to Pêro and spoke in a low voice. "He knew something bad was to happen. After you and Rafa go away from the Fabrica, the day before All Saints. A strange smell in the air. The cloudy water. Birds in the night sky. The signs talk to Jawoli. We want tell you but we know, you not to believe us. We hurry to the hillside that night before the earth shake in the morning like a possessed man and the river and sea go mad. We prayed. Spirits say, 'no go to the city, stay up on hill'. We made a camp. We watched. We listen and follow the earth's instructions," Kujaguo explained.

Jawoli peered up. "We saw destruction. We pray hidden, faraway. The hill quiet and easy to hear it speak. Days later the spirits say, 'go back' and we find the Fabrica broken. But Rafa working, cleaning, repairing."

The brothers looked with concerned eyes at Pêro. "We are sorry. We come now to help. I go find material to take Paulinha and girls home, to the Fabrica," Kujaguo said.

Pêro understood the brothers' words, the explanation, for he had seen and questioned the inland flying birds on All Saints Day too, but not noticed their evening flight while he was consumed with what to do about Bagamba and the order. Isabela too had exclaimed at the birds' flight. He'd sensed something different in the air also. His body tingled remembering this distinct moment with his dear daughter. People talked around him, but he could no longer hear — all was a jumble of words — with no meaning.

Kujaguo returned, his arms full of heavy crimson drapery. The cloth was sun bleached in streaks, exposed to the bright sunlight of Lisbon. But where the sun's rays could not reach, it retained its deep garnet color, hidden for years in the preserving folds. Kujaguo set down the reams of cloth and took a piece, draping it on top of his palms and forearms.

"Help, take the end." Kujaguo instructed Jawoli. They stretched the material out on the ground.

Pêro stood in a daze, as they extricated Constanza, he motionless — watching — in a distant dream. *How is this happening?*

Kujaguo and Jawoli laid Constanza on the cloth. Pêro stared down upon her — that is not her, but merely a body, not *her*. The two men set out another section of drapery. Kujaguo picked up Isabela's small body. He gently placed her onto the fabric.

Again, Pêro gazed down — *Where has my little girl gone? For that is not she.*

Now, poised alone, Paulinha, back rested against the other bodies hidden behind her. The rose color of life drained out of her, replaced with the ashen colors of transient clouds.

Another cloth was placed.

Kujaguo and Jawoli lifted Paulinha. She looked weightless, like sifted flour.

With a puzzled face Pêro took in her features. No, this is not Paulinha; it is a corpse, a vessel she'd merely occupied. The Paulinha he knew was not there. What was happening was in another place, another time.

"I'll fetch a cart," Jawoli said.

Pêro moved his hand over the wrapped tile hidden beneath his clothes, feeling for Paulinha there at his side, preserved in her brush strokes.

He knelt beside Constanza and stroked her hair. Gently, he untangled the white ribbon from her braid, and placed it in his pocket with the others he'd saved from the candlestick. He kissed her forehead. Her skin not yet weathered by time. Turning to Isabela he removed her ribbon and kissed her and drew his hand down her locks, and paused a moment, his head drooped forward.

He breathed in deeply and exhaled hard.

To Paulinha he shifted his attention, his love.

A whole creative life laid here in death, our girls, our family, our tile works. What cruel God would do this? What cruel God?

But Paulinha refused to get angry; she stared out through those crystalline blue eyes with the faint smile. He gripped her narrow shoulders. She — so fragile, delicate, precious. His hands large and rough, hers small and dry.

Jawoli returned with a cart and driver. Kujaguo and Jawoli stood by and waited. As Pêro got down and laid next to Paulinha, taking her lifeless hand into his, and he looked to the sky. The clouds nondescript, with billows of black plumes of soot like from the Fabrica's kilns. He watched the clouds and black streaks, waiting for them to shift, but it seemed that they were set like dried paint upon tile. Other workers turned and stared at the strange spectacle.

Two Padres' faces contorted, hands to mouths, and they started over toward Pêro. As they neared, Kujaguo and Jawoli stepped in, preventing them from going further.

"Leave him." Kujaguo ordered the Padres, his arm outstretched, insinuating a line not to be crossed. The Padres pressed their lips into sharp lines, but backed down, and waited with Kujaguo and Jawoli.

Pêro let go of Paulinha's stiff hand and placed it on her stomach. He got to his knees and moved the other hand on top. One more time, he looked into her eyes, and then he moved his hands to her eyelids and closed them: forever. A large tear fell on her pallid cheek. He kissed her in the center of her forehead, letting his tears fall upon her, and then he gently wiped them away. He got to his feet and folded the edges of the cloth around her. Turning to Isabela, he worked to place her hands together on her chest and wrapped the cloth up, doing the same for Constanza.

"Please, come help me," Pêro said to Kujaguo and Jawoli, his eyes wet.

Kujaguo and Jawoli lifted the bodies into the back of the waiting cart.

The Padres looked on but said nothing.

Pêro stared at them, knowing the Padres had too many dead to cope with. They would not worry themselves with where and what he and the two Mocambo men would be doing with the deceased. He climbed into the flatbed of the cart and sat in silence next to his family.

Jawoli and Kujaguo clambered onto the front plank with the driver.

His eyes fixed on the square, Pêro crossed himself, and placed his hand on the drapery, watching as the site disappeared behind the corner. Just like that, the plaza, the arduous week of hefting stones, the search for Paulinha, for Constanza, for Isabela ended.

CHAPTER FIFTY-THREE

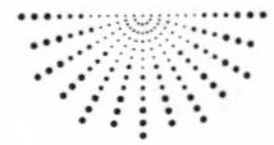

A vacant, remorseful feeling crept inside Pêro like an animal skulking off to the forest to die — alone. Nothing was fixed, nothing secure. Before him, an undirected quest of what to do with his life closed in on him. He at the bottom of a moat, water filling in, blurring his vision, drowning him, cutting him off from the light in the sky, the air, the world. Although he rested back-to-back with Jawoli and Kujaguo he sensed a distinct distance between them, protective walls he'd swiftly put up around his heart.

The cart meandered its way down a small tributary in an alluvial-like floodplain of debris that eventually deposited them near the Mocambo. Rubble still blocked the uphill ascent to the Fabrica.

Each man carefully retrieved to carry on foot, a faded rose madder-clothed bundle.

Pêro cradled Paulinha's cloaked body in his arms.

"My heart feels heavy," Kujaguo said, bearing his load.

Yes, the heaviest thing one will ever carry is a deceased loved one. Pêro nodded in agreement, heartbroken, and trod upward.

Jawoli held Constanza, Kujaguo, Isabela, both trailing behind

Pêro. Together they trudged, weaving their way, until they reached the Fabrica Santa María.

Rafa stopped working along with his four sons.

Pêro forced a sad smile as they entered the shop's courtyard.

A makeshift shelter was now in place. Timbers set into a grooved ledge cut from the slanted hillside. Mismatched clay tiles made up a patchwork roof and the old floor was now cleared of debris. The beehive kiln's dome was repaired with new adobe brick. The cylindrical chimney of the main kiln stood in mid-reconstruction with Rafa's second son mixing an earthen mortar for the repair work, while Diogo assisted as best he could. Two tables sat towards the back wall, their tabletops made with salvaged gesso tops and pieces of marble.

"You've all been busy, I can see." Pêro nodded his head in approval.

Rafa came towards Pêro. His sons looked on with somber faces. Diogo's brow deeply pinched as he leaned on his makeshift crutch.

"Pêro." For a moment that was all Rafa could manage, witnessing the loads they bore. "Things are in process here. But I can see we have more important things to do now. I'm sorry, so terribly sorry."

Tears streamed down Pêro's cheeks.

CHAPTER FIFTY-FOUR

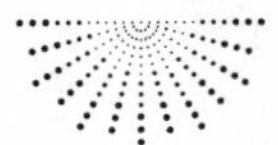

They moved in a snake-like procession, all bearing three sprigs of rosemary. Pêro prayed as he walked, fervently asking the Lord to forgive him for burying his family in unconsecrated ground and for his asking Gogo to preside over the proceedings. *I don't have the strength of heart to conduct this myself right now, if ever.*

Rafa and Bagamba escorted Gogo's small frame, her dark skin hanging loose from well-rounded bones. They held onto her upper arms. In one hand, she carried a bushel of dried basil and rosemary sprigs, in the other, a walking stick that she used to poke along the earth as they walked.

Jawoli, Kujaguo, and Rafa's oldest son carried Paulinha, Constanza, and Isabela. Pêro followed, head down, hands in prayer. Josepha trailed while assisting Diogo, and her middle son, Rui, who carried the pick and shovel.

Up the uninhabited hillside behind the Mocambo they climbed. Mid-way up, they stopped directly above the Fabrica Santa María. Gogo prodded the ground; her cloudy eyes like oceans covered in mist as she gazed blindly down.

"Dig here." She pointed with her stick to three places upon the earth. The earth sounding cold and hollow.

Rafa's son drove the pick into the frosted ground, breaking apart the shriveled browned wild thyme that gave off its scent with each strike. Rafa and the boys traded the shovel, relieving each other as they tired.

Pêro recited prayers next to Gogo whose brown leather-hard feet gripped the rocky soil.

Balancing on her worn staff, Gogo stepped forward, coming before the three holes. "Place our family, our Sisters, next to their respective resting places."

A chill breeze blew up the hillside, pressing the dried grasses towards the east. Steam rose off the working men.

Gogo shivered beneath her black woolen shawl, apron, and petticoats she'd worn since the day of her husband's death in the tradition of the local Portuguese fisherman's wives. "Turn back the cloths, reveal their faces for Our Mother Moon and Sky Lord."

Pêro crouched and drew back the fabric from each loved one, revealing for one last time the faces of Paulinha, Constanza, and Isabela, his beloveds. The wind stopped blowing; calmness presided over the site, as a kaleidoscope of white butterflies fluttered in and danced above the bodies, accompanied by the sweet scent of white roses.

They all froze and eyed one another, for the springtime butterflies had long since passed and the roses of summer had dried up months ago.

Gogo smiled, her milky eyes twinkling at the butterflies' presence.

"Their spirits are happy," Gogo said. "I'm warm now, let us begin. Oh, Great Mother, *María*...Welcome and receive our Sisters. May their spirits rejoin with yours...mother them, care for them, welcome them into your embrace." Gogo reached into her apron pocket, gathering handfuls of dried red beans, passing them around to the group. "Everyone take a few beans."

"Sons, place Paulinha," she said.

Jawoli and Kujaguo stepped forward and lifted Paulinha and placed her at the edge of the grave.

Pêro came forward. He dropped to the ground and felt alongside her light-blue linen dress. He paused, gripping his fingers over the cloth. Tears rushed from his eyes. He retrieved the little leather-bound sketchbook he'd given her and clasped it tight, placing it over his heart. He closed his eyes, lips moving, and folded the cloth back over her body. Drawing book at his heart, he stepped back alongside Gogo.

Jawoli and Kujaguo then carefully placed Paulinha in the ground.

Pêro, eyes hooded, wiped his cheeks. *Bury us both, bury this pain. I beg you Dear Lord, bury me with her.* He did not want to stay with the living; he wanted to depart with the dead. He wanted to escape this unbearable feeling of helplessness, of pain, of his heart closing in on itself.

Each girl was lowered in.

Again, Pêro fell to his knees before Paulinha's grave and whispered wishes, heart longings, forgiveness, and then dropped in one rosemary cutting along with a few beans. He hesitated above her; his head drooped like a dead palm frond. Then he visited Constanza's and Isabela's graves, his body visibly shaking.

Each member of the group followed suit.

Gogo began to sing, in a voice that crackled like dry wood in the fire, sung from the depths of the heart…

It is mine and yours this longing
No matter how much is lost
We are joined by the strings of our hearts
Now we understand this sadness
It is from the now lost love
Let us be consoled
Let our singing carry our hearts' songs to you
We would be less sad if you were here

Oh my People, Oh my Home
Of Our Hearts

With her staff, Gogo motioned for everyone to join in, and for Bagamba to come light her dried basil bouquet. Singing, she waved the smoking bushel over the three open graves.

"Come Pêro," she said, holding the burning herb, the breeze drawing the smoke out in opaque shrouds.

He moved before Gogo, allowing the incense to bathe him. He allowed her singing to enter his heart, each word, each line, each lament, while the dried basil smoked down to a nub.

The wind picked up and Gogo motioned for Pêro to begin to fill in the graves. With trembling arms Pêro filled the shovel's scalloped trough. He sighed with each subsequent shovelful as its weight increased. The sound of the cold earth as it fell onto each red madder encasing: lifeless.

"Here, rest." Rafa offered, taking over the shovel.

The men took turns as Gogo and the children continued to sing.

With the last trickles of dirt, a hummingbird appeared, dipped down, and zipped over the graves. It circled back and merrily flapped its wings at an unfathomable speed, paused, suspended in mid-air, and then flew backwards, past Gogo's ear and was gone. The old woman grinned and ended her song.

Pêro stared at the petite old black woman.

In silence, they listened to the wind blow through the grasses.

Gogo smiled knowingly, as she took Pêro's hands into hers. "All three spirits came. They are well. They are now going to rest with *Maria*. Now, Son you must rest and carry on."

"Please, Lord, give me strength to let it be so," Pêro said, strained with pain.

Together the group gathered up the wild thyme and scattered it over the graves.

Led by Rafa, single file, the group started down, Gogo on the arms of Bagamba and a great-grandson. Diogo and Josepha followed them.

Pêro remained behind next to the graves.

Diogo, the last in line stopped and hobbled back up to where Pêro stood.

"I miss the girls and Senhora Pires." Diogo hugged Pêro and took his hands into his small quivering ones. "I miss them *terribly*." Diogo's India ink-colored eyes filled with love and sorrow.

"Bless you child, bless you." Pêro took solace in the young boy's earnest gaze. He gently set his hands on Diogo's cheeks and kissed his forehead as he would his own daughters.

"Go now, your mother is waiting."

Diogo squeezed his maimed hand and then limped downhill after his mother.

Pêro stood vigil until the party was out of sight and then turned to the graves, dropping to his knees. He leaned into the cold dirt with his hands, his fingers and palms imprinting the mounds of each grave. He sobbed and reached inside his shirt, retrieving a wrapped bundle. He smelled each majolica tile, picturing the streambed in the Lapa that yielded the clay, running his fingers over the ultramarine flower-shell designs on white — Paulinha's painting. His body relaxed a little as he held the tiles in his hands, feeling the spirit of the earth, his family fired in the clay.

He turned a moment and watched as Rafa came into sight below, Diogo behind him in the distance near an exposed rock outcrop. Pêro looked back on the mounds and moved up hill, to where headstones should be, and he placed an *azulejo* on each grave. Falling on his knees, he lowered his head, hands gripping the sketchbook and he prayed. When the gray daylight shifted to the color of stone at twilight, the wind picked up and lashed at him, he rose, and started down.

At the halfway mark, he stopped and turned back, staring up

at the gravesites, all alone on the windswept hillside. One part of him felt lighter; the other heavy with grief. He called to the wind, his words riding on each gust. "I will love you forever — *forever*." The mistral picked up his words and carried them into the nothingness: the everything.

Pêro hurried down, the salt of his tears working its way into the cracks of his parched lips, the stinging feeling nothing in comparison to the ache of his heart. Darkness set in, everything more difficult to decipher.

Back in the Mocambo, Pêro wove through the throng of busy people navigating the piles of debris. Some carried bundles of cooking firewood, a fowl, a borrowed blackened clay pot. Makeshift hearths and terracotta braziers illuminated the winding trails, where folks sat upon the ground and on rubble piles, roasting skewered meats: chicken, goat, beef. How different it was to be amongst the living, a pulse existed, instead of penetrating cold silence. He gazed back up the hill once more and crossed himself.

Pêro searched ahead for Rafa and his family and Kujaguo and Jawoli. Out in front, he spotted the group paused in front of a vendor, who was perched upon a brick, selling salted cod from a wooden bowl.

Rafa spotted him, motioning him over.

Together they trod the pathways.

Gogo leaned on Pêro's arm. "Come to me, Son, when the pain is more than you can bear. I've been through the labyrinth of loss. I know your pain. Come as you need." Gogo patted his forearm.

Pêro looked into the old woman's chalk eyes, at the sparkle of life there despite the clouds. Tears welled and Gogo reached for his hand and held it tight.

"There, Son, it's going to be all right. I know it doesn't feel that way now, but in time it will."

What should I do now, Lord? Why have you taken my family from me? The pain is too much.

CHAPTER FIFTY-FIVE

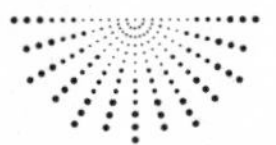

In the morning, sleepy-eyed, Pêro cast looks about the makeshift Fabrica, while he huddled under his canvas cloth on the earthen floor. Page through page, he went over Paulinha's designs, her unrealized visions, notes, delicate line work and vigorous shading — her marks left to *him*. A folded piece of paper fell from the pages. He unfolded it. Dear Lord, she knew. She found the summons note. He sat upright, staring out at nothing in particular, grasping tight the letter.

Carefully, he closed the sketchbook and squeezed it tight, then placed it back in his pocket with the white ribbons, remembering the collection of other design journals in the ornate cabinet at their home in the city center. *What's become of them? The other damning evidence?*

For a moment he just held his hand there upon the drawing book and the summons in his other hand. *How could the Lord have taken her and the girls? Why Lord? There's no sense to your selection, your ways. You take the innocent and leave the profane.*

He rose and lit a candle, holding the damning note to the flame, letting it fall to the floor, watching the fire burn every word. He stamped on the remains, letting the breeze scatter the ashes.

Pêro went to where Kujaguo and Jawoli lay. "I'm going to go see about the fate of the *Nossa Senhora da Luz* and the Amazon destined tiles. Inform Rafa when he arrives."

At the river's edge Pêro sought the *Nossa Senhora da Luz*.

Before the earthquake, the ship had been anchored out in front of the Mocambo. Now, as he surveyed the surviving vessels and their flags, he did not find it. There were ships from the colonies and the Portuguese Navy moored in the center of the channel, along with a few British and Norwegian merchant ships whose flags with red crosses fluttered in the onshore breeze. To the east, a massive ship was ablaze, bow sunk, her rectangular stern thrust upwards. Skiffs worked to pluck the fleeing from the water.

"Have you seen the *Nossa Senhora da Luz*?" Pêro asked, to a man tying up a boat.

"No, maybe check at the Tower of Belém? Many ships were swept out to sea."

Pêro joined a procession of mule-drawn carts filled with refugees heading towards Belém and its outlying areas and the camps forming in the countryside. Slowly they progressed, passing a group of *carpideiras*, professional mourners, who shrieked and cried keening wails as they clawed at their faces, their heads draped with black shawls matching their somber clothing — the entirety of Lisbon now their funeral grounds and responsibility. He held his head down and felt pain in each footstep, as they passed the dead and dying. The cries of the mourning women heard off in the distance. He mumbled prayers as they moved in the direction of the Atlantic.

At the Monastery of Jerónimos the group stopped to pray. The Tagus lapped within feet of the priory. Deckhands from every corner of the world milled at the water's edge.

Watermarks stained the side doors of the main nave. Grasses and grime were wedged into the door's crevasses and surrounding stone carved façade. Pêro noted a family of finches fluttering in and out of hidden nests in the intricately designed entranceway. The birds made their homes between chiseled angels, conch shells, grapes, and winged cherubs; the singing and chirping gave life to the stone, comforting him a bit.

Before entering the nave, Pêro looked to the river, dotted with ships. But they sat off in the distance and he couldn't decipher if the *Nossa Senhora da Luz* was amongst them. People streamed in before him, while a trail of others filed out from the cathedral's threshold. He stepped in, joining the flow of captains, sailors, and refugees.

Pêro searched for the stocky agent Lico in his black knee-high boots. He worked his way around broken parts of the upper choir balustrade now in pieces on the cathedral floor and took a seat in a back pew. He watched people come and go. The monastery's monks scuttled about in their white tunics with brown hoods and mantles, shepherding the distraught every which way.

Pêro knelt on the floor, the cold damp of the stone entered his body; he lowered his head and placed his hands in prayer. He mumbled scriptures and pleaded. "Please Lord, take away this pain. I beg for your mercy. I beg." Afterwards, he walked the perimeter of the nave and side-chapels, discovering no one from the *Nossa Senhora da Luz*.

Back outside, Pêro wended through the throngs of displaced people and edged into where skiffs pushed in through the mudflats.

"Pardon me, do you know of the whereabouts of the *Nossa Senhora da Luz*?" Pêro asked each incoming boat.

"There she is, out there. One of her skiffs is coming in, it looks like." A weather-worn sailor pointed to the waterway in front of the Tower of Belém.

Men worked and moved about on the deck of the ship. Squinting, Pêro could see a passenger boat being loaded on her port side. He waited and prayed.

"You there! Help us in. Macaco, throw him the bow line," the skiff captain said.

Pêro embraced the boat's nose as it eased into the mire. One of the skiff's rowers jumped out and took over.

"Is agent Lico or Captain Rocha aboard or onshore?" Pêro asked, as the men unloaded themselves.

"Ah, look' n for The Hairy Eyeball, are you? Or Lico?" Macaco the deckhand asked.

"The Hairy Eyeball?" Pêro raised an eyebrow.

"Yeah, The Hairy Eyeball. We call him that, you see, our Captain got this one eyeball that gets real big when he's suspicious or doubtin' your loyalty. That eyeball pops out with his big hairy eyebrow above it. Stare a man right down. Makes you shut up, all right. It'll damn convince you to tell the truth or make you think twice whether you is or not." Macaco grinned. "Ain't that right, Eel?" Macaco deferred to the skiff captain.

"Yeah, that's right," Eel said.

The crew burst out laughing. Their simple joy forced a smile from Pêro's leaden face.

"I see. Where is this Captain Eyeball or Lico?"

"They're out there. You can hitch a ride. We be loading up them barrels, then going back out," Eel said.

Pêro stepped aside and listened to the crew's banter.

"You know we all damn near died! God damn mother of a storm! *Nossa Senhora da Luz* did not hold one anchor. Not a one! But she stayed upright. That She did. Sea tried to suck us out! Keeled over on her starboard side, *María* to Jesus! I was swearing 'Hail *María* this! Hail *María* that! Inhaling me tobacco thinking to myself 'this be it, this be it.'" Macaco simulated sucking on a cigarette and wildly gestured with his hand.

The seamen were gruffer than the average clay worker mused Pêro, as he was awkwardly assisted to ride atop a water keg. They rowed the boat out into the channel. The crew seemed like a group of clashing waves, all slapping against the other, unpredictable, but good humored. He appreciated their light-heartedness and jokes.

The *Nossa Senhora da Luz* was a *Nau* vessel. As the skiff

approached, her bowsprit came into view; a painted figurehead of María dressed in sky blue, facing out to sea, serene and compassionate. Pêro whispered a prayer to her. He turned back to the shore as the boat eased into the shadow of the mother ship. He shivered from the coldness that dwelt there. The river water shifted under them, but only Pêro seemed to feel uneasy. He did not like to be so far offshore in such a small craft.

A rope ladder was draped over the ship's gunwales, waiting for the crew and their passenger to ascend. Pêro waited for the others to climb up, leaving him with Eel.

"Get on up there, fellow," Eel said.

Hand on the cord, Pêro placed his foot, pushing and pulling himself up the rungs, cresting the ship's side where he was greeted by a flurry of action.

Yells came from below deck and men dropped down a hole and disappeared. Wood smoke and the smell of drying wool suffused the sea air.

Captain Rocha was on the stern's upper level, pointing and belting out commands. "There! Starboard. Down!"

Pêro thought his one-word commands sounded odd, but the crew seemed to understand and did as they were told.

Pêro skirted the busy crew, working his way towards the captain. Standing below him, he waited for the right moment to speak, feeling uncomfortable without his habit. The captain's dark bushy eyebrow raised, and the hairy eyeball telescoped down onto Pêro.

"*Boa Tarde,* Captain Rocha. I'm Pêro Manuel Pires, the tile maker from the Fabrica Santa María. My shop made the tiles for your client in the Amazon," Pêro said.

The only answer he received was a long stare.

"We sent word, before All Saints Day, about the accident and cargo. You did receive the message? We still need to remake the pieces that were ruined. What are your plans for departure now? I presume the cargo is still aboard? How did it fair?" Pêro asked.

Captain Rocha had a large barrel chest and dark hair,

streaked white and pulled back under his tricorn hat. He was neither tall nor short. Large hands hung from strong arms. His head seemed slightly small for his body.

"Tile maker? Padre Pêro?" Lico asked. "Good to see you. You survived the disasters." The agent offered a handshake. Pêro stiffened as Lico's words opened the wound in his heart — Paulinha and the girls flashed before his eyes.

Captain Rocha turned his attention back to his crew.

"I've come to inquire about the Amazon commission."

Lico wiped his upper lip with a handkerchief. "We nearly lost the whole lot here. The most uncommon situation I've ever lived through. Most of us thought we were doomed as the second wave struck and sucked us out to sea. But Captain Rocha manned the helm and kept us upright, by God. We are all lucky to be alive." With reverence Lico looked to his captain.

Lico inched in close to Pêro. "Padre it was horrific before the waves even struck. As far as I could see along the shore every edifice seemed to be tumbling down before my eyes with great cracks of noise that thundered across the river and the hordes of people crying out for help…fathers and mothers screaming the names of their children as the city collapsed upon them. It was unbearable to witness from the water. I must see a confessor."

Pêro swallowed hard. "May you, may each of us be relieved of these horrors. May the Lord restore peace in Lisbon and within our hearts." Pêro blinked a couple of times and then peered up at Captain Rocha, who continued to blurt orders. He tried to imagine what this man could have done to save the ship during such an unpredictable and sudden situation. He turned back to Lico. "We've begun rebuilding our shop and we'll be able to produce the remaining tiles. I do hope the other crates have survived and are intact. When do you expect to sail?" Pêro could feel the Captain hovering above them, an eagle in his nest, his muscles tensed in his presence.

"The ship has suffered damages too that need tending. Let

me consult with the Captain." Lico excused himself and climbed up the short ladder to where he stood.

Pêro watched the crew work, but out of the corner of his eye he spied how Lico engaged the captain, curious to know how to converse with the man. A conversation seemed to unfold and within minutes the agent returned.

"We'll check the shipment and inform you. He says he plans to leave in a few weeks. As soon as the repairs have been made." Lico straightened his jacket and then leaned into Pêro. "Also, he knows and predicts Lisbon will be in need of lots of timber from the Amazon, in order to rebuild. You do know your tiles are headed to a powerful and influential wood baron. Once word arrives of Lisbon's leveling, there is going to be bountiful work and profits beyond calculation to be made in hardwoods and — tiles. Not only here but also in the New World. Captain's asked if you'd like to accompany the ship and co-broker commissions with us at a payout fee of two percent to him. I'll handle the rest at my normal rate. Get your shop back on its feet."

Pêro held Lico's stare. *Profits? Thinking of profits now?* The vision he'd had the other night flashed before him: he on a ship's deck tasting salt on his lips. He recalled clearly Paulinha's desire to see their tile works in the jungle, and from the sound of the captain's reasoning there might be many more tile works to be made than she'd ever dreamed of.

"There are opportunities for you and the Fabrica Santa María. I know how these men work," Lico said. "They love to display their wealth, as we know here in Lisbon. Remember luck favors the bold." Lico winked at him and nodded. Pêro looked up at the captain, who cast him a knowing glance.

Profits? How could anyone think of profits when so much has been lost? Pêro's stomach clenched and turned over. But it was true; he needed the Amazon commission's full payment. Funds, to be ready should the de Sousas resurface and demand payment for Bagamba, for he still did not have the funds to pay. Now more than ever, he needed Bagamba at the Fabrica. *Now it is essential to keep people together, not just for Rafa's family's sake but my own.*

Pêro whispered the words. "New World"...followed by the thought of *new life*... Never imagining the situation he now found himself in. "We'll do everything in our power to have them ready before you sail," Pêro said. "And I'd like to receive payment for the tiles that have been delivered. Tell the Captain I'll think over his offer."

"I'll see what I can do."

Pêro did not register Lico's response as he looked out over the lead-colored waters at the barges loaded with the dead headed to the open ocean. The Captain's foresight and suggestion of the profits to be made from these disasters horrified him as did this loss of life that would soon be cast into the sea. But now, he understood Captain Rocha. He did not necessarily agree with him, but the man displayed insightfulness and obvious ambition.

Pêro waited as Lico spoke with the captain.

"I can release half."

"Only half?" Pêro said in a low voice. "But there's only one crate left to deliver." Pêro raised an eyebrow and tried not to show his displeasure before Lico and the Captain.

"That's the best I can do, under the circumstances. I am waiting too for another payment to pay you. The Captain and I do expect to sail with the baron's order complete. Come now," Lico said, gesturing him forward.

Pêro pursed his lips and followed, knowing the partial payment would still not make it possible to manumit Bagamba, but it would put him one step closer.

Pêro waited, while the crew readied the skiff for shore.

Lico saluted him from the ship's rail. "Go with God!"

Go with God...here in this hell, the home of the damned and suffering the Lord's created. Where's the logic and reason to all this? Are there truly other forces and explanations as the philosophers of the north insist? As Jawoli and Kujaguo seem to know?

CHAPTER FIFTY-SIX

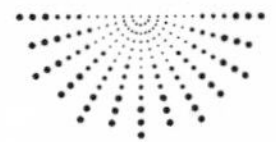

Pêro set out early in search of the needed supplies to remake the last tiles for the Amazon commission and those found broken upon the ship. On foot, he wound his way into the city center on one of the many trails. Makeshift huts marked the way: food centers and temporary hospitals for the wounded. Bakers and millers alike were forced to stay in Lisbon and help feed survivors. The king's army oversaw and directed the storehouses with grain to be milled; making sure the flour was delivered to the intact bakeries that produced bread for the population at little to no cost. They worked day and night to supply the long lines of the destitute and hungry.

Policia and military personnel guarded the entrance and exit ways into the center and along the river, inspecting everything leaving and entering the city, keeping watch for stolen treasures. Troops and lay people alike worked at ridding the city of stagnant pools of water, hoping to fend off illness and the plague.

Lico's words played through Pêro's head as he traveled. He took note of the endless downed and crumbled buildings and the tiles that would be needed to rebuild them. Captain Rocha was correct; the city would need many tiles.

Right now, though, finishing the order destined for the jungle and securing the final funds needed to liberate Bagamba, while managing his heavy heart, was all he could handle. He clutched his chest, his breathing labored at the thought of it all. Dizziness overwhelmed him, until slowly he regained his composure, taking in long deep belabored breaths.

At the burned-out Opera House, Pêro stopped alongside a man who held a sketch pad in the crook of his arm. He was broad shouldered with blond hair and wore a black smock and low-cut boots not from this region. With vigorous quick strokes the man filled in the blank space of the paper with hash marks. Pêro admired the results of the man's efforts. It most certainly wasn't how he'd depict the scene; for the man covered most of the paper with black slashed lines, yet this way of rendering the destruction did visually articulate the scene. He couldn't bear the hopelessness and finality of the dark lines, marking the irreversible destruction of his life, wife, and children.

Pêro nodded and mustered a half smile and moved on. For the artist had accomplished the artistic task of rendering and honestly recorded the reality of their lives, despite its harsh bleakness. Through art, lives lost in the destruction would not be forgotten.

Word spread like blazing fires throughout the Continent of Lisbon's plight and destruction. Northern European artists and writers rushed by horseback, carriage, and abroad incoming vessels to record and depict the plight of the "Queen of the Seas", the likes of this fair skinned man now wandered amongst Lisbon's ruins. For she now was a broken ship, no wind in her sails, no sails for that matter. Yet, as Pêro made his way through the city the determination and resilience of her people were everywhere, helping each other in every way imaginable.

Journalists interviewed and recorded the stories of the fall of Lisbon. Yesterday on Pêro's way back to the Fabrica from the ship, he'd happened upon another fellow who roamed from broken man to woman, asking questions, seeking stories of that Godforsaken day.

Pêro was struck by the pain and urgency of the personal stories he overheard, the anguish in each word, like his own pained memories. His plight mirrored so many others and this comforted him, helping him stave off self-pity. When the journalist adjusted his beret and turned in his direction, Pêro fled uphill away from the reporter and his inquires. Only when he was out of questioning distance, did he dare to look back at the writer. No, he could not bear to reveal and share his loss with the world.

Pêro inched his way along, finally locating the alleyway of the artist supply shop. A blanket covered the shattered display window. The entrance door frame was cracked at the top, the door hanging off one hinge. He ducked and slipped into the colorman's place. The shelves had been torn from the walls and the materials lay in piles of broken jars and containers, but there were signs of order too, salvaged supplies lay about the floor in groupings. The squawking parrots were nowhere to be seen. He longed to hear the grinding pestle upon stone mortar. But a sad silence suffused the space.

"*Bom dia,* Senhor Simões? Hello?" Pêro made his way to the back of the shop where the curtain rod that used to hold the velvet emerald cloth hung ripped from its brackets. He poked his head into the mixing room.

Senhor Simões met Pêro's inquiring eyes. The purveyor of paints stopped what he was doing, paintbrush in his right hand and looked down at the bandage that encased where his left arm used to be. He'd grown thin in the face, his welcoming jolliness absent.

"Oh, I am so pleased to find you. Dear Lord, what's befallen you?" Pêro moved towards him.

The artist supply man rose from his stool. "Padre Pêro blessed." He began to cry.

Pêro embraced him. "I know. It's all too much. But I am relieved you are here, still with the living." His heart skipped a beat.

Pêro looked at what Senhor Simões was working on, an ex-voto devotional painting to Our Lady of the Star, depicting himself moments before a large broken block of building fell upon him. He'd sketched the men and women and children running to his aid. Our Lady of the Star sat on a fluffy white cloud in a halo of golden light, a babe in her right arm and the left hand uplifted, open to God.

"It's a miracle I'm alive. I was hit, I was told, by large falling stone blocks from a nearby building that came down as I tried to escape, resulting in this." He gestured to his amputated arm.

"Oh, Senhor Simões, I know your anguish." He looked to his own hand with missing fingers and held it up.

Senhor Simões embraced his bandaging again. "I will adjust to this with time — I still have the sensation that the appendage is there, ever present, despite its absence."

Pêro pursed his lips, knowing the strange feeling of the loss of a part of one's body, what the art supplier was going through.

"How can I help you? Let's see if we can find some of the items you need."

On his way back to the Mocambo with a few of the needed materials in hand, Pêro stopped at a makeshift newspaper stand. He scanned the local paper and the headline article. *Who is really to blame for these incidents? The populace of Lisbon? Was this disaster heaven sent? Is this truly punishment from the Lord?* He then picked up one of the pamphlets, a translation of what the foreign correspondents and philosophers of the north were saying — that it was the earth itself to blame, that this all was a natural occurrence. *Could this be so?*

In an obscure alley, abandoned by people at this hour, Pêro came across a newly crafted shrine to María. He placed the newspaper and pamphlet in her care. *What to believe, Mother María?* As he turned to leave, a sharp point drove into the small of his back. Pêro gasped as an arm wrapped around his throat.

CHAPTER FIFTY-SEVEN

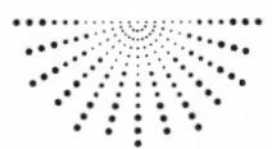

"What do you want!" Pêro asked. But he already knew.

The man felt along his trousers and stopped. "What's this?"

"Something my wife made, nothing of value that you'd want." Pêro choked on his words.

"Give it to me! And your package." The assaulter pressed the knife further into his back.

In one swift motion, Pêro swung to the side, throwing the man off balance and dropped the art supplies.

Before Mother María, the men fell to the ground. With a force of strength Pêro did not know he possessed, he flipped the robber onto his back and pinned him to the cobbles, with his knee to his chin. Pêro ripped the knife from the thief's possession. He gripped it with both hands and held it above the man's forehead, ready to plunge, Saint María to his back.

A woman screamed. Pêro turned, the man knocked Pêro off him. The assaulter scrambled on all fours and ran.

Pêro crumpled before the shrine, knife in hand, resting his forehead on its handle, regaining his breath. He sought the woman who'd saved him from committing an unforgivable crime. The alleyway was now vacant and silent. He thrust the blade beneath his canvas cloak and under his belt that held his beloved's tile work and retrieved his art goods. Only to find the thief had absconded with them. Hands shaking, he quickly felt along his pant pockets and then let out a long sigh, clenching Paulinha's sketchbook and his bag of coins hidden behind it.

He thanked Mother María for sending a savior, preventing him from acting out his fury and that he still possessed his beloved's creative work and needed funds. He then hurried on his way back to the Mocambo.

Days later at the shop, a deep despair swelled in Pêro like growing sea waves, threatening to drown him in sorrow. He could not speak, only motioning to things that needed to be done. He deferred Kujaguo, Jawoli, and Bagamba to Rafa's instruction and direction, while they all set to replacing the stolen art supplies and recreating the last few tiles needed to complete the order headed to the Amazon.

"Master, almost done?" Jawoli asked Pêro.

Pêro sat motionless staring at the work before him on the table.

"Yes, soon," Pêro said, in a weak voice. Pêro stepped away from the workbench and Jawoli and sat before another table doing nothing but staring out at the courtyard.

Rafa and Bagamba brought food for the men of the shop each morning, but Pêro just picked and left his portion half eaten or he offered it to Kujaguo and Jawoli. The string tied at Pêro's waist, securing Paulinha's wrapped tile, began to sag. He had to shorten it to keep it from dangling and getting in his way.

Pêro contemplated seeking out his Franciscan brotherhood and prayed that someone would come and look in on him. But no one came. As the days passed, he found himself unable to leave the Fabrica. His chest muscles felt tight as a drum, protecting his heart. Doubts of the goodness of God consumed his contemplations. The only positive at this point was the fact that the de Sousas had not returned to claim Bagamba or the agreed upon funds. *But would they? Was it just a matter of time? Or were they lost to the world like Paulinha and the girls?*

Pêro gave Rafa coins to find and buy or trade for food items they all needed daily, along with art supply materials to finish the commission: ternary-oxide for the yellow and precious cobalt-carbonate for the blue details, along with new paint-brushes.

After days of rooting around and begging, finally, the last needed things were gathered, and the time arrived when they could paint the new *azulejos* of Paulinha's shell and flower design motif. Pêro stared at the tiles before him on the table, glad it was this work of hers to redo and not of the sensuous. He started in on the line work, hunching over the first iron-oxide glazed white tile. His marred hand trembled as he held the fine tipped brush above the chalky ground. His fingers stiffened and his normally precise lines came out wobbly. Tears swelled in his eyes, his hand visibly shaking.

"Can you finish these?" Pêro asked. He turned to Rafa.

Rafa paused from what he was doing and gingerly took the paintbrush from him. Diogo stared at Pêro, eyes filled with compassion.

Abruptly, Pêro got up and rushed before the main kiln, burying his head in his hands, slumping down onto a stool. From the gaps between his fingers, Pêro watched as Rafa leaned down to Diogo, whispering in his ear, surely to not bother Padre Pêro in his moment of grief.

Diogo clutched the billowed shirt of his father, and turned his head looking back upon Pêro in deep sorrow.

Dear children, oh how I miss the girls, blessed Diogo and his concern.

Rafa painted the last five tiles. Diogo stole glances at him from afar, as Pêro busied himself with the preparations for the kiln's final firing.

Later that day, loading the kiln to fire the tiles, Kujaguo accidentally bumped into Pêro, causing Pêro to nearly drop one of the tiles in hand.

"Watch out! Watch what you're doing!" Pêro snapped.

Kujaguo and Jawoli stared at him, then at each other.

Pêro registered their disturbed glances, for he'd never responded to them in such a manner. But he couldn't help it. The pain was gnawing his nerves raw. Emotions swirled inside him like uncontrollable whirlpools. Anger and guilt swarmed Pêro's senses. *What is becoming of me?* He mumbled, "I'm sorry."

Kujaguo backed away without a word and from then on carefully tried not to cross his path.

In this way, the days passed.

Pêro continued to lash out at everyone. Rage boiled inside him. Work became more difficult for everyone. This he knew, yet he could not stop nor rein in his anger and pain. He announced flatly one day, after a particularly stressful morning. "I'm going. I don't know when I will be back. Rafa, please take care of things here."

Rafa, Jawoli, and Kujaguo caught each other's surprised glances.

Bagamba remained silent, broom in hand.

Diogo hurried to Pêro before he exited the Fabrica, and grabbed his bad hand, looking up at him with a smile filled with love, and then let him go.

CHAPTER FIFTY-EIGHT

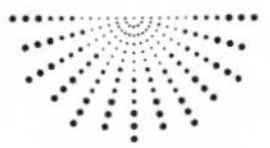

Weeks after Lisbon had been reduced to ruins, the royal family made a public appearance. Trumpets announced their arrival and the procession of repentance to follow. Pêro in a sea of people came to witness and participate in asking for the Lord's forgiveness. He looked around, feeling utterly alone despite the masses.

Today, the nobles traveled in simple unadorned black carriages. The crowd was silent as they rolled in. Pêro peered up at the gray clouds hanging over the countryside on the outskirts of Lisbon. He touched upon the hidden knife that he now carried at his waist when leaving the Fabrica and then gripped tight the tile made by Paulinha. The sharp edge cut into his palm. He eased his grip as the drumbeats began instigating the march.

Each member of the royal family fell into line and moved forward like a drugged snake, slinking along in time with the mournful rhythm. Barefoot with their heads hung and dressed in subdued drab wools, the House of Braganza walked to repent for their sins and the horrific punishment thrust upon their beloved city and its population.

Whispered prayers rippled through the crowd: "Lord save us,

have mercy!" Along with angry accusations pointed at the recklessness of the monarchy and the wealthy.

A man thrust a cross above the heads of the gathered crowd and yelled “Sinners!” He rushed forward, only to be blocked and carried off by guards. Embittered whispers erupted from the populace lining the long procession way.

At the end of the bitter cold route, the well-dressed Catholic clergy and Archbishop waited for the King and royal family.

Pêro pulled tight his canvas cloak around his shoulders as a light rain began to fall, making the chill of the day all the more insufferable. He watched the queen reach out for the support of her attendants as she padded down upon the cold earth, the onslaught of winter breathing its frozen breath upon them all. The girls of the royal house wept, continually holding their handkerchiefs to their eyes, or covering their nose and mouths. It looked as if they were stifling their internal wails of remorse for this redemption, for being implicated in bringing this destruction upon the land and its people.

The crowd around Pêro pushed forward as the royal family neared, the military pushed back. A coarse voice bellowed from the group: "Repent for our poverty! Repent for the greed that caused this destruction!" Two guards charged into the gathering after the belligerent woman, but the local populace closed in tight, allowing her to slip away.

Pêro wiped his tears with his canvas cloak as the family passed; flashing before his mind's eyes the beautiful, sculled boat and its handcrafted artisan work, he and Rafa had the good fortune of witnessing as it arrived at Terriro Square only weeks before. He remembered how he’d shared his excitement of the magnificent sighting with Paulinha.

At the Archbishop’s command, each member of the family knelt on the damp ground at his feet. In unison, they bowed forward, foreheads to the ground. A gasp rippled through the crowd — The House of Braganza reduced to such measures — a scene like never before.

"Repent! Bear witness of this prostration of the Highest Lord of this land, fashioned and in service to your command Lord in heaven, Our mightiest of Lords! Accept this humble prostration, a surrendering to the Mightiest of Lords! Repent, repent, repent!" the Archbishop threw up his arms to the dark skies.

The masses joined in: "Repent, repent, repent!" People fell to their knees and placed their foreheads on the ground too.

"Forgive them for their sins!" The Archbishop wailed.

With this closing plea, servants set to helping the royal family up onto their feet and escorted them back along the cold weary way from which they had come, and into their awaiting vehicles.

"Forgive us for our sins!" The crowd cried.

Pêro hung his head, repeating the words of forgiveness over and over. *Was this our punishment for freeing slaves? For challenging the Church on this matter? For supporting artistic aptitude and depicting risqué subjects? What Mighty Lord would inflict such pain upon them all?* Mangled hand to his heart, he fell silent, no longer able to speak aloud, for his and Portugal's loss was beyond prayer, beyond spoken words. It was incomprehensible and irreversible what had happened here. Pêro dropped his head into his hands and wept.

CHAPTER FIFTY-NINE

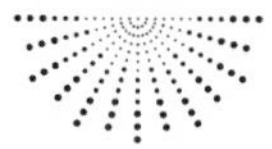

Rafa rushed after Diogo, placing a hand on his shoulder, as Pêro walked away from the Fabrica.

"Padre Pêro is very sad," Diogo said, looking up at his father.

"You're right, Son. Stay here, keep tending to Paulinha's favorite flowers. I'll see after him." Rafa hurried into the road as Pêro rounded the corner.

Rafa stopped. Better to let Padre Pêro be alone with his thoughts and instead carry out Pêro's wishes and keep things going here. It must be stifling and painful for him to be living at the shop now without his family. For his home in the city center was swallowed by the earth, along with all their possessions, connections, and memories.

Alone, on the deserted way Rafa turned towards a steely melancholy sound that floated towards him. He squinted, rubbing his hands together, blowing his warm breath into them. A cittern player came into view. The olive-brown skinned musician was clad in a worn black cape and tricorn hat, loose fitting cloth boots, playing a teardrop-shaped guitar with a scrolled end. Accompanying him was a stocky dwarf dressed in a floppy stocking cap and pin-striped knee length trousers and matching top, with a large dirty-white ruffle at the neck. The dwarf shook a tambourine vigorously. A little wiry dog trailed behind, and mournfully howled each time the music reached a low sad chord.

Closing his eyes, Rafa breathed in the winter air and the deep longing of each metal string's strum. His heart ached as he listened to the guitar's rueful song.

Rafa snapped open his eyes and hurried back into the shop.

"Parchment, parchment!" Rafa said to wide-eyed Jawoli.

Jawoli rummaged around and came up with a few scraps of paper.

"What about this?" Diogo said, holding up a medium-sized rectangular square.

"That's perfect." Rafa took it. "Hand me that board."

Kujaguo quickly fetched the wood and handed it over.

Rafa searched the tabletops until he found a piece of graphite. "I'll be back."

Bagamba smiled as he rested on a stool.

Kujaguo and Jawoli shrugged their shoulders, raised their eyebrows, and returned to fitting wood pieces together for a new crate for the last of the replacement tiles.

"Diogo assist them with the nails." Rafa rushed to the roadway, releasing a burst of steamy breath into the cool air.

The musical duo approached slowly. Rafa sat down in the dirt, back against the earthen concession wall, board resting on his thighs. He began to sketch as Pêro had instructed him: 'Watch your subject, not the paper, let your hand follow what the eye sees; only periodically looking down for a point of reference or to relocate your drawing utensil.' He moved the lead slowly, following the outline of the musician's cape, pressing a little harder at the shoulder and releasing force as he rounded to the neck and up over the head and down the other side. Quickly, he glanced down and set to drawing the dwarf. He stopped to see what he'd done, the music drifting closer. His eyebrows pinched in a frown. The proportions were off, the head too big for the guitar player's body and the dwarf came out, not as a man, but as a boy.

Rafa let out a sigh and shook his hands, letting the music sweep through him. His heart now acutely feeling the pain of the song, the *saudade,* the longing for those lost forever like Paulinha. She was correct, his heart was in this street music. He thought back to her by his side, encouraging him to design the figures now playing before him. A tear rushed down his cheek. *She'd believed in my ability as does Pêro.*

He turned the parchment over and began again. Drawing and glancing down, a dash here, a curve there, pressing hard and releasing pressure and spinning the lead between his fingers as he went. He shook his shoulders and watched the musicians intently, who now played before him. Looking, drawing, looking, drawing.

The dog let out a howl as the guitar player feverishly brought the tempo to a climax, strumming the strings and letting the sound vibrate out.

Rafa stared back down, and then held the paper out in front of him, looking again to the musicians. Better. Yet he still did not render the stout tambourine player as he wished.

The duo came to him. The music tapering off as they kneeled next to him.

"Can I see?" the guitarist asked.

With hesitation, Rafa turned the paper. The cittern player let out a belt of laughter, while the dwarf scowled like a dead fish.

"It doesn't look anything like me," the dwarf said. He grabbed the paper examining it closer. "Nope, nothing like me at all." He thrust the paper back at Rafa.

Rafa got up, brushed himself off, unable to look at the two men.

The guitarist ran his fingers over the metal strings and sang: "Of this bruised song I lament —" as he walked away, playing his somber tune.

The dwarf rattled his tambourine. The dog yelped. The trio walked away.

Rafa watched them go, and then looked back at his drawing. He mustered a smile; this was better than his first attempt. Practice, more sketches, as Paulinha advised. *If I am to take care of things for Padre Pêro I must tackle these drawings. I've no choice now the poor man needs me as much as we've always needed him.*

CHAPTER SIXTY

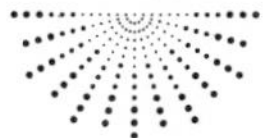

With quick steps Pêro advanced, peering over his shoulder occasionally and looking ahead into the dark spots along the way as he trod. *The time to see my mentor and Franciscan Brotherhood is long past due.* He slowed. *How will I explain burying my family in unconsecrated ground? That I chose to do so in direct opposition of the words spoken of "divine justice "that my wife and children's deaths were heaven sent because of Paulinha's artistic actions.* Holding tight in his hand the malachite stone, he knew it had been the right decision. *But how will this be received by my mentor? The one person I am required by the Church to confide in. Dear Lord, do you even exist?*

"Over here, keep coming!" A young Chamberlain ordered the stream of incoming people. Cart after cart waited in a disorderly line to enter the grounds of the Convent of Senhora of Jesus. Pêro walked alongside them in the Barrio Alto. His stomach clenched witnessing their heart-heavy loads of the dead: burnt, mutilated, and bloated bodies. *Dear God.*

The cross of the convent came into view. *How is Padre Dantas? Seeing him will be a relief of some measure.* Pêro covered his mouth and nose fending off an ungodly odor. Suddenly, he felt Paulinha's presence at his side, like the last time they were here together in the hospital ward. His deacon duties and responsibilities to the sick and poor now forgotten and overlooked in the urgency of the current situation and Bagamba's cause should the de Sousas resurface. He quickened his pace, desperate for council and condolence.

Pêro reached the holy grounds, where the arched entrance should have been. He picked his way through the broken pieces of the structure and throngs waiting to enter. He stopped abruptly at the courtyard's edge, slack-jawed at the scene: the earth opened like the belly of a whale, half of the cloister rooms in the southern complex had fallen.

Into the hole, cart after cart delivered their sickening loads. His Brotherhood, pieces of cloth to their mouths, repeatedly made the sign of the cross and repeated prayers. "Place them here." A monk pointed into the mass grave.

A magnetic pull drew Pêro forward to the pit's opening. His body began to shake. Dead in every disgraced form were jumbled together, a mass of parts, charred wood, and rubble. The stench of lye mixed with putrid flesh emanated from below. Pêro gagged and with his hand held back bile and stumbled away from the horrific scene. *This is consecrated ground, but beyond comprehension. No, I made the right decision to bury my family as I have.*

Padre Dantas? Where are you? Pêro sought his mentor. But only located a few of his Brothers performing death rites. Pêro brought his partially amputated hand to his heart, his breathing slowed.

"Padre Pêro?"

Pêro spun around. "Brother Leonard? Yes, it is I." Pêro tried to figure out who he was speaking to from behind the tied cloth. "Blessed to find you. How are you faring with all that's come to pass? What's happened here? The Order is in shambles and this gravesite —" He placed both hands on his Brother's shoulders, steadying himself. "I desperately need to meet with Padre Dantas."

His Brother dropped down his head and stood in silence, and then met Pêro's stare with his own pain-filled eyes.

"No." Pêro arms fell to his sides like dead weights. "Don't let it be so, Dear Lord —"

"I'm sorry Padre Pêro. We recovered his body a few days ago. He was in his personal place of prayer. I'm sure he died in peace. He's already been interred and received by the Lord."

Pêro grasped his Brother's hand. "Where may I find him and pay my respects?"

Brother Leonard led Pêro through the melee and back out behind the hospital ward into the orchard enclosed by crumbling cloister walls. The arbors were now devoid of leaves and fruits, trunks darkened by the rains, looking like skeletons.

At a mound of newly turned earth, Brother Leonard stopped. "Here is where he rests." His Brother then took leave.

Pêro lowered his head, hands in prayer before his heart. "Oh Lord…dear Padre Dantas…May you rest in peace; may the Lord hold you in His embrace." He then looked to the heavens. *Forgive me Lord and Padre Dantas for burying my family as I did and choosing to hold my silence now forever. Perhaps this is divine justice?* He gazed upon the grave. "God, you've taken everything from me. My heart aches with loss…I am weak and in pain…now my mentor is lost to me…my council, my direction. But I thank you for the crumb of mercy you've blessed upon me. But I don't know how to carry on —"

CHAPTER SIXTY-ONE

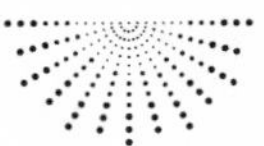

Pêro fled back to the Mocambo. At the base of the hillside backing the barrio, he stormed up. He quickened his ascent with each step, gasping in the frigid air. At the gravesite of his family, he crumpled upon the earth. Hot tears rushed forth. *Why Lord? Why? My family and now Padre Dantas too!*

He pleaded to the winter wind whose only response was a chilling cold breath. He beat his fists on the ground, until the skin tore at his knuckles.

Nothing was the same. He wanted this pain to go away. Instead, it coursed through him, settling deep inside each part of his body, festering there: raw and tender. *I no longer sleep through the night, as I anticipate Paulinha's small frame nestled next to mine.* Now there was only the chill of winter. He heard the girls' giggles as he lay awake in the dark. But after a moment the joyful sounds tapered off replaced by the vacant haunt of the howling wind.

Nightly, he replayed his last moments with Paulinha and the girls. They all in their cozy kitchen, the glow of the hearth, the warm dreamcakes, the girls' laughter, and how he and Isabela had played and joked, Constanza and her new womanliness, and Paulinha's small hand upon his forearm. How, his and

Paulinha's eyes, their souls had been joined there in the doorway, one last time, before he left, before they were separated from each other in life forever.

Dreamcakes.

Dreamcakes, that's all they were now: A dream.

Maybe if I go back to the city center, I can recover something? One small thing of our life together? Feel better? What of our friends? The Costa hat maker family? The wood guilder Alvaro and his brood? The Lopes who made bread? Senhor de Gomes the olive oil vendor? Padre Tomé and the congregation? What of the Martins sisters?

Terrible tales circled the living like vultures.

No, he would not go, it would just open the wound in his heart more, and besides, since being attacked, he knew it was becoming more dangerous by the day to be moving around Lisbon. He'd heard the recent horrific stories of murder at the hands of escaped thieves who robbed the weak and wounded, leaving them for dead while plundering their salvaged goods and homes. And the ongoing response of Sebastiao Jose de Carvalho e Mello as he attempted to instill order by ordering soldiers to behead and hang the guilty.

And prophecies of an even worse misfortune to come that would complete the punishment of Lisbon and her populace. The rumor now circling was that on the last day of the month there would be another colossal quake. Everyone was on edge, worried and waiting for the next disaster. Forcing the populace into themselves like animals into dens, while carefully creeping forth trying to care for the living and bury the dead. Pêro lashed at the earth, anger's bile erupting from him as he beat the frigid ground.

"Damn you, Lord! Damn You!"

God, you are the culprit who caused this devastation to my life, to Lisbon, to all that I love! But the outcry did not soothe his fury's fires, his singed emotions. A searing pain burst forth in him, and his mind fought to stay rational. Turning to the ground again, he punched until the madness subsided. Until he laid face down, crying.

Old memories surfaced, his dark secret, things he didn't want to remember. Like the time he'd impulsively struck Paulinha. It had surprised them both and the incident had turned him to God's forgiveness and instruction. One day they'd argued over something now lost to memory, but she had threatened to leave him, and he'd struck her across the cheek. Shocked and horrified, she stood and wept. As did he, for he was not a man who looked kindly upon such acts as other men did. Instead, he saw it as a man's weakness and his had been exposed. It took a long time for Paulinha to forgive him, and he himself. The memory creeping back when he least expected it. At the time, he did not understand why he'd reacted so, but now he understood; the fear of being left had frightened him beyond control. But now his fear had become reality. She was gone — he left alone with regret as his companion.

Paulinha had not been responsible for his reaction, just like she was not responsible for the earth's violent shaking; the taking of her life, but still he pounded the ground with his fists, unable to take back what he had done, or bring Paulinha back to life.

An inner voice bubbled up from within him: *I must sail with the Brazil shipment and away from this pain and regret, go for Paulinha, see what she longed to see. It's the least I can do for her.* He shivered violently and grasped his upper arms with his hands, shaking his head side to side, no —

Pêro stayed on the hill until the sky shifted to the colors of a bruise and the cold had numbed his limbs and emotions. Slowly, like a seedling surfacing from underground Saint Francis's wisdom blossomed in his mind: "We must rejoice when we fall into various trials and endure every sort of anguish of soul and body or ordeals in the world for the sake of eternal life." *Damn eternal life! Why didn't you take me too, Lord? What does this suffering have to do with eternal life?*

At twilight Pêro started down the hill. A thin band of pink shone over the Tagus, west to the open Atlantic. A bat swooped in front of him, so close he could see its furry body. It flew in jerky movements; the last bits of daylight highlighted its webbed wings, serrated with long black lines. He stopped to watch its flight: erratic and unpredictable. *What is it saying? Trying to communicate? I need to see Gogo.*

Days had passed since he'd really talked with anyone, and now before him the voice of nature, and as Saint Francis of Assisi had said: "The Earth speaks." This is what Jawoli and Kujaguo had also expressed and for the first time he saw a connection between their wisdom and his religious path.

Pêro made his way down to the base of the hill and then turned back towards whence he'd come, searching for the bat, but it had gone. Now, lead shadows draped the hillside and the graves of his family. He hurried to Rafa's house.

At the compound's earthen wall he called, "Hello?" He peered over and into where a fire burned between three stones set in a circle, a steaming pot at its center. The small house was abuzz with activity; children swirling about.

"Pêro, come in," Rafa said surprised and merry.

Diogo ran to the gate and opened it, grabbed Pêro's hand and led him in.

"I've just come from the hillside, visiting the graves," Pêro said, and rubbed the stubble on the side of his face, looking around with a shy smile as he entered.

Rafa observed him and stared at his torn knuckles.

Pêro tried to hide his wounds.

Gogo sat sunken in a chair that had been cleverly repaired many times with pieces of fishing net. Bagamba was stretched out on a pallet outside, gazing at the night sky.

"How are you, Son?' she asked, her clouded eyes welcoming him.

"I needed some time away. To be alone. To be with my family. I saw a bat as I was coming back."

"Tell me about this bat."

"I stopped to watch it. It was curious. I felt like it was saying something, but what I don't know."

"Come, sit here," Gogo said, gesturing to her side. Diogo brought over a footstool. "I'll tell you about the wisdom of bats."

Pêro perched alongside the old woman, folding his hands one on top of the other, feeling shame at what he'd done to himself and leaned over to listen.

"Bats are the helpers of people, the go-betweens of this realm and the next. They hear life's songs. They pass on guidance to those in need, pointing the way for us as they themselves hear their way through the world. This bat you saw, what did it say to you?" She looked at him with her smoky eyes.

"I don't know. That's the problem," he said in a beaten tone.

The old woman grinned at the night sky. "The bat often tells us to listen to the voice within one's self. What are you saying inside of you?" she asked, pointing a knobbed finger at his heart.

Pêro inspected Gogo's dark wrinkled face and glassy eyes. His brow furrowed, eyes focused and intent. Slowly, a whispering, a voice, his, from the hillside returned. "Pêro, you must go on with life: never forget Paulinha, Constanza, and Isabela but continue on. Finish the tile works destined for Brazil and set sail with the ship, see the jungle for Paulinha, for yourself, secure more commissions for the shop. The time away will help you heal." But he was afraid of this voice. It had spoken clearly. But he didn't trust it. He resisted its instruction, for his rational self said, "No, stay here, rebuild the Fabrica Santa María and see to Bagamba's freedom. Don't go to sea, it will be frightening and unpredictable. And you do not know how to swim. You are a man of the earth not the water. Remember how uneasy you felt climbing the *Nossa Senhora da Luz's* ladder." Yet, despite this voice of reason, the other voice pulled stronger at him, like the ocean's undertow, once caught in it one needed to surrender or perish. He longed to sail away from his pain, this place of vivid memories —

Pêro turned to Gogo and grasped her gnarled hands. "Yes, there is a guiding voice inside, actually two. One of reason, the other of the heart."

"Which one spoke first?" she asked.

Pêro gripped her hands tighter but could not speak. He knew the *Nossa Senhora da Luz* would sail with or without him. *Venture out to sea? Can I really?*

"Here, eat," Rafa said, handing him a roasted yam, the color of turmeric. It was warm, just off the fire and its skin pulled back easily. He ate it slowly, going over Gogo's last question. His response was there on the tip of his tongue. But saying it outright would somehow commit him to something he was not yet ready to do.

Gogo smiled knowingly and enjoyed her yam.

Walking back to the Fabrica, Pêro's stomach full, his anger dissipated, some of his feelings and doubts revealed, he looked to the night sky, to the stars as if seeing them for the first time since All Saints Day. His family was somewhere overhead, perhaps floating in the celestial heavens. He slept deeply for the first time since the disaster and dreamt of sailing on a calm sea.

CHAPTER SIXTY-TWO

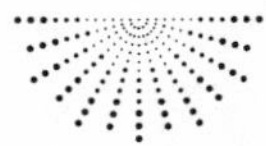

In the morning, Pêro helped Kujaguo and Jawoli with the last of the tiles.

"Luis never come back," Jawoli said, readying the *azulejos* for packing.

Pêro was silent, head down, fussing over organizing their humble collection of paintbrushes. "He perished with the waters."

Pêro looked up and met Jawoli and Kujaguo's surprise. "The last I saw of him, he helped me, saved my life and others. During the moment, he didn't know he was saving me. I know because I saw the surprise in his eyes like yours now. He rescued me from being trampled right before the waters hit. He was carried away from me with the panicked crowd. I'm sure he did not survive as he was carried downhill towards the river." They all stood silent. "Despite the betrayals, in his final moments his goodness returned, the Luis I knew all my life was there. Amends were made." Pêro wiped the tears from his cheek. "God bless him. May he rest in peace."

"Then Luis he go to be with his riverside ladies and eat grapes all day now in heaven." Kujaguo grinned at Pêro.

They all burst out laughing for the first time since the tragic day, laughter like sun rays from dark clouds.

"I wish that upon him, pampering women that he so adored," Pêro said. He liked to imagine that Luis was now in the care of an entourage of doting women.

A deep sense of peace swept through Pêro knowing why Luis had betrayed them, jealousy of Paulinha's talent and Rafa's aptitude and the threat it posed to him. He could still hear his parting words 'I am sorry! I was jealous of her! Of them!'. Now it was best to let things rest. Luis no longer around to testify against Paulinha nor she to be accused and questioned, the Inquisition's headquarters burned, and all record of her summoning disposed of.

"Still no word yet of the de Sousas?" Pêro asked.

Rafa shook his head, eyebrows raised. "Nothing yet."

"What of Senhor Guimarães?" Pêro asked.

"Rebuilding like us," Rafa said.

"Good."

As a group, they were luckier than most. Whole families and businesses in the city center had literally disappeared, their genealogical tree cut down forever. Not one person left to long for lost loved ones or to worry where they might be. Possibly, only a distant relative that lived in the countryside or up north along the coast, or down south in the mountains, remained of certain bloodlines.

Pêro tried to reflect on the losses of others to remind himself that he was not alone in his bereavement. Working at the Fabrica was starting to help ease his pain, his outbursts lessening. Instead of snapping, he took up Bagamba's job and swept relentlessly and sorted and organized, while Bagamba occupied himself with compiling salvaged wood to harvest nails from. Pêro volunteered to cut the clay from the earth, somehow his hurt lessened as he held the earth in his hands. It was cold to the touch but holding it extracted his sadness, as he knew he could shape it into something of beauty with long life potential and worth. It could make something so, if the de Sousas returned, he'd be ready with the funds to defend and free Bagamba.

Jawoli and Kujaguo closed the lid of the replacement tiles' crate.

Pêro scuffled around the Fabrica straightening up things obsessively.

Rafa arrived with a donkey and cart.

The box of replacement tiles was now ready to be delivered. The payment money for Bagamba's release was soon to be in hand.

Pêro jounced the donkey's harness and fiddled with its straps. This being Rafa's normal task, he stood by waiting for direction. Pêro stopped what he was doing and turned to Rafa. "I've decided to sail with the shipment."

Rafa stood in silence, reaching for the donkey's reins. He reworked what Pêro had already done, his strong hands fumbling. Abruptly he stopped. "Are you sure about this?" he asked, his voice strained. "What if they come for my father and there's a disagreement about something?" He wrung his hands together.

Pêro's gut clenched and he winced. "I've been worrying about this too. A part of me thinks I can't and shouldn't go." He closed his eyes and let out a sigh. "But I long to be away from this place of pain." Pêro took Rafa's hand into his and met his worried stare. "A voyage could do me good and there are opportunities that can benefit us all." He let go of Rafa's hand and ran his fingers through his peppered hair. "A month has passed with no word of the de Sousas' whereabouts. I'm afraid they've been lost too, as tragic as it may be, but freeing for your father and all of us. With this crate's delivery I'll be able to leave a negotiable sum with you should the de Sousas surface. And there are the other commissions to follow up on too."

Rafa rested his hand on the mane of the donkey. "You think I can really negotiate on my father's behalf? A man of my color? A man with this on his neck." Rafa revealed his slave brand, and then drew up his shirt collar.

Pêro looked to the gray sky for an answer, and then finally said, "Yes, with all that's come to pass, only men with the cruelest of hearts would not see to a fair compromise at this time. The de Sousas have been negotiable in the past."

The men held each other's stare.

"You'll just continue to fill in for me here. You can do it Rafa. You already are now."

Rafa stopped altering the harness and wiped sweat from his forehead. "Yes, the de Sousas have been negotiable but also unpredictable. What if the de Sousas refuse to hold up their end?" Rafa said.

"It will only be a short while." Pêro smiled encouragingly at Rafa.

Rafa bowed his head. "But I worry about...should the de Sousas return —"

"I'll leave a note of explanation for you that you're acting on my behalf. I desperately feel I need this time away to heal."

Rafa drew his hand up to his heart. "All right then, I guess we should arrange for your departure and make plans for your return."

"I am sure I'll be back before the springtime flowers," Pêro said. Tears welled in his eyes, his emotions he could no longer confine. In days past, at these emotional moments, he created a reason to fetch materials away from the men, some excuse to take leave, to be alone. But now, he wept openly.

"We take care." Kujaguo said, taking hold of Jawoli's hand.

Rafa waited patiently for Pêro to gather himself.

Pêro wiped his eyes and smiled at the three men before him, his family now. Their courage and acceptance of his decision gave him strength.

Later that day, Pêro and Rafa traveled to the Tagus with the replacement tiles through long lines of refugees. Pêro clasped his hands together tight going over in his mind his commitment to sail. The fleeing masses were juxtaposed against the busy waterfront. Stacks of cargo boxes awaited loading, men getting a shave, women selling bread and sardines, sellers vying for buyers. Cats and dogs dashed in front of the cart, weaving amongst the moving masses. Rafa brought the cart to a stop, as men rolled barrels around the earthquake and tidal mess. Pêro imagined the whole scene depicted in a large-scale tile mural, but who would purchase such a scene?

Refugees held onto the sides of the cart as they started slowly again on their way, the wheels creaking. Small dirty hands reached out from exhausted orphaned children, pleading for help. Others begged to enter the cart. Lisbon was now a city of displaced people of all ages. Pêro's heart constricted further in his chest. There were so many in need of help. "Jump in." Pêro reached for the weakest amongst the many and helped them into the cart.

People with festering wounds and swollen infected body parts lay on the ground dying, next to the dead, faces ashen with sunken eyes, muttering their last prayers. He covered his mouth with his canvas cloak. A Padre in a filthy cassock shouted into the crowd, demanding the survivors repent instead of taking leave of the city. The distraught hung their heads and trudged by the ranting priest.

Soldiers worked in the throng of the crowd, carrying the deceased to large skiffs already piled high with bodies. Pêro ignored the other holy man's accusations, as it took him back to the Sé Cathedral. But he prayed silently to those departed and taking leave. The cart approached a beached vessel loading cargo. Pêro scanned the bank for the *Nossa Senhora da Luz's* skiff.

The people upon their cart eased off the flatbed and continued on their way, each one helping the other along. Pêro called to them. "May the Lord see you to safety."

"Can you deliver a shipment to the *Nossa Senhora da Luz*?" Pêro asked, a man arranging his goods in a boat.

"Load her on her own skiff, here she comes," the sailor said, pointing to an incoming vessel. Today two men rowed the boat, pulling hard on wooden oars, propelling the craft towards the bank. She was full of passengers.

Pêro waited at the river's edge as the skiff eased in. He turned to Rafa, eyebrows raised. "Is that Padre João, and Princess María from the carriage?" His voice raised an octave.

"Yes, I believe so." Rafa rested the reins on his knees, eyes wide. "It's them."

They stared with surprise along with the shore's onlookers at the group wading through the shallow waters. Crewmen stepped aside as attendants rushed to Princess María and picked her out of the skiff like a newly arrived rare porcelain vase. Quickly, she was carried by an entourage of servants and taken off the mire and loaded into a red and black lacquered sedan. The crowd visibly infused with energy at the royal sighting.

Padre João was engaged in conversation with a man who wore a fitted black coat and carried a square bag with an ample brass buckle.

"Why do you think they're here? Do you think they're sailing with the *Nossa Senhora da Luz*?" Pêro asked Rafa.

"It looks that way."

"But why?"

Pêro's muscles tensed as Padre João and the man with the black bag came towards them. Pêro cringed at the thought of their last meeting. Mid-sentence, Padre João halted in front of them.

"Padre Pêro is that you?" Padre João inspected his face. "You're as light as a quill, but unscathed."

Pêro's body flushed with heat, looking upon Padre João's still corpulent face.

"Unscathed? I'd beg to differ," Pêro said. The very presence of this man before him tore him at the core. *How has Padre João been spared when Paulinha and the girls were not? What kind of God could do such a thing?* He wanted to scream into Padre João's face that he'd been terribly scathed; he'd lost his whole family, his mentor. While this plotting jealous man stood before him, the fat of his rosy cheeks bulging like bellows. Pêro shoved down the burning hurt and took in a long, controlled breath.

"I'm sorry. I've heard of your loss. It is a tragedy. Death does not pick age nor spare beauty," Padre João said with sincerity.

But his words were like a hot branding iron, scarring. Pêro sat still, time momentarily suspended. He then cleared his throat, where he felt a stone had lodged. "Thank you for your condolences. And what brings you here today?" he questioned, more bluntly than he would have liked.

"I shall sail to the colony of Brazil. In service to the Princess. There is much work to be done, now isn't there." Padre João leaned in towards him, smiling coyly.

Pêro turned his tongue in his closed mouth, trying not to ball his hands into fists.

"Padre Pêro, I'm truly sorry for your loss. But God's will is not for us to question. We are to obey his command and surrender to his plan, not ours," Padre João said.

A rain cloud hovered in; darkness pressed down.

Pêro briskly turned his head and stared ahead, while Padre João steepled his stumpy fingers together. From Pêro's peripheral vision he watched the Padre but refused to further engage. The man at the Padre's side patiently waited and observed the tense exchange.

"Shall we?" Padre João said finally, deferring to the waiting man. A sea breeze caught Padre João's black cape inflating it, giving his already robust figure extra volume.

Pêro frowned.

The accompanying man acknowledged Pêro with a slight nod. "Good day".

Pêro curtly nodded, as the men took leave.

"Anything else?" Eel called into the milling group on the bank.

"Should I unload?" Rafa asked, with hesitation.

"Yes, I suppose that would be the next thing to do," Pêro said exhausted.

At the back of the cart, they slid the crate out to its edge.

"We've some cargo to go to the ship," Rafa called to Eel.

"Bring it." Eel waved them over to the boat.

Pêro gazed far off, Padre João's words and squinting eyes still reeled before him, as heated raged inside him.

"That's it," Rafa said. The crew took over the crate of replacement tiles.

Eel and the old black sailor loaded sacks around the box of tiles inside the skiff's hull.

"The order is complete and shipped," Rafa said, attempting to engage Pêro. "The final payment now to follow."

But Pêro walked away and plunked himself upon the front plank of the cart.

Rafa took his place next to him.

In silence, Pêro, back straight, hands folded in his lap stared at his entwined fingers. Shouts of the sailors sailed by as they readied for departure. Pêro turned to Rafa. "You'll have to see about contacting Tiago's father about the damaged tiles. I should've confronted Padre João just now, for he's the true culprit behind the "accident". But from the sounds of things, I'll have plenty chance to do so upon the *Nossa Senhora da Luz*. I'll leave you a note for Tiago's father."

Rafa nodded in agreement.

"Cast off!" Eel pushed the bow of the boat.

"Is Lico aboard?" Pêro called to Eel.

"He is." Eel lifted one foot from the water and slung the other over the side of the boat.

"Tell him the tile maker, PMP, of the Amazon commission will be sailing with the *Nossa Senhora da Luz*. Tell him to draft our agreement. When's the ship's estimated departure and return?" Pêro asked.

"Be here then on the bank tomorrow at first light. We sail in the morning. Depends on how quickly we fill the hull four to six moons, give or take and we'll return." Eel pointed to the meeting spot along the waterfront.

"Tomorrow morning —" Pêro said under his breath to Rafa, who jerked the reins starting the cart forward.

Jawoli and Kujaguo were waiting for them at the rebuilt archway when they returned. They rushed over to the cart. Jawoli held out a red wax sealed note. Pêro sensed the men's uneasiness.

"This arrived just after you left." Jawoli handed Pêro the letter.

"I leave before daybreak tomorrow. It's sooner than I'd expected," Pêro said.

Pêro inspected the wax seal. *The King's…what is this?*

Jawoli and Kujaguo's eyes revealed their thoughts, their hearts, and their questions as to what would happen to them without Pêro as he broke the crimson seal. Kujaguo and Jawoli stole glances at each other.

"Rafa will lead in my absence. I plan to have more commissions for us upon my return," Pêro said. Then he gave his full attention to the note.

Pêro sucked in air, and slowly folded the fine parchment back up. He looked to Rafa, Kujaguo and Jawoli. "Sebastião José de Carvalho e Mello at the King's request has asked for our shop's assistance in drafting tile designs for the proposed rebuilding of the city center. He's inquiring to all surviving Fabricas to create tiles that can be easily replicated and inexpensive to make. One shop's design will be selected and then all Fabricas will work to produce the needed tiles."

Pêro's mind reeled. *How can I sail now?* Captain Rocha's words and foresight of Lisbon's needs clanged loudly in his head. *Now what to do?* Pêro looked at Rafa and then the letter. "This will settle some of the problem with Sehnor Guimarães, as no doubt he's received the same request."

Pêro pursed his lips together, scratched his head, looking around intently at the inside of the Fabrica.

CHAPTER SIXTY-THREE

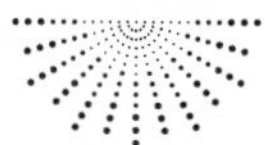

Rafa hurried through the dark of the new moon evening, stumbling on unseen objects, making his way to see Mother Conga Carlota the Astrologer. *I must have counsel before Pêro leaves tomorrow.* He pulled up the collar of his shirt.

Yes, he was free, but he'd never be free of this damning mark. The search for escaped slaves and prisoners was a daily affair now throughout the city and, even though he was neither, incorrect identification was an ongoing problem. His neck muscles clenched. He veered off the main throughway of the Mocambo, threading through the narrow paths and hidden back alleys of the quarter, ones only the residents of the barrio could navigate.

Shoulders brushing the broken packed-earth concession walls, Rafa halted abruptly before a wall cave-in that blocked the way. He retreated, taking an alternate route, and then turned sideways, slipping through a keyhole-shaped entranceway. He walked a few more steps, feeling along, until his hand reached a cloth tacked to the remains of a wall.

Rafa drew back the fabric and stepped into the Oracle's doorway. Immediately, he bumped into others who'd come at this late hour to see the stargazer, using the safety of the dark night to seek help, to learn what the stars would foretell to get through this difficult time. He took his place in the shadows of candlelight next to a gaunt-faced man of Moorish descent, a wrap of cloth upon his head. They nodded at each other.

Rafa squinted into the shadows trying to make out the people gathered here. He noted a gentleman who wore a powdered wig which glowed in the dark, alongside the man, his guide who'd led him here. Preceding the wigged gentleman was a hodgepodge of distraught seekers: a woman, her arm in a sling holding a mangy white cat; a mother with two distinctly different fathered children, one white as cream, the other as dark as café, each of the three wrapped in blood-soaked bandages; and an assortment of cripples with wooden boards attached to various body parts slouched on the ground leaning against the wall.

God's earth-shaking waves, and the subsequent uncontrollable fires of November had been cruel, unrelenting in their tyranny. Rafa gently shook his head in dismay. From his pants pocket, he retrieved the note from the king's council that Pêro had entrusted to him, the request for the new tile design to rebuild Lisbon. A design that could help begin to restore the city's beauty, to uplift the spirit of everyday people like these folks before him, like himself. Oh, how he wished Pêro would stay and assist to see this request through, for now it already bore down upon him.

Rafa looked to the parchment, his hand shaking, as he reflected on the King and Sebastiao Jose de Carvalho e Mello's order for the Fabrica to create new cost efficient, easy to reproduce tiles. He shivered. *Will I be able to fulfill this design demand of the King's court? And truly liberate my father from slavery? What will the stars reveal?*

When it was at last Rafa's turn, he was greeted by the same thin man with high cheekbones, Mercury, who'd led him through the underground chambers when he'd sought Carlota out about Diogo's condition. The visiting gentleman and his guide hurried by Rafa. Mercury received Rafa's payment and ushered him in, gesturing for him to remove his sandals.

When Rafa entered the astrologer's den, his senses were jolted at the starkness of this once opulent space that he'd first seen so long ago. He recalled the foreign cedar-mandarin smell, that of burning African beyo and the waves of blue smoke that had lingered in the air like swimming snakes. All that was now absent.

A woven mat rested on the hard-packed earthen floor, with Mother Conga Carlota on it, leaning her back against an adobe wall. She no longer lay on a raised earthen dais that connected with the back wall, littered with colorful leather and silk pillows surrounding her like gems. Her hands were not hennaed today; her head and body no longer wrapped in expensive indigo cloth with the plant dye visibly staining blue her forehead and the palms of her hands. But from her earlobes still hung the thick Viana gold hearts and about her neck a single gold chain where in the past multiple had hung with heart-shaped pendants like those of the women from the north. He'd not noticed any of these absent details while visiting her underground, his worry over Diogo consuming his senses. But now each missing detail stuck him, as though Mother Conga Carlota was a defaced work of art.

A brazier of coals sat next to her. As Rafa came before her, she sprinkled a few herbs over the hot cinders, herbal incense coils rising into the air. On the floor, alongside her, the life-sized wooden cross of the black Jesus was propped against the wall, instead of above her. Jesus's head was missing. Rafa then noticed it rested at the nailed feet of the saint, blood dripping from the crown of thorns seemingly into the earth.

"Come, be seated," Carlota said, her voice raspy.

Rafa knelt on the mat before her and noted the once voluminous woman had grown thinner in these six weeks.

"What is it you have there?" she asked, gesturing to the paper in his hand.

Rafa opened the parchment and held it out to her. "I've come for a star reading —"

Carlota shook her head and picked under her fingernails. "I don't need to see it." She glanced at the doorway and leaned forward. "It's a reading of the bones you need."

Rafa swiftly looked over his shoulder to the door and then back at her. Sweat broke out on his forehead. "*...the bones...?*" he whispered. "A star reading should be fine."

She raised a knowing eyebrow, and waved her index finger at him, smiling mischievously. A flash of a golden tooth caught the altar candlelight.

Rafa lowered the parchment, brow knit. He moved to get up.

She twisted the remaining golden ring on her finger. "Sit. Mercury, fetch my bag."

Mercury peeked behind the doorway's drawn cloth and then drew it closed. He rushed to the far corner of the room, to the altar of the Black María and Saint Anthony. The statues were no longer draped with rosaries of the "Brotherhood of Our Lady of the Rosary of the Blacks", and the regular sea of dancing candlelight at their feet was replaced by one burning candle. Mercury approached the statue of Mother María, reached behind, extracting a leather bag, encircled with fringed strips that dangled down. He brought it before his patron.

She spread a piece of leather, gently smoothing it out. "Stay guard at the door."

Mercury resumed his post.

Rafa bit his lower lip and wiped perspiration from his brow, and again, looked over his shoulder at the door.

From the weathered pouch, she produced a halved hollowed out gourd, with burned on symbols of x's, o's, arrows, and line dashes. She shook the leather bag. The bones rattled inside like a child's toy. She then poured the bones into the halved gourd, chanting in a language unfamiliar to Rafa. Suddenly, her eyes rolled back, and she thrust her index finger at the statues in the corner and began to mumble a Catholic prayer.

Mercury, wide-eyed and alert, held the entryway cloth firmly closed. From out of nowhere Carlota produced a bottle and uncorked it. She poured the liquid into her mouth and spat it out, the liquid substance raining down on Rafa's hot skin. It sizzled as it splattered upon the brazier coals, sending out a hiss.

She rolled the pupils of her eyes forward, released her hand from on top of the gourd, and spilled the bones upon the waiting cloth. They clattered into their formation. Mother Conga gazed upon the lines and symbolic formation. "Ah, yes —"

She looked to Rafa, who stared at the possessed woman.

"What do you see, Mother?" he asked, with caution.

She studied him. "Your success comes in the seasons of the dark, before the new blooms. The king's color purple and olive trees are your protectors."

"What do you —"

"The Lord's last day of the week is your luckiest day. You see good in others, but be careful not to be naïve, as all persons possess the light of the sun and the darkness of moonless starless nights like tonight. Be careful, Rafa, there are those around who don't want to see you rise," she intoned.

Instantly, Senhor Guimarães cruel words and accusations came barking back at him. Rafa stared at the Oracle...*'The king's color purple...' How could she have known this without me revealing the details of the letter to her?* He brought his hands to his face and smoothed them down his cheeks, drawing his brows together — the reading's message cryptic. "Can you —"

With the sweep of her hand Carlota ordered him away.

Rafa hesitated, and then got to his feet and headed back into the darkness of the night. His head confused and his heart heavier than when he'd arrived.

CHAPTER SIXTY-FOUR

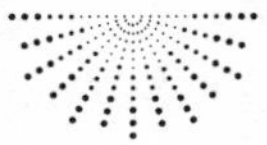

Throughout the night, Pêro tossed, his thoughts looping upon themselves. *I need to stay and help with the King's request and see to Bagamba's freedom. How can I possibly leave now?* He lay awake in the dark, tossing side to side. Before dawn he finally dozed off. In a deep slumber he dreamed of Paulinha, she as vivid as a masterpiece painting. *'Sail for me. See the tiles in the jungle I so longed to see, embark on the journey that for me will never be…'*

In the early morning darkness rain fell, awakening Pêro from his dream. The smell of clay permeated the air, the clay's odor changing from a dry ancient dust to an alive earthy aroma, what he'd heard the jungle was like. As the rain showered the roof's tiles, Pêro recalled Paulinha's face, her brilliant blue eyes, and her request for him to sail. The water rushed in straight silver rivulets hitting the ground and back splashing bits of gravel up onto the platform where he lay. He picked up his bedding and moved to the back where Kujaguo and Jawoli slept next to the earthen wall and kilns. The rain changed to a pounding downpour.

Pêro pulled the canvas cloth tight around himself against the penetrating December cold. *This is a good time to leave Lisbon with so much chilling misery.* He imagined the warmth of an immense forest. But here there were so many in need of assistance. *Where is my desire and dedication to help others?* Paulinha had spoken her heart's wish and he wanted to go for her. But he couldn't stop thinking of all the suffering homeless and winter winds and icy rain. He turned onto his side with difficulty, as he contemplated everything and leaving the Fabrica.

Monies for Bagamba's release had arrived last night from the captain, and a hearty portion was now safely hidden in the secret chamber in the floor. Rafa needed only to follow up on Tiago's outstanding payment to secure the remaining funds for his father's release. Pêro had extracted what he needed for his sea fare, leaving Rafa short for Bagamba's release now.

But what also now of the King's design request? Pêro lamented. Oh, how Paulinha would have loved to take part, she a fountain of ideas — his *amor*. The subtle shift in light arrived and with it an idea for a possible design to meet the King's request. Pêro quickly rendered the sketch, one he could leave with Rafa to work with.

It was time to gather his things and get down to the riverbank. The rain tapered and stopped. A soft mist floated in the open-air walls as a lone seagull skirled, cutting in front of the shop. Then the bird flew off in the direction of the Tagus, disappearing into the opaque white. Pêro placed his hand on the malachite stone in his pocket and thought of Gogo, Kujaguo, and Jawoli's advice. "The earth and its creatures speak and guide." The seagull went towards the water.

Fog shrouded the river and its bank in a gossamer veil.

Rafa, Diogo, Jawoli, and Kujaguo waited by Pêro's side in the mire, while other travelers flowed in on foot, cart, and sedan.

Pêro reached into his pocket, retrieving the velvet navy bag.

"Take these," he said, giving each of the men a coin. Jawoli puckered his lips, raising them in approval. Kujaguo's big smile caused his lizard facial tattoo to bunch up on his forehead. Rafa graciously lowered his head.

"Some food from my wife." Rafa handed him a worn cloth bundle. Gogo sends a message. "'Keep watching for signs, remember the animals speak as do the elements. Stay quiet. Listen. They'll guide you'."

Pêro smiled thinking of the morning gull. His heart longed to stay, but the undercurrent of what he must do — sail — was stronger and Paulinha had spoken. And the seagull had cried and moved towards the river. This time he would listen.

"U tienu wani len laffia, laffia, laafia, May God go with you and give you health," Kujaguo and Jawoli said in unison.

Pêro retrieved the design idea he'd sketched from his pocket and slipped from his left ring finger his signet ring. "I leave these in your care. Do your best to work with this or come up with something of your own. Sign off for the shop: PMP."

Diogo's eyes grew wide.

Rafa's eyes traveled to the band's monogram. Rafa gazed stunned at Pêro's trusting face. With care, he accepted the ring, gripping it tight in his trembling hand, along with the sketch.

Pêro smiled knowingly at Rafa's nervousness, looking deep into his eyes. They nodded at each other.

Pêro embraced each man and then crouched down to Diogo. "Help your father and mother with things. All right?" He embraced Diogo and his heart panged at the dearness of this little boy. His heart longing and wishing for his girls' presence. Blessed are the young, so full of love and joy, despite being forced through the crucible of life.

Pêro let Diogo go.

Rafa cleared his throat. "I'll start today on the King's request and follow up with Tiago's father this week. See if he can be located. Be careful, Pêro, please, don't be gone for long. Always remember we are here waiting for you."

"I will heed caution. I trust in you all and your abilities." Pêro placed a hand on Rafa's shoulder.

Pêro released Rafa and slipped his hand into his pocket, gripping the girls' white ribbons. Paulinha's *azulejo* was tied at his waist, her sketchbook hidden in his shirt pocket over his heart. Gogo, Kujaguo, and Jawoli's guiding wisdom now within him. He recalled the birds flying on All Saints Day, and how he'd wished he could have read their warning, as did Kujaguo and Jawoli. But now he would heed the call of the gull — and sail.

A dull light infused the mist. Passengers continued to gather and wait.

Padre João arrived in a black wool cape tied with a golden tasseled cord that shimmered in the day's somberness. He was in the company of a group of monks wearing simple coal-colored cloaks over their black habits, hoods hiding their faces.

Pêro observed how Padre João knotted up his hands into fists. And he couldn't help but think the Brothers now with him were the same ill-sent men who'd stood before his door.

The man with the black leather kit and brass buckle, most likely a doctor, waited alongside the Jesuits. His bag pulled his shoulder down, as though it contained heavy instruments and poultices. In the doctor's other hand, he held his frock closed tight around his neck, the skin on his hand pink from the cold, his knuckles white.

The ship's carpenter waited with his assortment of tools and repair materials: toothed saws, clamps, crates of nails, stack of boards and buckets of pitch. Multiple families huddled around their young and belongings, fending off the damp chill. More families than usual were gathered for travel on a merchant vessel at this time of year, those fleeing Lisbon, with hopes of a new life to be found in the colonies.

Nearby a boy whimpered. "But mama, *why* must we go?"

"Felipe, remember what I told you? We are sailing because father is going to work in the gold mines in the colony of Brazil. You like shiny things, don't you?" The mother patted her son's head in reassurance, but the boy scowled.

Military men with sheathed swords affixed to their belts shifted from foot to foot, moisture beading and running down their uniforms and dripping from their tricorn hats.

Pêro scanned the crowd for Princess María. *Will she be sailing with the ship?*

Out of the brume rowed in the mother ship's skiff, the Tagus splashing at her sides and bow. A light rain pocked the water. The *Nossa Senhora da Luz* invisible to them.

"Take care of yourself. We await your return," Rafa said.

Strong emotion welled up inside Pêro, for this good friend. Pêro could see clearly Rafa's questions, his doubts, similar to the ones he harbored about himself and his own journey before him. *Will we succeed? Can we endure?*

"Keep watch," Pêro said, in a forced stoic voice, his knees weak. Pêro's clothing hung from his wan frame. He further draped his canvas cloak over his shoulder and picked up his traveling bundles. He bowed his head to the men and Diogo. "Goodbye. See you in the springtime. May the Lord watch over us all."

Diogo reached into his trouser pocket and presented Pêro with a red geranium bloom.

"Blessed, wherever did you find this?" Pêro said, tears welling. He tucked the flower into his shirt pocket with Paulinha's sketchbook. "Thank you."

"There are still a few flowers to be found, if you know where to look," Diogo said.

Pêro grinned at the dear boy. He then joined the crowd pushing to the bank's edge.

The *Nossa Senhora da Luz's* crew helped women and children, first into the skiff.

Pêro sat facing the Mocambo. He watched as Rafa, Diogo, Jawoli and Kujaguo waved to him, as they became small, and then were lost behind a curtain of mist. An insular world engulfed him. At his back, he felt the Jesuits' eyes upon him, he the lowly Franciscan deacon, a tile maker, known by his monogram PMP, he without his habit, without his beloved family, and with a severely frayed belief in the Lord's plan.

Pêro hung his head, drawing the canvas cloak further over

his shoulders. He stared blankly at the choppy lead waters. Then he turned in the direction of the oncoming ship, only to meet Padre Joao's harsh stare. The skiff glided into the cold shadow of the *Nossa Senhora da Luz*. He placed his marred hand on the hidden tile at his waist, wishing for Paulinha's support. Oh, how he missed his daughters, his departed family. Now he sailed with Paulinha's sketchbook at his heart. No doubt, the Jesuits would love to get their hands on it. He looked back into the fog, trying to make out the shoreline. To see yet one more time where he and his family had spent their best and worst of days. But the moisture muted everything, like looking at a watercolor sketch, the blending of soft hues, nothing quite defined. Like his life now.

CHAPTER SIXTY-FIVE

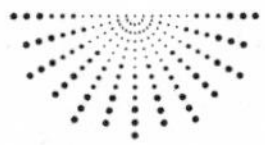

Rafa looked on holding tight in one hand the design and ring, and with the other took Diogo's hand into his, as Pêro became fuzzy, consumed by a cloud of white. A barrage of sadness overwhelmed him. The sea wrack smell was strong this bleak day, punctuating the deep loss of Pêro to this river and soon a sea of separation. *Will I ever see Pêro again?* Many say, "I'll be back," but it had been his experience that even with the best of intentions sometimes one did not return, for one reason or another — willpower alone did not override fate, one's destiny. *How to fare without Pêro and Paulinha at the Fabrica? And this new tile design request for the King? What will be my father's fate?* The passenger skiff vanished. His dark umber hands shook as he worked the signet ring onto his finger and turned to return to the Fabrica.

Hours later, Rafa stared at the simple sketch Pêro left him and the blank parchment before him, devoid of inner direction on how to begin filling it. An hour passed and a band of dogs barked incessantly outside. Nothing. He rested an elbow on the draft table, cupping his chin in his large hand, brow furrowed. He fixated on the paper before him, waiting for an idea — any form of inspiration to arrive. He doodled on a scrap of paper.

The hounds entered the Fabrica grounds. Rafa looked up to see the commotion. Canines circled and nipped at the heels of Senhor Guimarães. Kujaguo came out, brandishing a stick and the pack receded.

"Where's Padre Pêro? I need to consult with him," Guimarães said from the doorway.

Rafa noted the letter in his hand, clearly fine paper of the King's issue. "He's gone away for a while."

"When will he be back?"

"Sometime in the spring."

Brow pinched, the tile maker's face contorted into a snarl. "What? Surely that cannot be true." He wagged the note at Rafa. "Then who's been left in charge here that I can speak with?"

Senhor Guimarães strode into the Fabrica, seeking the person he could consult with, stopping before Rafa.

"He placed the care of the Fabrica with me, until his return." Rafa's nostrils flared, his eyes alert.

"What? He's left you in charge? I don't believe it. The city is in ruins and we've this court design to deal with, I will not consult with a slave over this." He gasped and thrashed the letter down onto the draft table and turned on Rafa. "Is this the design you are working on for the King? It's some sort of satanic design." He pointed at Rafa's scribbling. "Some occult curse, no doubt. Everything's gone to hell here. I'm going to the authorities. I will put an end to this once and for all. Slaves cannot and will not do this work for the King. He won't have it."

In familiar fashion, Senhor Guimarães spun on his heel and stomped out, waving the note in the air and ranting. "An end to this blasphemy! It's the likes of these actions that has brought the Lord's punishment down upon us!"

Rafa shook his head in dismay and slumped down. He'd foreseen this. *What to do now?* He sighed.

Pêro and Paulinha filled his mind, remembering how Pêro would launch into a design project. How designs sprang forth from him like the many green shoots of spring, and how they both believed in his ability. His mind seemed solid and impervious like rock. But patiently, he sat and waited and aimlessly made marks on the scratch paper.

Pêro's quoting of Saint Francis resurfaced. "He who works with his hands is a laborer. He who works with his hands and his head is a craftsman. He who works with his hands and his head and his heart is an artist." He wanted to be an artist, not a craftsman, not a laborer, and most of all, no longer a disrespected ex-slave. He pinched his eyes shut, bowing his head. *What to design for the King? Please, muse give me a gift. What would Pêro and Paulinha do if they were here?* He knew Paulinha was an integral part of Pêro's design process, but he'd never let on that he knew that she too wielded the drawing pencil.

"Kujaguo! Jawoli! Father!" Rafa called from in front of the blank paper. "We need to get some decent walls up here. I can't think in this cold."

"All right, what do you want us to do?" Jawoli asked. He pulled the red madder velvet remnant he'd saved from the Alfama tight around himself, trying to stave off the winter chill, adding another scrap of wood to the fire.

Rafa let his hand slide out from under his jaw, pushing himself away from the empty parchment.

"Let's go see about salvaging some adobe blocks from the downed building across the way," Rafa said. "Father, stay here, tend the fire. But stay out of sight, lest someone comes looking for you." Rafa locked eyes with his father, Bagamba.

Rafa, Kujaguo, and Jawoli exited the Fabrica, passing the broken pots that held the last of Paulinha's geraniums. Rafa smiled at the few red blooms hanging on. Down the cluttered road they made their way, the crumbled building coming into view. Off in the distance, Senhor Guimarães stood in the middle of the road, speaking to another man.

Rafa stopped and squinted trying to make out who Guimarães was talking to. Dear Lord, the caretaker from the de Sousa estate.

"Stop! I've got to go back and warn Bagamba." Rafa said. "That man could cause no end of trouble."

Kujaguo and Jawoli halted. "Should we all go back?"

"No, you two continue on, see what you can find and hear as you pass by them."

Rafa slipped back into the yard of the Fabrica and paused a moment before the geraniums Diogo lovingly repotted. An object from his past appeared in his mind's eye, one in particular, displayed in the window of the de Sousa's estate.

And like the magical opening of a desert flower after a long-awaited rain, Rafa's design idea for the King's court burst into full bloom.

CHAPTER SIXTY-SIX

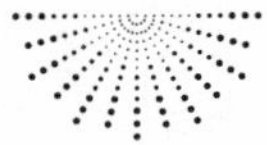

Pêro tried to meet the Jesuits' vexed glances with fortitude and ease, while his guts knotted. Swords of silver, *espada,* fish slithered and cut at the whitecaps next to the boat. Pêro waited his turn to board, he watched the black-robed Brotherhood ascend, and wished he had his own Order's russet habit. This time he did not hesitate to reach for the thick rope rungs but leapt up and scrambled onto the deck. Cresting the rails, he entered a sea-bound village.

Sailors set cords into neat piles like hand coiled clay pots. Deckhands tossed vinegary buckets of water across the decks, while others scrubbed down wooden planks. Seamen dangled from outriggers like monkeys. Pêro looked on as a man shimmied up a tall mast. Shouts and commands shot across the tri-level decks — like pebbles slung from slingshots.

Two-tiered chicken coops were bunched together and being lowered into an opening on the deck, with an occasional *cocoroka-caco* from a frustrated rooster, who could not access his clucking hens. Cages of pigeons and rabbits were aligned alongside the poultry. Crewmen rushed and cut in front of Pêro and the other boarding passengers, shuffling them and their personal belongings along the deck, and down into the belly of the ship.

Pêro positioned himself out of sight of the knot of Jesuits, who now awaited their turn to be shown below. He peered east and north; flashes of firelight illuminated the haze, as refugee campfires dotted the outlying hillsides of Lisbon. Then he and other new arrivals were hurried forward by a wiry deckhand, past the waiting group of Jesuits, their burning stares like wasp stings upon his back.

Below the main deck, on the cannon deck, tethered goats and sheep bleated; the air thick with the stench of wet wool and straw. Pêro held his hand over his mouth as they moved by. He ducked his head into the dimness and damp as they bustled down another steep ladder.

The passenger deck resembled a dim yet lively tavern. Lanterns with tallow candles sputtered, their glass coated with soot. The first thing Pêro sought was the altar: a carved statue of Mother María who wore a sky-blue dress, the paint peeling back from its folds. María's face was calm, her cheeks rosy. Three rows of short wooden pews sat before her. Refuge, he thought.

Pêro made the sign of the cross, inhaling the familiar vinegar air like that of the hospital ward of his Order where he and Paulinha had served side-by-side. He turned away from that thought and searched for a place to store his things. Brow pinched, eyes glistening, he gazed upon those traveling with family and children and felt an acute pang of loneliness, of despair.

"Padre Pêro!" Lico called through the crowd of jostling and settling voyagers.

"I was wondering if you'd make it. The tiles are all packed safely below." Lico talked over the noise. "Set to sail? Is it just you?"

Pêro stared at him.

Lico embraced his upper arm. "Eel told me you boarded alone."

"Yes." Pêro looked down to the deck.

Lico gently let go of his arm. "I'm sorry for your loss. Come with me, I'll show you where you can stay and stow your belongings."

Pêro forced a smile and followed Lico.

"Here you are. Place yourself next to the de Sousas' quarters. You can hang your hammock there alongside the wall." Lico slid in between the ship's hull and a table that hung suspended from iron bands, fastened to the deck above. "During the day, the tables are down for eating and you'll store it at night."

"The de Sousas?" Pêro asked.

"Yes, of the large estate in the Lapa."

The door opened from the private room and out stepped Senhor de Sousa. "Padre Pêro, what a surprise."

"Please excuse me, men. I must see to some tasks. Let me know if you need anything else. The accountant will settle with you soon. I'll go fetch our written agreement." Lico took leave, weaving through the melee of passengers.

The ship shifted beneath Pêro's feet, he staggered forward and steadied himself, a shiver spread through him as he thought of Bagamba. "You and your family are well and aboard?" Pêro asked.

"Dear Lord, yes. But our estate has suffered greatly. We fled north to our countryside home with our personnel and have now decided to pursue our investments in the colony while our help rebuilds here. I ordered our caretaker to see upon you and Benedito, today. Is he alive and all right? We still have this outstanding payment yet to be settled or for him to be returned to us immediately. We are desperate for assistance, like everyone, and must see to our finances."

Pêro's shoulders grew stiff, knowing full payment was still not available for Bagamba's release. He ran his damaged hand over his hair.

A choir of awed voices trickled down from the upper decks.

"Princess María is arriving!" A young man exclaimed from the deck above. Everyone stopped what they were doing and vied for the ladder.

"Perhaps we could settle over Benedito with some new tile works? Sounds like your estate is in need."

"Padre Pêro." Senhor de Sousa intoned and looked long at him. "What we need is Benedito back. Our caretaker has orders to recover him if payment is not received today. We can't go on like this with all that has happened. I am sorry, we have no other choice. I should have taken him back long ago."

Pêro bit his fingernail, tasting clay beneath it. He could smell Lisbon's springtime clovers and the scent of the green grasses drying in the summer's hot sun. He could see the bright light of a spring morning, the cooing pigeons nesting and feeding their young in the red clay roof tops. He tasted olive oil and green and black olives grown from the dry parched land. And escargot and the things of the sea: cod, sardines, and red snapper, and the women who peddled them, crying out their wares. And the fishermen of as many shades of color as the fish they caught. Lisbon, the Mocambo barrio. His home. Bagamba was part of his family now.

"There must be some sort of arrangement we can make under these circumstances we all are in now," Pêro said. His words echoed in the silence of the vacated space with only sounds of scuffling feet overhead from the upper decks.

"The arrangement is to pay what is still owned or give Benedito up. These were the orders I issued like it or not. I am sorry, Padre Pêro. They will be carried out one way or another."

The cold finality of de Sousa's words sent a shiver through Pêro. He couldn't leave Rafa and Bagamba to this fate. *Can I? Despite that Paulinha has clearly directed me to sail and the sign of the bird in flight.* But ultimately, he knew in the deepest part of his heart that she'd want Bagamba freed at all costs. He wanted his agony to go away, but instead here it was with him on the ship's rolling deck. An astute clarity filled him; his pain would not stay in Lisbon. It would hound him as relentlessly as de Sousa's demand for payment wherever he went.

Pêro looked at his stowed belongings then back at Senhor de

Sousa. "Let's settle here and now." He fished in his trousers for his velvet bag, retrieving the payment he had yet to make for his passage and the monies he'd allocated to live upon. "I need a receipt of payment and the written release of Benedito from your care."

Above on the main deck, Pêro inhaled the salt air, hands shaking as he held Bagamba's letter of freedom. He hung in the back rows of onlookers and a fair distance away from the Jesuits and Senhor de Sousa and family. He cast his eyes around the ship, trying to discover a task he could possibly take on to pay for his passage and living needs.

It was a regal Princess entrance like the one he and Rafa had witnessed that day while enroute to the Alfama to meet with a tile client. Children, despite being hungry and tired, had pushed through the crowd to the rails for a glimpse of the spectacle, their heads jutting between the deck's gunwale rungs. This is how he imagined Princess María would arrive if she was to sail with them. He'd been surprised — no — shocked to see her yesterday, ferried over the mired bank with common folks surrounding her, and being rowed in by the *Nossa Senhora da Luz's* sea-hardened crew. But it exemplified the desperate times Lisbon and her populace found themselves in.

Lisbon's cloak of piety and lavish use of wealth had succumbed to forces more powerful than pedigree. The Church, the saints, and the proceeds from gold, diamonds, and slaves were no match for the catastrophes unleashed upon them all. Yesterday, on the bank, Princess María had almost been one of them.

Today she arrived in royal fashion. The opulent navy-blue vessel was sleek upon the waters as the oarsmen spliced the craggy waves with gold leaf embossed oars, the fierce dragon eel design shone and glinted in the haze as the vessel glided alongside the ship. Pêro clenched tight in his hand, the receipt releasing Bagamba as cheers rang out from the deck crowd and people pulsed forward to catch sight of their royal guest. He needed to get this document immediately to Rafa and Bagamba.

Again, he went over why he'd boarded, the gull and Paulinha's wishes, knowing her deepest wish would be to see to Bagamba's welfare first. But she and the girls were no longer here. He was unfamiliar with this ongoing inner indecisiveness. He looked for clarifying details, to unravel the unease of his heart's torment. For he was a man who noticed the unnoticed, a God-given skill he'd developed through his clay works, painting training, through a life working in the arts. *But now, how to work with the inner pain and indecision?*

It was a dreary and sad day to be leaving Lisbon, a pall heavy upon him with his new set of problems: how to get word and this note ashore and pay for his passage and daily living. The haze lifted revealing the outlying countryside. Makeshift camps dotted the hillsides with haphazard tents, their open fires sending columns of smoke into the damp skies. The human wreckage of Lisbon was trying to survive. Water soon would be his only reference, with its constant shifting ways. He pushed through the throng and looked over the rail, he spied a string of floating objects like the sponges they used in the Fabrica to clean the edges of tiles. These were not sponges, but a fisherman's net set with square cork floats.

Perplexed, he stood there, the cold driving through the weave of his canvas cloak. He shivered. He would go now where explorers ventured, but he was not departing as an adventurer. But as a man in need of a cure for his agony — a seeker of another sort, under the guise of a tile maker and an uncloaked deacon in questionable service to God. This horrible realization overtook him — he could not float away from his misery — it would sail with him. He was forced to coexist with his unbearable pain, to somehow make peace with it. *But how?*

Pêro gripped the ship's rail as the royal vessel departed and the passenger boat readied to go to shore one last time. No, he did not want to accompany this tile cargo to its final destination, to such a lewd man nor pursue more opportunities outside of Lisbon. For suddenly, he could see clearly how the mural Paulinha had brilliantly applied her courageous creative hand to was now a symbol of the undermining of his wife's right to her womanliness and freedom to create. And despite how she had longed to see the works in the jungle. He looked to the water as it rushed and pushed upriver. Overhead a gull cried. Looking up, he gasped at seeing the bird flying inland towards the Fabrica with the turned tide.

CHAPTER SIXTY-SEVEN

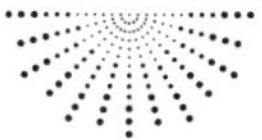

Rafa drew deliberate lines, creating a trellis of leaves on a vine, framing the inner design. Inside the square frame, he added rosettes surrounded by geometric clover shapes that could easily be repeated, a design rooted in simplicity. At the bottom of the drawing, he briskly shaded, making a base of swirls that imitated the trowel marks of masonry work. Rafa's lips curled upward as he created a drawing that honored the King's design request, as well as that of the traditional motifs inspired by the Chinese porcelain vase he'd seen daily in his youth poised in the window of the de Sousas' home. He'd grown up inspecting the exquisite vessel that had belonged to the man who had owned both him and his father, his family. It had sat in full view of the garden, overlooking the orchard of cork trees where he and his father worked, and he'd studied it as he pulled weeds.

It had been the straightforward repetitive designs of *azulejos* that had first captured his heart and called him to the trade. He let out the breath he'd been holding and gazed at what he'd drawn, wishing he could share this with his father right now. But Bagamba was already heading up the hillside to an outlying hill behind the Mocambo, following the plan they'd devised with Brother Sambo.

Rafa instead was forced to relish this moment alone, one he'd so long awaited. A moment he'd not, until now, been sure would ever come. He hoped the design before him would meet the King's requests of easily reproducible works to adorn new civic and apartment buildings throughout the city. The colors could be interchanged without much effort, ultramarine-blue, cornflower-yellow and browns. And he'd make an actual stencil to quickly repeat the pattern, if chosen.

Rafa tapped his foot, smiling over his sketch one more time.

There was a clapping at the Fabrica doorway.

Rafa turned towards the awaiting man. "*Boa tarde*. How can I help you?"

"I am here to see Padre Pêro."

"He's not going to be available for some time. Maybe there's something I can assist you with?" Rafa said cordially. "Please, come in."

The de Sousas' caretaker did not budge from his position at the door frame. "I know Padre Pêro is not here and won't be for some time. I've come for final payment on the de Sousas' property, Benedito. Or to bring him back to his rightful owner without refund what's already been paid. One or the other."

"I am sorry he too is not here right now. But do come in." Rafa gestured to the waiting stool.

"Are you going to pay up? Or am I taking back my master's property? Which is it?" the caretaker blurted. "I don't have all day to waste with another ill-placed slave."

Heat flushed Rafa's face, his heart beating rapidly. "I nearly have enough to pay off the last of the bill. We have one more outstanding payment yet to be received to finalize everything." Rafa gulped down his anger. "Give me a week to see this through with all that's happened."

"I can't. I have orders to return him back to the de Sousas' estate today. We are in desperate need of help, like everyone.

You're going to have to hand him over if you don't have the funds."

Rafa walked towards the caretaker. The man retreated away from the building.

"Fine. If you're going to be uncooperative, I'll get the policia. They'll settle this." The caretaker threatened before hurrying off.

Rafa stopped at the fallen arch entrance watching the caretaker go. *Dear Lord!* He rushed back into the shop and retrieved the payment documents and sought the letter of explanation of his overseer position left by Pêro. He set each one out on the table, attempting to create order while his thoughts ran wild.

Three policia entered the Fabrica grounds led by the caretaker. "There he is." The caretaker pointed to Rafa.

Rafa walked out to meet them in the yard.

"We need to see your papers."

"Which ones?"

"Tie him up."

"Wait." Rafa held up Pêro's signet ring. The gold sparkled in the dull daylight.

"Confiscate the stolen property."

An officer grabbed Rafa's hand, trying to wrench the ring from his finger. But it wouldn't come off, stopping at his first knuckle.

"You can't do this. Padre Pêro has left this to me to sign our works. I have Benedito's papers and those left by Master PMP. Give me the chance to retrieve them." Rafa shook the two men off and tried to step away. The men grabbed his upper arms, retaining him.

Hoofbeats sounded from the street and in rode a young man in a black tricorn hat and cape. He brought the mule to a halt before Rafa and the men holding him captive. The youth slid from his mount, reins in hand. With the other hand, he reached inside his cloak and produced a piece of paper and announced. "I have been sent by Padre Pêro on orders for me to deliver this."

Rafa's body went limp in the grip of the authorities, but still they held his arms tight.

The young man stepped forward. "This is for the man left in charge here by the name of Rafael Costa. I need a signature of delivery by the rightful recipient of this note. Is that you?"

Rafa nodded his head. "Please, may I see to my affairs? I am Rafael Costa."

The caretaker stepped in and snatched the letter from the rider's hand. He opened it and inspected and sneered at Rafa. "I am not sure if this truly is my Master's handwriting."

"Turn over the paper, see there…Senhor de Sousas' seal and signature. It's on the backside of the note." Rafa gestured to the underside of the paper.

The caretaker grimaced. "Hum. Well, it does seem to be Senhor de Sousa's seal and signature. By some luck of God —" Turning to the authorities, he begrudgingly conceded. "I guess things have been resolved."

"May I please?" Rafa gestured to the letter and requested release of his person. Letter in hand, he read and reread. "… receipt of full payment and release of Benedito Costa from the care of the de Sousa estate…"

The party disbanded. The mule rider was the last to disappear out of sight, leaving the yard quiet. Rafa clutched the note to his heart and fell to his knees and wept. A long-fought battle finally was coming to a close. How he did not yet know but held in his hand the letter of release for his father. The clouds dissipated, revealing the blue sky. He stared at the brilliant hue so like a shade of glaze they used. They'd seen the hard times through to liberation.

Rafa arose, returning to the draft table and placed the letter with the others laid out before the work. He reviewed his draft and waited for Kujaguo and Jawoli to return so he could seek out his father with the news. He smiled at the documents before him. Then carefully, he made the final touches to the sketch.

Outside a jubilant exchange was underway as Kujaguo and

Jawoli returned. Rafa lit a stub of candle and retrieved the piece of red wax, holding it over the flame. He kissed the signet ring and his large knuckle and pushed the PMP monogram into the soft substance and officially stamped the design for the King. He picked up the quill and dipped it and wrote Pêro's initials, "PMP" and "Fabrica Santa Mariá", at the bottom of the parchment. He returned the feather to its holder and blew on the letters and waved his hand over them. Gingerly, he rolled the design and tied it with a piece of twine, until he could locate a proper piece of ribbon. He paused looking at Pêro's signet ring upon his finger and shook his head. He raised it to his mouth and kissed it, saying a prayer of thanks to Mother Mariá.

Kujaguo and Jawoli appeared in the doorway talking and laughing and then fell silent. Rafa shifted his attention away from the drawing to the returning men. Kujaguo and Jawoli grinned wide and stepped aside, and in walked Padre Pêro.

CHAPTER SIXTY-EIGHT

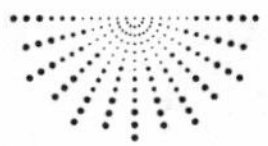

Pêro and Rafa locked eyes. Rafa's eyes growing large, he blinked twice. The men then clasped each other in a fierce embrace.

"I see the letter of release made it here in time," Pêro said. "Thank heavens. I crossed paths with the messenger as I made my way back here. He explained to me what was underway when he arrived with note in hand. I sensed urgency once I was back on shore and sent him ahead of me with the vital news."

Rafa fetched the important note, handing it to Pêro.

"The de Sousas were on board the ship. Senhor de Sousa revealed what would happen today. I settled matters once and for all. And I heeded Gogo's words. And yours. I noted and listened to the signs." Pêro grinned at Jawoli and Kujaguo. "The earth omens and animal signs changed. I caught a ride back with the last skiff." His heart swelled with happiness and certainty that he'd made the right decision. He knew now that there was worth in their ways and reasoning, as well as that of the ideas of the intelligentsia of the north.

"Senhor Guimarães has already come and gone and swirled up a storm. I'm relieved you're back to assist with the situation.

But despite all the turmoil I have something to show you." Rafa led Pêro to the draft table.

Rafa smoothed his hand across his design.

A wide grin broke from Pêro's face as he studied it. "Brilliant. It's perfect! I like what you've done here." Pêro pointed to the base shading. "Economical use of space that creates an enlivening decorative texture. And here —" He ran his finger over the repetitive flower and geometric clover pattern. "We can do a lot with what you've created."

"Yes, I'm imagining other linking patterns with a limited color palette of two to three colors which will be inexpensive to make." Rafa touched a rendered flower with the tip of his index finger.

Hunched over, Pêro and Rafa worked out the finer details of the shop's submission.

Rafa ran his fingers along the border. "I am thinking of shading here on the geometric clovers to create dimension."

"I like the dimensionality shading idea. You know it was originally Paulinha's, along with the creation of the *figura de convite*. It's time she's given full rightful credit for her contributions," Pêro said.

Rafa looked Pêro in the eye. "I've known for some time but kept it to myself."

Pêro let out a laugh. "I knew you could do this, Rafa. I've known for years." Pêro rested his hand on Rafa's. "Be proud. This is your creation and together, if it's chosen, we'll all see it through."

Rafa stood upright. "My father is in hiding. I'm going to fetch him and tell him of the good news and your return."

Pêro stepped back outside as Rafa left. He went over to the clay holding tank, bent down, and picked up a chunk of clay with both hands. He let his fingers sink into the malleable substance, his palms warming with the earth. He inhaled the live earthy scent, feeling the clay workable and healing in his hands. His home, his solution to this pain was to stay here and work this earth and allow the healing to come from the art, the friendships, the earth itself.

Pêro looked to the blue sky as a white dove fluttered into the yard and settled in the hollow of the old olive tree. He closed his eyes, listening to its soft cooing, then set the clay down and went to the few geraniums still full of life. He plucked a red bloom and rested it at the feet of Paulinha's noblewoman *figura de convite*.

"Through your art, my love, we live on…"

EPILOGUE

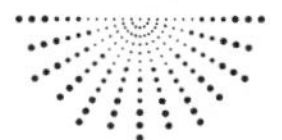

"Welcome, old friends." Pêro greeted Rafa and Diogo into his bedchamber filled with late afternoon sun.

"Look here, Padre Pêro." Rafa pointed to an article in the *Gazeta de Lisboa*. "It's a story about the royal decree of Marquis of Pombal and what people are calling *Pombalinos* tiles."

"Read it to me. My eyes are tired." Pêro lay back in bed, resting his white hair on the wall.

Diogo set a potted red geranium in full bloom on the nightstand and then brought over two chairs.

Rafa sat down alongside Pêro and read. "The Real Fábrica do Rato and the Fábrica da Bica do Sapato pioneered the large-scale production of *Pombalinos* tiles, the tile style named in honor of the King's Prime Minister, Sebastião José de Carvalho e Mello. Who was renamed by the royal court as the Marquis of Pombal, in veneration and celebration of his reconstruction contributions to Portugal fifteen years ago after the November 1st, 1755 disasters. The traditional patterned tiles, simple but elegant, with geometric designs of the previous century that had been nearly forgotten during the first half of this century were revived after the earthquake —"

"Yes." Pêro chuckled, and then coughed into a handkerchief.

Diogo got up and handed him a glass of water.

After drinking, Pêro smoothed out his blanket and rested back against the whitewash adobe. "Remember, it was your design, Rafa, that was chosen, and after that, the need for more tiles was so great we joined forces with other shops and developed —"

Rafa finished for him. "Efficient production techniques. Yes, yes, I know. I remember it all well. Shall I continue reading?"

Pêro nodded.

"*Pombalinos* decorated buildings that were the first-of-their-kind, built with protection against earth tremors engineered into them for the new city center." Rafa sat back in his chair, resting the paper on his lap.

Diogo frowned at Rafa. "Isn't there more? Neither of you nor the Fabric are even mentioned as the *Pombalinos* founding designers and shop."

Rafa's eyes gleamed with pride. "The city's demand for tile was great. We worked day and night, remember?"

Pêro held out his hand for the periodical, squinting to read it. "They've completely left you out and the Fabrica."

Rafa grinned. "I can still see the royal messenger who arrived at the Fabrica years ago. He was dressed from head to foot in royal blue, wearing a waistcoat with shiny brass buttons. Remember the two soldiers accompanied him, clad in tricorn hats, scabbard swords, and long canvas gaiters coming up to their thighs." Rafa's eyes sparkled. "I can hear each word of the messenger: '*Bom dia*. We've come on orders, on the behalf of King José'."

"Yes, I'd looked up from where I was painting a tile." Pêro held his hand as if holding a brush.

"It was warm that day. Springtime pollen filled the shop." Rafa shifted his face to the incoming sunlight. "I can still feel the navy-blue silk ribbon in my hand. Jawoli stopped trimming tiles. Kujaguo shifted from foot-to-foot. My father halted from sweeping." Rafa turned and leaned in toward Pêro.

Pêro sat up and reached into the bedstand drawer, handing Rafa a yellowed scroll with a royal-blue ribbon. "I remember how you carefully placed the fine linen paper on the draft table and washed your hands! Making us all wait with worry and excitement. Go ahead and read it to us."

Rafa laughed and held the old keepsake with both hands, closing his eyes a moment. "I slipped off the ribbon." He opened his eyes and undid the tie. "I distinctly recall admiring the elegant penmanship, imagining the quill that made it. My voice broke as I said aloud:

In the Year of Our Lord 1756

Royal Warrant of Appointment,

On the Behalf of King José I and the Royal Court we are pleased to announce the acceptance of Pêro Manuel Pire's design, monogram PMP of the Fabrica Santa María for use in the rebuilding of Lisbon.

His Majesty King José I Court

My hands quivered holding the parchment as tears came to my eyes. I remember the room fell silent." Rafa held out triumphant, the memento. "The royal court has chosen my design!"

Pêro's heart had exploded with pleasure with Rafa's. He distinctly remembered how he'd cast his eyes down at Paulinha's salvaged red geraniums placed by Diogo in new pots by the front door. Little green nubs already forming on the olive-green stems, and soon color, lots of color, would burst forth. Colorful life after so much loss. Despite all that was lost — new buds pushed forth.

"Pêro? Did you hear me?" Rafa patted his arm, seeking his

eyes. "It's wrong, unjust, that we aren't even mentioned in the article. Here's the proof of our part." He waved the scroll at Pêro.

Pêro's eyes glistened. "So is the way of men and history, Rafa. Often the creative sources of things are lost to us and the contributions credited to others." He took from the nightstand his worn copy of Voltaire's *Candide*. "Read this again. You know it was inspired by the great quake and illustrates the folly of people. I know and you know, and one day Diogo will tell your grandchildren. Those who are important to us know you were the designer and that the Fabrica played an important role."

Rafa clenched Diogo and Pêro's wrinkled hand, still holding the gazette. "I had the greatest of pleasure and reward in the moment I conceived of the design, and afterward, when we received this letter of acceptance. Those were my moments of glory, forever mine, despite what is remembered now and in the future."

"Yes." Pêro let the newspaper drift to the floor. A tear ran down his spotted cheek. "And as Paulinha said, 'Remember the thrill of creative grace is the greatest of gifts and gratification'."

Dear Reader,

We hope you enjoyed reading *Cut From The Earth*. Please take a moment to leave a review, even if it's a short one. Your opinion is important to us.

Discover more books by Stephanie Renée dos Santos at https://www.nextchapter.pub/authors/stephanie-renee-dos-santos

Want to know when one of our books is free or discounted? Join the newsletter at http://eepurl.com/bqqB3H

Best regards,

Stephanie Renée dos Santos and the Next Chapter Team

AUTHOR'S NOTE

Cut From The Earth is based on extensive research with multiple experts in Lisbon within the tile trade, art historians, and historical records, yet it is a work of fiction. Any oversights within these pages are mine alone. I have attempted to flesh out the lost and obscured voices of those creating the grand tile works during the artistic period of the "Cycle of the Masters" and the Great Lisbon Earthquake.

I'd like to share some known historical details and clarify some facts from fiction. Character Pêro Manuel Pires was inspired by a famous tile master who signed works with the monogram PMP. It's thought that these initials may have belonged to historical figure Padre Manuel Pereira, a priest and patron to a large tile making shop in Lisbon during the 1700's, but whose factory name is lost to history. The attributing of Paulinha as the designer who continued to mastermind new creations of the *figura de convite* and as the inventor of the mimicking of gold thread details in these figures is fictional. But historically, tile maker PMP is credited for the original conception of the *figura de convite*. The time period of these two tile design advancements is thought to have been around 1720 for the *figure de convite* and 1730 for the gold details, inspired by the vast amounts of gold extracted from the colony of Brazil at this time.

There are gray zones of unrecorded history, specifically around the artistic contributions of Africans and their descendants and women's roles in the production of tile during this period. But many of Lisbon's tile factories were located in the Mocambo, the first predominately black barrio in a European city. As I wrote the story locating the Fabrica Santa Maria in this neighborhood it became clear the local populace would have been integral in creating tile works, perhaps as overseeing and carrying out different aspect of production, firing kilns, delivery and management of supplies, and influencing designs.

There is no written historical record of a person of Rafa's character nor attribution to my knowledge to a single designer behind the inception of what would one day be called *Pombalinos* tiles. But there is a historical photograph of workers at the Fabrica Sant'Anna of mixed ancestry who inspired the creation of Rafa's character. Throughout Lisbon there are still existent tile works depicting the diversity of Portugal's population. They can be found at the Fundação das Casas de Fronteira e Aloma, Museu da Cidade, and National Tile Museum.

According to historical accounts, women healers and astrologers of African origin were prevalent in Lisbon in the eighteenth century. But these women, while sought after by the local populace for their abilities were also the target of accusations by the Church for practicing witchcraft and superstitious cures. Characters Gogo and Conga Carlota the Astrologer both were inspired by these facts, as was the mention of the medicine woman Doroteiada Rosa.

Moors from North Africa controlled parts of what is now today Portugal from the eighth to twelfth century. This history partly explains how some people of African origin may have been free while others were not during this time period of the story. I lived in Niger, West Africa from 1994 to 1997 with a little-known tribe the Fulmangani and Gulmancema people, along with the nomadic Fulani and Tuaregs. It is from this time in the scrub brush of the Sahel which informed aspects of the African and African descendant voices in the novel. During my time there, locals shared stories of people being forced across the Sahara into slavery, which is not a prevalently known route of the slave trade of Africans. The village I stayed in was the region's hamlet for healing exorcisms. Calabash drumming upon holes in the earth and dance while trying to revive character Diogo was inspired by real ritual practices.

Historically and even today, women's artistic contributions are co-oped by organizations and those in positions of authority and power. Paulinha's character represents all women of all time who've burned with the passion to create, but had to do so in secrecy and often forgo credit for their accomplishments, along with minority populations. I thank these voices that channeled through me. To be able to shine light on your forgotten and untold contributions to the enduring art and beauty of tile.

Many of the places and tile works mentioned throughout the story can be visited today in Lisbon and in outlying areas. Some of my intentions for this novel were to celebrate Portuguese tile making, its innovators and innovations and those who've gone unrecognized in its creation. To honor all women and disadvantaged people of all time whose art works have either been claimed or accredited to others, while giving thanks to those who've supported and valued creatives of all walks of life.

In addition, to commemorating the fortitude of the people of Lisbon when struck with such a life-altering and devastating disaster as the Great Lisbon Earthquake. It was one of the eighteenth century's most important historical events in all of Europe, affecting the whole of the Continent from writers, to artists and philosophers, architecture and theology alike. And most importantly to pay homage to all those who were fighting for their freedom and that of others, and to all those lost to the Great Lisbon Earthquake and everyone who carried on thereafter.

ACKNOWLEDGMENTS

I have many people to thank over the years of writing this novel. At the research stage, Portuguese tile expert, PhD Art Historian Luísa D'Orey Capucho Arruda at the Faculty of Fine Arts of the University of Lisbon fielded my questions over a number of years related to tile making in the eighteenth century. I am forever grateful for her expertise which clarified ambiguities and confirmed subtleties of this artistic era. Thank you to Alberto Brum at the Fabrica Sant'Anna, the oldest still producing tile factory in Lisbon since 1741, who kindly showed me around this historic place of creativity and commerce, inspiring the story's Fabrica Santa Maria. The Museu Nacional do Azulejo and accompanying museum library were instrumental for understanding the production processes of tile making, and provided rich inspiration for many aspects of the novel. A key one, the *figura de convite.*

Thank you to local Lisbon guides Mary H. Goudie and Rui de Castro Guimarães Cardoso for connecting me with proprietress Maria Mendonca, and gratitude to you for the personal tour, to view the national monument the Palácio Belmonte in the Alfama district. Home to some of the most well-preserved tile works from the eighteenth century in a public space.

These are the core reference texts I worked from to write this book: *A Herança Africana em Portu*gal by Isabel de Castro Henriques (Lisboa CTT, 2009); *O Terramoto de 1755 Lisboa e a Europ*a by Ana Cristina Araujo (Lisboa CTT. 2005); *Livro Azulejaria Barroca Portuguesa – Figuras de convite* by Luísa D'Orey Capucho Arruda (Edições Inapa, 1993); *A Herança das Américas em Portugal* by Isabel Drumond Braga (Lisboa CTT, 2007); *Lisbon before the 1755 Earthquake: Panoramic view of the city* introduction by Paulo Henriques and translation Marcia de Brito (Gotica – Chandeigne, 2004); *Azulejaria do Século XVIII, Museu National Do Azulejo Guide* by Paulo Henriques, Ana Almedia, Alexandre Pais, Fátima Loureio, João Pedro Monteiro (Instituto Português de Museus, 2006); *The Lisbon Earthquake* by T.D. Kendrick (Forgotten Books, 2012); *Wrath of God* Edward Paice (Quercus, 2008); *Blacks of the Rosary* by Elizabeth W. Kiddy (Pennsylvania State University Press, 2005); Sabores da *Lusofonia* by David Lopes Ramos (Lisboa CTT, 2009); *The Madness of Queen Maria* by Jenifer Roberts (Templeton Press, 2009).

A profound thanks to my first beta readers Christine Meier Smith, Richard Edward Smith (tenfold to you two!), Alexandra Sands, Dianne Englesen and Sue Noble whose comments were indispensable from the outset. To Valmire dos Santos a long extended thank you for keeping me in the supply of Omega-3s throughout the years of writing this novel. Thank you to early advice givers whose comments helped propel the story forward: Barbra Kyle, Stephanie Cowell, Alana White, Mary F. Burns, Heather Webb, Kris Waldherr, Patrica Hudson, Patricia O'Reilly, Shelley Schanfield, Dee Gillies, Sophie Six, Martin Lake, Jessica Stefani, David Cook, Nicky Moxey, and Lindsay Bennett.

I'd like to extend a special thank you in remembrance to the late author Susan Vreeland, a mentor who continually encouraged me and believed in this story. And to former Penguin Random House editor, now literary agent, Jane Von Merhan whose developmental editorial expertise helped advance the story's form.

My weekly writer's group was essential to getting the manuscript to completion, deep gratefulness to Fiona Claire (extra big to you!), Lisa Gibson Dutcher, and Sandra Clarke. With additional thanks to late readers, Michelle Cameron and Sarah Partipilo for your suggestions to polish the story. Robert Wright your encouragement kept me going; and thank you Catherine Mathis for your final manuscript advice. A word of gratitude to M.J. Rose, Richard Zimmler, Nancy Bilyeau, and Jeannine Johnson Maia for your query support; it buoyed me.

Thanks to Max Epstein, Mary Sharratt, and Jana Oliver for your expertise at crucial moments toward publication. A final thank you to author and acquisition editor Donna Russo Morin for championing these unheard voices and untold story; and to the publishing team of Next Chapter and Miika Hannila and for getting behind the whole venture. A shout out to anyone I may have forgotten who extended a helping hand in multiple ways for this book to make it into the hands and hearts of readers. I thank you.

A final bow to Shakti Kundalini whose creative force is responsible for this novel and forthcoming book two of this series, along with the upcoming anthology *When She Wakes: Women's Accounts of Kundalini Awakening.* Where I share how evolutionary energy is the crux of creativity and more.

ABOUT THE AUTHOR

Stephanie Renée dos Santos is author of *Cut From The Earth,* a Semi-Finalist for the 2019 Chanticleer International Book Reviews "Chaucer Book Awards". This is her first novel. She received her Bachelor of Arts in Studio Arts from Whitman College. She's an artist and yogini. A native of the United States, she divides her time between the Pacific Northwest and Brazil. She speaks publicly, to make arrangements and for book club discussion questions and to subscribe to her newsletter visit: www.stephaniereneedossantos.com.

Made in the USA
Columbia, SC
21 July 2021